TREASURED ROMANCE

ABOUT THE AUTHORS

ELAINE L. SCHULTE was born and raised in Crown Point, Indiana, and graduated from Purdue University. She has written hundreds of short stories and articles that have appeared in magazines and newspapers around the world. Her first novel, *Zack and the Magic Factory*, was produced for television. She lived in Belgium for several years and has traveled extensively in Europe, the Middle East, Africa, and North America. She resides with her husband in Rancho Santa Fe, California. They have two sons.

VELMA SEAWELL DANIELS has always been passionately in love with books. She is a native of Florida, where she has earned the title of the "Book Lady." She has been an NBC television hostess, librarian, book reviewer, newspaper and magazine columnist, and popular seminar and conference speaker. Velma is married to her first-grade sweetheart, Dexter, a championship golfer and business executive. Velma has written for *Guideposts* and is the author of three inspirational best sellers: *Patches of Joy*, *Kat* (the true story of her calico cat), and *Celebrate Joy*.

PEGGY ESKEW KING grew up in Anderson, South Carolina, where she studied art and fashion design at Winthrop College. She delights in creating and sewing original designs for her personal wardrobe as well as for family and friends. Peggy has won numerous awards, including the title of Mrs. Columbus and runner-up to Mrs. Georgia. She travels extensively and is a voracious reader, logging as many as four hundred books per year. Peggy now resides in Winter Haven, Florida, where she welcomes her minister sons and their families for frequent visits.

LYDIA HEERMANN was born in Winburne, Pennsylvania, and married in Wisconsin. She then lived in thirteen different states with her husband, Ray, a traveling salesman. Despite frequent relocations, Lydia worked sixteen years as a Braille transcriber. She also volunteered endless hours as church organist, soloist, and Sunday school teacher. She has had other books and several articles published through the years.

Contemporary Romance COLLECTION

TREASURED ROMANCE

VOLUME 1

On Wings of Love
Elaine L. Schulte

Love's Late Spring
Lydia Heermann

Fountain of Love
Velma S. Daniels and Peggy E. King

ZondervanPublishingHouse
Grand Rapids, Michigan

A Division of HarperCollins*Publishers*

Treasured Romance Volume 1
Copyright © 1996 by ZondervanPublishingHouse

On Wings of Love
Copyright © 1983 by Elaine L. Schulte

Love's Late Spring
Copyright © 1985 by Lydia Heermann

Fountain of Love
Copyright © 1983 by Velma S. Daniels and Peggy E. King

Requests for information should be addressed to:
ZondervanPublishingHouse
Grand Rapids, Michigan 49530

ISBN: 0-310-20952-8

This edition printed on acid-free paper and meets the American National Standards Institute Z39.48 standard.

Printed in the United States of America

96 97 98 99 00 01 02 /❖ DH/ 10 9 8 7 6 5 4 3 2

ON WINGS
OF LOVE

Elaine L. Schulte

To my dear Frank, a very great love

He had kissed her—then he had said he was sorry!

Katie blushed furiously as she recalled David's passionate kiss in the spotlight of the Antilles Lounge. Just as Stan had used her to charm his clients, she felt that David was now amusing himself with her naïvete. Katie was certain that she was a novelty with whom he would eventually grow bored. He and Giselle had probably enjoyed a good laugh together after Katie rushed to her cabin—utterly mortified with the intensity of her own reactions.

And what about that other kiss on the first night at sea? Was it an honor bestowed on the newest member of the travel agency? A memory to pack away with other mementos of the trip? A natural outcome of moonlight and mood music? After all, David was a man, and men seemed to share a number of disturbing similarities.

A kiss was a sacred thing, Katie believed, to be reserved for private moments and to be exchanged between two people who cared deeply for each other. Now she had dropped her guard with David more than once, overpowered by his irresistible good looks. But "beauty is only skin deep," Gran Lucy had often reminded her, and who knew what lay beneath the surface of the dashing and enigmatic David Wallace!

CHAPTER 1

KATIE ANNE THOMPSON sat staring at the sheet of paper in her typewriter, her thoughts on the silken wings of love. The words flitting through her mind came from something she had read about "the first consciousness of love, the first fluttering of its silken wings, the first rising sound and breath of that wind which is so soon to sweep through the soul, to purify or to destroy."

Longfellow. He was the poet who had written the disturbing phrases. Although she wasn't certain what he meant by love purifying the soul, she did understand about its power to destroy. Love had all but annihilated her only months ago, and once was more than enough!

Still, a voice within her whispered: Perhaps it would be different with another man. Perhaps it would be different with someone like . . . David Wallace.

David Wallace, the president and part owner of Wallace-Tyler Tour and Travel, would be driving from the downtown Los Angeles office for this afternoon's quarterly meeting of the board. She suspected that every woman in this, the southern district office, was secretly in love with him. Well, she would not be one of them! She ripped the ruined paper from her typewriter—her third attempt to type the quarterly report.

Slipping a fresh sheet of Wallace-Tyler Tour and Travel letterhead into the typewriter, she typed the date—October 15—her twenty-fourth birthday, and not a very auspicious one so far. It also occurred to her that she had worked here for exactly two months, prompting a new line of thought. It still seemed mysterious that she had been offered this job as office manager on the very evening she had returned from Northern California to her condo in Santa Monica.

Someone from the research company where she had worked must have told Bob Tyler that she had quit her job and was available for employment. Had that person also known that she had broken her engagement to Stan on that same horrid day? That she had fled wildly to her grandmother's house in Northern California for a month to recover?

She typed briskly and accurately, although as office manager, she was required to prepare only the most confidential reports. Scanning the page, she pulled the completed paper from the typewriter.

"All done?" Bob Tyler, her tall, sandy-haired boss, asked as he strode to her desk.

"Just finished." She ran a finger down the columns of figures to compare them with the rough draft. "I finally got the better of it," she added, sitting back with a sigh of relief.

Bob grinned. "Your reward is in sight. I'm taking you out to lunch."

She shook her head firmly, luxuriant sable hair rippling about her shoulders. "Thanks, but I'd really rather not." She didn't want to encourage his interest, nor any other man's for that matter. He was a wonderful boss, thirty-two

10

and attractive, but it was better not to become personally involved with a man who was separated from his wife. It would be dreadful to be the final straw between them, however innocently.

He looked crestfallen. "Giselle's coming along, and we're meeting David Wallace."

All the more reason not to go, Katie decided. The glamorous Giselle Vallon, another owner of the company and its top travel agent, was said to be interested in David Wallace. Katie did not care to watch the predatory female spinning her web.

"It's a business lunch," Bob added. "We'd really like for you to be there."

"Well, then . . . of course." Strange, she thought, grabbing her handbag from a desk drawer. She had never been invited to a business lunch before. "I hope there's time for me to freshen up."

"You've nothing to freshen up," Bob said, cocking an appreciative eye at her, "but I'll give you two minutes. We're supposed to meet David in San Pedro, and you know noontime traffic on Fridays."

"*Five* minutes," she called back, rushing off. She was grateful that she had worn her silk lavender dress, a birthday gift from her father and stepmother in Florida. Ordinarily she wouldn't wear anything so dressy to the office, but this morning her spirits had needed a lift—perhaps because it was a special occasion and because she was most definitely on her own and alone this year.

Opening the lounge door, a heavy French perfume assailed her senses before she spotted Giselle standing at the spacious wall mirror. She was pulling back her pale blond hair into a sleek chignon, and her amber eyes darted briefly toward Katie in the mirror before returning to her own lovely reflection.

11

"Hi!" Katie said. "It seems I'm going along for lunch."

"So I hear." Giselle's slight French accent put an elegant edge on the words. Her black silk suit, a designer creation, was terribly chic.

Katie rummaged in her handbag for her hairbrush, feeling awkward beside the poised woman. She had often tried to be friendly, but Giselle had always rebuffed such overtures.

"Where are we going?" she ventured.

"A surprise," Giselle answered, her eyes ignoring Katie in the mirror.

What have I done to make her dislike me? Katie puzzled. She knew that Giselle enjoyed the company of very few women, though David Wallace's late wife had been her best friend. It seemed that her life revolved around men, two of whom she had married and divorced before she was thirty.

Taking a final pleased glance at herself, Giselle turned and left the room.

"See you in a minute," Katie called after her, but the woman either didn't hear or didn't bother to answer, and the door swung shut.

Katie shrugged and ran the brush through her hair. Studying her image in the mirror, she recalled how her mother had once described her: " . . . the creamy oval face of your English great-grandmother, the dark hair of your Irish great-grandfather, and the gray-green eyes of your French and German forebears. But, most importantly, you have their fire and faith. You'll make it."

Well, her mother would be disappointed now if she happened to be looking down from heaven. Since the breakup with Stan her faith had suffered a mighty blow, and there was very little zest for life. She jammed her brush into her handbag and hurried out to the office.

Giselle and Bob stood near the enormous ficus benjamina plants by the plate-glass doors.

12

"Sorry to keep you waiting," Katie apologized.

"No problem," Bob answered. He held the door open as they walked out into the roar of traffic and the warm October breeze. She had the uneasy feeling that he was a little more interested in her than he ought to be.

Giselle glanced back at them curiously as she led the way to the parking lot, black high heels clicking smartly against the pavement.

Bob unlocked the front passenger door of his car, and Giselle quickly moved forward, slipping in with a flash of slim legs. He opened the back door for Katie, and she smiled up at him, content to sit behind the other woman.

As they pulled out onto Century Boulevard, Bob looked over at Giselle. "Excited about the cruise?"

She shrugged. "Not especially, although it does get me away from my desk."

Appalled, Katie couldn't help thinking how excited she would be if *she* were planning a Caribbean cruise. Ten days of luxury and adventure, the ads promised. She had accepted Bob's job offer as office manager in order to learn the travel business and eventually to become a travel agent. But, as she had told him, right now she needed a guaranteed income rather than promises of faraway places and distant commissions.

"I'm really looking forward to it," Bob said. "David and I need a better background on some of those islands."

Katie knew that as company attorney and district administrator, Bob rarely had time for travel anymore.

"Well, it's my fourth trip to some of the ports," Giselle said. "The business possibilities are what interest me now."

Katie suspected that Giselle, who owned ten percent of the company, was angling to move up in the hierarchy. She had been an early investor in Wallace-Tyler, although Bob and David were the principal owners. They had begun the first agency as a lark, and with its instant success, had opened affiliated offices throughout the West Coast. The two men were often featured in national business magazines as "the California travel tycoons."

Katie glanced out at the heavy noontime traffic, wondering why she was required for a business lunch. Perhaps, with all three of them literally at sea on a cruise, they would turn over more responsibility to her. Though she was new with the company, they had known her for several years. Ironically, Bob, David, and her ex-fiancé, Stan, had all graduated from UCLA together and often saw each other socially.

She recalled her attraction to David Wallace before she had learned that he was married and before her engagement to Stan. Then, for a while after his wife's death, Katie had suspected that the feeling was mutual. Once, at a large party, David's brown eyes had met hers across the room and held for such an intense moment that she felt as if he were looking into her soul. She knew that if she hadn't already been engaged, she might have walked right into his life. Later that night, Stan had questioned her. "What's going on between you and Wallace?"

She had attempted a reply, then finally laughed it off and changed the subject. Thereafter she had avoided David altogether, although Stan's interest in other women had not diminished. Strangely he had discarded her for a slightly younger version of Giselle—a sophisticated, hazel-eyed blonde.

Katie wondered if she should ever forgive Stan for his betrayal, for running around with other women while they were engaged. "Swinger Stan" was how she thought of him now. The bitterness that rose to choke her was almost a physical pain. Trying to forget, she asked Bob, "Where are we going?"

14

"It's a surprise!" he answered, turning onto the Harbor Freeway exit.

Did they know it was her birthday? Katie wondered. Maybe they were taking her out to celebrate.

Later, as they pulled into the Port of Los Angeles shipping area, the scenery took on a nautical air. Thick coils of rope swagged between weathered posts, defining the sprawling pavement into driving and parking areas. Across the water a magnificent white cruise ship was docked at the passenger terminal. Giant blue metal cranes jutted above warehouses and container ships in the distance. Overhead the gigantic green St. Thomas Vincent Bridge spanned the seaport scene and seemingly disappeared into the brilliant blue sky.

"There's part of the surprise," Bob teased as he maneuvered the car expertly into a parking space.

Katie saw the three white restaurant ships docked nearby and looked about for David Wallace. No sign of him anywhere. Surely Bob meant part of the surprise was eating on a restaurant ship.

Letting herself out of the car, she inhaled the salty air. "How lovely it is here," she said, relieved to be free of the heavy smog. Sea gulls cawed, wheeling over the channel. Here by the wind-rippled water, she might have been thousands of miles from Los Angeles. Quite suddenly she felt as if David Wallace were watching her.

"Haven't you ever been here with Stan?" Giselle asked.

Katie shook her head. It wasn't the glamorous kind of place that Stan frequented. He preferred chic city restaurants and night clubs to impress his advertising agency clients. A quiet seaside restaurant held no allure for him, although she had once talked him into going to a restaurant at Ports-of-Call Village.

Giselle waved toward the outside upper deck of the largest restaurant ship.

David Wallace! As he stood to greet them, Katie caught her breath, wondering if he had been watching her after all. He seemed to be smiling at her, and she mustered a timid smile in return.

The threesome passed under a sunny yellow canopy and entered the ship. Inside, gleaming brass fittings complemented the rich, dark mahogany paneling of the grand salon. Though intriguing specialty and gourmet shops lined the passageway, they disappeared like fading scenes in a film as the three made their way to the stairway where David would be waiting. Above the stairwell a French chandelier glittered, suspended from a three-deck-high skylight.

David Wallace stood at the top of the stairs, tall and rangy, probably two inches over six feet. His white teeth flashed against his deep tan, accentuating eyes the color of rich, dark chocolate. Despite her brave resolve, Katie felt slightly dizzy at the sight of him. By the time she was halfway up the stairs, she still did not have the faintest idea of what she would say.

"Happy birthday, Katie!" David said, his eyes shining.

So he did know about her birthday! "Why, thank you," she said, breathless from the admiring gaze he focused on her.

As he greeted the others, she noted the elegant cut of his gray slacks, pale blue long-sleeved shirt open at the collar, and navy blue blazer, hitched casually over his shoulder. He might have been posing for a fashion ad. Well, she was not going to be impressed! She could not risk being hurt again.

"Since our table in the dining room isn't quite ready," he said, taking her arm and guiding her through the lounge, "we can wait out on deck."

Soft music swirled around them from outdoor speakers as David escorted her across the crowded deck. She was dazed with his nearness. No other man had ever affected her so, Katie thought, as he seated her at a small table.

Bob held Giselle's chair for her, then sat down and brought out a large manila envelope from his leather portfolio, watching David as if awaiting a signal of some kind. But the other man glanced away, commenting on the cruise ship docked across the water.

Bob spoke quickly. "Giselle's just sold seventy incentive trips to Hawaii for an insurance sales contest!"

Something unspoken hung in the air. Katie sensed the tension, an undercurrent of excitement. She was certain that it had something to do with her. Yet she felt excluded from the conversation as they discussed various tour bookings. Evidently Giselle had pulled a real coup.

Giselle accepted their compliments, smoothing her hair with long, tapering fingers, magenta nail lacquer glistening. Katie was uncomfortably aware that David was watching her. How plain he must find her compared to Giselle—and even Giselle was no match for his stunning first wife, Eva. How could he ever forget Eva?

"You're very quiet for a birthday girl," David observed.

"I'm—I'm just overwhelmed," she stammered. "I've never been here before," she added, hoping to fill the awkward silence. She forced her gaze to the ship's channel where a cluster of tugboats were anchored. Nearby a red fireboat poked out of its station, much like a snail peering tentatively from its shell. Its seeming uncertainty reflected her feelings for David—and for all men in general, for that matter.

"It's one of my favorite places," he said, watching a small flotilla of sailboats. A harbor excursion vessel, packed with tourists and dwarfed by the great white liner, moved lazily through the shimmering water. "Makes me feel as if I'm sailing for faraway ports," he continued.

"It even sounds like it," she said. High above, on the St. Thomas Vincent Bridge, traffic hummed rhythmically; and there was an occasional staccato thump of a cargo container settling on the dock. A chugging tug guided an enormous coastal freighter out to sea, spreading a gentle wake to lap against crusty pilings and shoreline.

"Have you ever been on a cruise, Katie?" David asked.

She looked wistfully at the cruise ship with its strings of colorful banners waving overhead in the warm breeze. "No . . . just some family vacation trips to Yosemite and Grand Canyon when I was in grade school." She decided not to mention that her mother had been dying of cancer during her high school and college days.

"Then it's about time you saw a little more of the world," Bob said. "How would you like to go with us on the Caribbean cruise next Wednesday?"

"Me?" she asked.

He nodded.

"Why . . . I'd go in a minute! But you *are* teasing, aren't you?"

"I know it sounds preposterous, but at the last minute, the woman from our San Francisco office couldn't make it, so we have an extra ticket. You'd be a tour director like the three of us. You know that for every twenty-five passengers we book, there's a free tour director ticket. And we've booked a hundred passengers for this trip."

"But I don't know a thing about being a tour director," she protested, then realized that her honest declaration might undermine this marvelous opportunity.

"The three of us will fill you in," David reassured her. "And there's very little left to do, since our main jobs were to generate enthusiasm and coordinate the details."

"Wallace party?" the hostess interrupted.

They followed her through the lounge and into an en-

18

closed deck area that had been transformed into a sunny yellow-and-white Victorian dining room. As the hostess paused at their table, Giselle spoke quickly. "David, do sit by me. I hardly ever see you anymore."

Katie, still stunned and disbelieving from the sudden invitation to the cruise, meekly accepted the chair Bob held for her.

"You're really not joking about the cruise?" she asked again when they were settled with large, embossed menus.

"A travel agent *never* jokes about free trips!" David said, raising a hand in mock solemnity. "Just a hint of a free trip and most people have their suitcases packed."

Can this really be happening to me? Katie wondered, barely aware of the chatter of diners and the clatter of dishes. The enticing seafood choices on the menu swam before her eyes.

"The salmon is especially good," Bob suggested.

"That sounds fine," she said, too distracted to make a decision. Perhaps she had misunderstood about the cruise, or would have to pay for part of it . . .

Bob placed the large manila envelope on the table in front of her. "Happy birthday!" he said with a grin.

David was looking over the top of his menu as she opened the envelope. Slowly she drew out a brochure. On its cover a splendid white ship sailed between verdant islands in an indigo blue sea. *Sail the Caribbean,* it invited. A ticket, attached by a paper clip, showed a receipt marked "Paid."

"I can't believe this!" she exclaimed, finding baggage tags and a packet of information about the ship—the Golden Renaissance. "I've never received such a wonderful gift!"

David and Bob smiled at her delight, but Giselle continued to study the menu.

As the waiter took their orders, Katie flipped through the pages of the brochure. There were pictures of laughing passengers engulfed in clouds of confetti, photos of luxurious swimming pools, palm-covered islands, splendid ballrooms, sumptuous spreads of gourmet foods . . .

"You'll be Giselle's roommate," Bob said. "And you'll have all weekend for shopping and packing."

"You won't need a passport, just an I.D.," David added.

"I can't begin to thank you," Katie said, still bewildered. She was aware that Giselle, sitting opposite her, had not said a word.

When their food arrived, Katie only picked at her salmon. "What sort of clothes shall I take?"

Giselle blinked at her over a forkful of salad. "Resort wear, of course."

"Of course." Katie squeezed the lemon half over her salmon. Its pungent aroma reminded her of Giselle—sour. To begin with, Katie's "resort wear" consisted of lightweight California clothing, most of which she had sewn herself.

Suddenly famished, she dug into the salmon. The tang of lemon complemented the rich flaked meat; parsley and chives added piquancy to the white sauce. Her crispy salad greens with blue cheese and tomato slices were delicious. Even the cheesy broccoli spears were delectable.

After the table was cleared, a chorus of waiters appeared, bearing a cheesecake alight with six candles. Their voices blended in a unique rendition of "Happy birthday to you!"

"Make a wish?" Bob asked.

"How could I possibly wish for anything more?" she asked.

David smiled at her and, as their eyes met, her heart turned over. *No!* she told herself. *I will make no foolish wishes about him.* The only thing she could hope was that Giselle would be a pleasant cabinmate.

Katie closed her eyes. Opening them, she blew at the

candles, but David's intense gaze diverted her. The flames above only five of the candles went out.

"One year until your wish comes true," Giselle said.

By then it would be far too late for them to be companionable cabinmates, Katie thought.

After dessert, David asked, "How about my driving the birthday girl back to the office?"

There was an awkward silence before Katie replied, "Fine." She tried not to notice the tautness around Giselle's mouth. "And thank you all for bringing me here . . ."

"It was David's idea," Bob said.

"We thought this would put you into a seagoing mood," David explained as they stood to leave. "But I believe it has done wonders for all of us."

Had inviting her on the cruise been his idea too? Of course not. Bob was her boss, and he had told her when she was interviewed that certain privileges accompanied the job.

Walking down the steps to the ship's salon, she sighed, "I'm afraid that I'll awaken from a beautiful dream."

"Let's hope not," David said. "I'm looking forward to it too."

In the parking lot, he led her through the nautical rope barriers to a bright yellow Porsche. "Is this your car?" she asked.

"Doesn't it suit me?" he answered with a rueful smile.

"It's not that at all." She shook her head, thinking that the car looked somehow familiar. But yellow Porsches were not uncommon in a city the size of Los Angeles.

As she slid in she noticed that Bob and Giselle were parked nearby. While Bob unlocked his car, Giselle's amber eyes clouded in an expression of open hostility. Was she merely being protective of her late friend's memory? Katie didn't think so.

21

David climbed into the car gracefully for a man so tall, and Katie suddenly felt as nervous as a girl on her first date.

He appeared to delay, allowing Bob and Giselle to pull out of the parking lot ahead of them. Turning on the car radio, he played with the dial until he found some soft music.

The song called up memories of the evening she had talked Stan into dining at a waterfront restaurant at Ports-of-Call Village. A cruise ship had sailed out of the port past the restaurant's windows. Glowing with light, the ship had resembled a magnificent floating palace. Everyone in the restaurant had stood and applauded the spectacular sight, a romantic dream come true.

Now the dream appeared to be coming true for her. Yet her mind whirled with warnings. It was not safe to trust a man as irresistible as David Wallace. Not after her experience with Stan.

CHAPTER 2

As THEY DROVE through the parking lot, Katie watched David don a pair of sunglasses. She thought that there was something about dark glasses that made people appear remote and distant, something that masked their true identity. After her breakup with Stan, she had all but lived behind her dark glasses to hide red, swollen eyes. It seemed that she could die behind them and no one would even notice.

Seeing David in the glasses, she was reminded of Stan and of the sexy, worldly image he had tried to project. Unwillingly she felt a surge of the old bitterness.

"Something wrong?" David asked.

"No. Nothing," she answered, trying to relax. She must be careful not to be so transparent. She was grateful for the music from the car radio and for the diversion as David paid the parking fee.

She wondered if she had adequately expressed her appreciation for the lunch and trip. She tried again. "The cruise is the nicest, most unbelievable birthday present I've ever had."

"It's our pleasure," David replied.

As they pulled onto the freeway, it occurred to her that perhaps she would be expected to pay for the cruise in ways she hadn't considered—that he and Bob would assume favors she did not intend to give. There were so many wild stories about cruises . . .

"I still don't understand the duties of a tour director," she said, glancing away at the bustling port with its jumble of cranes, ships, bridges, and roads.

David was busy changing lanes. "Just be your pleasant and enthusiastic self."

"Surely there's more to it than that!"

He thought for a moment. "Well, let's start with Wednesday morning at the airport. First, we'll have to herd all of our passengers to the right plane and make sure that their luggage is checked."

"Good idea!" she agreed with a nervous laugh. "Then what?"

"Not much. The Golden Renaissance personnel will meet us at the airport, check the passenger list, and ferry us by bus to the ship."

"It sounds too simple," Katie said.

David was intent on the traffic. "The only other thing I can think of is your helping at the Wallace-Tyler party that we'll be giving our passengers. But that's catered by the ship's dining room."

"What if something goes wrong . . . if one of our people becomes sick?"

"The medical staff handles emergencies," he said. "It's rare for us to be very involved once we're aboard ship."

Katie felt relieved. It sounded as if she could carry out her duties with very little effort. Still, it didn't answer the question of David's or Bob's personal expectations of her. Because of her childhood faith and her current moral code, she was a virgin, and she did not intend to sacrifice her virginity in payment for a cruise or anything else. She had promised her dying mother, and she had promised God. Perhaps she had drifted away from Him since Stan ambled into her life, but she had kept her promise of purity.

She felt David looking at her.

"There's nothing for you to worry about," he said.

She wondered if he had read her mind. Or had he heard that her unwillingness to compromise had caused the breakup with Stan? In the end, she had learned that her fiancé was running around with far less virtuous girls. Hardest to take was the fact that he blamed *her*! "You should have been named Pollyanna!" he had stormed in a moment of frustrated yearning. She would have married him in a minute, but he had always found excuses to delay, to back away from the ultimate commitment.

She wondered now whether Stan had ever intended to marry her. Perhaps she had only represented a challenge for him—a treasure beyond reach—which only further excited his imagination. She knew, too, that he considered her an asset to his business, an appropriate girl for impressing the older and more exemplary clients of his advertising agency.

As David pulled onto Century Boulevard, she noticed a carful of young women staring at them. For a moment she was perplexed, then realized that it was David they were watching. His color rose under his tan.

Did women often throw themselves at him? Katie wondered. She had never heard such rumors, although there had been nasty ones about his late wife, Eva, and the man in whose private plane she had crashed. Was David, too, accustomed to a wild lifestyle?

The girls in the adjoining lane laughed and waved, to David's further embarrassment—or pretended embarrass-

25

ment. If he were a womanizer like Stan, he was probably enjoying the attention!

Back at the office David headed for the conference room where Bob, Giselle, and two of the other directors were taking their places behind the long conference table.

"See you later, Katie," he called.

"Yes . . . and thank you again!"

She sat down at her desk. Opening the top drawer, she noticed an envelope addressed to her. She recognized Bob's handwriting. Tearing open the envelope, she read the enclosed memo: "Let's not mention your trip until Tuesday afternoon. I'll put out a general memo then. Bob"

Good idea, Katie thought. No reason to stir up a rash of complaints and jealousy among the other employees, many of whom had been with the company for a much longer time. She would simply have to clear up her paperwork as inconspicuously as possible.

Smiling in anticipation, she dug in.

It was late when the quarterly meeting adjourned, but Katie was so preoccupied that she hadn't noticed the time.

"You must be one of our most dedicated employees," David remarked over her shoulder.

Startled, Katie looked around the room. Except for board members leaving the conference area, she was the only one there. "I'm trying to clear my desk," she explained.

"May I drive you home?" he asked.

"No. No, thank you," she answered quickly. "I have my own car."

He smiled. "See you at the airport on Wednesday then. I have a pile of work to finish at the downtown office too." He waved and was gone.

She sat wishing that she weren't so apprehensive, so

mistrustful of men. Surely he must think her not only absurdly naïve, but ungrateful as well.

Finally she grabbed the manila envelope with the cruise brochure, ticket and tags, and locked up her desk. In the supply room, she found maps and brochures describing the five Caribbean islands they would visit: St. Maarten, Antigua, Barbados, Martinique, and St. Thomas. She slipped the materials into the envelope for later study.

Back home in her condo, she threw herself into getting ready for the trip. Suddenly it occurred to her that she should share her exciting news with her grandmother! Gran Lucy would worry if she phoned later and there was no answer. No point in putting any more gray hairs on that dear head!

Sitting back on the pale yellow Victorian sofa that Gran Lucy had given her, Katie listened as the phone began to ring in Northern California. From the sofa, she surveyed the furnishings in the rest of her living room.

There were two light blue armchairs upholstered in floral needlepoint from Gran Lucy, along with some lamps and a charming little French iron table with painted leather inserts. The old walnut étagère in her dining area was filled with antique china, a recent birthday gift from her grandmother.

Katie cherished every piece, not only because of the sentimental value, but because each one had been crafted with such loving care. Her taste in furnishings aside, she often thought that she was a throwback to the turn-of-the-century; in the swinging city of Los Angeles, she felt like an alien from another era.

Finally Gran Lucy was on the phone wishing her a happy birthday. "I was praying for you, Katie," she said, explaining why it took her so long to answer the telephone. "You know me. Not even the telephone can interrupt my conversations with the Lord."

Katie smiled. "I should have realized how late it is, but I'm so excited. I think your prayers have been answered," she teased. "I'm leaving next week for a cruise!"

Gran Lucy seemed delighted to hear the news, but when Katie finished, she said, "It wasn't my prayers, honey. I never prayed for you to go on a cruise. What I pray for is that you will find the right man."

Katie paused, wondering if she should tell her about David.

"You still there, Katie?"

"Yes . . ."

"*Is* there a man involved in this?"

By the time she had explained how the cruise had come about, it sounded a bit strange to her too. To receive a free Caribbean cruise after only two months with the company seemed most unusual. Moreover, she had come to know these people through Stan.

"The men . . . are they married or divorced?" her grandmother asked.

"David is a widower," Katie answered. "Bob is separated."

After a long silence, Gran Lucy said, "I hear that some of the cruise ships have ministers and priests for religious services, so it must be all right." She laughed. Have a wonderful time, Katie, dear. I'll be praying for you."

Katie was still smiling when she hung up. Gran Lucy never worried long about anything; she gave it all up to the Lord in prayer. If it hadn't been for her listening love and her prayers . . .

By midnight she had planned her wardrobe, to be supplemented by the purchase of some black heels and white sandals, along with a respectable-looking suitcase and carry-on case. After studying her budget, it appeared there might still be some money left for the side tours and tipping suggested in the brochures—and even for a little shopping on the islands.

Saturday disappeared in a whirl of shopping, packing, and making the necessary arrangements to close her condo. But on Sunday morning it occurred to her that she hadn't asked anyone to care for her plants. How could she have forgotten?

She dashed down the hallway for Mrs. Sanders' door. They had met in the laundry room a year ago, shortly after Katie had moved in, and had been fast friends ever since. Something about her reminded Katie of Gran Lucy.

As Katie knocked at Mrs. Sanders' door, her elderly neighbor arrived from behind.

"Looking for me?" she asked with a delighted smile. She was wearing her Sunday best and was surely coming home from church.

"Yes. And I'm afraid that I'm looking for a favor too." She explained about the sudden trip and needing someone to water her plants.

"It's my pleasure," Mrs. Sanders said. "I know the routine, so don't worry." She gave Katie a hug. "You just have a wonderful time!"

Tuesday at lunchtime Katie bought a stunning white suit at one of the most expensive shops in the area. Mistakenly labeled a size fourteen instead of a size ten, the suit was marked down to a fourth of its summer price.

On Tuesday night there was a check in the mail for a hundred dollars from Gran Lucy. "Buy yourself something pretty," she wrote.

You've just paid for my suit, dear Gran, Katie thought happily.

It was after midnight before everything was packed in her new tan suitcase. Anticipation mounted so that she doubted she would be able to sleep at all. She laid out her new white suit and a jewel-tone turquoise blouse for the next morning. Perhaps white wasn't the smartest thing for traveling, but the suit was washable, and she had never felt so attractive in anything before.

Taking a final look around her apartment, she stopped in the kitchen for a mug of hot chocolate. Perhaps it would help her sleep.

Moments after slipping between the cool sheets, she was dreaming of David Wallace, although upon awakening she couldn't recall any of the details.

At six o'clock the next morning, Katie approached the airline reception area, her heart racing with excitement. When she saw David striding toward her, the night's dream flickered elusively.

"You look beautiful, Katie," he said, pinning a yellow Wallace-Tyler Travel and Tour badge on the lapel of her white suit. "Now it's time to earn your keep." He handed her a clipboard with a list of passengers' names. "Just send people who are wearing blue Golden Renaissance badges to Bob or to me, and check them off your list."

"Sounds simple enough."

He went on to detail the other arrangements. David and Bob would help tour group members with their tickets and luggage. Giselle was already at the departure gate to meet them with a duplicate list of tour members to be certain that no one was lost in the bustling terminal.

David reached for Katie's suitcase. "Now, if I may take your luggage, ma'am, I'll get you checked through right away."

She suppressed a giggle and waved to Bob in the distance. Moments later, excited tour group members wearing the blue badges surrounded her. She checked their names off her list and sent them on to Bob and David for further processing.

It became simple to spot the tour group members, not only by their badges, but from their beaming faces. It was as though all of them sensed that they were soon to step into another world—and were already experiencing the release of tension and daily anxiety.

Finally all one hundred passengers were accounted for and boarded, their luggage checked. Katie stepped onto the plane with David, Bob, and Giselle. Glancing at her ticket, Katie realized that, while the three of them were seated together, she had been placed far behind. She decided not to say anything to Giselle, who had evidently arranged the seating.

Katie found her row. She would just make the best of it, and proceeded by stowing her carry-on case under the seat in front of her. Still, she couldn't help but notice Giselle nestling comfortably between the two attractive men, toward the front of the plane.

An elderly couple, who introduced themselves as Ella and Edwin Goodman, sat down beside her. "It's our first cruise," Edwin said, his blue eyes sparkling. "And we mean to enjoy it."

"It's mine too," Katie confided, admiring her seatmates. Edwin was a distinguished man—tall and erect, with a silky thatch of white hair. His wife, Ella, was slim, tanned and lovely, her silver hair cropped stylishly.

"I have the impression that the two of you enjoy almost everything," Katie said.

"We do," Edwin answered, catching his wife's hand in his. "Don't we, honey?"

Ella Goodman's green eyes danced as she answered her husband. "Life's never been dull yet."

Katie pulled out her new paperback novel, but the Goodmans' animated conversation kept her entertained. Though they must have been well into their seventies, their youthful spirits belied their age. Gran Lucy would have called them "the salt of the earth."

Occasionally Katie glanced out her window. Once the city itself with its endless suburbs and smog was behind them, she marveled at the craggy foothills thrusting from the blueness of the earth. Mist lay in the valleys, rising in wraithlike wisps. Here and there the sun shimmered on lakes and rivers, transforming them into golden mirrors. Patches of white clouds floated in the blue sky. She thought that if she were to spend a lifetime flying, she would never lose the wonder of seeing the earth from high above.

"We are now flying at an altitude of 35,000 feet," the pilot announced.

Soon the mingled aromas of coffee and bacon drifted through the plane. As the pilot described the sights below, efficient flight attendants served breakfasts of fresh orange juice, cheesy omelets with bits of parsley and bright red cherry tomatoes, hot buttered English muffins, and curls of crisp bacon.

Katie sat back, relishing every bite.

Once, David passed down the aisle, smiling at her, and her pulse quickened.

"How's it going?" he asked.

"Wonderfully, just wonderfully, thank you!" she answered brightly and saw his eyes light up as if he, too, had been caught up in her excitement. After he was gone she couldn't help noticing the Goodmans exchange a curious look.

It seemed only a short time before the spicy aromas of pasta and tomato sauce greeted them, and the attendants were serving lunch.

Katie looked down at her tray. "But we've just eaten! We'll have to run around the airport ten times to work off the calories!"

Edwin chuckled. "From what we hear, we'll all be gaining a pound a day, if not more, on the cruise!"

"You're almost too thin, Katie," Ella said. "Weight is certainly not a problem for you."

Katie nodded. "Not too long ago I was nearly twenty pounds overweight." Just thinking about it caused her to forego the rolls and most of the dressing.

"Were you dieting?" Ella asked.

"No, I just couldn't eat for a while."

"There must have been a man involved," Edwin said.

She nodded. It was not as painful now recalling the last three months of her engagement to Stan, but the details were still vivid in her mind. At first she had refused to believe that he would betray her—especially not with the secretary who had the worst reputation in the entire company. Ironically it was Katie who had introduced the two of them at an office party.

When Stan's affair with the girl became obvious, Katie began to eat compulsively as if she were trying to destroy her body, or perhaps hide her old self under a layer of fat. In those three months of anguish, she had gained twenty pounds. Then, after she had returned Stan's ring and no longer had an appetite, her excess weight had melted away. A sad way to lose weight, she thought.

Edwin Goodman looked thoughtful. "There's usually a woman involved too."

"Sometimes even more than one," Katie replied bitterly.

She was grateful when they changed the subject to travel. It seemed that the Goodmans had traveled all over the United States, digging at archaeological sites and backpacking through the Rocky Mountains.

"We're getting old enough now to prefer a more leisurely pace," Edwin said.

Ella smiled. "You'll never be old."

After the flight attendant removed their trays, Katie set her watch forward to Florida time.

It seemed that she had no more than settled back to her book, a historical romance set appropriately in the Caribbean, than the plane began its descent over lush green vegetation and white sand—only a hint of the tropical splendors to come.

As the passengers disembarked into the brilliant sunshine, there were friendly Golden Renaissance tour guides to help them collect their luggage.

"Didn't I tell you they'd be here to take over?" David asked, as they were escorted to a bus. "From here on, we can sit back and enjoy the trip."

He was just behind her as she climbed onto the bus, and she was pleasantly disturbed once more by the deep rumble of his voice. He waited as Katie sat down at a window seat, then moved in beside her.

Glancing at him in profile, she noticed that a lock of dark, wavy hair had pulled loose and hung slightly over his high forehead. Her eyes wandered to his straight patrician nose, the high cheekbones and angular chin with its deep cleft, then to the full, sensuous lips. It was a strong face, but as he turned to her, there was warmth and tenderness in his expressive brown eyes.

"Excited about the cruise?" he asked.

"I've never been so excited in my life!" she replied honestly, but there was an element of suspense that troubled her.

For a moment she expected him to slide his arm around the back of her seat, but her apprehension must have been apparent. Still, he seemed pleased to be with her.

Looking out the window, Katie was barely aware of the bustle of passengers and porters hauling luggage. The heat and humidity enhanced the musky fragrance of David's aftershave.

She heard Giselle's voice and turned to see her taking a seat across the aisle. "It seems to me that you're managing very well for a novice," she said meaningfully.

Katie blushed and focused on the people boarding the bus. When Bob slid in beside Giselle, the uneasy moment passed. Either David hadn't noticed Giselle's caustic comment or had chosen to ignore it, Katie decided.

While David settled back to read through some paperwork, Katie opened the book she'd begun on the plane. But his nearness distracted her, and she was relieved when the bus neared its destination, giving her a glimpse of a startlingly beautiful ship.

"Is that our ship?" she asked.

David leaned forward to peer past the people in front of them, his arm against hers, its warmth and strength unnerving her. "That's the Golden Renaissance," he said as if their casual contact had no effect on him at all.

Everyone in the bus strained now for a better view, chattering and laughing, caught up again in the festive atmosphere.

Closer now, they could see the ship more clearly. The Golden Renaissance was as magnificent as its name, rising majestically against the blue sky. The bus braked to a stop, bringing the passengers to their feet in their eagerness to board her.

Hurrying off the bus, they were guided to a building in which they exchanged tickets for keys to their cabins. Katie looked at her large plastic key, stamped with the number of the cabin she would share with Giselle: E77. Europa Deck, Cabin 77. David was right behind with his key for E75, the adjoining cabin he would be sharing with Bob Tyler.

As they emerged into the sunshine, the ship's photographer snapped a picture of Katie and David, a life preserver bearing the name of the ship in the background. Too late, it occurred to Katie that they could easily be mistaken for a couple traveling together.

Flustered, she said for as least the third time that day, "Isn't this exciting!" Perhaps David would think her naïve, but everyone seemed infected with a spirit of enthusiastic abandon.

"The first time is always the most exciting for everything," David said, looking down at her.

Katie had the distinct impression that, if it had not been for the photographer waiting for them to move on, David might have taken her in his arms.

CHAPTER 3

KATIE WALKED UP the gangway of the great white ship, her hair flying in the balmy Florida breeze, her heart thumping with the beat of the calypso music spilling from an upper deck.

As the line of passengers in front of her came to an abrupt stop, David asked, "What do you think of her so far?" Katie looked at the Golden Renaissance. The ship was enormous, its bow rising gracefully in a sharp curve to the many open decks above. She smiled. "I feel as if I've stepped into a living travel brochure!"

David smiled. "You're just what we need," he said. "A shot of infectious enthusiasm."

She wished that he weren't wearing his dark glasses now so that she might read the expression in his eyes.

Just behind David in line, Giselle had removed her beige suit jacket, revealing a nearly backless beige silk halter blouse. Despite the brisk breeze, every hair of her blond chignon was in place. Her eyes flickered in faint amusement. "Really, David," she said, "*a shot of infectious enthusiasm?''* Her accent added intimacy to the husky voice, as if they shared old secrets.

Katie's heart plunged at the sight of David and Giselle—the cool, beautiful blonde and the tall, darkly handsome male. They looked so right together. If her enthusiasm had not infected her cabinmate, Katie was heartened by the exuberance of the laughing, jubilant people in the line ahead. Not even Giselle could ruin this moment. Katie wished that her hands were free to clap to the rhythms of the calypso music.

On board, crisp rows of white-jacketed attendants stood like an honor guard, their black slacks sharply creased, patent shoes gleaming. For each embarking passenger, the row moved forward in greeting. Suddenly an attendant was stepping toward her, his white-gloved hand outstretched for her cabin key and small case.

"Welcome to the Golden Renaissance," he said with a lilting Italian accent. His name tag read "Paulo." He led her into the luxurious salon.

Katie caught her breath. This was nothing like the little restaurant ship in San Pedro! This was a magnificent floating hotel, its elegant decor enhanced by elaborate crystal chandeliers and plush gold carpeting befitting a palace. Following her attendant through a maze of corridors, she realized that they had lost David, Bob, and Giselle.

The passageways and elevators were crowded with attendants ushering in new passengers. Others, who had been aboard for a short time, referred to maps of the ship as they got their bearings.

As Paulo unlocked the door to cabin E77, another white-jacketed attendant hurried past, carrying Giselle's white leather hand luggage.

"Excuse, please," he said, and placed Giselle's case on the bed by the porthole.

Katie stood open-mouthed as Paulo tried to apologize in his halting English. "Don't worry. It isn't your fault," she said. If it was that important for Giselle to have the bed by the porthole, what did it really matter?

He flashed a grateful smile, turned on the radio to soft music, then quickly showed her the cabin.

It was compact, but scrupulously clean. The attractive decor featured a gold, orange and tan Roman wall mural—a touch of ancient Rome amid the most modern of conveniences. A bowl of fruit graced the white formica coffee table. Paulo had placed her case on the twin-sized bed nearest the bath. A small dressing table and two occasional chairs left very little walking space.

"The suitcases . . . under the beds when they are unpacked," he suggested, then pointed out the life jackets in the closets which also contained hangers on top and drawers for additional storage at the bottom. The floor plan was so cleverly designed that everything could be quite comfortable—if only Giselle would be agreeable!

As Paulo closed the cabin door behind him, Katie decided to unpack her carry-on case and freshen up. At least she could learn where everything fit best. And she was eager to change from her high heels into more comfortable walking shoes.

In minutes she had decided where to store the few things she had brought with her. When she finished, she leafed through the pamphlets and brochures on the dresser. There was a ship's newspaper published daily, a deck plan, and other interesting information. It would take her a while just to learn the ropes.

She was brushing her hair when there was a knock at the door. Opening it, she found David and Bob in the corridor.

"We've come to escort you deckside," David said. "The first time out, you have to watch us sail."

"I'd love it!" she said, grabbing her key and deck plan, and putting them into her white canvas handbag.

Bob wore his usual boy-next-door grin, but David looked ill at ease for an instant before she preceded them down the narrow hallway. Behind her they laughed companionably. She knew the two of them had been friends since childhood, irrevocably bonded by a near-tragic automobile accident during high school in which both almost lost their lives.

Calypso music drifted through the air as they stepped into the sunshine. On this deck there was a shallow swimming pool for children surrounded by colorful lounge chairs. Beyond, there were two other open decks, each stretching out to the beautiful blue water far below. "It's even lovelier than I expected," she said.

"Let's go down to the Promenade Deck," Bob suggested, leading the way down the steps to the Ocean Deck, then to the enormous deck below. Here there was a large swimming pool, bright plastic chaise lounges, tables and chairs, and still plenty of room for the passengers who milled about, getting acquainted.

The calypso band played at the far end of the spacious deck. On the dock below men swarmed about, loading baggage and supplies. And on the other side was the Atlantic Ocean, its dark blue depths shimmering with the promise of adventure.

"Where's Giselle?" she asked. "She was right behind us when we boarded."

Bob chuckled. "Now that's one roommate you won't have to worry about. She probably knows the ship inside out already."

Almost too soon an announcement was issued over the loudspeaker, "All visitors ashore, please. All visitors ashore. The ship will be sailing in five minutes."

It seemed only moments before a loud blast of the ship's horn signaled that they were at last underway. The stately ship glided slowly away from the dock and into the open sea, guided by two large tugs.

As she walked around the deck with the men, Katie noticed again the openly admiring glances of women of all ages—stunned by David's good looks. She felt an odd twinge of jealousy and wondered if it had bothered Eva, his late wife. Probably not. Eva had always appeared so confident, but then she had had everything—wealth, beauty . . . and David. What else could Eva Wallace have needed to satisfy her?

"The peace of God," Gran Lucy would have said. She would have called Eva one of "the restless ones."

Watching as the tugs guided the majestic ship out of port, Katie turned to view the magnificent pink-and-gold sunset off the Florida coast.

Later, as the coastline disappeared, the refreshment bar opened near the swimming pool, and they joined the others moving toward the outdoor tables. They had been served when Giselle arrived, an exotic rum drink in hand. "I made our table arrangements with the maitre d'," she said. "Didn't any of you remember that's the first thing one does on a cruise?"

Bob laughed. "You're so well traveled, Giselle, that we knew we could leave it to you."

Giselle turned her eyes skyward in dismay. "You're incorrigible. But don't expect me to do everything for all of you." She sat down next to David and absently rested a proprietary hand on the arm of his navy blazer. There was certainly nothing absent-minded about the way she took possession of him, Katie thought. Giselle knew precisely what she was doing.

David seemed unaware of Giselle's hand on his arm. In

41

fact, if she didn't feel so resentful, Katie thought she might laugh at the irreproachable look on his face. Was he really so oblivious to her charms? Giselle was surely the most glamorous woman they had seen on the ship so far.

Katie glanced at her as she lit a cigarette. Giselle was one of those rare women with slim hips and a voluptuous bosom, now extremely conspicuous against her silk halter as she sat back exhaling smoke. Her bare shoulders were smoothly tanned.

"I'm still not thrilled about eating at the first sitting," Giselle pouted.

"We appreciate your giving in," Bob said. "We're unfashionable clods."

The conversation turned to their Caribbean itinerary. The first two-and-a-half days of the trip would consist of the leisurely cruise to St. Maarten, followed by four days of island hopping. That would give them another two-and-a-half days for the return trip to Florida.

"I'm glad for the rest before we begin to play tourist," Bob said. "We can spend the next two days eating."

David laughed. "Would you believe that it's only an hour before our first meal on board?" He turned to Katie. "Cruises are notorious for ruining one's figure."

Giselle stood to leave and stretched languidly. "Well, I've never gained an ounce on a cruise. As a matter of fact, I'm skipping dinner and turning in for a nap."

As Giselle strolled seductively beyond the swimming pool, a thought occurred to Katie: "How can I dress for dinner if she's sleeping?"

"No problem," David said. "We wear what we have on tonight. The luggage probably won't arrive in our cabins until after dinner."

"Tomorrow night is the Captain's Gala," Bob said. "You can dazzle us then."

"She's dazzling just the way she is," David said, his brown eyes frankly admiring.

She blushed. "Thank you," she said, glancing down at her white suit which looked amazingly crisp and fresh after a day of travel.

"Shall we give you a tour of the ship?"

Bob darted a questioning look at him.

"I'd love it," Katie said, curious about the nonverbal messages that so often passed between the two men.

The last rays of daylight lingered as the three of them started up the steps to the Ocean Deck. Here and there, lights on the ship began to glow.

"Are you game to start all the way at the top of the ship and work your way down?" David asked her.

"I'm game," she replied. "We've been sitting all day and I can use the exercise." From her handbag, she produced the deck plan to follow as they explored the ship.

After climbing the three flights of stairs to the top of the ship, she was surprised to find that the Sun Deck was not much more than an enormous wooden platform surrounding the stack from which huge clouds of smoke billowed, huffing and hissing, into the near darkness. A small building near the stack housed exercise equipment and mats. Otherwise there was only the railing around the deck, the ocean far below, and a sky sparkling with stars.

For a long time she stood lost in the symphony of night sounds at sea. After a while she turned to look at David. He stood some distance from her, studying the sky. His head was turned away, but he was so still that he might have been praying.

"David's something of an amateur astronomer," Bob said.

Katie was only half listening. "Astrologer?"

"No, *astronomer,*" Bob corrected. "He won't have a thing to do with astrology."

43

Katie breathed a quiet sigh of relief. Gran Lucy loved what she called stargazing herself, but was adamant in her distaste for astrology. "The Bible strictly forbids it," she had often said.

"David has a good-size telescope at his apartment," Bob said.

"Really?" How little she knew about him. She knew little, too, about stars, except where to find the Milky Way . . . and something about Venus, the evening star. Locating it now, she recalled that it was known as the wishing star, referred to by the poets as "love's harbinger." She quickly turned away, wanting nothing to do with a messenger of love.

Later, as they made their way down into the ship deck by deck, Bob excused himself at the purser's office. Katie and David continued their exploration, looking in on the library where a few people were already busily writing post cards. Farther down, there were boutiques, a gift shop and a perfume shop, all now closed.

"They'll be open later," David said, noticing her wistful expression.

"I doubt that I'll be buying much anyway," she said, then wished that her comment hadn't sounded so negative. It was the gift of a lifetime merely to be a passenger on this cruise.

David seemed to enjoy playing tour guide, she thought, as they took an elevator to the cinema at the bottom of the ship. It was dark and quiet, and as they stepped into the empty theater, their hands accidentally brushed.

"Sorry," he said quickly, but he didn't look sorry at all. His brown eyes filled with longing, and she thought that he must feel as unnerved as she.

"Katie. . . ?"

"Yes?"

"How about the movie after dinner?"

Katie suddenly felt shy, remembering the electric touch of his hand. But she found herself saying, "I'd like that." The words spilled out quickly, instinctively. Reproaching herself, she wished she had said *I'd like to think about it* . . . or, *Maybe I'll unpack after dinner* . . . or any one of a thousand other excuses!

Bells chimed over the loudspeakers. "Ladies and gentlemen, dinner is now served for those at the first seating. May I wish you a *bon appetito.*"

David chuckled. "After a while those bells condition everyone to drool like Pavlov's dogs, hungry or not."

She wondered if the flash of his smile conditioned women in the same way. As he guided her to the elevator, she was furious with herself for being so attracted to him.

She could think of nothing to say as the elevator doors closed behind them. She wondered what David was thinking. That she would be another easy conquest? The elevator stopped at the next deck, quickly filling with passengers on their way to dinner.

At the dining room entrance, the maitre d' appeared to escort them through the festive room. Colorful flags hung from the ceiling, and, below, a sea of tables were beautifully set with white damask cloths and tall, silver vases of red carnations. An air of expectancy filled the room as diners settled at the round tables, attended by an array of captains, waiters, and busboys.

As the maitre d' seated her with a flourish, Katie was delighted to see Edwin and Ella Goodman at their table.

"Katie! What a pleasure!" Edwin said.

"We feel that you're already a dear friend," Ella added, smiling in delight.

Bob Tyler rose from his chair and introduced the young honeymooners across the table, Marcie and Mark Bowden, and a middle-aged couple, Walt and Sondra Zelt, whose slurred response was apparently due to the rum drinks they had carried in with them from the bar.

The waiter, elegant in black suit and tie, presented huge embossed menus, and Katie puzzled over the selections—oysters, caviar, shrimp, lobster, steak, prime rib, fish, roast and other delicacies.

The busboy filled their goblets with tinkling ice water, then brought a tray of freshly baked rolls whose mouth-watering aroma had preceded him.

There was too much to choose from, Katie thought hopelessly. When she finally decided on the caviar hors d'oeuvre and prime rib for the entrée, she was surprised to find that David had made the same selections.

"You're not newlyweds, too, are you?" Edwin Goodman asked.

Katie felt her face burning. "Oh, no! We're just friends," and hurriedly explained that her cabinmate was resting.

After the conversation shifted, Edwin leaned over to apologize. "I'm so sorry. I didn't mean to embarrass you. It's just that you . . . you seem to belong together."

"Men!" Ella Goodman said, although with such an adoring look that it was obvious how she felt about her husband.

Edwin shook his head, turning to his wife. "You know *me*. If there's any possible way to put my foot in my mouth, I'll find it," he said, and they laughed congenially.

"Did I miss something?" David asked.

"Not at all," Katie replied, wishing that her blushes didn't betray her so. She would have to get a good tan—or even a burn—if she were going to continue to react like a teenager!

"You're very beautiful, Katie," David said softly, "especially when you blush."

"Never mind!" she protested with a helpless laugh. For an instant she thought that David was going to add something, but the waiter arrived just at that moment with their first course.

"It looks delicious," she said, concentrating her full attention on the tiny silver tubs of red and black caviar served with toast tips, sprigs of watercress, and slices of lemon. "I've only had caviar once before in my life . . ." She paused, remembering that it had been with Stan.

The conversation at their table turned to travel, and Katie could only listen, spellbound. With all the talk of exotic places and people, there was no question in her mind that she wanted to be a travel agent. How thrilling it would be to travel all over the world.

"It must be a lovely thought you're thinking," Ella Goodman said, speaking across her husband to Katie. "What is that quotation . . . 'If, instead of a gem or even a flower, we could cast the gift of a lovely thought into the heart of a friend . . .'"

". . . that would be giving as the angels give,'" David completed the sentence.

Katie turned to him. "You know poetry?"

"Only a little," he protested. "My mother wrote poetry and encouraged my sister and me to memorize passages. Comes in handy sometimes."

The waiter stopped to pour a glass of complimentary wine, but she waved him away. She had begun to drink while dating Stan and wanting so desperately to fit in with his crowd, but she did not intend to continue the practice. She recalled Gran Lucy saying, "Drinking is not only the devil's way into a person, but a person's way to the devil!" And Gran Lucy was usually right.

It was at dinner that Bob Tyler mentioned the heavy pitching of the ship. "I've been on many a cruise," he said, "but this is the worst pitching I've ever felt. It should smooth out when we're in the Caribbean."

"I hope so," moaned Sondra Zelt, although it wasn't clear what was causing her distress—the rum drinks topped by the bottle of wine they had nearly finished, or the movement of the ship. Her husband seemed unaware of her discomfort, intent on playfully harassing the newlywed Bowdens.

Katie finished her prime rib, green beans and potato puffs, grateful that the rolling of the ship hadn't affected her enjoyment of the delicious meal.

"Save room for dessert," Bob warned, to a chorus of groans.

After the entrées, the waiter served a selection of cakes, pies, petits fours and elegant little tarts, followed by an assortment of European cheeses and fresh fruit.

As they pushed away from the table, she half-hoped that David might forget about the movie or change his mind. But as he helped her from her chair, he said, "It's supposed to be a good movie; they only show first runs."

The elevators were crowded, so she and David made their way down the stairwells, struggling to maintain their balance against the pitching of the ship. Katie found herself wondering about his family, particularly his mother. His father's large accounting firm prepared the final accounts for Wallace-Tyler, but she knew nothing more about the Wallaces.

"What is your mother like?" she asked.

David's face clouded. "She passed away this year."

"I'm so sorry," Katie said. "Forgive me, David."

He smiled. "It's all right. You couldn't have known. I like to remember her. She was quite a lady." He was silent for a while as they continued down the stairs. "Now that I think of it, she was a lot like you, Katie. Enthusiastic,

48

interested in others, though she didn't blush nearly as often."

Normally, neither did *she,* Katie thought as the ship lurched, throwing her against David. She looked up at him as he steadied her, thinking that he seemed inordinately pleased. Then they were both laughing as he released her.

"Here, hang on," he said, taking her hand and tucking it into his arm. She couldn't very graciously pull it away, she decided as they walked into the lighted cinema.

Inside, they found seats near the back. As they sat down she removed her hand from his arm, but he caught it back and impulsively kissed her fingertips.

"David!" she protested, pulling her hand from his.

She moved her hands well away from him when the movie began, wondering what to expect next. Was he another Stan? After all, David had been part of the same party scene when he was married to Eva. Even after her death, he had appeared at the parties for a while before dropping out to concentrate on his business.

She forced her attention to the movie, although it was nearly impossible to forget the tall man at her side.

Later, when the movie was over and the lights came on, he said, "Bob's holding seats for us in the Antilles Lounge for the First-Night-Out Party."

Katie had to think for a moment before she remembered that there was a party scheduled there.

In the lounge Bob waved at them across the crowd. He was sitting with a young woman whom she recognized as a member of the Wallace-Tyler group, but he didn't look terribly interested in her. Katie wondered if he were still in love with his wife, Suzanne, a red-headed model who had become consumed with advancing her career. No one at work seemed to know if they were merely separated or if they had actually filed for divorce.

"Thank goodness, you saved seats," Katie said to Bob. Though the room was large, people were already standing against the walls. She sank down gratefully on the small love seat, David's arm resting on the back of it behind her. She fought the impulse to relax against him. *Remember,* she cautioned herself, *you've been hurt once. Don't trust him . . . don't trust him . . .*

Staff introductions were made from the front of the lounge, then the young cruise director took over, starting "fun, games, and prizes," as he called it.

"It reminds me of those television game shows," Katie laughed as cabin numbers were called out and prizes awarded to the occupants.

Moments later, the cruise director called, "Europa 77."

"That's my number!" she said, getting up and hurrying forward. She was halfway to the front before she realized that Giselle might be coming forward to claim the prize. Glancing around, she saw no sign of her.

The cruise director was waiting to introduce her to the audience, part of the ship's get-acquainted campaign. "Katie Thompson," he said. "Where are you from, Katie?"

"Santa Monica, California," she said and thanked him for the package.

Returning to the table, she unwrapped her gift—a bottle of cologne. "And I didn't bring any perfume," she said, delightedly spraying her wrists.

After a moment David took her hand to sniff the fragrance. "It's not soft enough for you," he said. "You should smell like flowers."

She withdrew her hand and sat back. Was he so knowledgeable about women that he could match the perfume to the individual? Perhaps he'd learned from Eva who, like Giselle, made it a point to be informed about such things.

Not that there was anything wrong with that, but she had never had the money to afford many luxury items. Besides, there were more important things in life.

At midnight they wandered into the dimly lit Calypso Lounge to hear the ship's orchestra, and Katie spotted Giselle dancing with one of the ship's officers. Her sensational silvery, low-backed dress set off her blond beauty to perfection. She might have stepped from the pages of an haute-couture magazine. Over the shoulder of her dancing partner, Giselle acknowledged their entrance with the lift of a speculative eyebrow.

"It's too smoky in here," David said. "How about some fresh air?"

"Fine," she said, wondering if their hasty exit had something to do with Giselle's presence.

They wandered out to the deck and leaned on the polished mahogany railing, looking out into the night.

"Bob tells me that you know all about astronomy," she said, gazing up at the velvety sky. The brilliant stars suspended above in the darkness seemed to be keeping watch over the sleeping earth.

"Certainly not everything," David laughed. "I suppose I'll always feel like a beginner, but I do enjoy the hobby."

A line of poetry flashed through Katie's mind. "Ye stars, that are the poetry of heaven . . ."

"Byron," he responded instantly.

"You *do* know poetry!" She tried to recall some other lines: "Silent, one by one, in the infinite meadows of heaven, blossomed the lovely stars . . . the forget-me-nots of angels."

"Longfellow, I think," he said with a grin.

She looked at him in amazement, this man who knew about stars and poetry. "You continue to surprise me," she said softly.

51

His arm moved around her, slowly turning her toward him.

No, David, she thought, as she appealed wordlessly, but then it was too late to think. His lips touched hers tentatively and, instead of pulling away, she tilted her head and leaned forward. His mouth, warm on her lips, was gentle at first, then grew demanding, possessive, sending tremors through her as though there had never been another kiss on earth. When they finally parted, her breath was as ragged as his; her knees, so weak that she had to grip the mahogany railing for support.

"I'm sorry," he said abruptly. "I didn't mean to do that."

She was too stunned to answer. For a long time they stood at the railing and stared out at the night sky. She must get away to sort out her thoughts.

"It's been a busy day," she finally said, "and I still have to unpack. Perhaps I'd better get back to the cabin."

"Of course," he said.

She noticed that he limped slightly as they pressed against the wind and recalled the accident that had almost claimed his life.

Outside her cabin door, she feared that he might try to kiss her again, but he asked only if he might take her to breakfast.

She unlocked the door, thinking that she had never been invited to breakfast by a man, but then she had never been on a cruise either. "Yes, thank you," she said, swallowing with difficulty. She was grateful that Giselle was not yet in the room.

As Katie began to close the door between them, she said softly, "Good night, David."

"'Night, Katie." He smiled. "See you in the morning."

She closed the door and leaned back against it, her eyes

shut. What was she feeling? Was it the first stirrings of love or only the magic of a starlit night at sea? It was a long time before she opened her eyes. Her reverie was broken by the memory of his words spoken with regret: "I'm sorry. I didn't mean to do that."

What had he meant? The words had stung like a slap. Why kiss and then apologize?!

Finding her suitcase key, Katie unpacked quickly. On her pillow was the program for tomorrow, every hour charted for anyone who cared to try to follow the scheduled events. But she could barely concentrate and placed it aside as she slipped into bed.

She tried to empty her mind, but there was too much that clamored for remembrance. As she drifted off into sleep, her last thought was of David holding her in the moonlight, his lips moving toward hers . . .

CHAPTER 4

THE MORNING LIGHT streamed in through the porthole, awakening Katie with the memory of David's kiss. She glanced at her wrist watch. She would have to hurry to be ready for the first breakfast seating at seven-thirty. She slipped out of bed, grateful that Giselle was still asleep.

Since she planned to lie in the sun after breakfast, she chose a white, blue, and green wrap-around skirt and a scooped-neck white blouse, which could be worn over her blue bathing suit. Her new white sandals completed the outfit.

She dressed quietly and was hurrying to the cabin door when Giselle rolled over, opened an eye, and said, "Don't get too involved with David. You're not his type. You'll only get hurt."

Katie stopped, staring in amazement.

"What do you mean?" she asked.

"I was one of his wife's best friends," Giselle said. "Eva and I were classmates in Switzerland. I was the maid of honor at their wedding. I *know* David Wallace."

"But . . ." Katie was taken aback. What she did was none of Giselle's concern.

"Eva was educated at the best schools. She was well-traveled and knew all the right people when David started his business," Giselle continued. "That's the kind of woman who appeals to him on a long-term basis." She rolled back to the wall, pulling the covers over her bare shoulder.

"Someone like you?" Katie asked, slightly indignant.

Giselle shrugged. "Perhaps."

Katie flared angrily. "And why are you telling me this?"

"Because I don't want to spend the last half of our trip listening to the wailing of a broken-hearted innocent," Giselle answered evenly. "Quite frankly, I find broken hearts foolish and boring."

You ought to know! Katie wanted to say, but managed to hold her tongue. A soft knock at the door deflected Katie's anger. Giselle mumbled instructions: "I have an eleven o'clock appointment with the masseuse, then another with the hairdresser. Tell David and Bob that I won't be available to help with Ports-of-Call information."

Katie grabbed her white canvas handbag and slipped out, quickly closing the door behind her, not daring to meet David's eyes.

"What's wrong?" he asked.

She forced a bright smile. "Nothing. Nothing at all." She was certain that Giselle was mistaken about David.

"You're sure?"

"Of course." She didn't like to lie, but how could she possibly tell him what Giselle had said? If Giselle loved David and wanted him for herself, she certainly had a strange way of showing it.

"Did you sleep well?" he asked.

"Like a baby! I think it was a combination of fatigue and

56

this marvelous sea air!'' She kept up the cheerful chatter all the way to the dining room. She was determined that David should not suspect anything about Giselle's warning, but as he glanced at her, Katie wondered if she had fooled him after all.

This morning, with the draperies pulled away from the wide windows, the dining room seemed less formal. There was a magnificent view of the ocean as the ship sliced through rolling swells. At their table, Bob Tyler and Edwin Goodman rose slightly as Katie was seated.

Ella Goodman smiled brightly. ''We five must be the only early birds at our table.''

''Seems a shame to sleep away the whole morning,'' Edwin said.

''Good morning, *signorina*,'' the waiter said, presenting her with a breakfast menu.

Over breakfast they discussed the morning's activities. There was an exercise class as well as a walk-a-mile on the Promenade Deck. In addition, there was a ship tour, dance class, bridge class, bingo tournament, and a ten-thirty briefing on the approaching ports-of-call.

''And that's only this morning,'' Edwin said. He showed Katie the activities for the afternoon listed in the ship's newspaper.

''It's better to take a half-day at a time,'' David chuckled. ''Otherwise it takes the vacation right out of the trip.''

She recalled Giselle's message. ''I nearly forgot. I'm to tell you that Giselle has appointments with the masseuse and the hairdresser. She won't be able to help with Ports-of-Call suggestions for our group.''

David and Bob exchanged exasperated glances, but said nothing.

''Maybe I can help,'' Katie offered.

''Maybe,'' David said. He smiled so warmly that her

spirits lifted. "We'll have to go to the Ports-of-Call talk. It's only a matter of our being around the purser's office later in case our tour people have questions."

"Then I'll be there," she said, anxious to repay them for this wonderful trip.

Bob said, "Giselle's the only one of us who is really knowledgeable about these island tours." He shrugged. "I guess we'll just have to use the travel agent's rule-of-thumb—put the swingers on the booze cruises and everyone else on land tours."

"If Katie's around to smile, everything will be fine!" David said.

She felt a blush rising to her face again, then everyone laughed good-naturedly. It would be a good day in spite of its unfortunate beginning.

As they lingered over breakfast, David asked, "What would you like to do this morning?"

She wrinkled her brow in thought. "Walk-a-mile, then be lazy in the sunshine by the pool . . . and attend the Ports-of-Call talk, of course."

"May I join you for the sunshine by the pool?" he asked.

She began to respond breezily, but when she found herself looking into the soft depths of his eyes, she could only nod. It seemed as if other people in the dining room had faded away and only the two of them existed. Remembering their moonlight kiss, Katie also recalled David's puzzling words: "I didn't mean to do that."

Stepping out on the Promenade Deck into the dazzling sunshine with David, she walked quickly to the railing and stared out across the inky-blue Atlantic, whipping up frothy whitecaps as rapidly as her mind was churning her tumbling emotions. In one sense, Giselle had been right: broken hearts were foolish. All of the passions of life—the agony and the ecstasy—wrung out a heart until living was unbearable. It was wonderful to be in love, but torment when it ended. Vowing never to be vulnerable to such anguish again, she clenched her hands until her fingernails dug into her palms.

For a long time she and David stood at the railing looking out at the ocean, lost in their own thoughts. Without warning, he tipped her chin and kissed her gently on the mouth. "I'm so glad you're here, Katie," he said.

She could only stare at him, disarmed by his tenderness, but more confused than ever. Giselle's warning sounded in her brain: *Don't get involved with David . . . You'll only get hurt.*

A crowd of energetic walkers bore down on them, led by an athletic young woman, undoubtedly the exercise instructor. "Step it up! Step it up!" she called cheerily.

"It's the walk-a-mile!" Katie said and, to avoid further confrontation, dashed off to join them. "See you later!" she called back over her shoulder, then saw the hurt and surprise on David's face. At least this time she hadn't given him the opportunity to say that he hadn't meant to kiss her!

By the time they had circled back, David was gone. It wasn't until the last turn around the deck that she saw him again. He had changed into bathing trunks and was settling on a lounge chair in the crowd of sunbathers near the pool. He tried to catch her eye, but she pretended not to notice. She moved on, even when the other walkers disbanded near him. She still didn't know why she was running, only that she had to get away from him.

Stopping in the Mediterranean Lounge to catch her breath, she found herself in the spot where she and David had lingered for a few minutes during their tour of the ship. They had stayed to listen to the mellow sounds of a jazz trombonist and planned to return on future evenings. Now, she felt ashamed. She had run out on David quite rudely. It

59

wasn't as if she had resisted his kisses. The problem was that she hadn't resisted at all! She was frightened—not so much of David—but of her growing infatuation with him.

She turned her attention to the far end of the room where a blonde hostess explained the dress code aboard ship to a group of passengers. "For evening attire, 'formal' means tuxedo or dark suit for men, and long or short evening dresses for women," she said. "'Informal' means business suit or sport jacket and slacks; for ladies, a dress, pants suit or sports outfit. 'Casual' suggests an open shirt and slacks, and skirt and blouse, or cotton dress."

Models wandered among the crowd, pirouetting gracefully to display the designer clothing that could be purchased from the ship's boutique.

"I thought that was you, Katie," Bob said, dropping to the couch beside her. "David said you'd disappeared."

"Sorry," she said, feeling a pang of guilt. "It's just that . . . I needed to get away by myself for a while." It wasn't entirely untrue, she thought.

Bob sat back with a sigh. "I need to simmer down myself." He glanced at his watch. "Unfortunately we ought to head for the Ports-of-Call talk in a few minutes or we'll have to stand through it all." He looked tired and a bit sad.

Did the models remind him of Suzanne? Katie mused. Bob had been married such a short time; it was dreadful that it seemed to be ending so soon.

Later, when she and Bob found seats in the Antilles Lounge, she saw David approaching. He had changed back into his white resort suit. His brow was furrowed, his eyes dull and flat. "Am I welcome here?"

She scooted over quickly. "Of course, David. I'm sorry to have run out on you . . ."

He didn't seem interested in hearing her explanation as he sat down, glancing around the room.

He has a temper too, she thought, reminded of Stan. Or was it that David was merely looking for someone else? Giselle?

At the front of the room, the cruise director tapped on the microphone, and the drone of the crowd subsided as they settled back to hear about island excursions, shopping tips, and the latest U. S. Customs information.

Katie noticed that David was careful not to sit too close. Why had she been so rude to him? Why had she run? Her eyes met his for an instant, finding them cold and lifeless. He continued to scrutinize Katie and Bob. Did he suspect there might be something going on between them?

Her guilt and David's quiet anger hung in the air as tangibly as if a curtain had dropped. As difficult as it was to concentrate, Katie managed to take copious notes. On St. Maarten, there were two tours—a land trip and a catamaran cruise past both the Dutch and French sides of the island; on Antigua, three tours; on Barbados, one; Martinique, two. St. Thomas offered five tours.

There was also much to learn about shopping on the islands. Although she would not be spending much money, she should be ready to answer the questions of the more prosperous passengers.

After the talk, people started for the purser's office to buy their island tour tickets. "With my notes," Katie offered, "I should be able to help a little."

"It won't be necessary," David answered coldly.

She stared at him in dismay, recalling his words at breakfast: "If Katie's around to smile, everything will be fine!"

She wanted to slink away, but she had to buy her own excursion tickets. Heartsick, she tried to study the Ports-of-Call sheet as she drifted with the crowd to the purser's office. Long lines had already formed.

As she checked off her final tour decisions, she noticed David moving among the lines of passengers to answer questions, then stopping at the purser's desk.

The tours were far more expensive than she had dreamed, and she realized she would have to use nearly all of her money. Perhaps she could skip a tour or two and stay on the ship those days.

"This is for you," David said, shoving an envelope at her. "If you don't like the selection, work it out with the purser." He quickly moved away into the crowd.

Opening the envelope, Katie discovered tour tickets for all of the islands. Wallace-Tyler had paid for them. Or maybe even David himself. She gave up her place in line and tried to catch him.

"David!" she called after him. "I can't accept this."

"Why not?" he asked angrily. "It's part of your free package as a tour director."

As he turned away, she reached out, touching his arm. "Please let me explain."

His brown eyes, flat and glittering now, met hers. "You're on!"

Nearby, people glanced at them curiously.

"Please . . . not here . . ."

"Where then?" he asked.

People all around had interrupted their own conversations to listen. She had no idea that David was the sort of man who would humiliate her publicly. He'd been so thoughtful, so gentle. She couldn't understand this steely side of him. She rushed blindly to the elevator, both hoping and fearing that he might follow—but she was alone.

Stepping out on the Promenade Deck, she walked to the port side. Now she had achieved exactly what she had been seeking all day—time to think.

Please, God, help me! Please help me to understand what

is happening to me—and to David. Taking a deep breath, Katie realized that this was the first time she had prayed in a very long time.

Looking out at the constancy of ocean and sky, she finally felt a peace stealing over her. She sat down to reconstruct the events that had prompted this miserable cold war: First, she had run from David; then, he had seen her with Bob . . . Of course! If Eva had been unfaithful as rumored, David would be especially sensitive and would have reason to be suspicious. Quite likely that was why he had been so distant when he found her sitting with Bob.

The loudspeaker crackled. "Ladies and gentlemen, luncheon is now served for the first seating . . ."

She was not at all hungry. Just the thought of food made her ill. She opened the envelope that David had given her and glanced at the excursion tickets, discovering that they matched those she had checked off on her sheet: St. Maarten's "Under Two Flags Island," Antigua's "Lord Nelson's Dockyard and Countryside," Barbados' "Island and Countryside," Martinique's "City of St. Pierre Tour," and St. Thomas's "Coral World Island Tour."

Surely David had chosen the tours for her. But how had he guessed her preferences?

Passengers carried trays of food along the port side now, no doubt from the outdoor buffet, and the tables in front of her were already taken.

"Are these chairs available?" an elderly woman asked.

"Yes," Katie said. "I was just leaving."

Giselle would probably still be with the masseuse or hairdresser. Now was the time to pick up her paperback novel.

In the corridor she was thankful that David and Bob were not in sight. When she unlocked the cabin door, she was relieved that Giselle was out too. The beds were neatly made, the dresser and table dusted, and the bathroom sparkling. She hung her blouse and skirt, and still in her blue bathing suit, slipped into the blue, green and white cover-up she had sewn from the same fabric as her skirt.

Grabbing her sunglasses and handbag, she hurried to the outside deck, jammed with passengers who had decided to eat their lunch in the sunshine.

"Looking for a lounge, Katie?" a cheerful voice called out from across the sea of sunbathers. It was Ella Goodman, who had at her side what was probably the only empty chair on the entire deck.

Katie waved, trying to smile. "Thanks! I'm coming!" She made her way through the maze of people. Someone ahead of her was heading for the lounge, but diminutive Ella was not to be talked out of it. She and Edwin seemed delighted to see her.

"Aren't you eating lunch?" Edwin asked.

"I'm not hungry," Katie answered, "I just wanted some sun."

"Where's David?" he asked.

Katie looked away. "I don't know. Maybe in the dining room."

"Why, he's right across the far corner of the pool . . ." Edwin said, then looked embarrassed as if he realized too late that he had again spoken hastily.

"You two aren't fighting, are you?" Ella asked with concern.

"We're only friends," Katie said lightly, darting a look at David, who was surrounded by a group of bikini-clad young women. One pretty brunette, in particular, seemed to have captured his attention.

"Looked to me like a lot more than that last night," Edwin remarked, despite Ella's warning frown.

Katie removed her beach cover-up and lay back, closing

her eyes, trying to relax and let the salty air and sunshine work its soothing magic.

Strange. She hadn't felt this uptight before the cruise. Cruises were supposed to be so relaxing; instead, her body felt tense. She tried to sleep, but she couldn't halt the troubled thoughts racing through her head.

"Katie, they're going to close up the buffet," Ella said. "Why don't you have some salad? You have to eat something."

"Maybe I should." Across the pool, David appeared to be having a fine time with the girls. Perhaps it was silly, but she didn't want to walk past him on the way to the buffet.

Ella, perceiving Katie's dilemma, was already up. "Let me get something for you. I want a fresh glass of iced tea anyway."

"Well, maybe just some salad and iced tea . . ."

When Ella brought her lunch on a bright yellow tray, Katie took it gratefully. "Thank you, Ella. You're a wonderful friend."

"My pleasure, dear."

She could only pick at the tossed salad and creamy cole slaw, but she drank the strong, icy tea. Feeling David's eyes on her, her hand trembled and she set the glass down quickly.

Later, the loudspeaker announced an informal champagne party for singles in the Caribbean Lounge, and many of the younger passengers got up from the chaises.

"Why don't you go?" Ella asked. "It might be fun."

"I tried being a swinging single for a while," Katie said. "I'm not much good at it."

"You're the prettiest girl on the ship," Edwin said with great conviction, then smiled at his wife. "Except for Ella, of course."

Katie smiled. "And you two are the kindest couple," she said.

When she looked for David, she saw that he had left. Feeling heartsick, she tried to settle down with her book, but her eyes moved absently over the pages. What had she done? Why had she been so willful and foolish? Perhaps if he hadn't pressed her so hard . . .

"I've had enough sun," Katie said to the Goodmans as she slipped into her cover-up. "I'll see you both later."

"You won't recognize us tonight at the Captain's Gala," Edwin said with a grin.

The Captain's Gala! She had forgotten all about the formal evening. And she had planned to wear a filmy green gown with her silver bag and high-heeled sandals. Well, she would just skip the whole affair and ask for a tray to be sent to her room, or sneak down to the grill for a slice of pizza.

After a refreshing shower, she strolled out onto the Europa Deck. There were few passengers here, and the children who usually splashed happily in the shallow pool were probably down for afternoon naps. Katie basked in the quiet, feeling the tension draining from her.

"Katie?"

Preoccupied, she heard his voice which seemed to be coming from far away. It took her a moment to realize that David was standing beside her.

"I'm sorry," he said. "I hope you'll forgive me." He handed her a small gift-wrapped package.

Katie accepted it reluctantly and closed her eyes. "Really, David, a present isn't necessary. Besides, it was *my* fault."

Smiling hesitantly, he perched on an adjoining lounge. "I'd like us to be friends again," he said, his eyes hopeful.

How could she ever explain? "I'm sorry I ran from you this morning . . ." She looked down. "I needed to be alone."

"I think I understand," he said.

They looked at each other for a long moment, weighing each other carefully.

"Open the package," he urged.

She tore away the exquisite gold paper and, seeing the contents, gasped. "It's Joy—Patou's Joy," she whispered. She knew only that it was one of the most expensive perfumes in the world. "Oh, David . . ."

She opened the bottle carefully, and the subtle flowery scent issued from it like the essence of a summer garden. "It's lovely, but you shouldn't have . . ."

"*You're* lovely," he said huskily.

She hesitated for an instant, then daubed a drop behind each ear, leaning toward him so he could catch a whiff. He bent down, and the fragrance enfolded them, weaving its spell. He moved away reluctantly.

"It's just right for you," he said, and paused. "Friends again?"

"Of course, David . . . and thank you."

"May I come by for you about six—that is, if you would allow me to escort the most beautiful girl on the ship to the Captain's Gala."

She nodded, trying to hide her happiness and the quick tears that had sprung to her eyes.

At the aft door, he flashed a careful smile, and she felt a momentary pang. Had he meant *exactly* what he had said? That now they were merely friends?

CHAPTER 5

THE FRAGRANCE OF JOY and the memory of David's parting smile lingered as Katie dressed for the Captain's Gala. Between Giselle's withering glances and thoughts of David, it was an effort to settle down at the dressing table.

Katie studied her reflection in the mirror. She had held up very well despite the day's torment. Her sparkling eyes were now nearly as sea green as the filmy dress that lay on her bed, her face, lightly tanned from the afternoon sun.

"Who gave you the perfume?" Giselle asked as she pulled several expensive dresses from her closet to make her selection for the evening.

"A friend." Katie's answer was noncommittal.

"Was it our dear David?"

Katie didn't reply and reached for her hairbrush.

"He's been known to be extravagant. Just don't come crying to me when he disappoints you."

Katie pretended not to have heard. There was no appropriate response, anyway. Brushing back her hair, she decided on a simple style. With Giselle's barbed comments so expertly aimed, Katie wanted only to escape the cabin as quickly as possible. She was grateful when her roommate headed for the shower.

Katie slipped into her evening gown, strapped on silver high-heeled sandals, and peered into the mirror. Her dark hair swung freely over one shoulder, and was brushed sleekly back behind the other. The sea green dress with its scooped neck, tiny sleeves, and skirt falling into subtle petals was enchanting. For once, she looked exactly as she had hoped she might.

"See you later, Giselle!" she called out.

Closing the cabin door behind her, Katie felt relieved to have evaded her roommate's scrutiny. Her ensemble certainly wouldn't be Giselle's idea of high fashion.

Standing in the corridor, Katie wondered what to do next. David wasn't due for another fifteen minutes. Down the hallway she noticed a young woman helping two children tape pictures to the walls. Of course! The youth rooms were just off the children's pool. The morning newspaper had invited passengers to view the children's artwork there.

As Katie approached, the youngsters gazed at her with undisguised admiration. Blue-eyed blonds with cherubic faces, they appeared to be sister and brother—the girl, about five years of age; the boy, perhaps four.

"You look like a princess," the girl said, her blue eyes wide.

Katie laughed. "Thank you. You're pretty enough to be a princess yourself."

The boy placed a small plump hand in Katie's. "Come look at *my* pictures."

The girl reached for Katie's other hand.

Their small, soft hands in hers, Katie glanced down the corridor to be certain that David wouldn't miss her here. "I'd love to," she answered.

Praising their drawings of ships at sea and islands with palm trees, she couldn't help hoping that David liked children. One of her greatest disappointments with Stan had been his attitude toward children, a home, and marriage. "You're crazy, Katie," he had said. "It's almost the year two thousand! Who wants to be saddled with kids and mortgages nowadays?"

Saddened, she couldn't imagine David wanting that either. After all, he was a wealthy businessman whose life had always revolved around travel. He hadn't had children with his first wife. Why should he want them now?

She realized how far her thoughts had wandered and turned her attention to the children's artwork. Minutes later she looked up to see David striding toward her, breathtaking in his midnight blue tuxedo.

"She's our princess," the little girl piped out as he approached.

The boy leaned far back to look up at David. "But *he* looks like the prince."

They laughed and David patted the child's shoulder. "Sorry, but I'm going to have to carry your princess away."

"Are you *really* going to carry her?" the boy asked.

David raised an amused eyebrow and grinned.

"We have to go now, but we'll see you again," Katie reassured the children.

As she and David walked down the corridor, he said, "That boy was right. You *do* look like a princess."

"I feel like one—right in the middle of a fairy tale," she answered, determined to hold the day's unpleasant memories at bay.

In the elevator, David leaned toward her with an appreciative whiff. "You smell wonderful," he said.

Seeing the women around them pretending so hard not to be listening, Katie suppressed a giggle. "Thank you," she

71

said. "It's Joy!" she added, wondering how her fellow passengers would interpret that remark!

At the Antilles Lounge door they joined a long line of people waiting to be introduced to the captain and to have their pictures taken with him.

"Well, look who's together again!" Edwin Goodman said.

Ella nudged her husband. Curing him of his lack of tact appeared to be an impossible mission, Katie thought, although Ella accepted the challenge with good humor.

"You look wonderful!" Katie exclaimed. "Both of you!"

Edwin, in his black tuxedo, and Ella, slim and lovely in a sapphire blue gown, chatted happily about the island excursions. David, too, seemed to be enjoying the elderly couple.

The reception line moved slowly, but finally she and David were introduced to the captain, whose white uniform and Italian accent lent a special dash to the festivities. Flashbulbs flared, then they were in the lounge where formally-dressed waiters hovered with trays of drinks. On stage, the ship's orchestra played soft, romantic melodies.

As she and David sat down on a small gold velvet couch, she observed Giselle's spectacular entrance in a slinky black silk dress cut in a deep V nearly to her waist. She seemed oblivious to the stares as she floated into the lounge.

Stopping in front of David, Giselle purred, "I do hope you were saving this seat for *me*."

Katie watched helplessly as Giselle sat with fluid grace and whispered in his ear. David seemed perfectly at ease, responding with muffled laughter to a private joke. As they sat together, pressed close on the narrow couch, Katie speculated on their relationship. Giselle was glamorous, worldly-wise, an astute businesswoman. She and David shared a host of memories. It seemed natural that he should be drawn to someone so like his first wife. But Katie found herself pleading silently: *Please don't let him be in love with her!* and wondering why she allowed herself to care.

The scenario ended abruptly as one of the ship's officers crossed the room to ask Giselle to dance. He spoke in fluent French and she responded in kind. *"Mais oui!"* She rose to accompany the handsome officer to the dance floor.

Katie studied David's dispassionate look. It was impossible to tell if he minded Giselle's being swept away to the dance floor. For a moment Katie wondered if David would ask her to dance, but he only smiled down at her. Perhaps he didn't dance, she thought, remembering his slight limp. It didn't matter. It was a pleasure just to sit quietly alone with him.

Suddenly Katie wanted desperately for David to refute Giselle's warning. "Have you known Giselle long?" she asked.

He nodded, eyeing her curiously. "Nine years. Why do you ask?"

"You . . . seem like old friends."

"I suppose it depends on one's definition of the word *friend,*" he answered.

Then maybe they *were* . . . romantically involved, she thought, and fought to hide her growing disappointment. "Gran Lucy, my grandmother, always says old friends, like old shoes, are best."

"Even old shoes can fall apart," David answered. "I guess I prefer Emerson's 'The only way to have a friend is to be one.'" He chuckled. "Now how did we ever get so terribly serious?"

Katie didn't respond, knowing very well that her curiosity about his relationship with Giselle had not been satisfied.

The ship's chimes rang out announcing dinner.

"You were right," she said. "Hearing those chimes does whet my appetite."

Laughing, they stood and merged with the crowd leaving for the dining room and the gala dinner.

"How elegant everyone looks tonight," she said.

"Clothes do make a difference," David agreed, "not only in appearance, but in bearing, in attitude."

"The ship is our stage and we're all playing parts?"

"Or life is a dream in the night?" he countered, with a smile.

She shrugged lightly. "I haven't thought about the meaning of life for such a long time," she heard herself saying.

"But you did once?" he asked, growing serious again.

"Yes. It seems a long time ago." When she was a freshman in high school, she had felt very close to God. It was when her mother's cancer had first been diagnosed. Instead of weeping in self-pity, her mother had calmly accepted the verdict. Later, she had even rejoiced at being ever closer to heaven.

At first Katie had been resentful, even skeptical of her mother's attitude. Then she found that the more she prayed, the more peaceful she felt, even as she dealt with the arrangements for her mother's imminent death. Praying for strength to go on, Katie had received it, along with a peculiar joy that illuminated the darkness surrounding her. Her church fellowship had offered support and practical assistance. It had been a time of great spiritual growth.

Then she had met Stan . . . After the long months of exhausting sickroom regimen and confinement, Katie welcomed his light-hearted approach to life. After dating him for several weeks, she began to sleep late on Sunday mornings, missing the church services. Gradually she had neglected reading the Bible at bedtime. Now she often failed to pray. Nor could she blame Stan for this spiritual lapse. She alone was responsible for her relationship with God.

As they stood at the dining room entrance waiting to be escorted in, Katie reflected on what David might think of Gran Lucy's philosophy—that the purpose of life was to glorify God.

"Impressive, isn't it?" David asked, gesturing toward the festive decorations. "A little touch of France."

Jolted into the present, she peered into the room. The draperies were closed, and the dining room glowed with candlelight. A profusion of French flags hung from the ceiling, giving the room a Continental look. Rumor had it that the dinner menu would offer excellent French selections.

As she and David stepped forward, the maitre d' smiled at them. *"Bon soir, mademoiselle et monsieur."*

"Bon soir," David responded.

Katie felt like true royalty as they were ushered to their dining room captain, who, in turn, escorted them to their candlelit table.

As she sat down, she noticed that the young Bowdens, totally engrossed in each other, had ordered an expensive bottle of wine. And the Zelts were already glassy-eyed from too many rum drinks. Walt, catching Katie's eye, winked at her.

"Bon soir, mademoiselle," the waiter said, presenting her with an oversized menu. The selections were staggering, and many of the dishes were listed in French. When David turned from discussing the menu with Giselle, Katie said with a hopeless laugh, "I don't know what to choose!"

"Do you like escargot?"

"I've never tried it." She knew only that escargot were snails, and that Stan had said that was where he drew the line with French cuisine. "I think I'll have the escargot," she found herself saying almost defiantly.

"You're sure?" David asked over his menu. The glow of candlelight accentuated his high cheekbones and angular chin. He was so striking that it took her breath away.

"Positive," she all but whispered.

He reached for her hand as if for a moment he, too, had forgotten that they were discussing dinner selections.

"Would you like for me to order for you?" he asked.

"Yes, please." She noticed that Giselle was now watching them over David's shoulder, and the romantic interlude dissipated like flower petals scattering in a sudden chill wind. She reluctantly removed her hand from the warmth of his.

It was a moment before he averted his eyes, and she wondered how she appeared to him in the flattering light. Once, in the glow of candlelight, she had glimpsed herself in a darkly marbled mirror; it had been like seeing an ethereal shadow, a crinkled photograph taken in another lifetime, another era. She smiled at the memory.

"What's so amusing?" Mark Bowden asked her.

"Unreality," she answered. She remembered the children in the corridor calling her a princess and David a prince. "You know, the other side of the looking glass . . . fairy tales . . ."

Mark rubbed his bushy mustache, peering at her strangely. "I don't know much about that. I'm in the stock market. A broker."

Marcie Bowden leaned over her new husband, her auburn hair falling forward, her brown eyes intense. "He's very good at it too. You wouldn't believe how much money he made last year, even with the economy down."

Mark beamed.

Katie wondered whether their relationship centered around money. She hoped the sparks in their eyes were true love and not dollar signs.

Glancing at David, she reflected on her attraction to him. Was it his money? She didn't think so, although his lifestyle undoubtedly had its effect. Physical attraction? Partly—but she had been physically attracted to Stan too. Authority? Observing the finesse with which he dealt with people had aroused her admiration. There seemed to be more, she thought, as their eyes met again—something indefinable and just beyond her grasp.

"Penny for your thoughts," he challenged.

Daring to be honest, she said, "I was thinking about you."

"Positive or negative?"

"I don't know yet," she confessed, hoping that she hadn't backed herself into a difficult corner.

"How do I find out?"

Time, she thought, absorbed in the flickering candlelight. Even though she and David had known each other casually for several years, she suspected that it took a long time to know if one were really in love. Yet, ironically, some couples who lived together for a lifetime seemed not to possess that deep understanding and commitment that characterized the Goodmans' marriage, for instance. Perhaps it was a matter of time—and discernment.

David waved his fingers in front of her eyes. "Where did you go?"

She was grateful that there was no time for an answer. The waiter was serving her plate of escargot. The hot garlic butter smelled so tantalizing that her mouth watered. "It smells fantastic," she said, changing the subject.

David looked at her strangely, then turned to his escargot.

Katie watched as he and Giselle deftly manipulated the special metal utensil and tiny fork for extracting the meat from the escargot shell. She felt a bit clumsy at first, then became more adept. The first luscious bite made it well worth the trouble. "I had visions of my entire meal flying across the table," she confided to David and, following his lead, mopped up the buttery sauce with pieces of French bread.

"You're going to be a very expensive date for a fellow when we get home," he said. "We're spoiling you."

Darting a glance at him, she wondered if he meant fellows in general or himself, but his smile was so disarming that she thought he surely meant himself.

Giselle was holding forth with Bob and the Zelts about the Cordon Bleu classes she had taken in Paris. As they discussed their favorite Continental dishes, David joined in with enthusiasm. Again Katie felt terribly inadequate; her knowledge of gourmet cooking was limited, to say the least. Noting again her cabinmate's revealing neckline, she wished that Giselle were more modest in dress and less knowledgeable about French cuisine . . . and David!

From across the table, she saw Walt Zelt eyeing her, a knowing smile on his thin lips, and she quickly averted her gaze.

The waiter brought brown pottery bowls of French onion soup still bubbling under their thick golden crusts of cheese. Then a simple but delicious salad with vinaigrette dressing which, Giselle insisted, should have been served after their entrées in the French manner. "Why does everyone have to Americanize perfectly good French styles of eating?" she demanded in a huff.

For the main course David had chosen Boeuf Bourguignon, an aromatic beef stew cooked with red wine, onions, and mushrooms, and served over freshly made noodles. "It's the best thing I've ever eaten," Katie said as the tender meat shredded easily beneath her fork.

David looked pleased. "And you haven't had dessert yet. Mousseline au Chocolat. Chocolate mousse," he explained.

78

"I do know chocolate mousse," she replied. He must think her utterly uninformed.

Finally they stood up from the table. "I don't think I'll ever eat again," Mark Bowden vowed. He and Marcie, the Zelts, and Giselle were feeling the effects of the bottles of red wine they had consumed. Giselle, staggering slightly, reached for David's arm.

"I need a walk on deck," Katie interjected.

He turned to her immediately, leaving Giselle staring first in disbelief, then in fury.

She had purposely outmaneuvered Giselle, she thought, although she took no joy from it. Gran Lucy would say, "Do unto others as you would have them do unto you." The world seemed to say, "Do unto others before they can do you in!"

"We're going to get some fresh air," David called to Bob, who was heading for the Antilles Lounge for the after-dinner show. "Hold seats for us."

As David caught her hand in his, Katie felt a warmth surging through her. They moved through the crowd and beyond the elevators, walking up the stairwell to the Promenade Deck.

When they stepped outside, the moonlight seemed a surprise, a wonder. "I feel like Cinderella at the ball," she said.

"Maybe you are! The travel brochures call this ship a floating palace," David said smiling, still holding her hand.

A rush of tenderness flooded her as they walked to the railing, bringing back the memory of last night's kiss. She wanted more than anything to be in David's arms again. Instead, he dropped her hand and leaned against the railing, looking out at the star-spangled night.

"David . . ." she began softly, wanting to apologize again for her childish behavior earlier in the day.

"Would you like to walk?" he asked, indifferent to her mood.

She was so astonished that she nodded. Then they were walking briskly around to the gusty windward side of the ship. Katie tried vainly to secure her wildly blowing hair, thinking that either he was taking her quite seriously about needing fresh air or was not interested in a romantic encounter.

The wind made talk impossible, and she had to run to keep up with him. As they rounded the deck to the protected leeward side, she stopped. "Please let me catch my breath!"

"Sorry," he said amiably.

She searched the dark sky for the Milky Way. Finding it, her eyes traveled on. "Is there a name for those stars?" she asked, pointing to a cluster of brilliance near the horizon.

"The Pleiades," he said. "Also known as the Seven Sisters. They're supposedly the seven daughters of Atlas, pursued by the great hunter, Orion."

Did the seven sisters regret the fact that Orion never caught them? Katie mused. How she regretted running from David this morning as she thought of what might have been! Trying to recall the little Greek mythology she had learned, she asked, "Wasn't it Artemis, goddess of the hunt, who killed Orion and placed him in the sky as a constellation?"

"Most people don't know that. Now it's my turn to be impressed." David's look was frankly admiring.

Katie pressed her advantage. "Where is Orion?" she asked.

He placed an arm around her so she could see where he pointed. "The three bright stars to the left are Orion's belt. See the upraised sword in his hand?"

"Yes . . ." The musky scent clinging to his smooth-shaven jaw was intoxicating. Yet he seemed unmoved by her nearness when all she wanted now was to be in his arms.

"There, beneath the belt, you can see the Great Nebula in Orion," he continued. Suddenly he swept her into his arms, holding her tightly, his chin resting atop her hair, then just as quickly released her. "Let's go in," he said curtly.

His sudden change of mood was perplexing, and the silence between them grew as they took the elevator to the Antilles Lounge. He looked terribly serious, as if he had firmed his resolve and reached some kind of clear decision.

She tried to concentrate on the passenger capacity sign, but her heart plummeted more rapidly than the elevator.

When they stepped into the lounge, the show was beginning. On stage, the ship's combo filled the air with the African rhythms of calypso. Across the room, Bob stood to wave them over, and they made their way through the lively crowd to the place where he and Giselle were holding seats for them.

"Hi, David!" a breezy, young voice called from the seat behind them.

Katie bit her lip as she recognized the cute brunette who had hung on David's every word at the pool this afternoon. She smiled at him, secrets dancing in her eyes, her low-cut dress shimmering in the dim light.

David brightened. "Hi there, Darlene!" And he stepped aside to say something further, leaving the girl in gales of laughter. Katie could not bear the sudden stab of jealousy.

Returning to Katie's side, he said, "I'm getting into the calypso mood!" His mood seemed suddenly light and carefree.

The tour director, taking the microphone, spoke over the music. "Welcome to Calypso Night! But before this African-Caribbean style of jazz gets the better of you, we'd like to play a little game. Some of you singles are still not getting around, and, after all, the object of a cruise is to make friends . . . to have fun . . . Now I want every unattached woman in this room to hop up and kiss a stranger."

Katie sat back in dismay.

Suddenly there was a plump redhead running around the couch to kiss David. Darlene was right behind her, waiting her turn. Katie turned a disapproving look on the girls, but it didn't faze them.

Without warning, Walt Zelt pulled Katie from the couch and kissed her hard on the mouth. She was so flabbergasted that it took a moment before she could twist loose, sinking back onto the couch with David. She wanted to wipe Walt's wet kiss from her lips.

Walt laughed. "I couldn't let the opportunity pass by," he said on the way back across the aisle.

Beside her, Sondra Zelt was kissing Bob and then David.

The tour director yelled, "Enough! Enough! I didn't dream that under those quiet exteriors lurked savage jungle beasts!"

Katie was appalled that so many women . . . and Walt Zelt . . . would run around the room to kiss strangers, who possibly didn't even want to be kissed.

Onstage, the ship's combo began to play an old calypso tune, and the tour director introduced their entertainer of the evening.

The handsome black singer from Trinidad ran forward down the far aisle, taking the portable microphone, and stunning the audience with his honeyed voice. His style, as he moved around the stage, was unbelievably sensual, almost steamy. His voice, reminiscent of Harry Belafonte's, moved in counterrhythm to the music. Soon he had the audience clapping, alive with excitement, as he interspersed old favorites like "Yellow Bird" with salacious folk songs that all but sizzled as he played with the words.

Clapping to the earthy rhythms, David darted a glance at

Katie, capturing her hands in midair as their eyes locked. He seemed to whisper her name, and she was lost in the primal beat and in the passion in his eyes.

The singer swayed down the aisle toward them, the spotlight moving with him. His provocative intonations suffused his words with sensual meanings, ". . . daylight come and I wanna go home."

As the singer stopped before them, the spotlight held them in its brilliant beam, while the singer's words hung around them like molasses, ". . . daylight come, and I wanna go home . . ." He grinned, improvising to the melody, ". . . man, you bettah kiss dat woman now . . ." He stood waiting as he sang on, the spotlight fixed on them . . . and there was nothing to do but for David to kiss her.

His lips came down on hers possessively and, caught up in the music and the moment, she responded with abandon, not caring what the crowd might think, not caring about anything except the warmth of David's embrace. They were floating, spiraling away through the spotlight and the sultry rhythms until she was aware of nothing but David.

The crowd around them applauded, laughing, led by the singer, who nodded his approval in tempo with the music. Amazed, then embarrassed, Katie moved away from David.

". . . daylight come and I wan . . . na go home," the singer sang out and moved on with the spotlight.

As she sat back in the darkness, she felt as taut as the guitar strings pulsating with the calypso beat. She turned to look at David.

"Sorry!" he said harshly.

Sorry?! She hadn't felt a moment's regret—until now!

CHAPTER 6

THE NEXT MORNING Katie blushed furiously as she recalled the incident of the evening before. Just as Stan had used her to charm his clients for his own personal gain, she felt that David was amusing himself with her naïvete. Katie was certain now that she was a novelty with whom he would soon grow bored. He and Giselle had probably enjoyed a good laugh together after Katie rushed to her cabin—utterly mortified.

A kiss was a sacred thing, Katie believed, to be reserved for private moments and to be exchanged between two people who cared deeply for each other. Now she had dropped her guard more than once with David, overpowered by his irresistible good looks. But "beauty is only skin deep," as Gran Lucy had often reminded her, and who knew what lay beneath the surface of the enigmatic David Wallace. He was becoming a mystery she could not afford to unravel.

Slipping out of bed, she picked up the morning paper which the steward had slid under the cabin door. Not wanting to wake Giselle by turning on a light, she read by the shaft of sunshine streaming in through the porthole.

Under the column that listed the day's activities, she found a notice of the religious service held daily in the cinema. If she hurried, she could make both breakfast and the service. Having bungled things so badly, she was looking forward to a time to collect her thoughts.

At seven-thirty she stepped into the dining room. Only a few people were seated at each table. "Where is everyone?" she asked Ella and Edwin Goodman as the waiter seated her.

"Sleeping late, I expect," Edwin said, buttering a bran muffin. "Say, what happened to you last night after that big kiss?"

Katie swallowed, pretending to concentrate on the menu. "Nothing much. I was tired and went to bed."

"You shouldn't let such a big handsome guy like David out of your sight for long," Edwin said. "The girls were asking him to dance! In our day, you never saw anything like that!"

"Never mind, Edwin," his wife interrupted, but too late.

The words on Katie's menu blurred out of focus. She was aware of the waiter standing behind her now, taking in Edwin's last words. "Just the cantaloupe, please," she ordered, her tone a little less than composed.

"You'd better have something else too, honey," Ella urged.

"This will be more than enough." She could visualize the girls lined up waiting to dance with David. "Shameless," Gran Lucy would call them. It occurred to Katie that she had behaved just as shamelessly.

Looking up, she saw Walt Zelt strolling to the table alone.

He grinned widely. "Well, if it isn't the prettiest girl on

the ship," he said, sitting next to her. "Maybe the most passionate too."

She felt the hot flush rising as rapidly as her anger.

"Surprised me," he added. "I took you for one of those nice, quiet girls."

Katie pried the fluted paper from around her blueberry muffin, holding back her retort. She deserved his low opinion. But there was something about Walt that revolted her, an oiliness in his manner. More than that, he reminded her of dirty-mouthed school boys whose delight it was to shock girls.

It was unusual for her to take such an instant dislike to someone. Perhaps she was being unfair, she thought. Buttering a blueberry muffin, she listened to Walt discuss last night's events with the Goodmans. Evidently the gala had become even wilder as the evening progressed. David's kiss would not be the most memorable event.

"You're mighty quiet," Walt said to her after a while.

"I'm not awake yet," she answered and bit into the warm muffin.

Something brushed against her leg and for a moment she decided that it was her imagination. Moving her leg away slightly, she glared at Walt. His hooded eyes and complacent smile made it obvious that his leg against hers had been no accident.

She gulped her hot coffee, and rose to leave, waving to the Goodmans. Walt seemed amused. What she needed was some fresh air.

"What's wrong?" Walt asked with a chuckle.

"Excuse me, please," she said, getting up from the table.

Minutes later she stepped out on deck into the dazzling sunshine. She inhaled deeply, her anger beginning to dissipate. How different things appeared when one was surrounded by the perfection of God's creation. It was man who took that which is precious and beautiful, and tarnished it with greed and lust. A man like Walt Zelt.

As she stood at the railing, she realized that something had changed. Of course! Instead of a dark inky-blue color, the sea was vibrant turquoise. During the night they had sailed into the Caribbean.

The few passengers who were out on deck were exclaiming over the surprising turquoise sea. Others lay on lounges, reading or dozing. Two joggers made their way around at intervals.

Katie wandered to the back railing and stood watching as the ship pressed onward through the water. Behind her, the wake flared, sparkling like diamonds into white cresting waves, then smoothing again to a glassy stillness. Would her life be like the passage of this ship—temporarily disturbing the surface of things only to fade quickly, leaving no lasting imprint? She knew she wanted more—to probe the depths, to discover the treasure buried within her.

She had seen no other ships, and there had been no sign of birds or fish since they had left Florida. It seemed as if they were moving through the beginning of time, as if the earth had just begun. There was only the sky with its high, white puffy clouds, the turquoise sea, and the big white ship passing through.

Time seemed irrelevant as she stood there. Nothing seemed important except being a part of this moment in existence. When she did glance at her watch, she realized the service was already in progress.

By the time she reached the Continental Deck, she could hear the sounds of singing. The familiar hymn had once been a favorite of hers—"Sweet Hour of Prayer." Strange that she never found sweetness now in her occasional perfunctory prayers.

A smiling young woman handed her a hymnal already opened. "Second verse," she whispered.

Katie's voice, a mellow alto, joined with the others: "Sweet hour of prayer, sweet hour of prayer, Thy wings shall my petition bear, To Him whose truth and faithfulness engage the waiting soul to rest . . ."

Without warning, tears flooded her eyes. Though her voice quavered, the words were comforting: "And since He bids me seek His face, believe His word and trust His grace, I'll cast on Him my every care, and wait for Thee, sweet hour of prayer."

What was it about the words that had touched her so? She examined them again. "Thy wings shall my petition bear . . ."

"God inhabits the praise of His people," Gran Lucy always said. "Prayers move on wings of love, on that golden shaft of joy that opens when you praise Him. I don't believe prayers of desperation are nearly as effective."

Prayers of desperation . . . That described her prayer life lately, Katie thought miserably as she sat down.

The pastor stood before them. "Heavenly Father," he prayed, "most glorious Lord God, at whose command the winds blow and lift up the waves of the sea . . ."

Katie sensed the presence of someone standing beside her. For a moment, she hoped it was David, though she had no idea whether he was a believer.

The words of the hymn continued to haunt her. "I'll cast on Him my every care . . ." She had not cast her cares on God for some time. She tried to do everything herself as if she doubted His ability to handle her affairs.

The pastor's prayer was a paean in praise of the beauties of the earth, sky, and sea. When it was over, she opened her eyes to find Ella Goodman at her side as they sat down.

"God is love," the pastor said. "Love is patient and kind, never jealous or envious, never boastful or proud, never haughty or selfish or rude. Love does not insist on its own way. Love does not delight in evil, but will barely notice when others accidentally do wrong . . ."

Why couldn't she have recognized Stan's boastfulness and arrogance? He had been all pride, all ego, yet she had loved him so much. She had grown more and more like him, and now she was holding grudges against him.

The pastor continued. "If you love someone, you will be loyal no matter what the cost . . ."

Stan had been totally disloyal! Katie thought in dismay. He had only pretended to love; he had made a mockery of it, a sham, but perhaps it had been her fault too. Only love misused could destroy.

"We can see and understand only a little about God now," the pastor said. "It's as if we were peering at His reflection in a dim mirror. But someday we will see Him face to face. Then we'll see everything clearly, just as clearly as God sees into our hearts right now."

Katie wasn't sure that she wanted Him to see into her heart. She was still so full of bitterness about Stan—and now David.

"There are three things that remain," the pastor said, "faith, hope, and love—and the greatest of these is love. Let love be your greatest aim."

After the service, Ella said softly, "I knew you were a believer. I just had a feeling about you."

"I've been away from God, for a long time it seems, Ella. I've made such a mess of things."

"You're not alone," Ella said, collecting her handbag. "For a time I tried to run the world around me, and it almost ruined our marriage . . ."

"*Your* marriage?" Katie asked, astonished. "It seems so

solid. You two are so right for each other, so happy together."

"It wasn't always that way. I suppose that if divorces had been more popular when we were young, our marriage would have been another of the casualties," Ella said. "Instead of turning to a divorce court, which doesn't seem to settle much anyway, I got on my knees every day and turned everything over to God."

"What happened?" Katie asked.

"I slowly found peace . . . a deep serenity I'd never had before. And joy! I hadn't even known what the word meant." Ella paused, "And I learned about love."

"About love?" Katie echoed, not comprehending.

Ella nodded. "First I learned that I didn't have to *like* everyone or what they did. Then I found that I could love people who hadn't even seemed lovable before."

"What happened next?" Katie asked as they headed out of the theater, lagging behind the others.

"Next Edwin and I *really* fell in love." She laughed. "We'd been married for twenty years by then. Everyone thought that we'd gone crazy, holding hands and acting like newlyweds."

"Sounds wonderful!" Katie said.

"It was and it still is," Ella said. "I think that Edwin's actually relieved that I love Jesus more than I love him. Poor Edwin was tired of being my knight in shining armor, trying to be perfect. You see, I had made a god of him. I forgot that we were mere mortals. But we finally have our priorities straight."

They walked on in silence for a while.

"You love David, don't you?" Ella asked.

"I don't know. I don't want to, yet . . ." She stopped. "You see, I just broke an engagement a few months ago." She found herself confiding in Ella what she had told no one

91

except Gran Lucy about Stan's unfaithfulness, her own hurt and bitterness.

The older woman raised her eyebrows. "Good thing that you found out before it was too late."

Katie dropped her head, anguish flooding her again. "I trusted him so much!" she blurted, struggling to control her emotions.

They stopped in front of the elevator and Ella pushed the button. "I trusted Edwin too," she said softly.

Katie was aghast. "Edwin?"

Ella smiled. "We were young once, you know, and temptation is always lurking around the next corner. Another girl. Another man. I expect that it's always been like that."

Katie nodded. "It's just that I can't trust men at all anymore." She thought about Stan and David . . . and Walt Zelt only this morning.

"I suppose it's going to take some time, Katie," Ella said. "What you're going to have to do first, though, is to trust God."

The elevator doors opened, ending their conversation. As Katie stood in the elevator she wondered, *How can I learn to trust God again when I haven't trusted Him for so long?*

CHAPTER 7

IN THE CABIN Giselle still slept soundly.

Katie changed into her swimsuit and cover-up. She slipped her paperback book into her handbag and stepped into the corridor.

"Katie?"

She stopped at the sound of David's low voice, not turning, trying to compose herself as he caught up with her. He was dressed for sunbathing in a white terry cloth beach jacket and blue trunks.

"Going to catch some sun?" he asked, looking as if the incident of the evening before had been erased from his memory.

"Yes," she replied, with cool restraint.

"Interested in some company?" he asked.

"Why not?"

Any woman sitting beside him last night could just as easily have been the recipient of that passionate kiss, inspired by the sensual music and the insistent singer. As for that first night . . . an honor bestowed on the newest member of the agency? A memory to pack away with other mementos of the trip? A natural outcome of moonlight and mood music? After all, he *was* a man, and men seemed to share a number of disturbing similarities.

Passing the children's drawings in the corridor, she glanced into the youth activity room. The two children sat with a group busily creating other artistic masterpieces.

"Look!" the little boy said. "It's the prince and princess!"

"Hi, kids!" David called as they waved their greeting.

Katie had enjoyed the pleasant interlude with the children, but they belonged to another woman. The entire evening had been a fairy tale . . . just a glamorous gala aboard a cruise ship. It had nothing to do with reality.

Down below on the Promenade Deck, late risers were served a continental breakfast from the buffet tables.

"Have you eaten?" David asked.

"Yes. In the dining room."

"Good girl," he said. "I'm afraid I just got up."

Not very surprising, she thought, as she settled on one of the lounges near the pool. Obviously, after she had left, he had partied late into the night. And if he cared for her at all, he wouldn't have risked hurting her by bringing that fact to her attention.

She took off her beach cover-up and sat down on the lounge, aware that David was admiring her trim figure. The look on his face was undisguised male appreciation. She may not have the generous curves of a Giselle, nor would she display them so flamboyantly, but she was beautifully proportioned and her modest swimsuit revealed the lovely lines of her body.

David appropriated the adjacent lounge, removing his beach jacket, while Katie slathered herself with suntan lotion, far too aware of how attractive he was.

"Can I get you anything from the buffet?" he asked, standing over her.

Disconcerted by his nearness, she answered, "Yes . . ."

He smiled. "Yes, what?"

"Just orange juice," she said, quickly pulling out her book and opening it.

When he returned, she was engrossed in the story.

By eleven o'clock all the chaises on deck were occupied, and the smell of suntan lotion mingled with the salty tang of the air. Katie brushed away the moisture from her upper lip. "Think I'll take a dip."

"It's a salt-water pool," he cautioned. "You'll ruin your hair."

"It's washable," she laughed, guessing that Eva and the glamorous girls he dated were overly concerned about their appearance.

"I'm glad you don't melt," he said, getting up with her.

She cast about for a retort. "I have to wash my hair for the Wallace-Tyler party this afternoon anyhow," she stated flatly.

She ran to the pool, the deck hot under her feet, but not so fast that she didn't notice Darlene and the other girls who had surrounded him on the deck yesterday. They watched him now, their eyes filled with admiration. She didn't even want to see how David dealt with their attention. Stan would have played it to the hilt to arouse her jealousy.

Noting again the "No Diving" sign, she decided it was posted because of the constant sloshing of water. All three of the ship's swimming pools were surrounded by tile decks and two-foot decorative walls. Despite the enclosures, water often splashed over them, sending squealing sun-bathers fleeing.

"I thought the Caribbean was supposed to be smooth," she said.

"There's probably a storm brewing somewhere," David responded.

Grabbing the handrails, she stepped into the pool. "The water is so warm!"

"It not the Pacific," he laughed, waiting for her to move away from the ladder.

She pushed off with a breaststroke in the buoyant salt water, then suddenly realized how little control she had. As the water tossed from one end of the pool to the other, she was lifted like a goldfish in a slowly tilted bowl.

"This is fun!" she called back to David.

"It's different," he admitted as he swam toward her. "But I like a little more control over my direction."

She considered his words in light of this morning's religious service. How much control did most people have over their direction in life?

As they lolled about in the pool, the swells increased, but the swimmers took the unpredictable shifts with good humor. Several clambered out after a particularly violent splash, while others climbed in to take their places.

Suddenly a huge swell lifted the ship, bouncing the swimmers across the pool, then heaved them forcefully at the wall. For an instant Katie was certain she would crash against the tiling, but David grabbed her, hauling her to safety.

"We'd better get out," he warned. "It's getting dangerous."

As he pulled her behind him toward the ladder, the water surged back, carrying them with it. With the force of a powerful undertow, they were thrust toward the pool wall once again. At the last moment David braced himself in front of her, taking the full blow on his back as the water pressed her heavily against him. She could only stare helplessly, her eyes wide. As the water shifted once again, he helped her up the ladder and followed quickly.

The ship's general alarm bells rang, and an announcement crackled over the loudspeaker. "Since we are experiencing heavy swells, we ask that all swimmers vacate the pools. We repeat: Swimmers vacate the pools."

They stood for a moment, catching their breath and licking the salt from their lips.

"High adventure! Just what the brochures promised!" David teased to ease the tension, brushing his wet hair from his face.

"Almost too much," Katie replied, remembering with embarrassment the instant she had been pressed into David's arms by the restless water. But he seemed strangely composed and unaffected by their intimate encounter.

Seating herself on the chaise lounge, Katie coiled her wet hair and fastened it on top of her head. Newly aware of David's presence, she couldn't return to her reading and was frustrated to see that he had rolled over onto his stomach and had apparently fallen asleep. She applied a liberal coat of suntan lotion, wishing that she could escape her turbulent emotions so easily.

It seemed only moments later that she heard David's voice calling her name. "Katie!"

He was moving slowly toward her through a crowded room, much like an airport terminal, searching the faces in the crowd. She was trying to reach him, to let him know that she was coming—but her legs were immobilized in warm liquid . . .

"Katie! Wake up! You're going to burn."

She opened her eyes, feeling the heat on her back and legs, tasting the brine on her dry lips. Raising her head, she found David watching her with concern.

"I hated to awaken you, but your back is turning red," he explained.

She blinked groggily and rolled over. "What time is it?"

"Twelve-thirty. Time to eat again."

"Oh, no!" She sat up, smiling sleepily.

"The good news is that the buffet lines are down to a reasonable wait," he said.

"I feel too lazy to move," she said, reaching for her cover-up. She noticed that he had donned his beach jacket. Good! She felt far more comfortable.

"Let's eat," he said heartily and pulled her to her feet.

In the buffet line, they found Bob Tyler. "Where's Giselle?" he asked. "I haven't seen her all day."

"She was still in the cabin sleeping when I changed around nine-thirty," Katie said. "Something wrong?"

"No," Bob said. "It's just that I hear she tottered in last night about four o'clock, and I was hoping that she'd help with this afternoon's party. Seems she had a little too much to drink. She's been known to be incapacitated the day after."

Katie ignored the remark and turned her attention to the sumptuous buffet set up in the shade of the overhang. The aroma of fried chicken, Italian sausages, meat balls, fish, lasagna, spaghetti, and meat loaf wafted from the enormous stainless steel serving dishes. There were salad bar makings as well as fruit salads, cole slaw, macaroni and carrot salads, and a luscious assortment of desserts.

"Come join us, Bob," David invited as their plates were filled by attendants.

"No, thanks. I'm on the Sun Deck with a good book."

"And a bevy of beautiful women, I'll bet!" teased David.

"Yep!" Bob grinned. "But none of them are my type."

It was strange to hear them bantering about women, Katie thought as she placed a glass of iced tea on her tray. Did they ever discuss her? Compare her with Giselle?

They were laughing again and she looked at Bob intently. With his sandy hair and boyish good looks, he was certain to attract many women, but she had the impression that he wasn't in the mood now. She recalled that at work he'd occasionally shown interest in her . . .

"See you later," Bob said and disappeared up the steps to the deck above.

"I wonder if anyone is eating lunch in the dining room today?" Katie asked. "It would be a shame to pass up this sunshine."

David nodded. "It couldn't be more perfect."

"No," she agreed. *It couldn't be more perfect.* She looked at him, wondering what he had meant, but his dark glasses masked his expression. Luncheon tray in hand, they wound their way back through the scattered lounges. As they ate, they chatted about the afternoon's party for clients and the island tours ahead. She was happy and fulfilled and knew that the dazzling warmth she felt had nothing to do with the sunshine.

"Time for me to wash my hair for the party," she said later, reluctant to leave.

"Why don't you try the beauty salon?"

She hesitated, not wanting to admit that her budget didn't allow for such luxuries.

"Just charge it to your cabin," he said, as if guessing her dilemma. "We'll consider it a company expense since you are playing hostess."

On the Ocean Deck, she found the salon easily. An hour and a half later, Katie marveled at the transformation wrought by the deft fingers of the British hairstylist. Her hair had been swept back, dipping slightly over the left eye, then pulled to one side to tumble in a heavy curl to her shoulder. A few errant tendrils had escaped to float provocatively around her face. Feminine. Definitely feminine.

"It's a distinctive look with that thick, dark hair of yours, ducks," the woman said. "Lovely, if I do say so myself."

Later, in her room, Katie had less than a half-hour to dress. She slipped into a white-on-white striped linen, its square-cut bodice appliqued with tiny flowers. She daubed a drop of Joy behind each ear and at the pulse point of her wrists.

Suddenly the cabin door opened. "Well, if you aren't the picture of the ingénue," Giselle smirked.

Katie managed a smile. Maybe she didn't look sophisticated, but, if clothes made a statement, the simple white dress said that this was a lady, not a swinger. She picked up her small clutch purse. "Aren't you going to the Wallace-Tyler party?" she asked Giselle, who was changing back into her nightie.

"I'm not feeling well," Giselle said. Her face was pale.

"What's wrong?"

"Motion sickness. The doctor gave me a shot and some pills. I can't help with the party."

"Is there anything I can do for you?" Katie asked with concern.

"Yes," Giselle yawned and turned away. "Let me sleep."

Katie closed the door softly.

Arriving in the Calypso Lounge a few minutes early, she found David and Bob there ahead of her. "Giselle can't make it," Katie said. "She's ill." The two men exchanged glances.

"Well, *you* look cool and crisp," observed Bob.

Katie laughed. "Giselle's word for it is *ingénuous!*"

"Aren't you?" David asked, leaving her to guess which definition he had in mind—*naïve, simple, trusting, innocent . . . ?*

David and Bob were genial hosts, and Katie loved play-

100

ing hostess to the Californians who had flown out with them. Nearly everyone attended the party, many of them delightful older clients like the Goodmans who were enjoying every moment of the trip. Waiters hovered solicitously with refreshing beverages and elegant canapés made in the ship's kitchens.

The party was nearly over when Katie noticed Walt Zelt heading in her direction. She quickly glanced around to find David watching closely from across the room. She smiled and tried to walk leisurely to his side.

"Having fun?" he asked, his eyes focusing just over her shoulder.

"Wonderful!" she exclaimed. When she turned, she saw that Walt had followed her.

"Well, if it isn't the passionate couple," he jibed.

David ignored the rude comment. "Are you having a good time, Walt?"

"Not as good as you two, I'll bet," Walt replied.

A muscle in David's jaw tightened. "I think you have the wrong idea," he said, grabbing Walt by the elbow. "Here, let me get you a fresh drink."

Katie was astonished to see how adroitly David maneuvered the heavy, older man through the crowded room to his wife, who appeared a bit dazed from too many drinks. Despite her irritation, Katie nearly laughed.

"Good party, wasn't it?" Bob asked, as the congenial crowd thinned.

"I thought so," David agreed. "What about you, Katie?"

"A smash!" she said. "Everyone had such a fine time that I'm sure they'll be booking another cruise with Wallace-Tyler."

"Spoken like a true travel agent!" The men smiled their approval. Then, arm-in-arm, they headed for the Mediterranean Lounge to recap the events of the afternoon and to enjoy the stylistic piano renditions. Before long the dinner chimes sounded.

As they were escorted into the dining room, Katie thought what a pleasure it was to be sharing the evening with David and Bob. There was something touching about their friendship—the playfulness of small boys, with overtones of greater depths of mutual understanding. They had clearly experienced both good and difficult times together. If anything, Bob seemed somewhat protective of David— perhaps a result of the accident in which he had been the driver, Katie mused.

In the dining room, the Zelts were already seated. Walt rose slightly and somewhat unsteadily from his chair, his eyes glittering as he looked at Katie. She was glad to be sitting safely between David and Bob. Something about Walt Zelt frightened her.

"There's an Agatha Christie movie on tonight," Bob said.

"How about it, Katie?" David asked. "Will you join us?"

"Delighted," she said. She sat back to enjoy the informal dinner which was delicious without being a major production. She noticed, too, that with Giselle absent, all three of them seemed more relaxed.

After the movie, they stopped in the Antilles Lounge to watch the floor show, a country singer and a comedian. The only sour note of the evening was when David and Bob escorted Katie back to her cabin. She was surprised to see Walt Zelt in the corridor. For some reason, she hadn't known that the Zelt's cabin was on the Europa Deck.

"Good night, Katie," David and Bob said as she let herself into the cabin.

"Thanks for a lovely evening," she said.

Giselle was in bed sleeping peacefully. Latching the chain securely, Katie wondered about Walt Zelt's reaction to the threesome. Whatever it was, she was sure to hear from him later.

CHAPTER 8

KATIE AND BOB TYLER stood at the railing of the Promenade Deck, looking out at the magnificent stormy seascape. Billowing gray clouds blotted out large portions of the blue sky.

"Surely it wouldn't rain for our first stop, would it?" Katie fretted as the ship plowed across the open sea toward the island they would visit in the Netherlands Antilles.

Bob appeared unconcerned. "October storms usually blow through quickly here."

A fat drop splatted on Katie's forehead, then another on her bare arm. Suddenly rain splattered loudly on the deck, starting a run for cover by everyone.

"It'll be over in a few minutes," Bob said as they stood watching from under an overhang.

Noticing wet splotches on her white blouse and old brown culottes, she was glad that she had decided on a practical outfit for the day. Her culottes would be comfortable for climbing in and out of the small boat that would tender them from the Golden Renaissance to the dock at St. Maarten.

Her white sandals would be sensible for walking, and her hair was held back by a huge tortoise shell barrette that Gran Lucy had given her. For fun, gold hoop earrings dangled at her ears.

She wiped the dark drops from the brown plastic cover of the small camera hanging from her neck. The fragrance of Joy on her wrists and behind her ears seemed intensified by the warm rain. She wondered if Bob knew that David had given the perfume to her.

"We'd better eat inside," Bob said when it appeared that the rain was not going to stop. They joined the throng of passengers who had made the same decision and rushed for the elevators and stairs.

In the dining room, Katie looked for David, but he had received a radiogram from the Los Angeles office. Evidently it required an immediate reply. As she sat down at the table, the Zelts approached.

"Let's sit over here," Walt said to the waiter, indicating the two empty chairs beside Katie.

"Ready for our first port?" Walt asked as he sat down heavily.

"All set."

"I thought you'd be bursting with enthusiasm." He glanced around. "But then your lover boy isn't here."

She bristled at the insinuating term. "I beg your pardon." She hoped Bob would come to her rescue, but he was discussing something with Giselle.

"Isn't David your lover boy?" Walt asked so loudly that diners at the next table turned to listen. "Maybe you're not the sweet little thing you pretend to be," he continued with a grin. "Maybe Bob is your lover boy too."

It was all she could do to refrain from slapping him. "It isn't any of your affair!" she blurted, then regretted her unfortunate choice of words.

He laughed.

"Is that husband of mine giving you a bad time?" Sondra Zelt asked with a sigh. "You just ignore him, honey." She patted her hand. "Actually, he only bothers the pretty girls."

Ella Goodman caught Katie's eye across the table, sending her a consoling look. Then the waiter was handing out menus.

Later, hurrying outside to the Promenade Deck, she was delighted to find that the rain had stopped. Overhead, the clouds parted, giving way to patches of blue. Despite the wet deck, an expectant crowd stood at the railing, waiting for a glimpse of the green, hilly island on the port side.

The first sighting of land since leaving the Florida coast brought a spontaneous burst of applause. In the tropical sunlight, St. Maarten glowed like an emerald, set in turquoise sea and alabaster sky. It was a sight well worth the wait.

"That you, Katie?" A tremor of joy stirred as she heard David's pleasant, rumbling voice. "Where have you been all day?" he asked, carrying a handful of cookies to the railing.

"I slept late," she explained sheepishly. "And then gobbled lunch in the dining room."

"Have some dessert then." He offered some of the cookies, and she selected one with chocolate chips. At that moment David reminded her of a small boy—a boy who might have raided Gran Lucy's cookie jar.

They stood watching as sailors rode down in one of the covered lifeboats being lowered to the water alongside the ship. Near the bow, the gangway moved into position.

"Guess we'd better head down and get in line," David said, grabbing another handful of cookies from the buffet table. "Everyone seems to think that if you're not on the first boat tendering to the dock, the island is likely to disappear."

The loudspeaker announced, "Now cleared to land passengers."

Down on the Riviera Deck, Katie and David joined the milling crowd moving out to the gangway which led steeply downward to a small boat below. Katie clung tightly to the handrails, noticing in the distance that one of their tender boats was already halfway to the dock. At the bottom, a crewman helped her into the boat. David was close behind.

"Over here!" Bob called out from his seat near the front. No sooner had they taken their places near Bob and Giselle than the small vessel was underway—a mere speck beside the Golden Renaissance.

"Something happen between you and Walt at the table today?" Bob asked Katie.

David turned to hear her reply, but she shook her head nervously. Glancing about the boat, she was glad the Zelts had not boarded. When she looked out across the water toward St. Maarten, she found David studying her curiously.

Pulling her camera from the case, she began to snap pictures of the glorious seascape—above, the rain-washed sky ablaze with sunlight; below, a hundred small sailboats gliding like white butterflies on the turquoise sea; and, in the distance, the luxuriant green hills of the island beckoning in welcome.

"It's beautiful!" she whispered reverently to David when she was seated.

"*You're* beautiful!" he said, leaning forward to catch her hand in his. Her heart pounded wildly, but at a wry look from Giselle, he dropped her hand and turned to view the port town of Philipsburg.

Nearing the dock, a woman read from the tour excursion sheet: "This island has been peacefully divided between Holland and France for over three hundred years. Philipsburg is the capital of the Dutch portion of the island of St. Maarten; the Dutch spelling the name of the island with two a's; the French, with one. Otherwise the differences are few . . ."

On the dock, the tour director called out, "Half an hour till the buses leave from the main street! Yacht cruise people can assemble over by the tour sign!"

Katie's legs bounced strangely under her as she walked across the dock. "It's moving!" she said, steadying herself by clinging to David's arm.

"It's your sea legs," David laughed. "We haven't walked on land for three days."

On the other hand, Giselle, wearing a low-necked, black T-shirt and scanty white shorts, seemed unaffected by the days aboard ship. With her blond hair pulled back into a Grecian fall, she looked fresh and alluring.

"I loathe bus tours," Giselle said, as they headed for the painted archway spelling out "Warm Greetings."

"Should have taken the catamaran tour," Bob shrugged.

"I took it last year," Giselle answered. "Anyway I wanted to be with you handsome men."

David and Bob chuckled, but Katie saw nothing funny about it.

The four of them stepped under the welcoming archway into the city of Philipsburg. Just beyond was a small white clapboard courthouse, only two stories high. Except for louvered shutters at the windows and nearby palm trees, the building resembled many pictures she had seen of New England architecture. A brown shingled church with a steeple was distinguished by unique white shutters that flared outward like angels' wings.

The narrow main street, jammed with cars, was a succession of cafés and tourist shops with Dutch names like "Natraj." Katie lingered at the window of a linen shop, spying a lace tablecloth for Gran Lucy, then followed the others down the street.

"What do you think of it?" David asked Katie.

"It's not at all what I expected."

"Tourist trap," Giselle said shortly.

Wandering back to the corner where they were to catch the bus, they passed the linen shop again. "Do you think there's time to shop?" Katie asked. "That tablecloth looks perfect for my grandmother's big, round table."

Giselle glanced at it in the shop window. "You'll do better in St. Thomas."

Katie bit her lip. She should have known better than to ask. Perhaps Giselle was right, but she had a way of making Katie appear so foolish.

On the bus Giselle maneuvered a seat beside David, forcing Katie to take the next vacant seat where she was joined by an elderly lady. The door flapped shut, and the bus jerked forward.

As they drove past the small downtown area, the driver turned on the microphone: "Welcome to St. Maarten," he said. "Unfortunately, on this humid day, our air-conditioner is not working . . ."

This announcement was met with loud moans, and Katie heard Giselle's "I'll bet!" from two seats away.

Katie opened her window wider. As the bus gained speed and headed for the green hills, the breeze was pleasant. The sun warmed her arm, though her spirits were chilled by visions of Giselle's hand resting possessively on David's arm, of her golden legs bare beside him.

Curving through the open country and small villages, the driver pointed out the Great Salt Pond and other sites of

110

interest as well as the magnificent vistas of green hillsides jutting into the turquoise Caribbean.

At International Point, most of the passengers climbed out to take pictures. Katie focused her camera on a velvety finger of land reaching out into the sea, then beyond to other distant islands.

She noticed that Giselle and David were not taking pictures, and, when they all climbed back on the bus, the woman sitting next to Katie said loudly, "I thought the tall, dark-haired fellow was your husband. Guess I was wrong."

Katie turned bright red. "No, we're all just friends."

Later, the bus descended to the French side of the island and they drove into the capital town of Marigot.

"This is more like it," Giselle said, loudly enough to be heard. "At least the atmosphere is a bit French."

Though the shops and houses bore a distinct aura of New Orleans, at least from what Katie had seen in pictures, she did not think them superior to the architecture on the opposite side of the island.

She followed the other passengers out for the half-hour rest stop, feeling increasingly forsaken as she was separated from the others by the crowd.

"We're going to have something cool to drink," Bob called to her as the three of them started out toward an outdoor café just above the town. It was a dubious invitation at best, and Katie had the distinct feeling that she was somehow intruding. Giselle talked rapidly, pointing out the sights. How enthralled David seemed with her!

Halfway up the small hill, David turned back, still laughing at a remark Giselle had made. "Aren't you coming, Katie?"

She nodded and followed them to the white clapboard café with its green-painted trim and trailing greenery. This was the man who had held her hand just a short time ago and called her beautiful. Was Giselle hearing the same words?

Bob stood under a white wooden canopy at the service counter. "What would you like?" he asked.

"Soft drink, please," she said, waiting with him while the busy counterman opened the bottles.

She had already seen David and Giselle in rapt conversation at one of the umbrella tables, and she hesitated, fearing that she might interrupt something. But Bob was carrying the tray of drinks to the table and there was nothing for Katie to do but follow. However, she was determined not to sit next to David and took the white metal chair near Giselle.

As she sipped her fruit drink, she realized that she had made a serious blunder. Next to Giselle, who looked cool and immaculate, she must appear wind-blown and travel-stained in her old clothes. She tried to smooth back the damp hair that had curled loose from her barrette. Worse still, she felt a headache lurking behind her eyes and fumbled in the bottom of her handbag for her aspirin tin.

"You all right, Katie?" Bob asked, sitting back after a sip of Coke.

"Just a little headache," she said, swallowing the aspirins that threatened to catch in her throat.

The shade, created by lush foliage trailing from the rooftops and trellises, offered some relief from the heat, and Katie was grateful for the brief respite. David and Giselle continued their discussion of ideas for Caribbean travel for Wallace-Tyler clients, punctuated by an occasional burst of laughter as they recalled other trips.

"Nice view," Bob said, motioning to the scene behind her.

Moving her chair so she could snap pictures allowed Katie to screen out the sight of the two so obviously enjoying their conversation. Indeed, the scene below was breath-

112

taking. Palm trees descended the hill, with the vegetation growing all the way to the water's edge. In the bay, sailboats lay at anchor. It was a tranquil sight in sharp contrast to the turmoil building within her.

"Let's check out the shops," Giselle said after a while.

"I suppose we ought to," David agreed.

Katie's head throbbed so now that she begged off.

"I'd rather sit too," Bob said as Giselle and David rose from the table.

Katie realized there was nothing she could do to change the circumstances. Later, from her vantage point above the main street, she watched David following Giselle from one shop to another, interested and attentive.

When the four returned to the tour bus, it was a strained reunion, Katie felt. Though her headache had subsided, Giselle had succeeded in commanding David's full attention, occasionally touching his arm to emphasize a point.

The rest of the tour, though there was much of interest to see and record on film, was wasted on Katie. The ache in her heart was not lessened by the beauty of the scenery, and it was almost a relief to return to the main street where they had begun their tour a few hours earlier.

"We have until ten-thirty," David said, checking his watch. "Giselle and I thought we ought to check out the bistros for tourist action. How about it?"

Bob shook his head. "Sorry. This darn climate has gotten the best of me. I'm going back to the ship for a siesta."

Returning to the ship with Bob seemed a perfect out for Katie as well. At least she could lick her wounds alone and take a nap. "Think I'll go back too," she said and glanced away from David quickly as tears threatened to spill.

"Are you sure?" he asked.

"Yes." She blinked hard and smiled. With a fast wave, she headed down the street.

"I have to pick up something in a store," Bob called out behind her. "Can you get back all right?"

"Of course!" She saw Bob's worried expression, but noticed that Giselle and David were already setting off, her arm in his.

Katie hurried through Philipsburg's welcoming arch and toward the dock, her heart so full of anguish that she felt physically ill. She saw that one of the Golden Renaissance tenders was nearly full of passengers and hurried through the throng of people waiting on the dock.

"Going back?" one of the ship's crew asked, as she rushed toward them.

"Yes . . ."

"Just in time," he said with an Italian accent. "Room for only one more here." He helped her aboard, then the tender was shoved off from the dock.

Back in her cabin, Katie decided that she must be the only young single taking an afternoon nap, but she was exhausted—wrung out from the humidity and her emotional turmoil. As she climbed into bed, the last thing she recalled was Giselle holding David's arm as they set off down the street in Philipsburg. Then she drifted off into troubled sleep.

It seemed days later when she heard a knock at the cabin door. Blinking awake, she finally realized where she was. "Just a minute!"

She opened the door, peering around it in her yellow cotton nightie.

Bob stood in the corridor with a large package under his arm, an apologetic smile on his lips. "Are you all right? I was worried when you skipped dinner."

She nodded groggily, her long hair tumbling about in disarray. "What time is it?"

"Eight-thirty. Look, maybe I shouldn't have awakened you . . ."

"No, I'm glad you did. Otherwise I'd be waking up in the middle of the night."

Bob slipped the package through the partly-open door. "It's a present for you," he said.

"Oh, Bob . . . But why?"

"Consider it a bonus," he answered. "Listen, there's a beachcomber party tonight and a barbecue on deck. You won't believe what they've done . . . brought in palm fronds from St. Maarten and even sand. I thought you wouldn't want to miss it."

Katie glanced at the box. "Thank you. And thanks for the invitation. It'll take only a few minutes to dress."

His blue eyes sparkled. "I'll wait in my cabin," he said. "Just knock when you're ready."

Dropping the box on her bed, Katie hurried to the bathroom to take a quick shower. She did feel better, she thought gratefully.

Opening her closet, she pulled out a long yellow-and-white flowered shift, slit to the knees on both sides. It looked comfortable and smart with her white sandals. She brushed her hair so that it curled simply at her shoulders and was surprised at how refreshed she looked. Suddenly she remembered the box on her bed.

The name and Philipsburg address of a Dutch shop on the box were useless clues to its contents. Removing the lid, she was amazed to find the magnificent ecru lace-and-linen tablecloth from the shop window! Gran Lucy would love it!

She grabbed her key and handbag, and hurried to Bob's door. When he opened it, she felt like hugging him.

"Bob, what a thoughtful thing for you to do! It's beautiful, just perfect. But I want to pay you for it. How did you ever guess the right size?"

He closed his cabin door behind him and started down the corridor with her. "You said a big, round table, and the saleswoman said this was for a big, round table that seated eight or ten.''

"It's exactly right. But why?''

Bob hesitated a moment before answering, "I've been learning lately that when you see something you really want, you should go after it. If you wait too long, it's apt to be gone.''

Katie darted a sideways glance at him. She had the definite impression that he was not discussing tablecloths.

As they stepped out the aft door into the moonlight on the Europa Deck, Katie marveled at the sight. Down below on the Ocean and Promenade Decks, the railings were lined solidly with palm fronds; even the ship's deck-support posts had been wired with fronds and fashioned into palm trees. An elaborate fountain spouted from the middle of the empty swimming pool, and romantic music swirled from the ship's orchestra. Colored spotlights transformed the scene into an island fantasy.

"I'm not sure if it's supposed to be Caribbean or Hawaiian,'' Bob said as the tour director handed them each a plastic lei. "Either way, it should be easy to get into the spirit of things.''

All the tables seemed to be occupied, and people were standing around the crowded dance floor; it looked impossible to find empty seats.

"Katie! Bob!'' Ella Goodman called out from one of the tables under a newly-created palm tree.

They made their way through the festive crowd to join the older couple.

"Thanks,'' Katie said, noting the perplexed look on Ella's face. She knew that Ella was trying to decide what might be going on now. She knew only that Bob was her boss.

"Where's the rest of your gang?'' Edwin asked.

Katie hoped that Bob would answer and looked at him.

"They're out casing St. Maarten for the tourist trade. We were too tired."

"I slept nearly four hours," Katie said quickly and thought Ella looked relieved.

"You must have needed it, dear," Ella said.

A waiter stopped by for their drink order, and the Goodmans excused themselves to stroll around the deck. Bob and Katie sat back to enjoy the balmy breezes and the music.

After a while Bob asked, "Dance?"

She shook her head. "No, thanks, but I'd love to walk." She hated herself for wishing it were David with whom she was sharing this romantic moonlight night.

They circled the deck slowly. Something about the moonlight and the island atmosphere made her feel deliciously languid, and she put aside all thoughts of David and Giselle. The thing to do was to enjoy this evening, she told herself. She would probably never experience such a special setting again in her lifetime.

"What are you thinking about so seriously?" Bob asked as they stopped by the railing to gaze up at the velvety sky.

Katie looked at him, thinking what an attractive man he was. "That I'm having a marvelous time." It occurred to her that under different circumstances, she might have been interested in a man like Bob.

"So am I," he said. They stood listening to the distant sentimental tunes played by the ship's orchestra. "What do you think of me, Katie?" he asked.

The unexpected question startled her, and she tried to hide her surprise. "That you're intelligent, attractive, kind . . ." She remembered the tablecloth. "And very considerate!"

He didn't answer, his thoughts far away.

Katie wondered again about the status of his marriage.

117

Word had it that his wife, Suzanne, was far more interested in advancing her career than their marriage.

"What do you mean by 'attractive'?" he asked.

She looked up at him, smiling indulgently. If he needed affirmation, that would be easy enough. "Tall, big shoulders, nice smile. To put it in one highly overused word—*handsome!*"

"You honestly think so?"

She nodded. "*I* think so. I suspect that *most* women would think so."

He was quiet for a moment. "I've never especially felt that way."

"But why not? It's true."

"I was one of those late bloomers," he said. "I grew up so darn fast all at once . . . all tall and gangly. My mother says I looked my best before five and after twenty-eight."

Katie sympathized with the insecure child within him—not so very different from her own fears of inadequacy. Strange how people viewed themselves.

"Katie . . ." he began, looking into her eyes. He caught her hands in his. "Do you think . . ."

"Yes?" She pulled away slightly, her breath in her throat, half dreading the question that seemed inevitable.

Diverted by a movement on the deck above, he dropped her hands. "Never mind," he said morosely, turning to brood into the darkness.

Katie lifted her eyes to the Europa Deck. Looking down from the railing were David and Giselle.

CHAPTER 9

STEPPING INTO THE dining room for breakfast, Katie glanced out the wide windows and caught glimpses of the green island of Antigua in the distance. The Golden Renaissance was to dock promptly at eight o'clock this morning. Apparently they would be on time again.

Bob, the Goodmans, and the Bowdens were already eating breakfast. She wondered where David was, then reminded herself that it really was not her concern; nothing about him was her concern. The idea of his deserting her for Giselle on St. Maarten still rankled, but her logic argued: *He's a free man, Katie. He hasn't uttered one word of commitment. He hasn't even said he loves you.*

"Good morning," Bob said, rising from his chair with the gentle smile she had come to expect from him. "I didn't think you'd make it down in time for breakfast."

"Barely," she admitted. "Giselle's having breakfast sent to the cabin, then she's taking the cruise around the island." *Thank goodness,* Katie thought, hoping that she didn't look too pleased.

"The Zelts are taking the booze cruise too," Mark said.

"Let's hope they don't throw their clothes overboard," Edwin said, and everyone chuckled.

Katie recalled the cruise director's outrageous tales of drunken passengers returning from island cruises. One elegant couple, full of rum, had a glorious battle on deck, ending only when they had thrown overboard every item of clothing they had brought except the clothes on their backs. Expensive evening gowns and suits had floated away in the Caribbean. Amazingly, after sobering up, they had laughed it off.

She noticed Bob watching her and glanced away. What was he thinking about last night? After seeing David and Giselle observing them from the upper deck, she had pretended not to have noticed. When she had looked again, they were gone. Terrified that she wouldn't find Giselle in the cabin, she had talked Bob into staying up for the midnight barbecue, although he hadn't required much urging. Fortunately, when she returned to the cabin, Giselle was sound asleep.

Katie smiled at Bob as the waiter brought her a breakfast menu. "Where's David?"

"Handling some tour group problems," Bob answered. "He's meeting us out on the dock. If he can't get away in time, he said that we should go on."

She fervently hoped that David would be there. She didn't want to be alone with Bob today. Her feelings about both men were growing increasingly complex.

Later, walking down the gangway into the dazzling sunshine, she was pleased to see David waving to them from the midst of the taxis assembled to transport cruise passengers on tours.

"It's a good thing that we're the only cruise ship in today," Bob said as they made their way through the traffic jam to the cab that David was holding for them. Ella and Edwin were already settled in the front seat.

"Good morning," David said, helping her into the back seat of the black cab, and smiling as if nothing of consequence had changed between them.

His eyes moved over her, approving her white slacks and deep turquoise T-shirt with its softly curved short sleeves and scallops at each side seam. She had brushed her hair back, and her only jewelry was a white bracelet and white enameled hoop earrings.

She climbed into the middle of the back seat, camera dangling around her neck again. In the front seat, Ella and Edwin chatted happily with the native driver. Bob got in on one side of Katie, David on the other, and she wondered uneasily what the day might bring.

When they were all settled, the driver turned to the back seat. "Good day," he said. "My name is Adam, and I bid you welcome to St. John's, Antigua." His clipped British accent was delightful. He turned to his driving and maneuvered through the traffic.

Katie felt David slip his arm casually over the back of the seat behind her and pretended not to notice. Did he think that he could pick up with her as if nothing had happened yesterday? Didn't he know how abandoned she had felt when he left with Giselle?

She recalled, too, that she had spent most of the evening with Bob, and others might have misinterpreted that. Perhaps David had felt betrayed when he had seen them together. Or perhaps he didn't care.

She felt curiously torn, sitting between them. Each of the men seemed to be wearing the same musky aftershave, and the fragrance sent her senses reeling. There was Bob's strong tanned arm close to hers on one side; on the other, David's arm around the back of the seat.

121

Darting a glance at David's angular profile as he looked out the window, she reminded herself that he had not made any promises to her. She wondered if he ever would.

Bob seemed more open, more vulnerable than David. Or was that only because of his present separation?

She tried to concentrate on what Adam was saying as they took a shortcut through St. John's, the capital and major city of the island.

"When Columbus first saw this island, he be glad he was worshiping in a church in Spain, Santa Maria of Antigua. So he calls this island Antigua."

Katie felt David's fingers drifting down the seat back to touch her shoulder. She turned to him, but he was looking out at the passing scenery, seemingly oblivious of her.

Adam continued his talk. "We are in the Leeward Islands, formerly the British West Indies, but now we got the independence. Over the years comes along Sir Francis Drake, then those pirates, then Lord Nelson . . ." Adam paused.

"You still have pirates around?" Edwin asked, smiling.

Adam laughed uproariously. "No more pirates here," he said. "Only tourists drinking up too much rum."

They all chuckled.

The suburbs of St. John's behind them, they drove through verdant countryside and small villages with names like All Saints and Liberta.

"What are those trees, Adam?" Katie asked. The dense trees with enormous tropical leaves supported round, green fruit far larger than grapefruit.

"Breadfruit," he replied. "Most every house got one of those trees. We fry breadfruit and mash 'em and eat 'em every which way."

As they drove at a leisurely speed through the countryside, the sun beamed on old sugar cane plantations and

122

cotton fields. There was a mystical feeling in the luminous morning as natives, dressed in their bright Sunday best, walked the road to their small churches. There was a poignancy to the scene and a sense of unreality, too, as if the pages of National Geographic had sprung to life.

In the next village, the sound of fervent gospel singing filled the warm air. The small church was set back from the road among palm and breadfruit trees, its doors and windows open wide to catch the morning breezes.

"May we stop to listen?" David asked.

Adam pulled over to the side of the road and turned off the motor.

The small congregation was singing "What a Friend We Have in Jesus" with a hint of calypso in the musical accents. But there was something more. She listened intently.

"What a privilege to carry . . . everything to God in prayer . . . Oh, what peace we often forfeit . . . oh, what needless pain we bear . . ."

David opened his car door, getting out to stand in the breeze.

What is he thinking with that inscrutable look on his face? Katie wondered as she slid to the edge of the seat and swung her legs out into the sunshine.

"All because we do not carry everything to God in prayer . . . Have we trials and temptations? Is there trouble anywhere? We should never be discouraged . . . take it to the Lord in prayer."

Her eyes closed at the transcendent joy in their voices. The beauty of faith, of love rang in their voices. She recalled Gran Lucy saying that God rejoices in prayers sent on wings of love.

"Can we find a friend so faithful, who will all our sorrows share? Jesus knows our every weakness . . . take it to the Lord in prayer."

123

The hymn drifted through the balmy air with such over-powering love that Katie's spirit rose with it, feeling a benediction with the harmonious "Amen."

Adam started the motor. "We've got to move on."

Katie thought that if she saw or heard nothing else of interest all day, just the sound of love in those voices would have been well worth the trip. She wished that she had such faith.

David said nothing as he climbed back into the taxi, although he seemed moved.

"What beautiful voices," Ella said to the driver.

"Oh, yes," he said as they pulled away. "And they mean what they sing."

They rode in contemplative silence for a long time. They drove through several other small towns, then pulled into a long private driveway that ended in a great parking lot full of taxis and their fellow passengers from the ship.

"Clarence House," Adam announced. "Named for the Duke of Clarence who became King William IV. It be the governor's country house now. Princess Margaret spent some of her honeymoon right here."

David helped Katie out of the taxi. Her eyes quickly moved away from his, and she fixed them firmly on the one-story house. Its screened verandas and shutters made it look more like plantation houses she had seen in pictures than a residence for royalty. With Bob on the other side, they followed a native guide who led them through the house, explaining the unique features and pointing out antiques brought from England.

"Isn't it lovely?" Katie whispered.

"If you like this, you should see the country houses in Europe," David answered, making her feel hopelessly naïve, although she was certain that it wasn't his intent.

The guide told humorous anecdotes about the illustrious

people who had been guests of Clarence House as he led the group through the rooms, ending in back with the outdoor kitchen.

Outside, David and Bob seemed to be vying for the chance to seat Katie in the taxi, and she sensed a new tension between them, fearing that she was the cause. She was glad when the cab took off again, and she could lean forward to chat with Ella to avoid the silence growing between the two men.

"Next is Lord Nelson's Dockyard," Adam said. "Lots of boats still in there."

Minutes later, he parked outside the entrance to the Dockyard and explained where to meet them later.

Getting out of the cab, Katie joined Ella. Ahead, there was a long brown brick wall hung from one end to the other with a clothesline full of colorful dresses for sale. Perhaps twenty native women stood waiting for them in the shade of nearby trees.

"Hello, dearies," a buxom dress vendor flashed a toothy smile. "Buy dresses from me first. I give you good price."

"Not now, thank you," Katie said as they walked on.

The woman pressed forward. "You remember my name, Pearla."

"One size fits all," the next vendor said as she tried to force a bright blue dress with great white flowers emblazoned across it into Katie's arms. "Beautiful dress for beautiful lady!"

"It is," Katie said, trying to get away without much success.

Edwin stepped forward. "We're not letting our women do any buying," he said in such a gruff, chauvinistic voice that Katie laughed.

His ploy to avoid the overzealous dress vendors worked temporarily until they met some women selling tamarind seed and bead jewelry from tables, tree stumps, and their own brown arms, which they used as display racks.

Ella stopped to admire an elderly woman's armful of tamarind necklaces and discussed the price.

"How much for ten of these?" she asked.

"Oh, no!" Edwin moaned.

Edwin began to object, but Ella said firmly, "We don't let our men interfere with our shopping. I'll take all ten of them."

Everyone laughed so that Edwin gave in with a helpless wave of his arms. When the sale was consummated, he asked, "What on earth are you going to do with ten of those necklaces?"

Ella didn't look at all flustered as she put the jewelry into the commodious, yellow canvas handbag that matched her skirt. "I'm collecting gifts for the international table at the church bazaar."

"Well," Edwin said, "ask a silly question . . . No wonder you brought that shopping bag of a purse along!"

The vendors stood listening and laughing, spreading merriment in waves all around them.

Katie was still amused as they entered the two-hundred-year-old dockyard, then amazed to find that the harbor in the distance was full of modern yachts—everything from eighteen footers to a two-hundred-footer with a small helicopter on the forward deck.

As Katie wandered along between David and Bob on the broken sidewalk, her shoe caught on a chunk of concrete, throwing her forward.

David grabbed her.

"Thank you!" she said, regaining her balance.

"I don't intend to let you break your neck," he said, tucking her hand firmly in his arm.

She looked up and noticed the muscle tensing in his jaw,

a look of determination on his face. She thought that Bob saw it, too, before he walked away to inspect an old sundial.

Pulling out her camera, Katie took pictures of the historical buildings. Dark brick trimmed in white, they had blue shutters at the windows. Near the water, still standing, were giant stone pillars of what had once been a two-storied boathouse and sail loft. There were enormous old cauldrons for boiling pitch and old cannons sunk into the ground as bollards.

"Let's take a look in the naval museum," David suggested, and they moved ahead of the others to an ancient building. After a while he said, "I'm sorry about yesterday . . . about deserting you at St. Maarten."

When he looked at her so remorsefully, she was speechless. "You owe me no apology," she finally answered. After all, there was no reason for him to be at her side constantly. She was the one who had grown to expect it. No doubt Giselle expected his attention too.

As the doors creaked shut behind them in the musty museum, she realized that they were alone. David turned to her, his brown eyes full of warmth. "Katie . . ." His arm moved around her, and at his touch, she melted. Voices drifted in as the doors creaked open again, admitting other tourists, and David moved away, his eyes darkening with disappointment.

She moved on around the exhibits with David, berating herself for her foolishness. How could she have been so anxious for him to hold her again? He was obviously not to be trusted, and she was foolish to yield to her fickle emotions.

Nevertheless, she wandered through the museum, far more aware of David's presence than of the two-hundred-year-old muskets, pulleys, sextants, uniforms, and original drawings of the buildings. Studying a miniature model of the old shipyard from Lord Nelson's time, she thought of the English women who had been left behind to await the sailors' return from the sea.

Later, at the Admiral's Inn, an old brick restaurant with outdoor tables and chairs, Katie and David stopped for refreshments. A verdant lawn extended to the turquoise bay. There were old pillars of a bygone boathouse and, beyond the water, green hills seemed to climb to the bright blue sky.

They carried their glasses of punch outside, sitting down in the shade of a willow tree. A slight breeze stirred the willow leaves, and birds twittered overhead.

"What a beautiful place," Katie said. The grounds, studded with palm trees and the giant stone boathouse pillars, drew them back into another era. She sipped the cool fruit punch, then leaned back to enjoy the breeze.

"May we join you?" Edwin asked as he, Ella, and Bob approached the table with their glasses. Katie noticed that Bob took the seat at the end of the table farthest from her, although he didn't seem angry, only reflective.

Fifteen languorous minutes later, they climbed into Adam's taxi, settling down for the rest of the morning tour.

Katie sat uneasily between David and Bob again, although there was plenty of interesting scenery to divert her. She took pictures of native villages and tropical countryside with banana tree plantations and coconut palms. Ruins of sugar refineries from earlier times protruded like crumbling towers on overgrown hillsides. On the road, black boys rode scrawny donkeys, some carrying enormous clusters of ripe bananas on their heads.

As they returned to St. John's and pulled up by the Golden Renaissance, David made arrangements for Adam to wait while they changed into their bathing suits aboard ship. The cruise director had recommended a swim at Buccaneer Cove and the famous lobster dinners served at the beach.

At Buccaneer Cove, David, Bob, and Edwin walked on ahead as Katie and Ella scuffed along the sandy path leading through a thick grove of trees to the beach.

"What is going on with the three of you?" Ella whispered.

Katie shrugged unhappily. "I wish I knew."

"If I'd taken you for such a man-maddening character, I would never have let Edwin close to you," she said, her eyes twinkling.

"It's not funny," Katie sighed. She liked both David and Bob, although David was the one who had set her head spinning. But it was difficult to trust him—or herself when she was near him!

A native band pounded out a calypso beat, filling the soft air with its sensual rhythms as Katie stepped out to the white sandy beach. Distant peninsulas tamed the turquoise sea here, slowing the waves so that they whispered into the cove, lapping at the fine sand. Small sailboats lay at anchor to one side, near a residential area, but otherwise the meandering shortline was as pristine as it might have been in the beginning of time.

"It's glorious," Ella said. "All we need now is some of that lobster they were talking about."

"Where do you ladies want to sit?" Edwin called back to them over the calypso music.

"In the sun!" Katie said.

"Shade!" Ella countered.

They found a place to suit everyone next to a round wooden picnic table under a sprawling shade tree. It was close enough to the steel band, yet far enough removed that they wouldn't be deafened by the music.

Katie slipped out of her beach robe, and ran across the creamy sand, splashing into the turquoise water. She swam out until she felt alone in the exquisite beauty of the cove.

Treading water, she found David and Bob rapidly closing the distance between them.

"Where did you learn to swim like that?" Bob asked.

"A swim team," David guessed.

She laughed. "Right. A long time ago it seems . . . in high school."

Later, when they swam back to the beach, they were famished, and the Goodmans were already exclaiming over their giant buttery lobsters.

"I'll get ours," Bob said, taking off for the rustic beach restaurant.

Katie dried herself, then spread the oversized towel on the hot sand. Lying down sleepily, she watched David spread his towel beside hers. She closed her eyes against the blazing sun.

Katie drifted between consciousness and sleep. She heard the steel band, the voices all around her, yet Giselle's face came clearly into view. The blond beauty stood between Katie and David, scornfully flinging Katie aside.

"He loves me!" Giselle screamed at her. "David loves me!"

"No!" Katie announced. "No, it's not true!"

Jerking awake, she opened her eyes and saw David watching her.

"What on earth were you dreaming? What isn't true?" he asked.

Katie blinked, shaking her head. "Just a nightmare," she said gratefully. But it seemed so real.

Across the beach, Bob was bringing their lobster dinners. "They look fantastic!" he called out.

Katie stood up groggily and slid onto the bench by the table. "How long did I sleep?" she asked David. It seemed as if the nightmare had repeated itself hundreds of times.

"Ten or fifteen minutes," he answered.

She wondered what other monsters lurked in her head as Bob placed before her the succulent white meat, swimming in hot butter. She dug in with her fingers and feasted until the reality of the dream faded.

Ella and Edwin, satiated with the sun and full meal, leaned back to listen to the band.

When Katie finished, she sat back between David and Bob, watching the young red-shirted natives casually beating out the sensual rhythm under a canopy of bright green trees. Except for the tension that she was obviously creating between David and Bob, she wished that time could stand still.

All too soon David said, "Time for a last swim. We have to be back on the ship at three forty-five."

She walked slowly out to the water, wanting to fix this scene in her memory forever. She turned to Bob. "I can never thank you enough for bringing me on this trip."

"All part of being a tour director," Bob said and raced ahead into the water.

"Aren't you going to swim?" David called back to her.

She blinked. "Race you!" she shouted.

An hour later, they were back on the Europa Deck of the Golden Renaissance, watching the island of Antigua growing smaller. The twin spires on the cathedral in downtown St. John's reminded Katie that they had not had nearly enough time to explore the small island. "Someday I'd like to come back," she said.

"Perhaps you will. Giselle's working out Caribbean land tours for clients now," David said.

At the mention of her name, the nightmare returned, obscuring the beauty of the day and the little town fast disappearing below the horizon, until there was only a green hilly island in the distance and a sky full of great white clouds above.

Suddenly the one dark cloud overhead gave way, releasing warm drops of rain. Everyone scurried for cover until she, David, and Bob were the only passengers remaining at the railing. Sun filtered through the swirling clouds, beaming through the rain.

For a moment, Katie wondered why there was no rainbow. Then there it was—a brilliant bow of bright colors reaching from the sea up through the clouds and arching to the Caribbean again. It spanned the distant island of Antigua, a symbolic promise of the future. But what . . . and with whom? Meanwhile Katie stood, transfixed—on the deck between Bob and David.

CHAPTER 10

INSIDE THE CROWDED Riviera Deck, Katie moved along slowly in the disembarkation line toward the gangway with David, Bob, and Giselle. The other passengers, refreshed from the night's rest, were eager to explore yet another of the exotic ports—Barbados. The very name of the island conjured images of tropical enchantment. Katie was determined not to let Giselle spoil this day for her.

Scanning the brochure, she noticed again the Barbados Tourist Board's recommendation that tourists "avoid scanty attire, especially in towns and churches." She hoped her yellow eyelet sundress was appropriate. Giselle, clad in very brief black shorts and a deep V-necked T-shirt, had tossed her blond pageboy and laughed at the ruling. "Why worry about it? It's our money they're after!"

From across the crowded deck, Katie saw Walt Zelt watching them. It seemed that he was always at the edges of her life lately.

"Let's have the history, Katie," Bob said. Giselle glanced up in disgust, but David appeared interested.

Katie opened the brochure and grabbed a deep breath. "The Portuguese discovered the pear-shaped, twenty-one-mile-long island in 1536 and, before sailing on, named it Barbados after the beardlike growth on the aerial roots of the hairy fig tree."

"Now there's a fascinating fact, Giselle," Bob said with a grin.

Katie read on, ignoring Giselle's exasperation. "The island was uninhabited when the English settlers arrived in 1627, although there is evidence that Arawak Indians had lived there."

She skipped the more boring details. "Barbados remained under British rule until 1966 when it became independent . . . So it's not surprising that British influence remains strong among Bajans, most of whom are descendants of African slaves brought in to work the sugar and tobacco plantations."

"No doubt we'll be riding on the left side of the road," David said as they stepped out to the gangway. "Here we go!"

The city of Bridgetown shimmering in the morning sun revealed docks, warehouses, city buildings, and roads with snarled traffic—nothing at all like Antigua or St. Maarten. So-called civilization had obviously set in.

On the dock, Giselle hailed their tour taxi. "Let's go," she said. "Why don't you sit up front, David? You'll have more leg room. And, Katie, since you're the shortest, you can sit in the middle."

Irritated, Katie scooted into the back seat. How dare Giselle assign their places as if they were children! She wondered why David and Bob put up with it. Was Giselle's ten percent ownership of the company that important to them? Was that why David had taken off with her at St. Maarten?

In moments their taxi edged through the congestion and headed into the heavy traffic of Bridgetown—driving on the left side of the street. At first Katie braced every time they turned a corner, positive they would careen into another car.

Their native driver seemed either sullen or shy, giving occasional information in a kind of pidgin English. "Bridgetown," he said, "got our own Trafalgar Square with a statue of Lord Nelson, just like London. And we got our parliament there, and the other government buildings.

"On the corner of Bay and Chelsea there, we got the George Washington house, where he visited."

Katie craned her neck to see it. "Is that it?" she asked, noticing only a cleaning establishment.

"Yes, ma'am," the driver answered. "General Cleaners now."

Bob chuckled, and David turned to smile sympathetically at her.

"I knew that Washington slept in lots of places," she said, "but I never imagined him sleeping at a cleaners."

"Travel not only broadens," David observed, "it sometimes disillusions."

"Our David is quite the philosopher today," Giselle said with an intimate look at him.

Katie glanced out Bob's window at the shops. She was not in the mood for Giselle's seductive ploys. Bob seemed terribly quiet, yawning frequently as if he had not slept well.

Later they drove by St. Michael's Cathedral near Queen's Park. "Washington went to Anglican services here," the driver said. "And here in the park we got the giant baobab tree. Over one thousand years old."

"Now that is surprising," Giselle said. "I always think of baobabs as indigenous to Africa."

Never having even heard of the trees, which Giselle

explained were the source of cream of tartar, Katie again felt naïve and untraveled. It wasn't merely her ignorance of native trees; it was a total lack of sophistication. How could she have ever imagined that David, president of a travel company, might be seriously interested in her?

She was glad when they drove north—out of the city. A little later, when they stopped at a monument dedicated to the island's first settler, she changed her mind. There, in the tour taxi behind them, was Walt Zelt with his wife and other Golden Renaissance passengers.

At Fortress Hill, they turned inland to the east. Although the road was narrow, there was very little traffic, and Katie relaxed. It was quiet as everyone looked out at the hilly countryside.

After a while, the driver stopped at a turkey farm for more picture-taking.

"*Let's go on to something more interesting.* We'd rather spend our time visiting places like Villa Nova," Giselle said coldly, ignoring the hurt on their driver's face.

As they drove on, Katie noticed David's keen interest as Giselle expounded on Villa Nova, a sugar cane great house from early plantation days in the Caribbean. She had studied the area extensively in a recent university class and spouted interesting, if obscure, details.

Bob leaned back, closing his eyes.

As Katie watched Giselle and David, again engrossed in conversation, she felt invisible. Tuning out their words, she listened only to the deep rumble of David's voice, her eyes roaming to the back of his head where his dark, thick hair fell into a wave several inches above his shirt collar. Suddenly she had the urge to caress his neck. Appalled, she looked aside, wondering how she could become so captivated by a man who was obviously only interested in her when Giselle was not around. It was ludicrous!

She glanced at Bob, who drifted in and out of sleep. He had been more quiet than usual this morning, more serious. She wondered if his interest in her was only loneliness because of his separation from his wife.

She reminded herself that shipboard romances were notoriously short-lived. They did not last long once the passengers returned to the realities of life ashore, leaving only beautiful memories and, more often than not, broken hearts. She must remember to protect hers.

At the Villa Nova estate, the cab driver dropped them off by the main entrance. Flowers bloomed along walkways and great trees sprawled over bright green grounds. It was an impressive place.

Noticing the Zelts just behind them, Katie tried to concentrate on the distant stone plantation house. White-trellised verandas surrounded the first floor; on the second story, the upper white shutters swung up like canopies to block out the mid-day sun, and the lower shutters folded out neatly against the dark stone.

"Exactly as a Caribbean plantation house should look," Giselle said, taking David's arm as they walked along the path to the house.

Katie said nothing and, beside her, Bob was equally silent.

Women volunteers with clipped British accents showed them through the house, pointing out the exquisite antiques.

"Villa Nova was once the home of former English Prime Minister, Sir Anthony Eden," their guide explained.

In the garden, orchids and hundreds of other exotic flowers and shrubs bloomed in a profusion of riotous color. Under an especially lush shade tree, there was a marble bath tub in which the prime minister had taken his baths. Water lilies now floated on the water.

"Now that's the right place for a tub," Walt Zelt said

from somewhere behind them. "I wouldn't mind taking my baths in the great outdoors."

Just the thought of Walt in the tub was loathsome, Katie thought.

When they climbed back into their taxi, Giselle expounded on the beauty of the house and grounds. "Didn't you enjoy it?" she asked Katie.

"It was marvelous," she said, but there seemed to be nothing more to add to Giselle's glowing comments. Moreover, she was feeling oddly nervous with Walt Zelt in the vicinity.

Later, as they pulled into the shaded parking lot next to St. John's Anglican Church, the driver said, "Be sure to see the old cemetery in back."

The church, built of massive gray stones that had blackened over the centuries, had a broad tower rising from the middle, dwarfing the main structure. Battlements on the rooflines and thickly buttressed side walls gave the aged church a look of solidity.

"Ugly old thing, isn't it?" Giselle asked as they climbed out of the taxi.

"Well, it was built in 1650," David answered.

"I suppose the thing to do is to see it anyhow," she said.

David eyed her black shorts and revealing T-shirt. "Do you think you're suitably dressed?"

Giselle, surprised by his comment, laughed, but dropped back.

Bob, who had opened one eye to observe their stop, decided to nap in the car.

Inside, the church appeared to have been renovated. Its white walls were freshly plastered, and the stained-glass windows and lacy grillwork in front of the chancel had certainly been added more recently than 1650.

Katie sat down on a wooden pew and ran her fingers

lightly over the worn wood, wondering how many thousands had prayed here over the centuries—and for what? Had they found Gran Lucy's peace—and Ella's joy?

For a time she sat quietly, trying to shut out the boisterous tourists who viewed the church as another tourist attraction and wanted only to whisk through, snapping pictures for their scrapbooks. Bowing her head, she relaxed, allowing the hallowed atmosphere to seep into her very being, quieting her soul until every distraction disappeared. *Heavenly Father,* she prayed, *I want to be as close to You as I once was. Help me to become the person You want me to be . . . I know You want me to forgive those who have caused me pain—Stan . . . David . . . even Giselle.*

She paused. She didn't *want* to forgive Giselle. That was one woman who knew precisely what she wanted and didn't mind hurting others in the process.

Father, please help me to want to forgive . . . she amended.

As voices nearby shattered the silence, she rose sadly, knowing that she was not yet ready for her prayer to be answered.

As she edged out of the pew, she was surprised to see David sitting several pews behind her, his head bowed. She had never really considered the state of his spiritual life.

She walked slowly up the middle aisle to the lacy grillwork at the chancel, admiring the narrow stained-glass windows that ended in peaks pointing heavenward. She hadn't felt as if she were pointed in that direction lately.

Someone stepped up beside her. Turning, she saw David, his eyes glowing warmly.

"To borrow your favorite word, it's lovely," he whispered.

She smiled as they stepped outside. "Very different from

our old California missions, yet born of the same kind of faith, I think.''

"Shall we take in the cemetery?'' he asked.

"Why not?'' she answered.

The sides of the church were even blacker with age, and greenery grew against the buttresses. In back, the cemetery was a tangle of green trees, bushes, and ferns. Moss thrived among the cracked stones on vaults, headstones, and granite crosses.

"Look at this,'' David said, stopping near a blackened stone vault.

Under the name, the inscription read: "A native of this island and for more than forty years a resident in the colony of British Guiana. 'I am to be gathered unto my people. Bury me with my fathers.'''

Strange, Katie thought. A man who had left his island, yet wanted to be buried with his forefathers. Surely there was an interesting story behind it.

Looking up, she found David watching her. What does he want of me? she wondered. Surely he was more interested in Giselle, who had been right about one thing—on a long-term basis, he needed someone sophisticated and well-traveled.

They peered down over the thick grove of trees marching down to the deserted beaches, and the turquoise sea beyond.

"It must be the most beautiful cemetery view on earth,'' he said.

She nodded and busied herself taking pictures. As she started back toward the church with David, there was Walt Zelt snapping pictures that surely included her. She felt apprehensive, somehow violated.

When they reached the parking lot, Giselle handed out small candies. "Picturesque place for shopping,'' she said.

"Where's Bob?'' Katie asked.

140

"Asleep on the back seat," Giselle said.

"He hasn't been sleeping much lately," David said, then reluctantly awakened him.

"Going next to Sam Lord's Castle," their driver said as they piled in.

Driving southeast, it seemed only a short time before they arrived at the Castle, a national museum and resort.

As they started down the path, Giselle took David's arm, and Katie hung back with Bob, still groggy with sleep.

"What's wrong, Bob?" Katie asked, concerned. "Something must be troubling you."

He looked out over the formal gardens of the resort, his eyes raw with pain. "I miss Suzanne," he said. "I can't get her off my mind, no matter what I do. I keep thinking that if only I had brought her, if we had had more time together . . ."

Katie glanced away. If she suggested her first thought, she would ruin forever any chances for romance she might have with him, but it seemed more important to ease his torment if she could. "It's not too late, Bob. It's never too late." She remembered his poor opinion of himself, and added: "You're a wonderful and attractive man."

"Sure," he said skeptically.

She had an inspiration. "Why don't you send a radiogram from the ship?"

"What would I say?"

"That you love her, that you'd like to try again." Katie looked at David and Giselle, wandering through the gardens. "I wish someone loved me so much that he went mooning all over the Caribbean." She forced a smile, knowing she had put an end to any possible romance with Bob. And everything with David was apparently over too.

As they caught up with David and Giselle, she said, "Well, let's hear about Sam Lord's Castle:" At least she might be able to learn something of value to her career.

Giselle seemed delighted to fill them in. "Sam Lord was a pirate of sorts," she explained. "He supposedly lured ships here to his plantation by hanging lanterns on trees and even on his goats. Ship captains, thinking they were lights in a safe harbor, would founder on his beach."

Just like some girls who lure men to destruction, Katie thought.

"And for that he was knighted?" David asked.

"It seems he was!" Giselle answered with a laugh.

Strange that the pirates of the world are so often rewarded in one way or another, Katie mused.

"The important thing here, of course, is the resort," Giselle said silkily.

The world-famous resort was composed of villas set in seventy-two acres of formal gardens, with swimming pools, tennis courts, and every possible amenity. Below on the beach, turquoise waves caressed the white sandy beach.

"It's all very nice if you want to be idle," Katie said as they paused in a garden bar for a glass of punch. "But I'm afraid I'd be bored in a few days."

Giselle's brown eyes glittered. "You probably have had very little experience as a resort guest."

Katie felt as if she were cutting her own throat. "None," she answered and sipped her fruit punch. "But I do like the castle."

Giselle shook her head, her blond pageboy drifting like gossamer over her tan shoulders. "It's so gauche, Katie."

She winced, knowing that she had left herself open for that jab. She looked across the grounds to the white, two-story mansion known as Sam Lord's Castle. The house had a certain charm and elegance despite the battlements notching the rooflines, giving it a raffish look befitting a pirate pretending to be genteel. She was certain that was how

Giselle viewed her—a pretender. Gauche. And David? It no longer mattered what he thought of her.

Inside the mansion there were valuable paintings, period furniture and other antiques, which, according to Giselle, had been seized from the shipwrecks on the beach. Giselle was extremely knowledgeable and articulate, and David seemed more and more impressed.

Climbing into the cab, Bob confided, "I'm going to do it, Katie. I'm going to send the radiogram."

After lunch in Bridgetown, he was eager to get back to the ship. Since Katie did not want to interfere with Giselle's and David's plans for the afternoon, she decided to accompany Bob.

"Are you sure?" Bob asked.

"There's shopping just outside the ship near the dock," she reminded him. Before Bob could question her further, she called to David and Giselle. "We're heading back. See you later."

She tried to decipher the expression on David's face. Surprise. Nothing else.

Early the next morning as they climbed onto a tender boat for Martinique, Katie stayed with Bob, who was in far better spirits since sending the radiogram. It was too soon to expect a response from Suzanne, though he clearly felt relieved to have made an attempt at reconciliation.

In front of them David sat with Giselle, drifting ever deeper into her sensuous web, Katie thought. She tried not to look at them. As the boat moved away from the Golden Renaissance, she decided to look forward to the day ahead. She gazed out to the island of Martinique, where a centuries-old fortress lined a cliff, then to the modern city of Fort-de-France.

On the dock, Walt Zelt pressed through the crowd to them. "How about letting me ride along with you?" he asked Giselle and David. "Sondra's sick. She's staying on the ship."

Giselle paused momentarily, then agreed. "Sure. Come on."

It wasn't surprising that Sondra was sick, Katie thought. A number of the passengers had come down with flu, including Edwin Goodman. Ella was remaining with him today.

Climbing into their taxi, Katie found she had no choice but to sit in the middle of the front seat since Giselle was already settling in the back with Bob and David. Katie smiled at the friendly native driver, trying to ignore Walt who was pressing in beside her.

"We start with our countryside," the driver said as the cab took off with a shriek of tires. "Later you have time to shop in Fort-de-France."

As they turned a corner, Katie found herself thrown against Walt, who laughingly caught her and said to the driver, "You can keep that up all day."

She jerked away, glaring at him.

They drove crazily through the city, past modern office buildings as well as bustling outdoor markets displaying a colorful array of vegetables, flowers, and fruits. Here and there on the crowded sidewalks, native women wore bright native dress. From the open windows of the taxi, they heard French and a rapid Creole patois—a blend of Spanish, English, and French. Music with a subdued African beat could be heard from car radios.

"The Carib Indians named Martinique the island of flowers," the driver said, "and to this day, the magnificent flowers are one of our main attractions."

"Not to mention the beautiful women!" Walt added.

"Oh, yes!" the driver agreed. "You do know that Josephine, the Empress of France, was born here?"

"They know how to get around men, don't they?" Walt asked.

"Oh, they surely do," the driver agreed with a savvy grin.

"She sure knew how to get around Napoleon!" Walt exclaimed, and the driver laughed uproariously.

Katie was relieved when their conversation about women ended, and she concentrated on their drive through the suburbs.

Turning inland, the driver explained, "First, we are going to St. Pierre. As you might know, that whole city was destroyed in 1902 when the volcano Mount Pelee erupted. Forty thousand people were killed in that eruption."

As they drove through the misty green countryside, Katie tried to ignore Walt, but his proximity made it difficult. If he understood her angry glances, he showed no sign of retreating. She wondered if David or Bob had noticed her plight, but they were busily discussing the Wallace-Tyler tour possibilities in Martinique with Giselle.

When they finally arrived at the town of St. Pierre, Katie gratefully slid out of the front seat and hurried to the Mount Pelee museum.

"No museums for me," Walt said. "I'll meet you back here."

Inside the museum, Giselle stepped into the restroom, and David drew Katie aside. "Is everything all right?" he asked, with a worried look.

Katie backed away. Why should he care? "Just fine," she said coolly and excused herself, heading for the sanctuary of the ladies' room.

Later, in the museum, she avoided David assiduously, turning her back on him whenever he came near. The

145

charred artifacts of the annihilated town added to her depression. When the guided tour was over, she stepped outside. David was taking Giselle's picture as she posed seductively on the museum wall with red bougainvillaea and the turquoise Caribbean for her backdrop.

When they returned to the taxi, Walt smelled of liquor. "Oh, man, that rum," he said with a boozy grin. Even the broken veins in his bulbous nose seemed redder.

They drove on through a tropical rain forest, during which Walt dozed, bobbing ever closer to Katie so that it was all but impossible for her to enjoy the tangle of tropical greenery and misty mountains. When Walt's head was nearly resting on her shoulder, she requested a picture stop.

Getting out, she ran to the nearby stream, ostensibly for a shot of the hulking green mountain through the valley. She didn't know how much longer she could endure sitting next to Walt, but when she reached the cab, everyone else was settled in the back seat; and Walt was holding the front door open for her.

Walt was awake as they drove on through the lush countryside to Balata. By now his thigh was pressed purposefully against hers. At Balata, they stopped to visit the miniature replica of Paris's Sacre Coeur of Montmartre.

"No churches for me!" Walt said, starting down the street toward the bars.

Katie was grateful to enter the cool church building and sink down on a pew alone. *Please give me the strength to get through this day,* she prayed. She felt dazed and sat for a long time before she could enjoy the simple painting in earthy Indian tones on the white arches and dome. The momentary retreat from the humidity and Walt soon ended and it was time to return.

Walt stood waiting near the cab's front door. She had to remind herself that the tour was nearly over. As he sat down beside her, she could smell the sickening stench of rum. She fixed her gaze straight ahead, sitting as far from him as possible.

On their return to Fort-de-France, they followed the coast, passing fishing villages on the white, sandy beaches. From the corner of her eye, she saw Walt's hand slowly moving closer and closer. Suddenly he spread his hand and squeezed her thigh.

Without even thinking, she stamped on his foot hard.

He removed his hand with a quiet chuckle. "Hellion, are you? I like spirit in my women!"

She could barely refrain from slapping his grinning face. If he said one more foul thing or tried to touch her again, she would hit him with all of her might. Her fury must have been obvious because he sat stiffly beside her, looking out at the scenery the rest of the way into Fort-de-France. Perhaps he wasn't willing to take chances with David and Bob so near.

In town, they set out for lunch and shopping.

Katie drew Bob aside. "I can't stand to be near that Walt another moment," she whispered. As they looked up, Walt was watching.

"I've got some shopping to do," Walt said. "See you all later."

"What's wrong?" Bob asked.

"He's . . . disgusting."

"You should have told us," Bob said. "What did he do?"

Katie shook her head. "I just want to forget about him." She saw David looking at them. "Come on," she said, managing a smile. "Let's shop."

In the stores there was colorful native jewelry made of beads and seeds. The more elegant shops offered French crystal, clothing, jewelry, and perfumes. Giselle purchased a bright Martinique caftan and brass slave bracelets. Bob, full of hope, bought a bottle of perfume for Suzanne.

"Aren't you buying anything?" David asked Katie.

She hadn't intended to, but with sudden pique held out a brass bracelet to the sales clerk. "Yes, this." She dug in her purse for money. What a fool she was to buy the first thing at hand to avoid facing him! When it was time to leave, she was even more disgusted to discover that her bracelet was identical to Giselle's.

On the tender, Katie found a seat with Bob as far from David as possible, although he was so busy discussing something with Giselle that he didn't appear to notice.

When they boarded the ship, Bob said, "Come to the radio room with me. I need you for courage."

"Do you think there will be an answer this soon?" Katie asked, hoping to soften the blow.

Leaving David and Giselle behind, Katie could barely keep up with Bob in his rush. What if there were no answer? Yet, in the radio room, an envelope was waiting for Bob. As he tore it open, Katie closed her eyes, breathing a prayer, *Please let it be good news!*

He stared at the message and burst into a wide grin, thrusting the paper in front of her eyes.

It read: "I love you too. Yes, yes, yes, yes! Love, Suzanne."

"She used all ten words!" Katie laughed.

Bob beamed. "I hadn't noticed that."

If only things had worked out that beautifully between her and David, she thought as they hurried to the Promenade Deck for a late lunch.

Half an hour later, the ship sailed, and they bade farewell to the island of Martinique.

That night at dinner, their table seemed strangely empty with the Goodmans and Zelts missing. At the last moment,

Walt ambled in alone, taking the empty seat beside Katie and grinning companionably.

"Miss me, honey?" he asked.

She glared back. "How is *your wife* feeling?"

Walt threw back his head and laughed, the smell of liquor heavy on his breath.

She wished that Bob were on the other side of her instead of Mark, who was preoccupied as usual with his bride. Across the table, she felt David's eyes on her, but every time she looked up, he was talking to Giselle.

Hurrying through her shrimp cocktail, she listened with dismay as Walt ordered a bottle of red wine for the two of them for dinner. He had obviously been drinking all afternoon as it was and ignored her "None for me, thanks."

When the waiter arrived with the wine, Katie said, "I don't care for any, thank you," but Walt insisted that the waiter pour for her too.

"It's good," Walt said, taking a hearty gulp. "Most expensive wine on the ship."

"Don't you understand?" she asked, losing patience. "I don't want any!"

He backed away, his eyes glittering with anger.

Katie ate her steak dinner quickly, hardly tasting it as she watched Walt consume the entire bottle of wine. His words slurred more and more as the wine had its effect. He thought himself clever, a delight to all women, Katie realized, although she couldn't understand why he should have that impression.

The dinner dragged on interminably. As Katie stood to excuse herself, Walt was watching her every move.

"Going to the movie, Katie?" Bob asked from across the table.

"Not tonight," she answered, "I'm tired. Think I'll wash out some clothes and write a letter, then just go to bed."

For the first time, Katie felt apprehensive as she stepped off the elevator onto the Europa Deck. Checking about, she found the corridor deserted.

Hurrying to her cabin, she considered what she might write to her grandmother, who would be hoping for nothing less than a grand romance—the answer to her prayers for Katie.

As she turned the key in the cabin door, Walt Zelt sprang from behind, muffling her cry of surprise with his hand over her mouth and shoving her roughly into the cabin.

"David!" she screamed instinctively when her mouth was free. She fell back across the bed, while Walt lurched convulsively to shut the door behind him.

"Get out of here!" ordered David as he kicked the door open against Walt.

Walt clutched his shoulder in pain, but David grabbed him by the collar, shaking him furiously. "If you ever come near Katie again . . ." He did not finish the threat, but thrust Walt from the room and slammed the door.

Katie was shivering uncontrollably, too bewildered to speak.

"Are you all right?" David asked gently.

Without warning she burst into tears and threw herself into his arms.

"I should never have left you," he said, holding her close. "After dinner, I was almost certain that he was following you, so I . . ."

"Just don't leave me," she begged. "Don't leave me, David!" She felt safe, sheltered in his arms.

"I never *wanted* to leave you," he said softly.

She pulled away slightly, looking up at him.

"I love you, Katie," he said, his brown eyes earnest.

"But . . . But I thought you and Giselle . . ."

He shook his head. "Giselle's only an old friend."

"I thought you loved *her!*" Katie half-sobbed.

He pulled her against him again. "Never," he said. "I feel sorry for her . . . but I could never love her."

Katie blinked away the tears clinging to her lashes as she nestled close. "I've been so jealous of her!"

"I have to take some of the blame for that," he sighed, "but I didn't know what else to do. You resisted me so much at first. I knew about Stan. I know what it's like when someone you love and trust is unfaithful to you . . ."

Then the rumors about his first wife Eva and the pilot in the plane crash were probably true, Katie thought.

"I knew that you wouldn't be able to trust men for a while," he added. "I was afraid of scaring you away, like that morning on the deck."

Katie held him closer, remembering how she had almost lost him, how she had all but handed him over to Giselle.

"I decided that I'd have to wait for you to make the first move," he continued, "but when you didn't . . ."

She tried to explain. "I've been so confused, David. I swore that I wouldn't fall in love with you or any other man." She searched his eyes for understanding.

"I almost waited too long," he said. "One minute longer . . ."

"But you didn't wait too long," she protested. "Oh, David, don't you know that I love you too?"

His eyes widened with amazement, then joy, and his lips moved hungrily to hers.

CHAPTER 11

IN THE MIDDLE of the night, Katie awakened, remembering the warmth of David's arms around her, his fervent kisses. As if to retrace them, she touched her lips.

"I love you, Katie," he had whispered over and over. They would meet for breakfast again, like the first morning on the ship. This time she would not run. This time he wanted to discuss something "important" before they docked at St. Thomas.

As they had walked in the moonlight on the Promenade Deck, the calypso singer had recognized them. "If you could can that happiness on your faces and sell it, you'd be rich, my friends," he said and moved on.

Katie and David had smiled at each other, barely aware of Giselle sitting in a nearby deck chair. Katie didn't care. The glamorous Miss Vallon was no longer a threat.

It was overwhelming to think that David had loved her all of this time, that he had purposely backed away, understanding her ambivalence—wanting love, but fearing the risk. She knew in her heart that it was true. She remembered the first day of the cruise when his kiss in the moonlight had been so full of yearning, so full of love—then the next morning when she had fled in confusion.

Katie wandered in and out of sleep into the morning hours. When she finally awakened, it was six o'clock. Sitting up, she vaguely recalled Giselle coming in during the night, but now her bed was rumpled and empty. At least the bathroom was available, Katie thought, standing and stretching luxuriously.

Wanting to look her best for David, she chose her slim white linen skirt and the silky scoop-necked violet blouse with short drifting sleeves.

Pulling on her white sandals, she thought about the wonderful day together they had planned. The ship would begin disembarking passengers on St. Thomas at eight. They would take the Coral World Island tour in the morning, then shop the afternoon away.

She glanced into the mirror. Her face glowed, her eyes danced; she looked like a woman in love. Though it was too early for perfume, she daubed a drop of Joy behind each ear and was encircled once more by the fragrance of flowers.

She looked at her watch. Only six-thirty. She smiled. How anxious she was to see him again. Picking up her white canvas handbag, she decided to go to the Promenade Deck.

As she stepped into the elevator, she was surprised to see Bob.

"You're up early," she said. "Expecting another radiogram?"

He smiled sleepily. "No, I'm expecting Suzanne."

"You're joking!" Katie said.

"I called her last night, and she's going to meet me in Martinique. I'm flying back there this afternoon.".

The elevator doors opened for Katie's floor. "Bob! I'm so happy for you!" She left him, beaming as widely as he.

She felt incredibly happy. Not only had things worked out beautifully for her and David, but also for Bob and Suzanne.

Starting down the corridor, she suddenly recalled that she had forgotten her St. Thomas shopping guide. She would need it for the shopping expedition. Returning to the Europa Deck, she hurried down the corridor and, opening her door, noticed that Giselle wasn't back yet. Grabbing her guidebook, she hurried out again.

As she passed David's cabin, the door opened. At first she refused to believe her eyes, but there was no mistaking it. Giselle! Giselle, wearing her short beige nightie and filmy robe, was just leaving. And David was right behind her in blue pajamas, his brown eyes sleepy, his hair tousled. When he saw Katie, he looked aghast.

She stood rooted before them for a moment, Giselle's eyes meeting Katie's with defiance. Then Katie fled in panic.

"Katie!" David called after her.

She didn't stop, hardly knowing where she was going. She rushed outside and climbed to the next deck, then to the Sun Deck. It was vacant. She hurried to the shadow of the smokestack.

How could she have trusted him? And after all of his fine explanations last night! He had said he loved her. If this was how he showed his love, she wanted no more of it!

The stack roared dully beside her as smoke billowed into the blue sky. Her white linen skirt would be covered with droplets of oil if the wind swung the smoke over the deck, but she didn't care. She thought about the couple who had thrown each other's clothes overboard as they argued, and she knew just how they felt. At this moment she would gladly throw herself overboard.

Oh, didn't David think he was wonderfully heroic to save her from Walt Żelt! But he was infinitely worse. At least

155

Walt had not pretended he loved her. Nor was it surprising that Giselle had warned her about David's preference for sophisticated women. Obviously she had misjudged Giselle.

Dispirited, she watched the green island of St. Thomas in the distance and pulled the guidebook from her handbag. She would wait until everyone had disembarked, then she'd dash into town for a short while. She glanced dully at the book which touted St. Thomas as a shoppers' paradise. "Even if you spend the whole day shopping in the town of Charlotte Amalie," it read, "you would not be able to cover all of the shops and see what is certainly the most complete range of merchandise displayed in one small town in the whole world."

Well, she was going to see it, if only to buy a little gift for Mrs. Sanders for taking care of her plants.

As the ship neared St. Thomas, she wished that she could cry, but her heart felt cold and hard. The island was fantastically beautiful, she thought dispassionately. She stared at its green hills, the harbor full of yachts and great white cruise ships. It was a magnificent sight. But she felt nothing. Only a vast emptiness.

Remaining in the shadow of the stack until everyone was ashore, she decided that it would be safe to leave. David, Giselle, and Bob would have left for the morning tour of Coral World Island by now.

She made her way through the strangely silent ship to the gangway door. The crew stared at her curiously, but she ignored them. Swallowing hard, she walked down the gangway alone and flagged a taxi, her guidebook in hand.

Once in the waterfront town of Charlotte Amalie, she was glad that the shops were jammed with tourists; everyone was so crazed with bargain-hunting and sampling every perfume on the store counters, that she might have been invisible, floating among the shoppers like the wafting fragrances.

In a shop that carried everything from diamonds to rum, she found a tiny English china vase for Mrs. Sanders. There were so many other things to shop for—endless selections of watches, scarves, china, T-shirts, woolens, linens, jewelry, cameras, leather goods. . . . But she had spent most of her remaining money yesterday when she had insisted on repaying Bob for Gran Lucy's tablecloth. It had been far more expensive than she had dreamed.

As she paid for her purchase, she spotted David, Giselle, and Bob through the shop windows. They hadn't gone on the Coral World tour after all! She turned away quickly, unsure whether David had seen her, and rushed for the door that opened onto the next street.

Hurrying out into the narrow street, she pressed through the crowd of shoppers and looked frantically for a taxi.

"Katie!" David yelled from behind her in the street.

She ran blindly through amazed tourists whose arms cradled parcels and whose hands gripped colorful shopping bags. Finally she saw a cab and flagged it. Hopping in, she slammed the door behind her. "Golden Renaissance! Hurry!"

The driver looked at her strangely. "Yes, ma'am," he said, "although I do believe she won't be leaving until around eight o'clock tonight."

"Hurry!" she said again, glancing back.

David was nearly to her door, shouting as he ran.

She turned away and the cab moved into the heavy traffic.

"Sure does look like that man's trying to catch you," the cabbie said, glancing at her in the rearview mirror.

"Never mind!" she snapped. She was not going to listen to another thing David Wallace had to say.

"He was a nice-looking fellow," the cabbie commented.

"Oh, be quiet!" she cried, then was ashamed of herself.

They rode in silence the rest of the way to the dock.

When she paid the cab driver, he shook his head. "I think you missed it with that fellow."

She whirled away, sorry that she had tipped him.

"*Bon voyage!*" he called out behind her.

Men! Katie thought. She would like to throttle all of them.

She walked angrily up the gangway, threading her way through the quiet corridors to her cabin. By the time she arrived, she was still livid with rage and disappointment.

In the cabin, she stuffed the package into her closet. If she was going to be stuck here all day, she might as well lie out in the sun, she decided, and put on her blue bathing suit and beach cover-up.

What would Gran Lucy have to say about all of this?

Katie knew the answer. Gran Lucy would pray. But she *had* prayed and everything had gone wrong again!

Full of bitterness, Katie slumped down at the dressing table and looked into the mirror, remembering the joyous face that had greeted her this morning. It had been a face glowing with love. The one peering back at her was grim with hatred.

Her heart twisted with pain. A sob escaped, then another and another. She buried her head on her arms at the dressing table, weeping uncontrollably. If God loved her the way Gran Lucy said, then how could she have been so hurt *twice?*

It was a long time before she sat up and wiped her eyes, still trembling. She knew Gran Lucy's response: "Have you surrendered everything to God, or are you still trying to run your own life?"

Tearfully she thought it over. The answer was obvious.

"You have to surrender *everything* to God—that means

your past, your present, *and* your future!'' Gran Lucy would have said firmly.

"Then I surrender!'' Katie wailed. "I give it all to you, God! I give up my resentment toward Giselle and my anger at Walt Zelt!''

"And David?'' Gran Lucy seemed to ask.

It broke her heart, but she answered firmly, "David . . . I give up David!''

"But do you *forgive* them?''

Katie knew that she must deal with forgiveness, that it was the key to the elusive peace and joy she had sought. "Yes,'' she whispered. "I do forgive them.''

Gran Lucy wouldn't let up. "But you must forgive Stan, too, you know.''

Katie sat straighter, incredulous. "How do you know whether I forgave Stan or not?'' she asked aloud as if her grandmother were in the very room.

"Because you haven't trusted men ever since,'' Gran Lucy seemed to be saying. "You haven't even trusted Jesus.''

Katie blew her nose. "Very well then,'' she said, mustering all the conviction she could, "I do forgive Stan too.''

"And now what?'' Gran Lucy continued as if Katie were still a little girl in her arms.

"Now I can pray.''

Gran Lucy persevered. *"How* should you pray?''

"Joyously,'' Katie said, "praising Him.''

Gran Lucy's voice seemed to soften with love. "And how will God answer you?''

Katie smiled as she remembered the answer her grandmother had given her so long ago. "God answers the prayers of His children on wings of love. Even in the most bitter of circumstances, if you're right with Him and ask for help, He'll give you the peace to live with a situation or

He'll deliver you from it entirely. Or sometimes He says, *Not now; someday you'll see it all come to good."*

Katie stood up. Her reflection filled the dressing table mirror. How enraptured she had become with herself lately instead of with God! She wished that she were outside in the sunshine and fresh air where she had so often felt His presence, but she reminded herself that He was everywhere, especially in the praise of His people.

Dropping to her knees, she closed her eyes. It came to her that the perfect prayer had already been given. She took a deep breath.

Our Father, who art in Heaven, she began, feeling a small spark of warmth opening her heart to Him again.

Hallowed be Thy Name, she whispered, the warmth in her beginning to flicker and spread.

Thy kingdom come . . . Thy will be done . . . It doesn't matter about my will, Father, she thought, aglow with love.

When she finished, she knew that she had never really meant those words before. Now she truly wanted only His will. It didn't matter about Stan; it didn't matter about David. If it was God's will that she should never marry, she was willing to accept it.

She washed the tears from her face, and her heart grew more and more peaceful. It occurred to her that she had loved Stan more than God. She had made an idol of him, expecting far more of him than any man could give. That was one mistake she did not intend to make again.

As she let herself out of the cabin, she decided that it was a good time to count her blessings. For one, this cruise . . .

"Katie!"

She glanced down the corridor. It was David!

He and Giselle walked toward her, laden with packages. David looked grim; Giselle, uncertain.

"I'd like to talk with you," he began.

"Fine," she answered with such serenity that it surprised her.

Giselle raised an elegant eyebrow. "Didn't I warn you?" she asked.

"Yes," Katie said quietly. "You did. You implied that I was an innocent, and that you and Eva were more David's type—on a long-term basis." Once the words were out of her mouth, she realized that she had answered a question that Giselle had put to David.

He looked at Giselle. "And you warned me that all Katie cared about was my money." He glanced at Katie.

She gasped. "If anything, David, I considered your money an obstacle between us. You're so knowledgeable . . . you've seen so much of the world . . . I couldn't imagine your really being interested in anyone so . . . so inexperienced."

Giselle quickly unlocked the cabin door. "Excuse me, I have to pack," she said, but her departure went unnoticed.

"You might have trusted me a little more," he said quietly. "Edwin Goodman became much worse during the night, and we had to help Ella make arrangements to get him to the hospital in St. Thomas this morning."

"Oh, no!" Katie cried.

"It's not as bad as the ship's doctor suspected at first, but Edwin's going to have tests for a few days. Giselle will stay here with Ella until he is well enough to fly home."

"If only you had told me," she said. "You must have known how it looked to me with Giselle coming out of your cabin in her nightie and you . . ."

"You took off running too fast," David protested. "I tried to find you. I searched the whole ship."

How stupid she had been. "I'm sorry, David. I just went crazy when I saw the two of you like that."

"I guess I should be flattered," he said.

"But why didn't you tell me about Edwin?"

"Bob and I thought you'd had a bad enough time last night with Walt Zelt. And when Bob knocked on your door this morning, Giselle answered."

"I guess I didn't hear it," Katie sighed.

He caught a deep breath. "The truth of the matter is that selfishly I didn't want anything or anyone to interrupt our happiness."

Katie reached for his hands, and they stood silently for a moment in the hallway.

"We had a lot to work out with Giselle too," he added. "She's going to set up a Caribbean affiliate travel agency here."

"That's what she wants?" Katie asked, amazed.

"That's what she wants."

"Since she can't have you?"

The color in his face deepened. "She didn't put it that way. But I suspect that she has contributed heavily to the complications between us. Seems I'm too trustful of women again, and you're too distrustful of men."

"I'm sorry," Katie said. "Giselle told me you needed someone like her, so when I saw the two of you together, I assumed the worst."

"Would I have arranged to bring you on this tour if that's what . . ." He stopped, appalled at his transparency

"You arranged the cruise for me, David?"

He looked down sheepishly. "I've admired you for a long time, Katie," he said. "Mrs. Sanders at your apartment building knew. I drive her home from church on Sundays . . ."

So that's where she had seen his yellow Porsche before! "But how did you know I lived there?"

"I saw you one Sunday morning and asked Mrs. Sanders about you. She told me when you broke up with Stan."

162

David colored again. "I'm afraid that I talked her into letting me know when you returned from your grandmother's. Then I had Bob call to offer you the job."

"Oh, David," she whispered, and he caught her against him.

"I love you, Katie," he said. "I've loved you for a long time, I think since the first time I saw you years ago."

Looking up at him, she saw the same glow in his eyes that she had noticed after he'd prayed in the church in Barbados. She suddenly knew in her heart that he had been praying about her there, that he would never knowingly hurt her, that she had only to reach out . . .

"Oh, David," she whispered, "I love you too."

"I didn't think there was anyone like you left in the world," he murmured huskily. "When I was healed from that accident, I never thought I'd pray so fervently for anything again as I've prayed for you."

He is a Christian! Katie exulted. *And not just a Sunday Christian. He believes in prayer.* He had prayed for her! He had waited patiently for her!

"It's the prince and the princess," piped a little voice in the corridor. "They're hugging!"

David tousled the boy's hair as the children passed by. "I can see our children already. . . . A little girl like you . . ."

"Our children?" Katie asked.

"I've always wanted children. Don't you?"

"Oh, yes, David!"

He kissed the top of her head. "God willing, we'll have them. There's time . . ." Suddenly changing his tone, he said happily, "There's even time for a shopping expedition!"

She waited for him to explain, but he only stood there smiling down at her. "Anything special in mind?" she teased.

163

"An engagement ring?" he replied hopefully. "I can't bear to have you run away again. And St. Thomas is said to have some of the most beautiful gems in the world."

She hugged him. "And would we have time to see Edwin and Ella at the hospital?"

"If you can change in a hurry."

"Five minutes?" she asked before truly realizing that he had proposed.

Instead of responding, he lifted her and whirled her around in the corridor.

"Do you know that you've just agreed to marry me?"

"I didn't think that you'd even need an answer," she replied joyously, "but, yes, David . . . oh, yes!"

When his lips met hers, the wondrous prayer of thanksgiving filling her heart seemed to soar higher and higher. Like her joy, it ascended on wings of love.

LOVE'S LATE SPRING

SPRING

Velma S. Daniels and Peggy E. King

CHAPTER 1

PAULA RUSSELL TOOK A deep breath, exhaled slowly, and slid some papers into her briefcase. It was always a relief to settle a customer complaint before it came to the attention of Mr. Wilkins. As assistant to the branch manager, Paula knew him to be a hard man—one of those efficient business machines, programmed to operate without further thought —or feeling. He would not welcome a late-day complication in his well-ordered routine.

Then a quick appraisal in the mirror, an expert stroke of her lipstick, and she was on her way out of the bank. She slipped into her smart, black, all-weather coat on the way.

After claiming her Mustang in the parking lot, she drifted easily into the daily race toward home in the suburbs. She enjoyed the stimulating challenge of the traffic, the constant maneuvering for an opening. It reminded her of a game of checkers; she almost expected to see one car "jump" another.

The moist feel of spring was in the air. A few curious crocuses were already showing color. In a few weeks tulips and daffodils would send their green fingers out of the earth, testing for warmth and light.

Paula turned her car into the driveway and stopped near a brick house. The setting sun made golden squares of the windowpanes. She opened her door and stepped inside to be greeted by a small, white kitten.

"Hi, Susie Cat. Happy to see me? Come on, out with you. Have a nice run in the yard."

Susie rubbed her head on Paula's ankle and purred contentedly for a moment before walking sedately out the kitchen door, tail high and flirty.

Paula had a special feeling of warmth and security inside the walls of this apartment. The round table in the center of the kitchen was bright with a colorful fringed cloth and a small African violet. Going through the living room she switched on lamps and placed some records on the stereo. She pulled a few pins out of her heavy auburn hair and shook it free; then she changed into pale green lounging pajamas. The heavy, sweet chords of Rachmaninoff were just beginning to work their soothing magic when the phone rang.

"Hi, Tony," she said. "What noise? Oh, my records. Listen," and she held the receiver out into the room.

"Tonight? Oh, Tony—can't we make it tomorrow? You know Friday night is usually late. I just came in."

"Oh," she continued, on a falling note. "Okay, I understand. Well, call me. 'By now."

She shook her head slightly. *Poor Tony. Thirty-six years old and still at his mother's beck and call. When she needs to go somewhere, dutiful Tony is required to take her.*

Susie was crying to be let in the door. Purring loudly, she went looking for her supper.

"Just a minute, young lady. Puss'n-Boots comin' up for you."

After a leisurely meal, Paula read the evening paper,

4

listened to more records, and finally settled in bed with a book, her hair in rollers and cream on her face.

"That's one nice thing about living alone," she mused aloud. "I don't need to think about pleasing a man."

She was deep in her book when the phone rang once more. *Tony again?* she thought.

"Hello, Paula," her mother said.

"Why, Mother—how nice! But you don't usually call as late at this. Is anything wrong?"

"Nothing wrong at home," Mrs. Russell stated. "But something did happen here in Woodruff that I thought you'd like to know about."

"What?" Paula asked with a note of concern in her voice.

"Amy died," her mother answered softly.

Paula faltered a little. "Amy! John's wife?"

"Yes," her mother replied. "Late this afternoon. She was in the hospital for just a day. An acute attack of appendicitis. She never came out of the anesthetic. John's mother was just here. The funeral will be on Monday. I thought you'd like to come."

"Why, why, yes, I want to come. I'll have to call Mr. Wilkins at home tomorrow and tell him. I'll come, Mother. Thank you for calling. Good-by."

She hung up, staring at the Van Gogh print on the wall but seeing only John Adams.

"Oh, John," she whispered. "Your beautiful Amy."

Tears came to her eyes. Absent-mindedly she got up and walked around the room. She straightened a picture, watered her favorite Pothos plant, and uncurled a corner of a rug. Her hands were occupied with small chores, but her mind raced into the past. She was back in church sixteen years ago, watching Amy Clark, a white satin doll, float down the aisle to the altar where John was waiting. She had slipped out quietly then, unnoticed. To hear the words: "I now pronounce you man and wife,'' would have twisted the knife already deeply embedded in her heart. She could still feel some of the pain.

When she finally returned to bed, she lay there as again her mind rushed to review the past. John had always been there. The Russells and Adams had been neighbors before Paula and John were born. Her first walk to kindergarten was with her hand in John's. He was eight months older than she, and as much a part of her life as her parents were.

A smile came to her lips as she remembered him standing on the rug inside the kitchen door, impatiently waiting for her to be dressed for school. His snow pants were tucked into heavy, clumsy overshoes with metal buckles; a scarf was wound around his face, and only his eyes showed. On his head was a heavy, hand-knit tassel cap. Her outfit was almost a replica of his.

Together they braved many a snowstorm. How many times her wet, soggy mittens were in his pocket. How often he held her hand, helping her cross puddles of slush in early spring.

She recalled homemade valentines, picnics, Sunday school programs, Christmas gifts—through grade school to high school.

There was never a thought of anyone else in her heart. John filled her life completely, and she his—she thought —until . . . Paula squirmed uncomfortably now, to remember, with a pang, their senior year in high school.

Already in March plans were made for the prom in June. Then in April a new student arrived. A princess out of a fairy tale. Petite; shy; enormous gray eyes; soft, golden blond hair. Every boy in school became tongue-tied in her presence. Every girl envied her; however, none disliked her. Her genuine warmth and gentle friendliness won all hearts—including Paula's.

6

Yet when John, full of eagerness and exultation, confided to her that Amy Clark had promised to go to the prom with him, she had been filled with such hatred and envy that it frightened her. The night of the prom she feigned illness, aided by her understanding mother.

John and Amy were married three years later. Three years, during which Paula's sparkle dimmed. She became an extraordinarily efficient machine, a secretary unequaled in dedication to responsibility.

A few years later, after Connie, and then Denise, were born to John and Amy, Paula abruptly decided to remove herself from the scene. She found a position in a bank in Chicago, one she still had, and moved to Elmhurst.

Away from Woodruff she finally came out of her shell. At a bank Christmas party she met Tony Anglietti, head of the savings department. They dated frequently, more often lately—when his mother did not need him. Paula had her apartment; she was as contented as she'd ever be, she thought.

And now? All right, and what now? What are you thinking of? she asked herself. *Be honest. You're already thinking that John is free.*

"God forgive me," she whispered, horrified. "I won't think about him. It was over a long time ago, really never was anything in the first place."

After much tossing and turning, she managed to sleep fitfully for a few hours.

In the morning she called the Wilkins' residence, and in her husband's absence, Mrs. Wilkins assured Paula that it was all right. However, if he needed her on Monday, Mr. Wilkins would call back by noon.

When he failed to call by one o'clock, she watered her plants, turned down the thermostat, placed Susie in her covered basket, and backed her small car out of the driveway.

The wind was blowing gustily, drying the muddy fields. Here and there a winter-weary gardener, anxious to feel again the surge of life in the earth, was testing its workability by crumbling a piece of it in his hands.

Women, their hair tied back with headbands or colorful scarves, were raking lawns, cleaning the yard, preliminary to turning the house inside out. Children with sweaters flying in the wind were racing madly on roller skates and bicycles, exuberantly rejoicing in life.

Life—Paula thought. *Life is all around, new and exciting, but not for Amy.*

The highway brought her into Woodruff in a few hours. John and Amy Adams lived in another part of the city, in a new house built after Amy's parents died; the old Adams' house next door looked forbidding and cold. Every window shade was drawn. It reminded Paula of eyes closed in death.

Mrs. Russell, using her apron as a cape, ran out to meet and embrace her daughter. "I'm glad you're here," she said. "John is in shock. It will be good for him to see you."

"You think so?" Paula was dubious. "What about the girls?"

"They seem to be all right, but when it's over, I'm afraid John will find his hands full. It was so sudden. One day Amy was fine, making plans for Easter outfits, and a day later she's gone."

Paula's father, tall and lean, cheeks creased by smiles, enclosed her in his strong, hard arms.

"Paula, child, it's good to see you," he said. "You should be here all the time. We miss you."

"I almost wish I could be here, Dad," she answered.

Susie stepped daintily out of her basket when Paula set it down, greeted them all with a rub and a purr, and set off to explore the yard.

In the warm, familiar living room Paula felt a surge of

homesickness. Her own apartment was functional, attractive, and satisfying. But her heart strings were attached to every detail in this room. The old upright piano on the short wall near the dining room. How gleefully she and John had pounded out "Chopsticks" or "Jingle Bells" on it. The scratches from their shoes were still visible on the bench and legs of the piano.

"Do you want to see them tonight?" Mrs. Russell asked. Suddenly, inexplicably, she felt shy. "Wouldn't it be kinder to leave them alone tonight?" she asked. "I'll see them tomorrow."

Mrs. Russell understood. "As you wish, dear. I'm taking a casserole over and I'll tell them you're here."

Later, in her old room, Paula removed the dainty, flounced spread from the bed and thought, *I should not have come—at least not until tomorrow. I don't belong in John's life anymore. Too many years have been torn off the calendar. He has his children and his memories. I can't help him. I'll attend church services with Dad and Mother in the morning and go to the funeral home in the afternoon, then drive home.*

Sunday was a raw day. The wind was now driving a cold rain from the east, and a few late snowflakes fluttered down and disappeared.

Paula and her parents were seated near the front in church. After the sermon and general prayers, the congregation was hushed when Reverend Winthrop recited the words: "It hath pleased Almighty God to summon out of this vale of tears, to His favors in heaven, the soul of Amy, wife of John Adams, who departed this life on Friday, March 18th, bringing the days of her earthly pilgrimage to 35 years, 10 months and 4 days. Let us pray."

The Adams' were, mercifully, absent.

Paula dreaded the visit to the deep-carpeted, comfortably

9

furnished funeral home. The strong odor of many flowers filled the air with too much sweetness; it disturbed the senses.

She saw John before he noticed her. His tall frame was stooped a little, but his hair was as black and wavy as in high school. Connie, fourteen, was his image: tall and slender, with dark hair and brown eyes. Denise, four years younger, was a blond angel holding onto her father's hand.

Paula's heart beat a little faster at the sight of John, but she controlled every impulse to hurry. Instead she deliberately stood and gazed at Amy—beautiful even in death.

When John saw her, he dropped his daughter's hand and came to her quickly.

"Paula," he said softly, "I'm so glad to see you. You remember Connie and Denise, don't you?"

"Yes, of course I do," Paula replied. "But they're almost young ladies. I haven't seen them for a few years."

"Isn't she beautiful?" Denise asked. "Did you know her a long time ago?"

"Yes," Paula answered, "I knew her—in high school."

To John she said, "What can I say, except that I'm sorry? If I can ever help in any way, please let me know."

"Thank you," John replied, "we'll remember."

Others were waiting to offer condolences and Paula moved away. *There is nothing for me to do here,* she thought. She hurried to find Susie and be on her way home. Her parents had a rare perception of her mood and did not attempt to dissuade her.

"We hoped to have you for another day," her father said, "but maybe some other time."

"Where's Susie?" Paula wondered. "I can't wait much longer. I'd like to be home before the traffic gets too bad in this rain."

Susie, however, was not to be found, and Paula reluctantly left without her.

Her mother's small frame was a silhouette in the window as she drove away. On the way she thought of her snug apartment waiting, her pleasant work at the bank, and of Tony. "I forgot to tell him I was going." She was talking to herself as she often did. "Wonder if he was worried about me?"

Clouds were heavy and darkness came swiftly. The rain fell steadily on the windshield. Street lights showed arcs of shiny, wet pavement; she was happy to turn into her own driveway.

While unlocking the door, she heard the phone ringing and hurried to answer it.

"Paula?" It was Tony, in a demanding voice. "Where have you been? I've been calling every half-hour. Even drove out last night when you didn't answer the phone."

She laughed delightedly. "You mean you were really worried? That's a good sign." Then in a softer tone she said, "I'm sorry. I forgot to call you. Mother called to tell me about a friend's death, and I drove to Woodruff yesterday afternoon."

"Now I'm sorry," Tony said. "Forgive me. Do you feel like going out tonight?"

"Why don't you come over here for a while and watch TV with me? I'm sort of tired."

Tony jumped at the suggestion. "I'll be right over," he said.

"Give me thirty minutes," Paula begged, "and I'll be ready."

"Okay, see you," he replied and hung up.

He was true to his word. She heard his cheerful whistle exactly a half-hour later and ran to open the door. "Come in, come in," she called out.

Tony stepped in quickly. His horn-rimmed glasses enhanced the twinkle in his brown eyes. His stocky body, inherited from his Italian parentage, was hard as a rock and flexible as a young sapling. He was the eligible and sought-after bachelor in the bank; Paula was envied by many of the young girls.

Now he caught her in a firm embrace and swung her around.

"What do you mean—forgetting to call me?"

"I'm really sorry, Tony," Paula told him. "My mind was so filled with thoughts of Amy that I simply forgot. She was a nice person. Her husband and daughters will miss her very much."

"That's too bad," Tony said. "My aunt died when my cousins were only seven and nine years old. I still remember Uncle Antonio and Francesca and Mario following the casket into church and weeping all through the service. It's easier when a man dies; a wife can at least make a home for the children, but most men are helpless then."

Paula thought of John and the girls sitting down at the table with the vacant chair and a pain crossed her heart.

Tony looked around the room and asked, "Where's Susie on such a night?"

"She was out visiting somewhere when I left. I couldn't wait any longer, so Mother and Dad will keep her for me. She's stayed there before. How about some coffee?"

"Fine, I'd like that," Tony said.

She was pouring the coffee when Tony looked at her closely and told her, "You know that you're one of the most beautiful women I know."

The cup rattled dangerously in her hand. "Why, Tony," she gasped. "That's the nicest compliment anyone ever gave me. Thank you, kind sir," and she bowed her head to him.

Tony's gaze was intent. "I didn't mean it as a shallow compliment, Paula; it's true. You have that clear, almost translucent skin that often goes with red hair and blue eyes. Your bone structure is . . ."

"Tony," she interrupted him, flushing, "please stop. What brought this on? You embarrass me."

"I've often thought of it," he said, "but never found the courage to tell you."

Paula was deeply moved. All her life she had been "that red-headed, freckled-faced kid," and to hear the word "beautiful" ascribed to her upset her opinion of herself. To Tony she said, "Let's keep it light. Someday you'll meet a really beautiful woman, and then you'll see the difference."

"Hmpf," Tony snorted, "I doubt that."

They listened to the news and weather report—"more rain." The living room with its warmth and friendliness was a cozy island, and Tony was unwilling to leave. However, Paula stifled a yawn and suggested that it was getting late.

"Okay," he said, "drive me out. If I sneeze at work tomorrow, it will be your fault. A man could get pneumonia in this weather."

"Out—out," Paula insisted. "I'll see you tomorrow."

He gave her cheek a warm touch with his lips and ran out to his car.

Paula closed the door gently, then leaned against it and hugged Tony's words to her heart. Beautiful! Such a word to describe her! She could still remember her nightly childhood prayer: "Please, dear Lord, let my freckles go away."

Now she ran to the mirror and searched for the despised freckles which had made her girlhood miserable. Odd— they were just about gone; a mere dusting remained. She remembered how they always popped out on a windy spring day. Had her prayers been answered after all these years?

"Thank you," she whispered.

Mr. Wilkins gave her a surprised stare in the morning. He

13

took out a clean handkerchief and wiped his glasses.

"Why, Miss Russell, I thought you were at a funeral."

After ten years she was still "Miss Russell." It suited her; she didn't appreciate familiarity in the office.

"I didn't stay for the funeral. There wasn't much I could do."

"That's right," Mr. Wilkins agreed. "We're all helpless then. It's later on that we can often be of assistance. Nevertheless, I'm glad you're here; there are some important matters that need attention."

Paula was grateful for the challenge of work; she refused to dwell on the picture Tony had given her of a lonesome man and two confused children slowly walking down a church aisle, following the beloved.

At the end of the day she found a measure of relief. It was over. She realized that her subconscious mind had been with John all day. In the evening she felt compelled to call her mother.

Mr. Russell answered. "Hello, Dad. Is everyone all right?" she asked.

"As well as can be expected, Paula," her father said. "I'll let your mother talk to you. Just a moment."

Paula understood a man's discomfort about such things.

Her mother came to the phone and said, "I'm glad you called. It's over; now life must go on again. John and the girls are spending the night next door with John's mother. Somehow time and God's grace will heal the wound."

Paula spoke softly. "Thank you, Mother. You always say the right thing."

Then she asked, "Did Susie come back?"

"Yes," her mother answered. "About an hour after you left. Are you coming for Easter? She can stay until then."

Easter was still two weeks away, but Paula agreed to come home, and said good night to her mother.

14

CHAPTER 2

RESURRECTION DAY DAWNED WITH a breath-taking sunrise. Sharp golden beams pointed fingers of light into infinite space; higher and higher they rose, filling all the world with brightness.

As the sun poured its light and warmth across the nation, chilled bands of worshippers in sunrise services sent out their anthems of praise. From the teeming eastern seaboard, across already green fields of the Middle West, over cloud-tipped mountain peaks, on to the Pacific Ocean the "Hallelujahs" soared to heaven.

Paula listened and thrilled to the familiar announcement "Christ is risen!" as she carefully followed Sunday traffic.

John, together with Connie and Denise, attended Easter services. They were seated a few pews ahead of Paula and her parents. It was difficult to keep her mind from wandering. She noticed how broad his shoulders were, how affectionately he bent his head to hear a whisper from Denise, as her fingers smoothed his coat sleeve. Occasionally he placed an arm across the back of the pew, and Paula saw the

15

wedding ring still on his finger. His hands seemed as hard and strong as years ago when he helped her climb a snowbank.

After church John's mother invited them for a late Easter breakfast. Again a shyness overwhelmed Paula, and she thought of refusing. However, her parents accepted immediately, and hesitantly Paula accompanied them.

John's smile was warm and friendly. "Happy Easter, Paula," he greeted her. "You look wonderful. That shade of green always was your color."

She was wearing an emerald green suit which set off her red hair beautifully. Her eyes shone.

"Thank you, John. How nice of you to remember."

Connie drew near and said, "Hello, Paula. Daddy, may I get you some coffee?"

John chuckled slightly. "Never mind, Connie. We'll get it later on. Paula and I would like to visit a little first."

To Paula he said, "This child seems to think that I'm senile. She waits on me hand and foot."

Connie blushed. "Daddy—you know I'm only trying to help you."

She walked away, appearing disappointed, and Paula said, "It's perhaps for her own sake. She feels lost and misses Amy," and immediately felt awkward.

However, John's acceptance of Amy's absence was realistic as he replied, "We all miss her very much. By the way, the girls enjoyed Susie last week."

"Then I'm happy she stayed here." Paula smiled. "I'm sure Susie also enjoyed their attention."

Leaving the house a bit later, Paula shook John's hand and withdrew hers quickly. She flushed deeply. It was the first time in more than sixteen years that their fingers had met, and she felt a distinct tremor in her heart. It dismayed and disturbed her.

16

In the afternoon, having settled Susie in her basket, Paula pleaded heavy holiday traffic and left early. She was uneasy all the way home. *I'm acting like a teen-ager,* she chided herself. *Act your age, woman. You have everything you want now; you've created a good life; let sleeping dogs lie. Just because a man you once loved gives you goose pimples merely by shaking your hand, doesn't mean that he's aware of you. I'll call Tony; we'll go out somewhere and I'll forget this foolishness.*

However, Tony was not at home when she called. She watched TV for a while, then settled Susie in her accustomed place under the kitchen table, and retired early.

In the following weeks Paula's tranquility returned somewhat. Her work load at the bank increased, and she was grateful for it. Occasionally she dreamed of John, but sternly admonished her heart and deliberately thought of Tony.

The sweetness of lilacs was followed by the fragrance of roses. Paula worked in her small garden, filling it with perfume and color. Beaches were again covered with young bodies simmering under the hot sun and turning a golden brown. Soft summer nights cried for hearts to share their sensuous scented beauty.

Paula and Tony soaked up sunshine and stargazed in dappled moonlight. They listened to music under the stars. They dined in every mysterious, exotic place they could find.

If the indoors was too warm for comfort, they sat in Paula's exquisite, tiny, mint-scented garden and watched the quivering shadows of moonlight through the trees.

"Ahhh," Tony sighed contentedly, stretched out full-length in a lawn chair, "who could ask for more? When I retire, I'm going somewhere where I can do this all year long."

He gave Paula a sidelong glance and asked, "How about it? Would you go with me?"

"Hmmmm," Paula answered sleepily. "Would you be surprised if I said 'yes'! You'd run like a scared rabbit. You're the perennial bachelor. Remember?"

Tony grinned at her. "Why don't you try to change me? Others have. Maybe that's why you intrigue me; part of you is never here. You look at me; we have fun together; but it seems you're always listening or waiting for something, or someone. What is it, Paula?" He was serious now.

"I don't know," Paula said dreamily. "Nights like this always make me feel like crying—they're so beautiful."

"I don't mean just tonight," Tony replied, "but always. I hold you in my arms, your head rests on my shoulder, but your heart is somewhere else. Where?"

Startled, Paula stiffened slightly. Without turning her head she asked, "Whatever makes you ask that? We've had such good times this summer. We even took our vacations at the same time."

Tony looked over at her and said. "You're avoiding the issue. Yep! We had our vacations at the same time. So what did we do? Stayed in Chicago—at home. We should at least have gone to some resort in northern Wisconsin for a few days."

"Together?" Paula asked.

"We're adults," he answered. "We can do as we like. But never mind. I wouldn't violate your principles. I found out long ago that there's more to you than sex."

And suddenly he spoke earnestly. "Paula, you know how I feel about you. Would you marry me if I asked you?"

She held her breath a moment, then said, "Tony, I'm very fond of you, but don't ask me—not just yet anyhow."

Carefully her fingers pleated a crease in her cotton slacks. The wind rustled the leaves of the poplar tree nearby.

"It's getting late; we'd better call it a day," she told him.

"Okay," Tony replied, "but think about it, will you, Paula? Really think about it? We could have such a good life—carefree and entertaining."

"What about your mother?"

"Mom would understand. Oh, she'd fuss for a while. But she'd gain a daughter. That would please her; someone else to take her shopping."

The moon was sliding behind a cloud. The wind was becoming stronger.

"Looks like it might rain; you'd better get going, Tony," Paula urged.

"I'm going, I'm going," he answered, getting up slowly. He kissed her cheek gently; suddenly he pulled her into his arms, bent his head, and kissed her lips long and hard. Then without waiting for her to catch her breath, he released her and said, "That's what you need. Think about it. See you." He strode away as if in anger.

Paula stayed in her garden until the first raindrops fell. She was in utter turmoil. Never had she been kissed in such fashion. Did she love Tony? Enough to marry him? It was true, they could have a carefree, interesting life. Both of them were beyond the first, young love stage. They could be realistic. But was that enough?

When the rain came she called Susie, who was already ahead of her, waiting at the door. Together they entered the warm rooms. She allowed doors and windows to remain open as long as possible. The cool, rain-washed air flowed through the apartment, and in a short time it was fresh and comfortable.

Before falling asleep she again thought of the pleasant life she and Tony could have. Instead of dreaming about him, though, she dreamed that she and John Adams were flying, floating, zooming through space under their own power.

They touched their heads on the blue heaven and fell to earth, landing in a heap, laughing for pure joy.

She sat up in bed and wept. "Stay out of my dreams, John," she scolded. "Why shouldn't I take what is offered to me? You had your life; leave me alone now. What if I don't love him the way I once loved you? I could make him happy."

In the morning she awoke and picked up the thread of thought which had tangled in the night and attempted to unravel it. Over a cup of coffee she thought of Tony's brown eyes. Toying with her spoon she tried to see into the future. *Would I be happy to have coffee with Tony every day for the rest of my life? It wouldn't be too bad,* she thought.

John's face appeared across the table, and her heart quickened.

"Tony asked me," she protested to the vision. "Would you ever do the same? I wonder."

She heard a church bell and decided, "It's Sunday; I'm going to church."

The sky was clean and blue. Small clouds still hovered over the city, like white butterflies over a cabbage patch, but the dry west wind soon swept them away. She walked the few blocks to her church.

At the entrance she hesitated and wondered how it would be to walk down the aisle to the strains of the wedding march. She tried to picture Tony waiting for her at the altar, and instead, John was there. *That's enough,* she thought. *I came here to worship, not to think about men.* But her mind kept wandering. It was only when the benediction was pronounced that she felt a quietness and peace envelop her. She walked home smiling and knew not why.

After lunch she slipped into shorts and went out into her yard. She removed the dried blossoms from her prized day lilies. Gently she shook the sand from the bedraggled petunias, clipped the wilted roses, and pulled the mulch back around them. A few of the begonias in front of the house needed staking. Her hands were grubby, for she couldn't bear to work with gloves, and her knees were covered with earth and grass stains.

Later, showered and dressed in a cool sundress, she was lounging in a comfortable chair and thinking. *Why do I need a man around? I'm fine just the way I am. Life is pleasant; living alone is quite satisfactory.*

Tony called in the evening, disconsolate. "Mother wants me to take her to her sister's," he said plaintively.

Paula couldn't help it; she giggled. "All right. I don't mind. I've been working in the yard. I'm ready for bed in a short while."

"But I wanted to see you," he said sadly.

"Well, that's up to you—and mother," she replied gently. "Don't worry about it; I'll see you at work in the morning."

In September Paula was given another raise. Her salary astonished her. *Am I worth that much?* she wondered. It was pleasant, however, to know that she was capable, and appreciated. She celebrated by cooking a thick porterhouse steak for Tony and herself. Her small dining alcove was festive with the silver and candlelight.

"You're not only beautiful and bright, with a great career," Tony told her, "but an excellent cook, too. With all that talent, how could we miss in a marriage?"

He said it lightly, but his eyes were serious.

"I'm thinking about it," Paula answered, "but when I marry—if I marry—the job goes. I do not intend to be a working wife."

"Oh, oh," Tony laughed. "There goes my carefree life."

"Let's keep it like this, for a while anyway. Shall we?" Paula asked.

Tony patted her hand. "Providing you cook me a steak like this once a week."

"Is that a bribe or a threat?" she asked laughingly.

"It's a compliment, my sweet," Tony answered seriously.

CHAPTER 3

THE FIRST HEAVY FROST of the year came unexpectedly. Paula looked out the window one morning in mid-October and saw a silver sheet of hoarfrost covering the lawns and housetops. *I didn't cover my begonias,* she thought regretfully. They were still standing straight and firm, but she knew that when the sun warmed them they would fall, blackened and dying.

In a few days leaves fell gently, as one by one they released their hold on life and floated to the ground. Bare outlines of trees were again visible. The fine tracery of small branches was etched on the horizon.

Paula worked in her garden again. This time it was to lift bulbs, cover roses, and put the garden to bed for the winter.

She planned to go home for Thanksgiving and asked Tony to accompany her. His eyes lit up. "I'd like that very much," he said quickly.

"Fine, I'll tell mother to expect you."

Thanksgiving Day was cloudy. A cold front pushed through during the night lowering temperatures by ten degrees or more. Tony's Wildcat was a warm refuge, carrying them to Woodruff. Susie dozed contentedly in her basket on the back seat.

"I hope your mother is not alone today," Paula said.

Tony laughed. "Alone! You don't know how many relatives I have. My sisters, Gina and Lola, and their families; my two uncles and aunts, cousins. . . . There will be at least fifteen at my mother's table today."

"I'm glad," Paula said.

"Of course, I'm a most disrespectful son," Tony added, mockingly.

"Why?" Paula asked with concern.

"As head of the household, since father died twenty years ago, it is my solemn duty to preside at all family gatherings," he mimicked.

"You must enjoy it," Paula remarked. "It has a special honor, doesn't it?"

"Honor?" Tony weighed the word. "Maybe. But it also reminds me of my constant responsibility to my mother. Kept me home—to run errands. And where is my own family?"

The last few words were said somewhat bitterly. Paula was silent. It has never occurred to her that Tony could be unhappy in his seemingly carefree bachelorhood.

"Turn right at the next corner," she directed him. "It's not far from here."

"Nothing's far in a small town," Tony replied. And then remarked, "For a small town, that's a good-sized factory. What is it?" They were passing a large, modern plant.

"That's the Woodruff Paper Company. It's been here for years. John Adams, the man whose wife died, is president."

"Looks like a busy place."

"I believe it is," Paula said. And in a few minutes told

him, "The third house on the right, in the next block—that's where my parents live."

It was an old house. The bottom half was white siding; the top, brown shingles. A huge chestnut tree stood in the front yard. Some of the branches touched the windows of Paula's old room. The backyard was dwarfed by a huge spruce tree.

Paula and Tony entered to find a crackling fire going in the fireplace in the living room.

"Anybody home?" Paula called out.

"Paula!" her mother answered. "Here in the kitchen. Come through the den; the dining room door is closed. Leave your things in the hall."

The old hall tree was still there, still tipping a little to one side. Paula knew just how to balance it by handing coats a certain way.

They walked through the den. The library table where Paula's books were found every school night was still under the windows. Her mother's sewing machine was in its place near the radiator; her father's comfortable chair, with the old bridge lamp near it, showed the contour of his body.

Mrs. Russell was in the large kitchen. The table in the middle of the room was covered with pots, pans, casserole dishes—everything needed for a successful holiday dinner.

"Mmmm—I'm glad you're here," she said as Paula kissed her cheek. Her hands were filled with pie crust.

"Mother, this is Tony," Paula said.

"Hi, Tony. We're happy to have you. You'll have to excuse me—I must get this mince pie into the oven."

"Thank you for asking me," Tony said. "Mince pie is my favorite."

"Good," Mrs. Russell said, her blue eyes twinkling, "it's also our favorite. Paula, call Dad. He's in the basement."

Paula went to the wall switches and flicked the middle one. Immediately a shout was heard in the basement. "Okay, okay. I'm coming."

"That's the best way to call him," Paula laughed. "Turn off the light."

Mr. Russell came up the stairs, both arms filled with fruit jars—pickled peaches, apple butter, and beets.

"Thought I heard voices," he said. "Nice to have you, Tony."

They shook hands.

"Let the men go to the living room, Paula," her mother said. "You find an apron and help me."

"He seems nice," her mother told her later. "Is it serious?"

Paula shrugged her shoulders. "I haven't made up my mind yet. I like him. But I think I've been a bachelor girl too long; I enjoy my solitude."

"Solitude and loneliness are first cousins, my dear, and may become inseparable later on," Mrs. Russell stated. "Better think about it now."

"I am thinking about it, Mother," she replied. "Really I am. But somehow I must wait."

"Don't wait too long," Mrs. Russell advised her.

Paula walked through the den into the hall to find a tissue in her purse. Coming back she looked through the window to the Adams' house next door. John was seated at his mother's table. He saw her. As by a prearranged signal in childhood, he raised his hand and, with upturned palm, pointed the fingers at her. The meaning had always been: *I'll come over later.*

Paula flushed slightly, then smiled at him and nodded her head.

After dinner—dined and sated—they relaxed in the living room and watched the football game on TV.

"Do you still have the traditional Thanksgiving Day walk, Mother?" Paula asked.

"Yes, we do," Mrs. Russell answered. "Dad has given it up, but most everyone still goes."

"What's this 'traditional walk'?" Tony asked from the depths of his chair.

"Every Thanksgiving Day, after dinner at noon, or shortly thereafter," Paula told him, "while the women do dishes, everyone else walks downtown to see the first Christmas display at Thurows, the main department store."

"You mean they actually *walk*? Both ways?" Tony was horrified.

"Yes, lazybones," Paula laughed, "we walk both ways. And when we get back, we start right in on the leftovers."

She did not realize that she had aligned herself with friends and neighbors.

"Are you going today?" Tony asked.

"I think I shall. Don't you want to go?"

"Oh," he protested, "how can I? All that food, and this game on TV. If you don't mind I'll keep your father company."

"That's fine with me," Mr. Russell told him.

"All right, see you later," Paula replied.

Slipping into her coat and walking shoes, Paula stuck her hands into her pockets and walked out. It was still cloudy and cool, and the brisk walk brightened her eyes and brought a flush to her cheeks.

At Thurows, eight or nine blocks away, the crowd was gathered in front of the windows. Fathers held small children on their shoulders. Animated toys and figures in a pre-Christmas setting stimulated anticipation of joys. A tiny, moving figure of a girl sat before a small piano and with one finger searched for the melody of "Silent Night, Holy Night."

Paula stood on the fringe of the crowd. Most of the faces were unfamiliar. She had been gone long enough for a new generation of parents to appear.

A hand was placed upon her shoulder lightly, and she turned and looked into John Adams' smiling eyes.

"Hi," he greeted her. "I thought I recognized that shining red hair ahead of us."

"I didn't see you," Paula said. "Where are the girls?"

"Around somewhere. Where's your friend? I saw you when you came."

"Tony decided the game was too important. Besides he was too comfortable to move."

Connie and Denise came. "Hi, Paula," Denise cried out. "Isn't the window beautiful?" Her eyes were sparkling with pleasure.

Connie said, "Hi. It's pretty, but don't you think we're getting a little too old for this, Daddy?"

John laughed. "Right now you feel too old for it. When you get our age, you'll realize nobody's ever too old for it."

"I'm getting cold," Connie said. "Let's go."

Quite naturally they fell into step. The girls walked on ahead, and John and Paula followed.

Many old landmarks had been replaced by new buildings, and many buildings had new fronts. However, the block of Fountain Park still remained. The bubbler of mineral water was still there, stained with the iron content of the water. Casually, as in the past, they stooped and drank of the salty, slightly bitter, slightly medicinal-tasting water, and made the usual wry faces.

"Still tastes the same," Paula said happily.

Denise and Connie met friends and were far ahead of them. All Paula's shyness vanished as she and John slipped into pleasant reminiscence. *Remember this? Remember that?*

When they reached home, Paula suddenly thought of Tony: she felt a bit uncomfortable. The girls were waiting for them.

"Grandma's over at Russells," they said. "We're supposed to come too, Daddy."

When Tony and John were introduced, they appraised each other, as men do—the firm handshake, the scrutinizing eye, then the smile.

John's mother, tall and spare, with gentle, brown eyes, kissed Paula's cheek. "You smell so fresh and look so clean. That walk was good for you," she said.

Tony looked at Paula and asked in a low tone. "Did I just cut my throat by staying home? That walk was more important than any game, I'm afraid."

Paula merely smiled at him. "Let's have more turkey," she said.

Susie came in slowly, greeted everyone with a switch of her tail, and rubbed her head on Denise's ankle.

The girls were seated at the piano, trying to imitate the figure of the small girl playing with one finger. John walked over to them and said, "Play something we can sing, Connie. How about the Thanksgiving prayer—'We Gather together to Ask the Lord's Blessing'?"

Tony's tenor complimented John's bass. From this they went into folk songs and popular choruses. When Connie and Denise left the piano bench to play with Susie, John sat down and began to play "Jingle Bells."

"Come on Paula," he urged her. "You still remember it, I'm sure."

"Oh, John, it's been years and years," she protested.

Nevertheless, she sat down next to him, and after a few attempts, they played their childish version of the song. John banged the bass notes and Paula played her own variation of the melody. Her fingers skipped over the treble keys, ending in an imitation of tinkling bells on the high notes.

The girls left Susie and watched in amazement. "Daddy," Connie exclaimed, "I didn't know you could play the piano; you and Mother never played."

"Play it again," Denise begged.

Clowning a little, they repeated the performance.

"Did you and Daddy play together when you were small?" Connie asked.

Mrs. Adams answered for them. "They played together, went to school together, fought each other over marbles, and cried together afterward."

Connie's response was a small, "Oh." Then she walked back to Susie in the den.

It was soon time to leave. Mrs. Russell wrapped part of the turkey for Paula and included a large piece of mince pie. Susie was back in her basket.

Out on the highway Paula leaned her head back and exclaimed, "What a day! What a glorious day! Wasn't it?"

Tony hesitated a moment before answering. "Yeah. I think it was—for you. Paula, is John what you've been waiting, listening for?"

Paula sat up in surprise. "We were friends for many years, Tony. I feel sorry for John."

Most of the ride home was in silence. Each was busy sorting out thoughts. Finally Tony said, "I hate to say this, but Connie is suspicious of you."

"Suspicious! What does she have to suspect?"

"Can't you see that she's taking care of daddy, and the woman who steps between them better be prepared for a fight?"

"When did you notice all this?"

"You couldn't see her eyes when you and John played your 'Jingle Bells.' She was jealous. Once a girl her age takes mother's place, it's not easy to dislodge her."

"She needn't worry. Poor child. I'm not thinking of dislodging her. But John is still a young man. She must realize that he could marry again."

"I'd like to make you a bet that she'll try to prevent it," Tony said.

"I'm not a betting woman," Paula answered, "but I think you're mistaken. I think she still misses her mother dreadfully and clings to her father for assurance."

"Denise is the one who misses her mother," Tony answered. "Did you notice how she stayed near her grandmother?"

"No, I didn't. She's very different from Connie, however."

It was after eleven when they arrived at Paula's apartment. Tony brought Susie's basket and let her run in the yard.

"I think I'll go right home," he said. "I'm still sort of 'food-groggy.' But, Paula," he added, "it was a glorious day."

"I'm glad you went with me, Tony," she answered.

He kissed her cheek lightly and walked slowly to the car.

Paula placed the turkey in the refrigerator, but ate the pie. By then Susie was ready to come in, and Paula opened the back door for her. She walked in slowly. "Come on, come on," Paula urged her. "It's time for bed."

CHAPTER 4

THE WEEKS BETWEEN Thanksgiving and Christmas were always a magical time for Paula. She felt the world holding its breath, waiting for the first shy note of a Christmas carol. As the time drew nearer, the music became fuller and sweeter.

For her parents she found a set of beautiful TV tables and a lace cloth for the dining room table. Tony loved good sweaters, so she shopped carefully and found a smart, golden brown cashmere. A soft, light shawl, the color of coffee with cream, caught her eye. She let her fingers smooth it, then decided to buy it for Tony's mother.

Often she admired small, precious figurines which she pictured in Connie's and Denise's hands. However, a sense of inappropriate intrusion prevented her from buying them.

As a child the tree enchanted her early Christmas morning. Now she began trimming her small home three weeks in advance. Tall, thin tapers, surrounded by tiny, silver balls, shed a soft glow in the dining alcove. Cherished, fragile figures created a crèche on the desk in the subdued light of the copper lamp.

The stereo was loaded exclusively with Christmas music.

Tony's car stopped at the curb outside Paula's apartment. Inside the car they finished singing "Deck the Halls." The bank Christmas party was over. Contrary to the usual office parties, Mr. Wilkins insisted upon strict decorum. Punch was served without spirits, and a smorgasbord of Christmas dainties surrounded the punch bowl near the huge decorated tree in the lobby. Gifts were generous. Mr. Wilkins had a piano wheeled in and everyone gathered around to sing. Solos, quartets, descants, complete choir—all took part.

The happiness of the occasion removed social restraints. It was surprising to note the increased skill of the pianists and to hear the enthusiasm in the singing. Several girls discovered they had courage enough to kiss Mr. Wilkins and wish him a "Merry Christmas" when they left.

Flooded with a delightful feeling of warmth and well-being, Paula and Tony laughed pleasantly now at their artistry.

"Do you feel about Christmas music as I do?" Paula asked.

"I don't know. How do you feel?"

"I wish I could explain it," Paula answered. "Every year when I hear the first Christmas music, I feel a curious easing of tension, even my facial muscles relax. I can feel a smile on my lips, spreading way up to my ears. A delicious sense of weightlessness and peace washes over me."

They entered the apartment. Paula lit the candles and the low light near the crèche. Then she turned on the stereo and the room was filled with the soft music of strings.

Tony sighed and sat down slowly. "Now I know what you mean by peace. Ahhh."

33

"I'll make some coffee," Paula said.

"Are you really going home for Christmas?" he asked as they drank coffee and nibbled on fruit cake and cookies.

"Yes, I am. Mother and Dad are expecting me tomorrow. I'll be back sometime on Monday."

"You'll be here for New Year's Eve, though, won't you?"

"I expect to be," Paula said.

"Don't forget we have a date. My sisters are throwing a party at their club that evening."

"You spoke about going out, but I didn't know it was your sisters' party."

"They just decided this a few days ago."

"I better find something to wear," Paula said. "A party deserves a new dress."

Tony fumbled in his pocket and brought out a small package.

"Can you use this with a new dress?" he asked.

"What is it?"

"Open it."

She held the box in her hand for a moment and looked at him. Then she unwrapped it carefully and gasped. A beautiful green sapphire pin and earrings lay in the cotton.

"Oh," she exclaimed. "Tony, they're gorgeous. How lovely!"

She held the pin in her hand. It glowed. "Tony, you shouldn't. It's too much," she protested.

Tony's smile was warm. "Please wear them, Paula. Sapphires were made for you."

Paula's eyes were bright. "How will I ever find a dress worthy of them?"

She felt she ought to refuse, but to reject the gift would inflict pain upon him. She raised her eyes. His face was very near. Her eyes closed. She seemed to sway toward him a little, and he reached for her hungrily. His lips were on her hair.

"Paula, Paula, I love you so," he whispered.

Her face was hidden in his shirt front. He smelled of shaving lotion and fresh, wintry air.

"Oh, Tony, I'm such a fool. Sometimes I think I love you very much, other times I think I'm destined to remain an old maid. How can you be so patient with me?"

"For you, darling, I'll wait forever," he said.

She gave him a bright smile. "Thank you, thank you for everything."

He turned to the door.

"Wait a minute," she called to him. "I have something for you and your mother. But don't open it 'til tomorrow."

"For Mother, too? You'll be on her preferred list from now on."

She laughed. "It's not much, but it made me think of her. I thought she'd like it."

"I won't see you, then, until after Christmas," he said. "Greet your parents for me."

Once more he held her close and whispered, "Merry, Merry Christmas, darling."

After he left, Paula again looked at the earrings and pin. She shook her head wonderingly. *Why am I such a stupid thing?* she asked herself. *Why can't I tell him that I'll marry him? I could learn to love him. He'd be so happy. Why can't I? Why not? He's good; he's kind. We have much in common. What's holding me back?*

Susie glided into the room and eyed Paula through half-closed lids. Her pink tongue curled as she yawned. After a few moments of purring, she returned to her basket.

"All right," Paula told her. "I get the message. I'm going."

The next day, Saturday, was a gray, cloudy day, promising snow. "Maybe we'll have a white Christmas," Paula told Susie as she packed gifts into her Mustang.

The highway was crowded. Everyone was in a hurry to reach the warmth of a certain destination before dark. By the time Paula turned her car into the streets of Woodruff, Christmas decorations were lit. The small town was transformed into a fairyland. Twinkling, shimmering lights glowed everywhere. The magic of yesteryear returned to Paula. Nostalgia for childhood's magical enchantment engulfed her, and her eyes were misty when she stopped in front of the old house. The huge spruce tree near the garage was ablaze with lights, welcoming her.

Mrs. Russell saw the car stop and ran to open the door. "Merry Christmas," she called out.

"Hi—to you, too," Paula answered. "Don't come out. I'll bring Susie, then get the rest."

"All right," her mother answered. "I'd ask Dad to help you, but he's not feeling too well."

Paula came to the door. At her surprised look Mrs. Russell added, "Nothing to worry about. Just needs rest and vitamins."

"Is he in bed?" Paula wanted to know.

"No, not now. He did stay in bed for a day or two last week, but he's downstairs now."

"He didn't put those lights on the tree out there, did he?" Paula asked.

"No, John did that. He was helping his mother with her tree so came over here later and helped us with ours, too."

"How are they?"

"Well—the first Christmas will be strange, I suppose. Connie and Denise seemed sort of quiet last Sunday when I saw them."

"I'm sorry," Paula said. Then in a moment of sudden

decision she asked, "Do you think they'd like to have Susie?"

Surprise showed in Mrs. Russell's voice. "You mean you want them to keep Susie? Wouldn't you miss her?"

"I suppose I would. But if it would make the girls happy, I'd like them to have her."

She opened the basket and allowed Susie to run through the house. Then she went into the living room to call out, "Merry Christmas, Daddy."

He smiled at her happily and returned the greeting.

"Now we can have Christmas," he said. "Let me get your things."

"Thank you, Dad, but there's not much. I can manage easily."

Paula's sharp glance noticed a slight change in him. He seemed smaller, or thinner. His hands felt lighter on her shoulders.

"Are we going to Christmas Eve services?" she asked, after the gifts were placed under the small, beautifully white-flocked tree in front of the large window.

"I think we better not," her mother said. "The services at 7:30 are mostly for the children. There is a midnight service at 11:30. I'd like to go to that one."

After a pleasant, leisurely supper, Paula and her parents exchanged gifts. "This year we decided to give you several small gifts rather than one large one," her mother said. She handed Paula four colorfully wrapped packages. Slippers, a Grecian type robe and gown—in a blue to match her eyes, a golden velvet pillow for her davenport, and another soft pillow for Susie's bed. Paula kissed them both. "Thank you. Everything is lovely; and I adore the robe and gown."

"How did you know we wanted just this kind of TV table, and a lace cloth?" her father asked.

"I heard Mother muttering something at one time," Paula laughed.

"Don't you think Connie and Denise would like to have Susie?" she asked her father.

"I think it would be the best thing for them," he said. "They'd have something other than their father to think about."

"We'll fix her up tomorrow with a ribbon and the new pillow," Paula said excitedly.

Mr. Russell declined their invitation to the midnight service, saying he was tired.

When Paula and her mother left the house to walk the four blocks to church, the snow was falling quietly and slowly. There was no wind; not a branch stirred. Each feathery flake appeared to be spaced in exactly its own spot. Softly, gently, they settled lightly on the town.

Paula stopped and whispered, "Mother, have you ever seen anything so beautiful? So hushed? It must have been a night like this when the angels sang."

Seated in church later on, hearing the choir, singing the carols, Paula thought, "*This* is Christmas Eve. *This* is real. *This* is what it all points to: Christ is born—Love and Peace."

At the close of the service the lights on the two tall trees, one on either side of the altar, were slowly turned off, until only a few in the form of a cross remained. Then the entire congregation began to sing "Silent Night, Holy Night" as they filed out of the pews.

One by one the bells began to ring. More and more were added until the night was alive with the sound.

Old friends welcomed Paula, and John and his mother greeted her warmly. However, they seemed a little apart—as if alone in all the festivities.

"We'll see you tomorrow," John said briefly.

Christmas Day Paula found a large red-and-green ribbon which she tied onto Susie's collar. The basket was decorated with a wide red ribbon and a few small bells. The new pillow was placed inside, and a large tag with "Merry Christmas to Connie and Denise" was tied to the side.

"Shall we take her over to their house?" Paula asked.

"Why not?" Mrs. Russell asked. "Let's go."

"Come on, Dad," Paula called to her father. He appeared fresh as a youngster today.

"All right. I want to see their faces when they see Susie," he answered.

It had stopped snowing, and the low December sun was shining on trees piled high with eiderdown. Snow shovels scraped on sidewalks, and snowballs bounced off billboards. The air was clear and cold.

The Adams lived on the edge of town, where the house stood by itself. John opened the door to them in joyful surprise.

"How nice. Come in, come in. Connie and Denise, come down," he called, "we have company."

Paula set Susie's basket down near the tree.

The girls came down the stairs slowly. Both were quiet and unsmiling. They seemed to have been crying. At sight of the basket and at the sound of Susie's voice, they ran down swiftly. Incredulously they looked at their names on the tag.

Denise was down on her knees first. Speechless, she opened the basket and lifted Susie out. "You mean she's ours? We can keep her?" Connie asked. They both looked at Paula with tear-bright eyes.

"Yes," Paula said. "If you want her, and if your daddy agrees."

"Oh, Daddy, may we?" Denise cried.

"Of course you may," John told her. His own eyes were bright.

"Thank you, Paula," he said, "this is the happiest moment we've had here today."

Susie was already inspecting her new home. It was a large house, furnished with exquisite taste. Square, brick colonial style on the outside, it was warm and gracious inside. The center hall showed a good-sized living room to the right. To the left was the dining room with superb modern furniture. A carpeted stairway led to the second floor. Beyond the dining room was a swinging door to the kitchen where Susie was heading.

"Is she hungry?" Denise asked.

"She's usually fed just twice a day, morning and evening, but she recognizes a kitchen odor, I suppose. That's where she sleeps."

"Couldn't she sleep in our room, Daddy?" Connie asked.

"We'll make her entirely your responsibility. How's that?"

"Good," the girls agreed happily. "Thank you, Paula."

Paula saw a large, cream-colored sofa opposite the fireplace in the living room. A long, narrow, marble-topped table stood in front of it. Behind it, on the wall, hung an excellent painting of an old fisherman and a tiny, wistful girl. The rug was a deep pile in a soft green. In one corner of the room stood a small grand piano—with the keyboard closed.

John noticed Paula's glance and said, "The girls closed it. They haven't played since—since their mother . . ."

"May I try it?" Paula asked.

"Please do," John replied.

She looked in the bench for Christmas music, then began to play softly.

Suddenly Connie ran into the room. When she saw Paula at the piano, her face paled. She cried out, "No, no, don't play it! Stay away from Mother's piano!"

John was shocked and appalled at his daughter's behavior.

"Connie," he scolded, "Connie, stop it."

Paula, however, let her fingers slip off the keys. She put the cover down again and apologized to Connie.

"I'm sorry, Connie," she said. "I was admiring your mother's wonderful taste in furniture and music. She was very good, you know."

"Don't tell me anything about my mother," Connie replied hotly.

Then as quickly as her anger had come, she burst into tears and ran up the stairs, crying out, "I'm sorry, I'm sorry, Daddy!"

Denise also had tears in her eyes as she stood in the doorway holding Susie.

"Do you want Susie back now?" she asked.

"No, dear," Paula answered. "Of course not. Keep her. She's very fond of you all."

John's eyes wandered to the stairway several times. Paula noticed and said, "Leave her alone, John. And don't let it worry you. She misses Amy very much. I understand."

Mr. and Mrs. Russell had remained silent. Now Paula's mother said. "Just assure her, John, that everything's fine. We'll go now. Are you stopping by the house later on?"

"I'd like to," John said. "We're going to Mother's for supper, and the girls have something doing at church. Maybe I can see you then."

"I was hoping you'd say that," Mrs. Russell said.

They rose to leave. Denise was still playing with Susie.

"Oh, Paula," she cried. "I'm glad you gave Susie to us. We'll take good care of her. And you can come to see her often."

"I'll try to, Denise. 'By Susie—be good now. You hear?"

She gave Susie an affectionate pat and rubbed her head.

"'By, John, see you later.''

In the car Mrs. Russell said, "Poor child. It must have been a miserable day for her. Everyone else talking about what mother made and did and she, unable to join in.''

"I'm surprised that Denise is so different, though," Paula said.

"Well, she's younger," Mrs. Russell answered, "and always leaned more on her father than Connie did.''

"Are you tired, Dad?" Paula asked. He was very quiet.

"A little, and hungry, too," he answered.

"We'll have some herring salad for supper with that caraway rye bread you like," Mrs. Russell said.

"Did you make the salad with apples, pickles, and potatoes, Mother?" Paula asked.

"Yes, and whipped cream!" she answered.

"Ohhh," Paula cried. "There goes my waistline—but I'm going to have a lot of it.''

John and Mrs. Adams came in while the three of them were finishing their late supper.

"Come, have some salad with us," Mrs. Russell invited them.

They found chairs at the large oak table.

"Where are the girls?" Mrs. Russell asked.

"The young people are having a Christmas party in the church hall," John said. "I'll pick them up later.''

"Is Connie all right?" Mrs. Russell wanted to know.

"Yes," John replied. "She's fine. It was a childish outburst, but she's all right now.''

"Don't you want your tree lit?" he continued.

"Oh, yes," Mrs. Russell said. "Will you turn it on please?''

He was almost as familiar with this house as his mother's. In a few moments the tree was bright. The snow covered it, and the varicolored lights shining through their white blanket transformed the tree into a rainbow.

"Do you remember when we planted it?" John asked Paula.

"That's right, we did. About, let's see—about twenty-eight or twenty-nine years ago," she answered. "We were only about seven years old, weren't we?"

"Six or seven. I remember Mr. Rosenthal, on the corner gave it to us. He was planting some seedlings, and this was such a scrawny one that he gave it away."

Paula smiled. "How we dug that day!" she said. "The hole was three times larger than necessary."

"And were we proud of our tree!" John reminisced.

Their eyes met, held a moment in remembrance, then parted.

Paula's father arose to leave the table—and swayed a little.

"What's wrong, Dad?" Paula's mother's voice was anxious. She was up and near him in a few seconds.

"You all right, Mr. Russell?" John asked.

Mr. Russell looked at them rather strangely. "Of course I'm all right. Shouldn't I be?"

Very steadily he walked to the living room and sat down in his large chair to watch TV.

Their eyes were puzzled as they looked at each other.

"How about a short walk, Paula?" John suggested later.

The house was warm and smelled deliciously of Christmas. They were all a bit drowsy.

"I'd like that," Paula replied immediately.

"Did you bring boots?" Mrs. Russell inquired.

"No, I'll wear your flat ones. Okay?"

"Fine, they're in the hall. John can help you find them."

Booted, but hatless, they walked out. John's dark hair was a head higher than Paula's auburn one. Innumerable

43

times they had walked out this door and down this street. They fell into step as easily as they had walked to school twenty-five years ago. Words, however, did not come as easily as then. For a long time they walked in silence. It had turned colder, and the wind drove the fine, powdered snow into their faces.

Finally John asked, "You're happy, aren't you, Paula?"

"Yes, I guess so."

"Is Tony very special to you?"

"I don't know what to say. Yes, he's special, in a way. I like him very much," she answered.

"Have you known him long?"

"About five years. A short time after he came to work at the bank."

They were walking quite rapidly and didn't see the curb covered with snow. Paula felt herself slipping and put out her hand to hold on to John. He caught her quickly, and for a few seconds held her tightly. Then he looked at her as though he saw her, really saw her, for the first time in his life.

"Are you all right?" he asked, a little out of breath it seemed.

"Yes, I'm fine. Awkward of me. My heel slipped in the boot."

"I'll have to pick up the girls in a short time. Maybe we better go back," he said.

After the girls were asleep that night, John stayed in the living room for a long time. The late movie and the endless commercials went on and on. He heard the sound, but nothing touched his consciousness as the feel of Paula in his arms.

Great guns! he thought, *she's beautiful! And that fragrance in her hair!* He couldn't understand why he felt this way. She had always been there, as much a part of him as—as his mother. They had been friends for as long as he could remember. She was always just "Paula," his companion. Their near brother-sister relationship had continued through their school years—until Amy came.

Amy! The hurt was still there, but buried a little deeper. The throbbing sharp pain was replaced by a dull, nameless ache. He still missed her so very much. How well he understood Connie's feelings when she heard her mother's piano.

Yet—the irrevocable truth remained—she was gone. Never again would he touch her face or hold her in his hungry arms. He thought again of catching Paula. *Was that why I felt that way about her? Was it only because my arms ached to hold Amy?*

Very much bewildered, John Adams went to bed—to dream of a snowball fight with Paula.

The next day, still called second Christmas Day in Woodruff, Paula's father was up early and had breakfast ready when Paula and her mother came down.

The sun was dazzling on the snow. A few small drifts were piled under the dining room windows.

"I wonder how the roads are," Paula said.

"They'll be all right," her father answered. "It didn't snow long enough to cause trouble."

"Isn't it a bit early anyhow for the first snowstorm?" Paula asked. "Seems to me we usually have the first one right after the new year."

"I think you're right," her mother said. "By the way, what are you doing New Year's Eve?"

"I'm going to a party," Paula answered gaily. "Tony's sisters are giving one at their club. I think it's called 'Traveler's Club.' Anyhow, it's on Highway 66, I know that."

"You really like him, don't you?" her father asked.

45

"Yes, I like him a lot. He's good fun."

She waited a long moment, then said, "He gave me a beautiful pin and earring set for Christmas. Green sapphires. I'm still not sure if I did the right thing in accepting them. They must have cost half a fortune."

"Oh, Paula, should you?" her mother asked quickly.

"I don't know. I might as well tell you—he wants me to marry him."

"And you're not sure," Mrs. Russell told her.

"That's just it. Sometimes I'm very sure; then again I'm not. I don't seem to be able to make up my mind."

Mr. Russell observed his daughter thoughtfully. "Child, if you are at all undecided, then don't do it. Don't settle for anything but the best—at any age. When you're sure, you won't even think of anything else. Your answer will be there even before the question."

"That's right," her mother agreed.

Paula looked at them, considering their advice. "Thank you both. I'll try to remember. Anyway, I must buy a dress this week to match the jewelry."

When she was ready to leave, her mother helped her carry the gifts to the car.

"Wonder how Susie likes her new home?" Paula asked.

"You're going to miss her, aren't you?"

"Yes, I will. But if the girls are happy, then it's fine with me."

"Drive carefully, and have a good time at the party," her mother called as she drove away.

The highway was good. Whatever snow had fallen was ground to powder and blown away by traffic. She drove slowly. Her mind wandered. *Wonder what's wrong with Dad?* she thought. Last night after he was seated in the living room, she thought she had seen him slip something into his mouth—furtively. Come to think of it, he hadn't gone hunting this year, or even fishing. She remembered how much those sports had been part of his life when she was small.

She felt sorry for Connie and Denise. The house was clean and warm, and doubtless they were all cared for very well. Yet something was missing. Like a chain with a link missing. Both ends were clean and shining; yet without that link they were not a chain at all—merely pieces of metal.

When she had stumbled last night, John caught her. Did she only imagine it, or did he seem to look at her very closely? Why?

Tony? What am I going to do about him? I must make up my mind. It's unfair to him to waver so.

At home later, she packed gifts away and changed into her old lounging pajamas. The apartment was strangely quiet without Susie. *I'm going to take a long, hot bath and go to bed. Work tomorrow.* As always the thought of her work steadied her. She liked her job—it was interesting, challenging, and it demanded her concentration.

Tony waved from across the lobby as she walked out for lunch the next day, and after work he waited for her at the entrance.

"Hi. Did you have a good time?" he asked.

"Wonderful!"

"I missed you."

They fell into step. "Aren't you going to the parking lot?" Tony asked.

"No. I'm going to Fields to look for a dress for New Year's."

"Can't I help?" he pleased.

"Nope. I want to surprise you," she said. "Besides, I've never gone shopping with a man; I wouldn't know how to act."

She found a dress of sheerest wool. The lines were elegant, with long, full sleeves cuffed tightly at the wrist. Gold threads ran through the soft creamy confection. With a narrow, intricately woven chain that served as a belt and gold buttons spaced down one side of the back yoke, it was a dress of which dreams are spun. She was shocked at the price, but it would be a perfect setting for Tony's pin and earings.

Work between Christmas and New Year's was merely a place to go during the day. Evenings were meant for living. Paula and Tony were together every evening. They made old-fashioned Christmas calls. His mother and sisters welcomed her warmly. Mrs. Anglietti was as delighted with her shawl as a child with a toy. It was draped over a velvet chair and shown to every holiday visitor.

"Is it not soft? Is it not beautiful? My son's friend gave it to me."

She was soft, plump, and deceptively helpless.

CHAPTER 5

The last day of the year! Paula was listening to the radio. Every announcer was reflecting on the happenings of the 365 days that were now part of history, and how the past would affect the future.

The economy was showing no immediate signs of recovery, despite a temporary upsurge during the Christmas season. The President's popularity seemed to fluctuate with the Dow-Jones average. Sports reviewed, ripped apart, and put together again for next season. Great strides in medical technology, the space program, education. But reports of border skirmishes in Ireland and other hot spots in various parts of the world were only grim reminders that peace on earth was forever elusive. Mankind had not come so far, after all.

She thought of her own life, less than a grain of sand in the universe, yet important in its particular spot. *What did the year bring to my life? What will the new year bring?* And again a haunting, longing, yearning came to her. A soul-searching; a hunger of the deepest, innermost recesses of her heart. *Is this what Tony means when he says that I listen or wait for something? For what? Dear Lord, for what? I should be content. I have a really good life, a nice home, a man who wants to marry me, wonderful parents.*

We skim over our lives lightly, she thought, *merely on the barest surface. Underneath is so much more depth; in beauty, in the cry of the soul—for what?* Sometimes she felt that she could almost capture the fleeting reality—then it receded into the subconscious again.

I could never talk to Tony about this, she thought. *He'd tell me to snap out of it. And that's what I'd better do right now,* she concluded. *Tony will be here in an hour. We're going to a party—to have fun!*

Wonder what John and the girls are doing tonight? What a year it had been for them.

She dressed slowly and deliberately. *Tony wants to be proud of me tonight. All right—he will be.* She was glad she had allowed her hair to grow out. It had been brushed until it blazed and flamed, framing her face in a coppery aureole. The dress clung in the right places; the earrings and pin looked like they were made for the dress. She placed a dab of perfume behind each ear and in the curve of her arm.

When Tony walked in a few minutes before eight-thirty, he gasped and stared at her.

"Paula! You're beautiful! I'm going to be one proud Anglietti tonight. Am I allowed to touch?" he teased.

"Silly," she laughed. "Is it cold? Do I need boots?"

"Yes, it's cold," he answered, "and yes, you ought to take boots. We might have to park quite a distance from the club."

"I'd better take a scarf too," Paula decided.

Tony took her coat and boots from the closet. As he held her coat, he inhaled deeply.

"You know, I could find a piece of your clothing anywhere by the perfume. Everything you wear smells—like you," he said, "heavenly."

The Traveler, Paula discovered, was many miles out on the highway. The night was cold, but a clear, stinging cold, without snow.

"What a party!" Paula exclaimed, when they finally found a parking place a block from the building. "You mean these cars all belong to relatives of yours?"

"Relatives and friends," Tony answered. "Nearly a hundred, I bet."

"That's not a party," Paula laughed, "it's a convention."

Once inside, they fought a good-natured battle to find a place for their wraps. Paula thought, *Why it's better than a convention, lots more fun.*

A long table was placed across one end of the hall. On it was every dish possible, from hot savory Italian sausage, to pasta, to desserts and coffee.

Tony's mother, and his sisters and their husbands were at the head of the table in a sort of receiving line. Paula was admired, secretly and openly. She felt flattered and extremely shy.

Tony's face was flushed with pleasure. Proudly he presented her to uncles, aunts, cousins, and friends—whose names she promptly forgot.

There was an orchestra playing, and the room was filled with young and old. Tony and Paula were standing at one end of the hall when Tony said, "You're listening again."

"I hear a phone ringing," she said.

"Let it ring." Tony replied. "Someone just wants to wish us a Happy New Year."

Paula persisted, "Tony, don't you think you should answer it?"

"All right, if you wish." He took her hand, and they

threaded their way through the room. The phone in the office was still ringing. Tony picked up the receiver.

"Hello."

"Hello. Is this the Traveler's Club?" a man's tense voice asked.

"Yes, it is," Tony answered.

"Please listen carefully," the voice continued. "Is Miss Paula Russell there?"

Tony looked at Paula. "Miss Russell? Who wants her?"

"This is John Adams, in Woodruff. Please, it's very urgent. If she's there, may I speak to her?"

"Just a moment," Tony said. He handed the receiver to her. "It's for you—John."

At the mention of his name, Paula's heart beat faster. Her hand flew to her lips.

"Hello, John," she said. "What's happened?"

"It's your father, Paula. He's in the hospital—he's had a heart attack. Dr. Parker asked me to call you."

"I'll be there just as soon as possible, John. Please," she almost whispered, "please keep him for me."

"We'll try, Paula. Come quickly."

She turned away from the phone, her hands wet with perspiration. "It's Dad. He's had a heart attack. I must go right away."

Tony flew into action.

"Find your coat and boots and meet me at the front door. I'll tell Mother why we're leaving."

Fortunately they had come later than many of the guests, so her coat was not too difficult to find. In a few minutes she was at the door. Tony was already there.

"Wait here. I'll run for the car," he told her.

She made use of the time to slip into her boots and tie her scarf. In a short while Tony was there. He turned out of the driveway and headed west.

"Tony," Paula cried out "you're going the wrong way."

"No, I'm not," he replied. "We'll pick up Highway 31 a few miles out, then go straight up through Elgin. We'll gain a good half hour or more that way."

"Oh, Tony," Paula said in a small, grateful voice, "you mean you're driving me up there? You wouldn't need to. What about your party?"

"What party? Without you there is no party for me."

She laid her head against his sleeve and said softly. "Thank you. I must admit it would have been unpleasant to drive alone."

They rode in silence most of the way. Tony drove fast but carefully, and traffic was light on this less-frequented road.

"So he did sway," Paula said.

"What do you mean?"

"Last Sunday when he left the table, Dad swayed a little. We all noticed it. And later I thought I saw him put a pill into his mouth. But he insisted that he felt fine. I wonder how long he's been sick. Poor Daddy," she added. "I hope he'll be all right. What would Mother do without him?"

The bells in Woodruff were just finishing their greeting to the new year when they reached the outskirts of town. Tony looked at Paula and said, "I'll say it anyhow—Happy New Year, Paula. There's more I want to say, but it will have to wait now."

"A Happy New Year to you, too," Paula said.

In a few minutes she directed him. "Turn right on North Avenue, then go straight to the hospital on 7th Street."

Tony drove into the circular driveway and stopped at the entrance. Paula had the door open before the car stopped. She ran into the hospital. The waiting room was dim, but at the switchboard was Grace DenBoer, an old friend. She saw Paula come in and said, "Hello Paula. He's in Room 202."

53

The elevator was too slow. Paula ran up the stairs, a terrible urgency at her heels. She turned the corner at the nurse's station and saw her mother and John come out of the room. Instinctively she knew it was too late. "No," she cried out to them, "no."

She felt she had been running all night, and now she was up against a stone wall and had to stop. Her mind whirled and came to an abrupt halt. She walked into the room, where the nurse was already covering the gray, empty face.

"Dad," she whispered to him. "Daddy, forgive me for not being here." Her throat felt tight and hard.

Tony had parked the car and now came to the door of the room where the rest of them waited. The nurse stood by, waiting tactfully until John led them into the hall.

Paula and her mother clung to each other for a few moments, silently. Mrs. Russell, constant in her inner strength, was calm, even though her eyes were brimming with tears.

"Mother," Paula reproached herself, "I'm sorry I wasn't here. When . . . ?"

"About eight this evening," Mrs. Russell answered. "We had planned to go to church services, but he said he was not feeling too well; he was tired. Then, while watching TV, he . . . he just crumpled in his chair."

She put her hands in front of her eyes; her voice broke.

"I tried to help him, but he slipped to the floor. John was at his mother's next door, so I ran over to get help. When we called Dr. Parker, he immediately sent an ambulance and told us to call you."

"Did you call the apartment?"

"Yes," John answered. "About eight-thirty."

Tony and Paula looked at each other. "We left a few minutes after eight-thirty," Paula said. "If we had only waited. How did you know where to find me?"

"Your mother remembered that you had said the party was at a club on Highway 66," John said. "The operator was very helpful."

"What can I do?" Tony asked.

John inclined his head a little to one side and Tony went to him. "Will you take Mrs. Russell and Paula home?" he asked. "Someone must make preparations and give instructions. I'll stay here."

"I'll be happy to," Tony replied.

He walked over to Paula and asked, "Shouldn't we take your mother home? John will attend to everything here."

Paula nodded gratefully.

In the living room at home Paula slipped out of her coat and noticed her dress, its perfection inappropriate now. She remembered a skirt and blouse in her closet upstairs.

"He was here a few hours ago," Mrs. Russell said to Paula when she came downstairs. She sat in the big chair, dry-eyed and withdrawn, not yet fully comprehending her loss. "His glasses are here; his paper is still open to the sports page. He's not really gone, is he, Paula?" She knew otherwise, but her heart recoiled from reality.

When John came in, Dr. Parker was with him. He went to Mrs. Russell and said, "He did not suffer. Be grateful for that."

Paula asked, "How long had he been sick, Dr. Parker?"

"For about a year. He would not allow me to tell you."

"Poor Dad. I wish I'd known."

"What could you have done for him?" Dr. Parker asked. "He didn't want to be babied or pitied."

"I would have been here much more often. I would have stayed longer when I was here."

Dr. Parker turned to Mrs. Russell. "Let me give you something to help you sleep," he suggested.

"No, thank you, Doctor, I'd rather not. It won't hurt me

to keep vigil one night—or more. I have many, many wonderful memories to sustain me."

"All right," Dr. Parker said, "but if you need me, just call."

"We will—thank you," she told him.

John went to the door with him. "We'll help her, Doctor."

"I know you will, John. It's kind of you."

Tony was uncomfortable. He didn't belong. The three of them spoke intimately of friends and relatives who must be notified and plans to be made. He stood in front of the darkened fireplace, near the forgotten Christmas tree, with his hands in his pockets. His fingers grasped a small, square box. He swallowed several times, then said, "I think I'll go now, Paula, I'll be back for the . . . on Tuesday."

Paula looked at him, a little surprised. "Oh, Tony, must you go?" Then added, "I suppose so."

Mrs. Russell said, "Thank you very much for bringing Paula."

He held her hands warmly and said, "I'm just sorry that we didn't get here sooner. I'll be back on Tuesday."

Paula walked to the door with him. "I'll never forget your kindness, Tony. Thank you again."

He looked at her for a long moment, thinking of the small box in his pocket, then shook his head slightly and said briefly, "Yup," and walked out.

Shortly after Tony left, Mrs. Adams came over with coffee and a few sandwiches. It was then, when the two women, neighbors for so many years, looked at each other, that Mrs. Russell's composure broke.

"Aggie, Aggie," she said, and they fell into each other's arms. Tears came easily now. Mrs. Adams remembered her own grief years before. Her understanding comforted her old friend more than the presence of her own child.

Paula and John sat at the kitchen table, trying to eat but managing only to drink coffee. Dryly Paula commented, "Death is so demanding, so instantly important. Many other plans one makes are subject to change, but not Death. Death is *now*, right now, no vacillating, no procrastination."

"Yes, I know," John said. "It's pitiless, but honest. It cuts and scrapes, but brings with it maturity as a small compensation."

Suddenly Paula remembered Amy and said, "I'm sorry, John."

"It's all right," he comforted her. "As your mother once told me—time and the grace of God heal all wounds."

Toward morning Mrs. Russell was finally able to rest a little. Mrs. Adams and John left, promising to return in a few hours. Paula tried to relax. Sleep would not come, so she curled up in the big chair in the living room. *Was it only yesterday,* she thought, *that I wondered about the future, what the new year would bring? Is it less than twelve hours ago that Tony and I heard that phone?* It all seemed a life time away, an unpleasant dream.

What will happen to Mother? I can't leave her alone, and I must go back to work. I cannot ask her to live with me in the apartment; she'd miss her home and friends too much. It would be cruel. Someone must see about the funeral—I can at least relieve her of that.

Her mind rambled on and on; inevitable problems arose. A living being is torn out of his place in Life. It leaves a ragged tear in the tapestry of Time, which must be mended and repaired. The broken threads must be drawn together by other lives, the ends tied and worked into the tapestry to complete the picture.

I must call Mr. Wilkins—I must have more clothing—I ought to drive in and get some things. Maybe Mrs. Adams will stay with Mother for a few hours. I could take Dad's car.

She dozed a little and awoke when her body rebelled at the cramped position. The smell of fresh coffee came from the kitchen. Mrs. Russell was sitting at the table, staring out the window.

"Didn't you sleep at all, Mother?" Paula asked.

"A minute at a time, I think," Mrs. Russell replied. "I made a list of people we should call. Aggie said she would take care of it for us."

"If she stays with you for a few hours," Paula suggested, "perhaps I can take Dad's car and drive home. I must have more clothing; and I should call Mr. Wilkins. Before I leave I can see about necessary arrangements for the—the funeral."

"Of course you can take the car. And I would be grateful if you would take care of the arrangements. But I do not like to have you driving alone today."

When Mrs. Adams came, she suggested that Paula allow John to drive her to her apartment.

"What about the girls?" Paula asked.

"They'll be all right," Mrs. Adams said. "They're old enough to take care of themselves for a few hours."

John arrived within the hour and instantly agreed that Paula should not go alone.

"I'll call the girls," Mrs. Adams promised.

By nine-thirty they were on the way. Arrangements were brief for the funeral—and with the pastor. John had taken care of many details the evening before.

It was still windy and cold. Even with the heater turned high, Paula was grateful for the small fur rug which John placed over her knees.

"Your mother is taking it very well, isn't she?" John stated.

58

"Too well," Paula said. "I'm afraid she'll break later, when I'm gone. It worries me. I don't like to leave her alone. I wish now that I would have come more often, spent more time with Dad."

"Don't reproach yourself," John said. "No matter what we do, it never seems quite enough. And then, too, how do we know what would have happened had we done otherwise? Perhaps I'm too optimistic, but I have a peculiar feeling that everything is meant for our good. That in some way God will turn misfortune into good fortune."

"Did you reproach yourself after Amy's death?" Paula asked.

John was quiet for a moment, then said, "Yes, I did, at first. *Reproach* is probably not the word. I was sorry that we didn't take the trips to the West Coast and Mexico as we planned; that we didn't buy some of the things she wanted for the house. No, it isn't reproach; you just miss them dreadfully. There is a great sadness and deep loneliness. But like recuperation from a serious illness, every succeeding day brings additional strength, serenity, a release from petty anxieties—a sort of mental and spiritual maturity. Things which seemed highly important no longer trouble you."

Paula's heart was extremely heavy. "You loved her very much, didn't you?" she asked.

"Yes," he answered, "I did. But already she seems more a memory of a wonderful dream than a reality. Even though the girls are there, she seems distant. Perhaps the heart and mind build up a resistance to grief in self-defense—I don't know."

Paula directed him to her address.

"I thought you lived in an apartment," he said when he saw the low, rambling building.

"This is it," Paula expained. "It's a duplex. The land-lord, Mr. Sikes, lives on the other side."

"It suits you," John said later in the living room. He was admiring her Christmas decorations. "I remember some of these figures in your manger scene. They were under your tree for many years."

Paula was delighted. "Remember this one?" she asked, pointing to a white velvet lamb with a tiny, golden bell on the collar.

"Didn't I give that to you when we were about ten years old? The year we had the measles?" he asked eagerly.

"Yes, that's the one," Paula said, smiling.

They were bending over the crèche on the table, close to each other. John turned to look at her, his dark eyes a little above hers.

"We had a wonderful childhood, didn't we?" he said. "All through grade school, into high school . . ."

Paula interrupted, "Yes, we were happy."

She was a bit uncomfortable. High school memories were not all pleasant for her. "I'll make some coffee," she said, "and we might as well have lunch before going back."

"Why don't you let me look through your refrigerator? I'll find something while you're packing a few things."

Paula was pleasantly surprised. John's culinary abilities had been nonexistent years ago.

"Okay, I'll start the coffee," she told him.

Before packing, she called Mr. Wilkins and was grateful when, after expressing his sympathy, he suggested a week's vacation.

She quickly changed into a dark suit, packed, and went back to the kitchen. John was busy cracking eggs into a bowl.

"We might as well have scambled eggs and bacon," he said and laughed. "That's about all I can make."

A magic descended. Scrambled eggs, bacon, toast, coffee, and Christmas *stollen*, together with golden apricots in delicate blue bowls, were transformed into ambrosia—a banquet. A curious light-hearted feeling came over them.

John smiled at Paula across the table and said. "This is the most delightful meal I've had in a long time. It's perhaps not the right time to say it, but I'm happy. It feels good to be here."

Paula's eyes were bright. "You know, I think you're right. This is the best meal I've had for ages, too. More coffee?"

They finished the coffee, and together they cleaned up the kitchen. Paula watered the plants heavily.

"Shall I drive my car back?" she asked. "Then I won't need to bother anyone when I come home next week."

"Bother!" John exclaimed. "It's no bother. I'm looking forward to bringing you home again. Where is your car?"

"In my garage."

"Let it stay there," John said.

Paula and her mother were alone. The last eloquently commiserating relative had been kissed and bade farewell. The remains of the funeral visits and refreshments were evident everywhere. It had always seemed a barbaric custom to Paula—this gathering of friends and relatives for a meal after the funeral. Neighbors, who felt the loss of the departed one more keenly than did most of the relatives, supplied the food and the service. Mrs. Adams took complete charge.

"About the only time we see each other these days is at a wedding or a funeral," was heard again and again.

"Aunt Edna, how are you?"

"Uncle Frank! Haven't seen you since Hattie's wedding."

One of the teen-age cousins brought with him the ubiquitous guitar, and the younger folk soon gathered around him and began their mournful folk songs.

Paula thought, *I don't believe it! It's not possible! How can they?* She didn't know whether to be shocked or angry until John, who stopped in for a few minutes after the service, said to her, "They're not being disrespectful, Paula. It's their way of expression. And listen, they're singing of love, life and death. These belong together. Death is a part of life, isn't it? In the final truth—we are born to die. Death is as much a part of life as birth and love—and just as important."

"It's morbid," Paula stated strongly.

"No, it is not morbid, it's realistic," he told her. "For anyone who does not believe in immortality and Christ, yes, it's morbid, but not for us."

She made a second appraisal of the group and decided it would be inhospitable to allow them to leave without at least some small refreshment.

Tony also had been there for a few minutes. He was talking to Mrs. Russell, but Paula sensed his uneasiness and came to his rescue.

"Thank you for coming, Tony," she said.

He turned to her quickly. "You have almost as many relatives as I," he said with a half smile. "Your mother says you're staying for the rest of the week. Are you?"

"Yes, Mr. Wilkins suggested it," Paula told him. "I'll help Mother get things straightened out a little."

"Want me to come back for you?"

"It won't be necessary. John said that he'll drive me home," Paula told him.

Tony's eyes sought something in hers. Then he said a short, "Oh," and added, "Well, I better be getting along. Call me when you come home."

A slightly uncomfortable, undefined, vague feeling of guilt disturbed her, as if she had failed him in some way.

She watched him as he said a few more words to her mother; then he turned, smiled at small groups of visitors, and left, closing the door gently.

Now, an hour later, Paula and her mother surveyed the room. Mrs. Russell sighed, "Sort of a mess, isn't it?"

Chairs were everywhere; coffee cups were stacked on the piano and windowsills. Part of a sandwich had found a resting place in a flowerpot.

"Quite a mess," Paula agreed. "Let's leave it and try to get some sleep. Mrs. Adams said she and the rest of the neighbors would come in the morning to help."

Mrs. Russell looked helpless and very tired.

"Tonight you ought to have something to help you sleep Mother," Paula suggested.

She looked at her daughter and sternly replied, "Child, I've never taken sleeping pills and do not intend to begin now. What if I do stay awake for a night or two? When my body gets tired enough, I'll sleep. Right now I'm all right."

Paula studied her mother for a moment, then said, "I'm sorry, you're right. I was thinking of Dr. Parker's advice, but I can see your point. Even if we can't sleep, our bodies are resting at least. I'm sure you'll be fine."

"In time I'll be all right, I know," Mrs. Russell replied. Then she added in a forlorn voice, "What hurts most is not to be able to hear him breathing in bed, or to reach out and pull the blanket a little higher over his shoulder. But I'll get used to it."

Tears were brimming in her eyes, but her back was straight as she walked up the stairs ahead of her daughter.

Contrary to expectations, the days followed each other rapidly. Mrs. Russell decided to take her time and tackle each problem as it appeared. Paula wondered about finances.

"Why are you worried, Paula?" her mother asked. "I have the house and insurance. That's all I need. But I'll be so lonesome for a while. Couldn't you come back home?"

Paula sat up straight and looked at her mother in startled surprise. "Why, Mother!" she began. "I don't know what to say. I never thought of it. What would I do here? Where would I find work?"

"I don't know that," her mother replied. "But it would be wonderful to have you home once more."

They were eating a light supper in the warm kitchen. The house was in order. Mrs. Adams and several other neighbors had come in the morning, and in a few hours everything was in its accustomed place. Connie and Denise had taken the tree down when John and Paula drove to Elmhurst. The large spruce in the back yard was still adorned with lights and would remain so until warm weather.

"It's such a pretty thing to see when we have a late snowstorm," Mrs. Russell said. "We light the tree then, and it's Christmas again."

Paula lay awake a long time that night. Her mother's suggestion that she return to Woodruff was tantalizing. *I could walk to work on tree-lined streets,* she thought. *No traffic problems to worry about. Instead of the strident city sounds, I could hear the "cheer-cheer" of the cardinal and see the fat robin fall back on his tail when he succeeds in pulling his dinner out of the moist earth. I could look out of my window and see the squirrel in the chestnut tree again.*

And finally she came face to face with the thought she knew had been there from the beginning, and which she trembled to think about. *I could see John.* She almost whispered it to herself.

But my job—Mr. Wilkins—and my lovely apartment. For ten, almost eleven years it's been my home.

"Oh, Mother, Mother," she said aloud, "you started something."

Saturday afternoon John called to ask Paula and Mrs. Russell to have dinner with them.

"The girls want to go to the country club," he said when they were settled in the car.

As soon as the car stopped, the girls were out and running ahead to watch the skaters on the ice-rink. Mrs. Adams and Mrs. Russell were deep in conversation. Paula and John followed them.

"I've never been here," Paula said.

"Amy and the girls enjoyed our membership here," he said. "And you'll probably see some of your old friends in the dining room, also."

When John and his companions walked into the club, Paula's bright red hair shone like a beacon. Several men in a group raised their eyes and arrested their conversation to stare.

"Will you look at our John?" one of them said. "Who is she?"

"Why, that—that's Paula Russell," another volunteered, amazement in his voice. "Her father just died."

"Who's 'Paula Russell'?" a comparative newcomer asked.

"She left here a number of years ago," the former answered. "We all considered her John's girl until Amy Clark came. But, wow! What happened to her? She's a beauty!"

Paula looked around the room after they were seated, trying to find someone familiar. She recognized a pleasant round face at the next table. The man smiled widely and immediately came to the table.

"Paula Russell, as I live and breathe!" he cried out.

"Skeeter!" Paula exclaimed, "Skeeter Jenkins!"

Skeeter's eyes took them all in. "Hi, John, it's good to see you, and with so many lovely ladies."

"Still the flatterer," Paula laughed, while the rest of the women beamed.

"Where's your wife?" John asked.

"Around somewhere," Skeeter said as he scanned the room. "There she is, with Bill Schoen and Walt Zerner. I'll get her."

"Do I know her?" Paula asked John.

"I think so," he said. "Mary Hansen? She was a year or so behind us in school. They were married about eight years ago."

Not only Mary, but Bill and Walt also came with Skeeter.

Paula was overwhelmed. An absurd tingle of excitement brought a sparkle to her eyes and a pink flush to her cheeks.

"Mary Hansen!" she cried. "Of course I remember you. You were the cheerleader who jumped the highest at our football games."

"Hi. It's been a long time since high school days," she smiled warmly as she embraced Paula.

Skeeter interrupted jokingly with, "Jumped the highest and screeched the loudest."

"Just loud enough to make you hear me, Skeet," she smiled at him. Paula saw her firm, hard hand reach for her husband's, while she wrinkled her nose at him.

Connie and Denise looked on in wide-eyed astonishment as Bill and Walt kissed Paula's cheek.

"Boy, Paula," Walt exclaimed, "are you looking good! Remember the time you and John quarreled and he climbed that chestnut tree near your window to get your attention, and then he fell down and got a black eye?"

John answered him. "That's not all. I ripped my trousers, too, and heard about it from Mother the next day."

Mrs. Adams and Mrs. Russell joined in reliving happy

66

memories of the past. They nodded and smiled at each other in mute understanding of the years gone by.

"We're sorry about Mr. Russell," Bill said soberly, "but he had such a full life; I can't imagine him wanting it any other way."

"Thank you," Paula's mother said with her usual composure.

Denise took advantage of the lull in conversation to report that she was hungry.

"We'll order right away," John said.

"Are you planning to stay awhile?" Walt asked Paula. "I'd like Judy to see you."

"Judy?" Paula asked quickly. "Judy Blair? I knew she'd get you." And soft rippled laughter came with the words.

"What do you mean?" he asked.

"You didn't know it, but she was in love with you from the first day you stepped into Woodruff High."

"Yeah?" he asked. "How come I never knew?"

"Well," Paula hedged, "if you fellows were so stupid that you couldn't recognize love—" she shrugged her shoulders, "why should we tell you?"

At her words John observed her intently for a few seconds —then lowered his eyes and said, "I think the girls are hungry. Shall we order?"

"Say 'Hello' to Judy for me," Paula told Walt as he left.

Later, on the way home, Connie said to Paula, "You must have been pretty popular in high school."

Before Paula had opportunity to answer, John said, "She was one of the finest scholars we ever had in Woodruff High. Made the National Honor Society, too."

"John, stop it," pleaded Paula. "Others were on the honor roll, too."

"Was Mother on it?" Denise asked.

John said, "No, your mother and I were not on it."

"How's Susie?" Paula asked, to change the atmosphere in the car.

"She's fine," Denise replied. "She sleeps in our room every night. When are you coming to see her?"

"I should have come this week," Paula said. "Tomorrow I'm going back home. I'll see her next time I'm here. Okay?"

Mrs. Russell asked, "Is Tony coming to get you, Paula?"

Quickly John replied, "No, I'm taking her home, right after lunch."

A thoughtful John Adams brewed himself a cup of coffee and sat before his television, completely oblivious to the characters and commercials flashing on and off the screen. He was trying to pin down his feelings for Paula. Brotherly love indeed! In a few seconds at the club when he had looked at her, his heart had turned a somersault. He was surprised that no one had noticed his trembling.

Now he allowed his mind and heart to travel backward. *She was always there—we were always together—I always loved her—and I never knew it.*

Was this being disloyal to Amy? *No I did love Amy; she filled every moment of our married life, and would have continued to do so. And yet there were many times when I seemed to be waiting for something—someone.*

"Dear Lord," he said softly, "can this be true? Can a man love two women at the same time? I don't know."

He ran his strong fingers through his dark hair, took a long swallow of his coffee, and slid down deeper into his chair. Slowly he became aware of Connie's presence in the room. Her hair was in rollers; her feet were in huge rabbit fur slippers. He noticed that her wildly striped pajamas were a bit short on her. *She's growing too fast,* he thought, before he asked her, "Anything wrong, dear? I thought you were asleep."

Connie slid to the floor in front of him.

"No, nothing's wrong. I-I just wanted to talk a little."

"About what?"

She clasped her hands in front of her knees, rocked back and forth a little, and began hesitantly, "Daddy, are you really taking Paula home tomorrow?"

"Yes," John answered. "Your grandmother will stay with you."

"Oh, we're old enough to stay alone. But—" she hesitated.

"But what?" John prompted her.

Instead of answering his question, she looked at him with serious eyes and said, "We're getting along all right, aren't we? I'm taking care of everything real well. Don't you think so?"

John leaned forward and cupped her chin in his hand. "You're doing very well, darling. I know that, and I appreciate it, too. But it should not be necessary for you to think of taking care of us."

Nimble as a kitten she jumped to her feet. "But Daddy, I like to do it. It's fun to take care of you and the house."

"Thank you, Connie. Now you better run up to bed, unless you would like to open the piano and play something for me. Don't you think it's been closed long enough?"

At his request she stopped short. "That's Mother's piano," she protested. "No one else should play it."

John rose and placed his hands on her shoulders and said, emphatically, "Connie, listen to me. This is *our* piano, always was *ours,* not just Mother's. She would be the first one to scold you for keeping it closed."

"Daddy," she cried, "how can you talk that way about Mother? You don't love her any more."

"I can't *love* her any more, Connie; she's not here. I think of her often and miss her very much. I'm grateful for the years we had, and for you and Denise. But we cannot live with invisible spirits. Life goes forward—it doesn't stand still—nor does it go backward."

She clung to him wordlessly. Two large tears slid down her cheeks.

"All right, dear," John said soothingly, as he gave her a little push. "Up to bed with you now. We'll talk about the piano some other time. Good night."

He kissed her wet cheeks and turned her toward the stairs. Then he walked back to his chair, picked up his coffee, and finished it in two long gulps. He turned off the TV and walked over to the piano. His hands moved across the smooth surface of the cover. "Nothing but a piece of wood—if it's closed," he mused, "a highly polished, unnecessary piece of dead wood."

CHAPTER 6

PAULA AND HER MOTHER were enjoying a cup of coffee in the living room after the club dinner.

"It was good to meet old friends, wasn't it?" Mrs. Russell pointed out.

"Yes," Paula agreed, lifting the cup. "Yes, and no. It was good to see them, but it made me realize that I've been gone a long time; and, much as we'd like to deny it, the fact remains, we're all changed."

"Wouldn't you really like to come back?"

"Mother, that's not something I can decide tonight, or even in a few days. I enjoy my work—the surroundings—everything connected with it. And I like my apartment and my life there."

"And Tony?" Mrs. Russell prodded gently.

Paula kicked off her shoes, put one foot on the chair, and sat on it. She drew a long breath, held it a moment, then let it out slowly.

"Tony!" she said. "I'm fond of him, but I know now that that's not enough. I'll have to tell him, and I dread it.

71

"I also dread to think of you being here alone. Why don't you come with me tomorrow and stay for at least a week? Mrs. Adams will take care of your plants, I'm sure."

Mrs. Russell stared at her daughter. "For a whole week! What would I do there all day?"

Paula laughed. "You could clean my kitchen cupboards for me. And do some badly needed repairs on my clothing."

"Maybe I should," Mrs. Russell spoke thoughtfully. "It would probably be easier to be alone all day in strange rooms than here, with a memory in every object." And immediately changed her mind. "No, no I can't. The memories are all that I have left. I want to enjoy them."

"But Mother, what of the lonely evenings, the nights?"

"Of course they'll be lonely," Mrs. Russell admitted. "I don't expect them to be otherwise. But Aggie is next door, and other friends are near. No, I'll stay here. I wish you would decide to come home, but that's up to you. I'll be all right."

"I admit that the thought of being here in Woodruff is pleasant," Paula said, "but I must be sure."

"Of course you must. Don't do it simply because I'm lonely, or because I suggested it. Perhaps I should not have voiced my wishes at all."

"No, Mother, don't feel that way. You'll never know how lonely and homesick I was the first year or two after I left."

"Poor child," Mrs. Russell murmured. "It was rough on you, I know."

They both understood what she meant.

"Well," Paula said decisively, after a few moments of thought, "I better pack my few things. Are we going to church tomorrow?"

"I'd like to go," Mrs. Russell said. "Will you go with me? It will be the first time without Dad."

"Yes, I want to go, too."

The next morning in church John and his daughters sat a few rows behind Paula and her mother. John understood the quivering lips, the tear hastily wiped away, but he also knew that time and the grace of God would soften and heal the pain.

At the close of the service, after many friends again expressed comforting words to Mrs. Russell, John and the girls walked up to them. Paula's eyes lit up and she smiled.

"Would you like a ride?" John asked. "I'm taking Mother home."

Mrs. Russell accepted readily for both of them. While waiting for John to bring the car, Paula was pleasantly surprised to feel Denise's hand near hers. She smiled down at her and clasped her fingers tightly.

"Is two o-clock too early, Paula?" John asked when she and her mother left the car in front of the house.

"No, that's good," she answered.

"Can't you see Susie before you go?" Denise asked plaintively.

John and Paula looked at each other. He nodded his head and said, "Why, sure, sweetheart. I'll bring Paula over before we leave."

Walking to the door at home a few minutes later, Denise looked up at John and said, "Daddy, I like Paula. She holds my hand like Mother used to. And when she smiles, her eyes smile, too."

John caught his breath and said, "Bless you, darling. I like her, too. And come to think of it, her eyes do smile."

Connie, walking behind them, gave her sister a disdainful glance and said, "Baby! Everybody's hand is the same."

"No, that's not so," Denise argued. "Paula's hand is soft and hard at the same time; and it fits mine just right. Anyhow," she added defiantly, "I like her."

John's voice was light as he suggested, "Let's have one of those chicken TV dinners."

"Good," Connie told him. "I like them. They're easy to do."

Susie was in and out under their feet.

"When Paula comes, I'm going to put a big ribbon on you," Denise told her pet, and laughed at the thought.

After the TV dinners and milk (both of which were becoming obnoxious to John), he said, "You get the dishes into the dishwasher, Connie. And Denise, you straighten up the papers in the living room. I'll go for Paula."

Paula had again urged her mother to come with her. However, Mrs. Russell was firm in her refusal.

"No, dear," she repeated. "Let me stay here in my comfortable old house, my familiar surroundings. I know it will be easier here."

"Will you at least promise to call me anytime you need me—or feel lonely?" Paula insisted.

"Yes, that I will do," Mrs. Russell conceded.

When John came, Paula held her mother close for a few seconds. She kissed her cheek and said, "Take care of yourself, Mother, dear. You're all I have now."

Mrs. Russell smiled through tears as she waved to them.

"Poor Mother," Paula said as they drove away. "She wants me to come home."

John looked at her, sharply aware of a quickening pulse.

"Will you?" he asked.

"I don't know yet. As I told her, there is much to consider. Where would I find the interesting work I now have?"

"Woodruff is small, that's true," John replied, "but I'm sure you'd find something very soon."

Denise was waiting for them inside the door. She opened it and gleefully held Susie out to Paula.

"Here she is," she announced.

Paula dropped her bag and reached for Susie. "Hi, Susie girl. How are you? And what a beautiful ribbon you have."

Denise giggled.

Susie purred her pleasure at recognition of Paula. When lowered to the rug, she persisted in her ingratiating bid for attention by rubbing her head, her ears, her entire body across Paula's ankles.

"She likes you very much," Denise said.

Connie, seemingly shrinking from a display of affection, watched them wryly.

"When will you be back, Daddy?" she asked John.

"If we get started now," John said, "I should be back about seven or eight o'clock."

"'By Paula, 'by Daddy," Denise ran up to them and raised her face.

"'By," Paula kissed her cheek gently and smiled at her.

John dropped a kiss on Denise's hair, blew one at Connie, who was sitting stiff and straight in a chair and said, "'By, see you later."

"I'll have to stop at the plant for a minute or two," John said as they drove through town.

"I'm embarrassed to admit it," Paula told him, "but I am incredibly ignorant about the product you manufacture."

"Right now we're doing so much, and such diversified business, that I myself feel ignorant at times."

"That sounds as though business is good."

"For these times, it *is* good," John admitted. "We work with hardboard, paper, plastics, combinations of these, and impregnations. Many of them have replaced metal, glass, rubber, wood, and other expensive materials. It is unbelievable how one product spirals, merges, and leads into other avenues of business.''

''Just what do you make?'' Paula asked.

''Oh,'' John blew out a deep breath, ''wall paneling, TV and radio panels, chair backs, certain auto parts, toys. The potential is absolutely fantastic. And, unlike some less fiscally sound companies, we have been able to avoid layoffs. . . . I'll be back in a minute,'' he said as he stopped the car. He was out in a moment with a quick, strong movement.

Something in Paula's heart leaped. He was vitally alive, a man to whom loyalty could be given easily and unhesitatingly.

In a few minutes he was back, buttoning his coat, eyes sparkling.

''Everything's fine,'' he said. ''We had a little trouble with one of the presses, but it's fixed. Running like a clock. Without our excellent engineer, we'd be in trouble.''

A deft turn of the wheel and they were on the road again, driving through a soft, milky haze, born of snow and clouds. Fence posts marched along the fields like toy soldiers. Flocks of winter birds, small bodies mysteriously enduring the cold, wheeled in flight across the highway. A lonesome pony, head down, stood at the corner of a fence, in a barnyard. White birches were outlined against the solid gray of other trees. Poplars, like cathedral spires, pointed to the sky.

For the most part they drove in silence, mindful of each other's presence. Finally John said, ''Remember the time we walked home from school in such heavy fog that we thought we were lost?''

''Oh,'' Paula exclaimed, ''wasn't that terrible!''

Smiling a little, as if to himself, John said, ''We gripped each other's hands all the way home. Remember? And on the corner we met our mothers.''

"Did you ever tell your mother how we sneaked into the movie?" Paula asked slyly.

John laughed. "No. Did you?"

"Nope." Paula replied. "You said you'd clobber me if I did."

"And I would have, too," John admitted, laughing with her.

"Did you ever tell your mother how sick we were the time we stayed on the merry-go-round for four rides in a row?" he asked.

"No, I didn't," Paula giggled. "We weren't supposed to go to the carnival alone. Remember?"

They laughed easily in mutual amusement at their childish secrets.

In the apartment later, Paula looked around carefully, examining every detail with new interest. The crèche still slumbered under the glow of light on the table.

"I've lived here for a good number of years," she said. "It's home to me. And yet, basically, I think I'm small-town stuff. I like to walk down a street and occasionally meet someone I know. I don't even know everyone at the bank, and yet we're under the same roof."

"Does Tony enter in at all?" John asked.

An unreadable flicker crossed her face. She picked up the white velvet lamb and examined the tiny, golden bell on the collar. Then, more to herself than to John, she said, "I used to think so."

"And now?" John prompted her in a near whisper.

She was so intensely aware of him that she hesitated to speak, for fear of the trembling in her voice. At length she said, "Oh, John, I don't know. I'm all confused."

She raised her eyes to look at him—and an avalanche of emotion swept over them. In one swift, hungry movement they were in each other's arms.

"Paula, Paula," John whispered in her hair.

As their lips met, nothing in the world mattered to Paula but the feel of John's arms holding her close to him.

Through tears and laughter she finally pulled away from him a little and said, "John Adams, are you sure you wanted to do that?"

His eyes were misty-bright and seemed to look into the depths of her soul.

"More than anything in the world. I love you. My arms have been aching to hold you."

He drew her into his embrace once more and asked softly, "Paula, will you? Would you? Paula, will you marry me?"

Every fiber of her being thrilled at his words. And suddenly she remembered her father's statement: "When you're sure, your answer will be there even before the question." She smiled tremulously and with joyous love said, "Yes, yes, John, I will."

Long after seven they were still sharing exquisite tremors of excitement. They renewed and strengthened the cords which had bound them many years before. Paula opened doors which for a long time had been forbidden territory for her. Together they· discovered new paths of understanding and tolerance. New vistas of love promised happiness and contentment.

Finally John remembered that he had told Connie that he expected to be home by seven or eight o'clock.

"I better call home," he said.

Connie was miserably indignant. "Daddy, you said seven, and it's eight-thirty. Where are you?" she asked.

"I'm here at Paula's," he told her.

"Still there?" Connie asked in amazement. "What are you doing?"

He chuckled. "Never mind that. Is your grandmother with you?"

"Yes, she is."

"Good," he said. "I'll be home around ten-thirty or eleven. You and Denise better hike to bed. Homework finished?"

"Just about," Connie replied, slightly annoyed.

"Okay, dear. Say good night to Denise, and tell your grandmother everything's fine. Goodbye, Connie."

"'By, Daddy," her reply was faint.

He turned from the phone and said, "I better leave. It *is* getting late. When will I see you again? Will you be coming home now?"

A bit of shyness remained. Their new status was still somewhat strange and unreal. However, Paula's uncertainty was completely erased by the events of the few preceding hours.

"Yes," she answered now. "I do want to come home, and as quickly as possible. I'll talk to Mr. Wilkins tomorrow."

"I would like to tell Mother," John said. "In fact, I would like to announce it from a huge billboard."

"Couldn't we wait and tell it to both our mothers at the same time?"

"Yes," John agreed. "That's better. We can also tell the girls at that time."

He pulled her into his arms again and pleaded, "Let's not wait too long, though; I want you near me."

Paula's eyes were bright as leftover sunlight. A warm happiness spread through her. "Oh, John, John," she whispered.

After he left, she remembered the warmth of his arms. She didn't know whether to laugh, sing, or cry. The suddenness of his words of love so astounded and enraptured her that her mind was incapable of grasping it all. Only her heart was vibrantly alive, pulsating with excitement. Dreamily she cleared away the remnants of their coffee and leftover Christmas cookies. Suddenly she caught her breath and slipped into a chair, sobbing deeply. Years of repressed emotions were washed away.

After the healing tears came relief and joyful anticipation of the future.

CHAPTER 7

THAT PAULA AND HER Mustang arrived intact at the parking lot the next morning was due not to her driving ability, but to the presence of her guardian angel. The air was clear, the sky a vivid blue, polka-dotted with small clouds. Paula's heart danced along with the light wind which playfully picked up a vagrant, shredded leaf and whirled it into the wake of a car.

She walked into the bank radiantly alive, her feet barely touching the polished floor. Tony, in a corner of his cage, had a momentary glimpse of her before she entered her office. He held his breath at her loveliness, and yet a perplexing feeling of anxiety—some increasing sense of distress—began to gnaw at him, a bothersome thought that refused to leave. He was impatient for their lunch hour when he could talk with her.

When Mr. Wilkins came in, his cursory greeting halted at the look in Paula's eyes. He glanced at her carefully.

"Good morning, Miss Russell," he began again. "You're looking uncommonly well. I'm glad you're back."

"Thank you, Mr. Wilkins," Paula's voice had a definite ring in it. "May I see you later?"

"See me?" His gaze was critical. "Why, yes. Come in now."

She followed him into his office.

"Sit down," he urged her.

She sat directly facing him, in the large chair reserved for special clients.

"What is it, Miss Russell?" he asked, a bit puzzled.

"Mr. Wilkins," she said, "I—I don't know how to say this, but I'm going back home."

Mr. Wilkins look at her in amazement. "You mean you're leaving? Miss Russell, do you want a raise?"

"No, no," she replied quickly. "No, Mr. Wilkins. My salary is more than adequate. No. My mother is alone, and," she blushed furiously, but kept her eyes on him, "I'm going to be married."

Mr. Wilkins gazed intently at this young woman with the promising future. He had had great plans for her. She was his most capable and conscientious employee, though at one time the thought of recommending a female as branch manager of his bank would never have occurred to him. *If only young Anglietti were more dedicated . . . If only Miss Russell had waited until he retired in another year or two . . .* He should have acted sooner. Ah, but anyone could see from her radiant face that it was much too late for that now!

"You're being married! At your age . . ." He caught himself. "Why, Miss Russell, that's fine. That's fine. But must you leave? Can't you continue here?"

"No, I can't," Paula answered. "I'll stay, of course, until you find a replacement, but no longer than the first of the month."

"This is shocking news, Miss Russell," Mr. Wilkins

said. "Shocking!" He let his hands fall to the edge of the desk in a gesture of finality. "But if you are determined, we shall, of course, groom someone else for the position. Although after so many years, it will be a most unsavory change."

Paula's spirits were somewhat dampened by her employer's attitude, but not for long. Not as long as John's face appeared before her.

At noon Tony was waiting for her at the bank cafeteria, where he had already taken possession of a corner table. He looked at her, mentally rejecting the queer feeling of loss which had come to him earlier.

She said down opposite him. Her presence stimulated him, as always.

"Hi!" she greeted him. "You look beat. Are you ill?"

"Hi!" he answered with a grin. "Am I beaten? I don't know. Am I?"

Paula's glance fell. "What do you mean?"

"Well—you seem to have JOHN spelled out in capital letters all over your face," he replied stiffly.

"Oh, Tony." Her heart ached for him.

For what seemed an age they sat in silence.

"It's true then, isn't it?" Tony finally asked.

Paula's eyes were dimmed a little, but her smile was bright as she said, "Yes, it's true. I'm leaving the bank as soon as a replacement can be found."

Tony shifted his legs. He took off his glasses and wiped them over and over with a clean handkerchief.

"Somehow I expected it. He's what you've been listening and waiting for, isn't he?"

"Not consciously, Tony," she replied. "I don't think so. At least I didn't think so."

He drew a deep breath, then spread his hands wide in an effect of emptiness and said, "Well, congratulations to

John. And I do wish the best for you, Paula, dear. If ever John beats you, or your stepdaughter, Connie, gets out of hand, remember Uncle Tony.''

"That's right," Paula said, "I'll be a stepmother. Why does the word always suggest spite and meanness?"

"Who knows?" Tony shrugged his shoulders. He stood up. "Will you excuse me, Paula? I have something to do."

He walked around her chair and patted her hair lightly. "See you around. Be happy!"

"Goodbye, Tony, dear friend," Paula whispered after him. She discovered that to her, also, the thought of food was distasteful. She picked up her purse and left.

The day seemed to have more and longer hours. Paula was impatient to be home. John would call and already she reveled in the sound of his voice. When he did call, she had a momentary shyness. Inane statements seemed to be the extent of their conversation, but to them they were world-shaking truths. *How are you? I'm fine.* All that really mattered was the sound of the voice at the other end of the wire.

"I'm driving in Saturday afternoon," John said. "Will you be home?"

"Yes, I will," Paula said. "It's about time I packed away my Christmas decorations."

"I'll see you then."

"Have you seen Mother? Is she all right?" Paula asked.

"I didn't see her," he said, "but I called to tell her that you were home and all right. She's okay. I was tempted to tell her about us, but I'll wait. I love you, darling."

"Oh, John," she spoke softly. "I love you, too."

Paula spent the next few days cleaning out the unnecessary accumulation of papers in the cubbyholes in her desk, and sorting and discarding clothing which had hung in her closets for years. She surveyed her kitchen cupboards and was surprised at the collection of unused items gathered in ten years of residence in one place.

Her landlord was disappointed when she told him about vacating the apartment. "I'll never find another like you," he said.

When John came on Saturday, he brought a ring set with a diamond surrounded by small emeralds. He placed it upon Paula's finger and lifted the hand to his lips.

"Paula, my darling. I feel like a new man in a new world."

Paula's eyes were stars as she raised her lips to meet his.

"When can we tell our mothers?" John asked.

"Can't we wait until I come home? I spoke to Mr. Wilkins."

"How much time did you give him?"

"Until the first of February."

"All right, sweetheart. We've waited this long; we can wait another three weeks."

"What will the girls say?" Paula wanted to know.

"They'll be delighted," John answered. "Especially Denise. She says you hold her hand like her mother did—that it just fits hers."

Paula's heart beat faster at the words. "And Connie?"

"After she gets used to the idea, she'll be happy. She's too young to be taking care of her father. She'll be fine."

"I know Mother will be pleased." Paula told him.

John smiled. "My mother will say, 'It's about time, John.' She's always loved you."

Because of Amy and Paula's father, they planned a small wedding toward the end of April.

"It will give the girls time to get used to me in the role of future stepmother," Paula said.

John pulled her closer to him. "Mother—stepmother—

what's the difference? All that matters is that you love me."

He was content and very happy.

Paula's impending departure from the bank was announced by her ring. It furnished excitement for the young and hope for the not-so-young.

"If she found someone," one of the older female employees said, "there's a chance for me, too."

Shoulders were straightened and eyes faced the world with new confidence.

CHAPTER 8

CHICAGO ENJOYED A FEW days of warm weather, and downtown traffic increased considerably. Paula decided to find a parking lot off the Eisenhower Expressway and take the El to the Loop.

A week later the weather bureau began forecasting rain or snow. Her decision in finding a parking lot was a good one, she felt. *It won't take me so long to get home.*

Wednesday morning the forecast was for snow mixed with freezing rain. Thursday morning she listened to the announcer forecasting heavy snow. *I better wear boots,* she thought. It was slow driving; the windshield wiper worked hard against the wet snow. The four inches predicted by afternoon seemed to be already there.

By ten o'clock the prediction was for thirteen inches of accumulation. Already tires were spinning in the streets, and a queer muffling of sound was felt. It was as if the city was slowly falling asleep under its white blanket.

By noon streets were strangely empty; shops were closing for lack of customers. Then the word came: Go home—it's getting much worse.

Outdoors it was unbelievable. Snow was coming down faster than it could be shoveled away. Long lines of pedestrians waited for long-delayed buses and cabs. Cars resembled huge mounds of meringue.

Paula walked to the El as quickly as possible through deep snow, and miraculously managed to get in before the doors closed. When she left the El, she walked with her collar up and face down against the wind now beginning to blow. It wasn't too cold yet, but heavy, wet snow continued to pour out of the heavens. The city was ghostlike, outlines of buildings were indistinct, abstract.

She found her car in the lot and was happy to see that the attendant had shoveled a little. Her Mustang started immediately, and she drove out carefully. A half block away three cars were stuck; hers was the fourth. Fortunately, a heavy truck laden with cement blocks came along. With charity born out of his fellow-man's need, the truck driver pushed all four out into the middle of the street. Each one waved his thanks to the trucker.

About a mile farther on, while waiting for a light, Paula's car again sank into the deep, white carpet. She spun her tires, but only succeeded in digging deeper into the snow. A group of young black boys came toward her. She locked the doors. Abreast of her, they stopped and stared at her predicament. One came to her window and said, "When I yell, give her the gun, lady."

He yelled—Paula gunned—they pushed. The tires spun so furiously she smelled burning rubber.

"Okay," the youth called out, "once more. Now!"

With superhuman effort they pushed. She was out and going. *I must thank them,* she thought, but was urged on by their shouts of "Go, baby, go!"

It was dreamlike. The snow swirled, danced, whirled, ran ahead of the lights, straight into them, circled, billions of frenzied flakes on a wild spree. She drove without thought, without feeling; her only instinct was to stay in the middle of the street and get home.

As she turned the corner a few doors away from the apartment, a drift caught a front wheel and the car swerved. The motor sputtered and died. It was impossible to see the curb, but from the direction of the street she realized that the car was standing crossways, with the headlights pointing to the right.

Like a sleepwalker she took the key out of the ignition, gathered up her purse, and stepped out into the snow—up to her knees. *The car will have to stay here,* she thought, *at least for tonight.*

She was only two doors away from the apartment, but with every step she had to look up to be sure she was walking in the right direction. When she finally reached her door and stepped inside, she was trembling. Snow was melting in her boots; her feet were standing in water.

"I'm home," she breathed out. "Thank God, I'm home."

The snow continued, hour after hour. Radio announcers spoke of bitter cold to follow; schools closed; traffic halted. Paula felt isolated. The walls which had always been security seemed a prison now. *I wish I were home,* she thought, and realized she meant Woodruff. *I want to be with my own people—to hear their voices, see their faces.*

When the phone rang later in the evening, she picked it up eagerly. It was John. The connection was bad.

"Paula?" he seemed relieved. "You're home. Are you all right?"

"Yes, John," she cried out.

"I've been trying to call you for hours," he said, "but our lines were out."

"How bad is it in Woodruff?"

"Very bad, but not as serious as in Chicago," John told her. "How did you get home?"

"I got stuck several times," she could laugh about it now, "but someone always helped me. I'll tell you about it sometime."

"I was worried about you, darling. As soon as possible I want you here at home," John said.

"I do want to be there quickly, John," Paula said. "Will you please call Mother and tell her I'm all right?"

"Yes, I will," he answered. "Good night, my love."

Suddenly she felt warm and cherished. The wonder of John's love was indescribably sweet.

The wind was driving snow like powder into drifts that obliterated all landmarks. Paula watched the dancing flakes around the streetlights, fascinating in their contempt for human weakness, for man's puny resistance to natural forces.

A little later, already half-asleep, she heard the phone again and was awake instantly.

"Paula?"

"Tony?" Surprise showed in her voice.

"Yes," he said. "You all right?"

"I'm fine. Took me about two and a half hours to get home, but I made it."

"I'm glad. I'm supposed to tell you that the bank will be closed until Monday."

"'Til Monday? Is it that bad?"

"Worse than anyone expected it to be," Tony said. "Will you be all right?"

"Yes, I will, Tony," she replied. "Thank you for calling."

"Glad to do it, Paula," he said shortly.

Paula heard the wind in the night and snuggled down deeper.

"Dear God," she prayed, "let everyone have shelter and a warm place to sleep tonight."

In the morning the snow was smothering the city in a soft, but deadly embrace. Paula listened to radio and TV reports throughout the day. A state of emergency was declared. Silent, clean, the snow was unmerciful in its power to force an incredibly vast metropolis to its knees. Mountainous drifts closed airports and stalled trains. Thousands of vehicles were trapped—six or seven in her block alone.

Paula was grateful that her car was near home. She could see only the top of it. *Even if I shovel it out,* she thought, *I couldn't go anywhere, so I'll wait until tomorrow.* When she opened the door, she found the snow waist-high on the outside of the storm door. She knew that she'd need help in getting out of the house. Her landlord called in the afternoon to tell her that he had arranged for the neighbor boys to shovel them out later.

"When did you plan to move, Miss Russell?" he asked.

"Sometime after the fouth of February," she answered.

"I hope it stops snowing by then," he laughed.

The boys also shoveled her car out and helped others who were in the same unfortunate situation. She had no difficulty in starting her Mustang and soon had straightened it out so it was parallel to the curb, although the street was still impassable.

In the evening she called home.

"Paula? Are you all right?" Mrs. Russell asked anxiously.

"Yes, Mother," she answered. "I'm fine. No work today—in fact nothing going on anywhere. How are you doing?"

"Oh," Mrs. Russell began, slowly, "so-so, I guess. I miss him so much, Paula."

"Mother," Paula said, softly, "I'm coming home."

91

"Child!" her mother cried. "Are you really? When?"

"As soon as possible, in about a week—two at the most."

Mrs. Russell had difficulty in speaking. "Paula, you don't know how happy this makes me. Bless you. I'll get your room ready."

Paula laughed. "It's always ready, Mother. Don't work so hard. I'll let you know exactly when to expect me. Mr. Wilkins is looking for someone to take my place."

"I'm sure you'll not regret it," Mrs. Russell said. "In the end you'll be happier here in Woodruff."

The temptation to tell her mother about John was great. However, all she said was, "I know I'll be happy there. I'm very anxious to be home."

By Monday, after an unprecedented twenty-four to twenty-five inches of snow, the giant was beginning to awaken. He stretched and stirred, but was still weak, tottering, and reeling from the knockout blow dealt by the blizzard. Without movement, a city is dead. Initial attempts to restore order and fluidity of traffic were only partially successful. Backbreaking labor would still be necessary.

Paula thought, *Snowflakes! Such an innocent, lovely sounding word! One flake is a marvel of nature; multiplied by millions it becomes a curse. Yet we must be thankful. What if a fire—or a number of fires—had occurred? Instead of snowflakes, what if a bomb had immobilized the city? How would the giant react then? What of the panic?* The picture was too horrible to behold.

By following the main arteries she was able to drive to the parking lot on Monday. From there she walked to the El platform. *Just a few more days,* she thought, *then I'll be home.* No more rush-hour traffic problems. Yet every morning through all these years she had looked forward to the day at the bank. *Is it true then that woman's place is in the home,* she wondered, *and when the right man comes along, she is willing to renounce her career for his love?*

I don't know about other women, she thought, *but I am loved, and I love a man, and I shall have a home, a true home.* A peculiarly tender feeling washed over her. She knew that what she was doing was right.

Mr. Wilkins nodded to her when she came in, then said, "Oh, Miss Russell, will you come in please."

Without preamble, he announced: "Well, Miss Russell, you may be interested to know that I'm moving Tony Anglietti into your old position. I've been watching the boy and I've noticed a new attitude of late. Thinking of grooming him for top management—though I must admit you were my first choice. If I had any idea . . . well, just know that you'll be greatly missed around here. Oh, and you'll find two months' salary in your envelope when you leave."

Tony! How marvelous for him! A challenging opportunity to develop his potential, to discover himself—and perhaps to remove some of the sting of their parting. Guiltily, Paula realized her thoughts had been wandering and that Mr. Wilkins was waiting for her reaction.

"Why, Mr. Wilkins. I couldn't be more pleased. Tony is a splendid choice! And I am grateful for the training I've had here. The experience has been both pleasant and profitable. I won't forget any of you . . ."

Paula had expected at least a small jab of uneasiness when Friday came and she began to clean the personal things out of her desk. However, her only regret was Tony's closed, withdrawn glance when she met him. *I'm sorry, Tony,* she thought, *but this is better than you and I could have done. Your ideas of life are not mine—I know that now. We would have skimmed across the surface, asking life only to entertain us.* The deep involvement in every phase of living is different. Merely picking the rose and enjoying its fragrance is not the same as planting, weeding, caring for the flower—actually getting your hands into the earth, knowing what makes that rose live, grow, and bring forth its beauty. *No, Tony,* she wished she could tell him, *it's far better this way. Someday you'll understand.*

After her years at the bank, Paula said her farewells to a few close friends and left, smiling.

Mr. Sikes, her landlord, had bought most of her furniture. It was necessary only to pack personal possessions and her stereo and records.

She called her mother Sunday evening and told her that she would be home the next day. "John is sending a small truck for my things," she said.

Mrs. Russell sounded surprised. "John is?" she asked.

"Yes," Paula stammered a little. "Yes, he called on Saturday."

"He did? How nice." Mrs. Russell's voice had a happy note in it.

Paula was afraid to say more. She would surely entangle her tongue in phrase after phrase which would need explaining.

"I'll see you tomorrow, then, Mother," she said.

CHAPTER 9

THE NEXT MORNING, before leaving her apartment for the last time, Paula had a small moment of discomfort. She walked through the rooms thinking of the many years she had lived there. *Lord,* she prayed, *bless the next occupants; let them enjoy it as much as I have.*

Later, home in Woodruff, after all the planning to surprise their mothers, John and Paula had not been able to hide their feelings; Mrs. Russell had guessed immediately. One glance at their faces when they came in, and the light in their eyes was enough to make her catch her breath. Then when they smiled at each other she was certain.

She clasped her hands and said. "Tell me, is it true what I'm thinking?"

They looked at each other. John put his arm around Paula and laughingly asked, "And what would you be thinking?"

"That you—you," it was her turn now to falter, stammer confusedly. "Oh, tell me please," she finally cried impatiently.

From the shelter of John's arm, Paula said, "Yes, it's true. We're going to be married."

Mrs. Russell could not suppress her emotions. Tears glistened in her eyes. She embraced them and said, "I wish your father were here. He would be as happy as I am. Let's call Aggie. Does she know?"

"Not yet," John answered. "We wanted to tell you at the same time, but you were too much for us. I'll get her."

When Mrs. Adams came in, she also needed but a glance to realize that her dreams of many years were finally to come true.

She drew Paula into her arms and said, "Welcome home, my dear. I've longed for this for months now."

To John she said, "It's about time, Son."

Paula and John laughed aloud.

"You're not going to look for work now, are you Paula?" her mother asked.

"No, of course she isn't." John answered for her. "We're going to be married as soon as possible."

"I thought we had decided on the end of April," Paula said.

"Let's make it the beginning, can't we?" he asked now.

Connie stirred in early morning sleep. A sound foreign to the house aroused her. With a slight frown she raised her head to listen.

"Denise," she called to her sister. "Denise, wake up. Listen."

"What's wrong?" Denise was only half-awake.

"Listen—Dad's whistling and singing in the shower."

"What's wrong with that?" Denise muttered and turned over to the other side of the bed.

"What's wrong with that?" Connie was shocked. "He hasn't whistled since—since Mother's been gone. That's what!"

Both girls sat up in bed. From the bathroom across the

hall came sounds of splashing water, aimless whistling, and then a few bars of "Jingle Bells."

The girls looked at each other.

"Jingle Bells!" Denise's eyes were puzzled. "What happened to him?"

A memory stirred in Connie's mind.

"That's the way he and Paula played it that night. Remember?"

"No, I don't remember," Denise shook her head. "But I might as well get up." She swung her feet out of bed and reached for her robe and slippers.

Connie was quiet and thoughtful. She opened the drapes and looked out. Light snow was falling. The room the girls shared was large. Its walls were soft yellow with white trim. A deep, white cotton rug covered the floor. On a table near the window, in a glass frame, was a tinted portrait of their mother. In a doll bed near Connie's bed, Susie was still asleep.

Noises across the hall had ceased. They heard dresser drawers being opened and closed in their father's room.

Denise rapped on his door.

"Come in, come in!" John's voice was cheerful.

Both girls stood in the doorway and said, "Good morning, Daddy."

John was standing in front of the dresser buttoning his shirt. When they entered, he turned and grinned at them.

"Good morning. Did I wake you?"

"Well—" Connie said, slowly, "sort of. Are you all right?"

"I sure am, darling. Never felt better. Hurry down; we'll have breakfast soon. I have something to tell you."

His step was firm, yet bouncy.

"What in the world does he have to tell us?" Denise wondered, wide-eyed.

Connie was dressing silently. She waited a moment before answering.

"I bet it's something about Paula," she said. Her voice was tight and low.

"Paula?" Denise was mystified.

When they came down a few minutes later, their father was turning bacon while executing a fancy step. He smiled happily.

"Come on, help a little," he urged. "Your juice is there. Now, plates and cups; come on."

In silence they obeyed.

Denise couldn't wait any longer. "Daddy, what did you want to tell us?" she asked.

And suddenly John was serious. "Connie, Denise," he began. "I don't know how to begin this—how it could happen to me."

He looked at his daughters as though for help. Connie's eyes fell to her tightly clasped hands. "Paula—Paula and I are going to be married. Isn't that wonderful?"

Connie's head came up swiftly. Her eyes were cold as she stared at him.

"Daddy," she exclaimed in a horrified voice. "Daddy, how can you? Mother didn't mean a thing to you." Then she turned and ran from the room, sobbing loudly.

John looked at Denise uneasily.

"I'm glad, Daddy," she told him. "We'll have a mother again."

"Thank you, dear," John hugged her. "But Connie doesn't seem happy about it. Eat your breakfast; I must talk to her."

Muffled sobs could be heard in the girls' room. John rapped and asked, "May I come in, Connie?"

At the sound of his voice, her sobs increased in volume and haltingly she said, "I - don't - care. I - don't - care."

He opened the door gently. She was lying on her bed, her face down under the pillow. John sat down slowly.

"Child, how can I make you understand that it will be good for all of us to have Paula here?"

"But we *don't need* anybody here, Daddy," she answered, her face turned away. "You yourself said that I was taking care of everything real well. You did, you did," she emphasized every word.

John's shoulders slumped a little. "Yes, I did say that. And you are doing well. But I also said that it should not be necessary for you to do it. A girl your age needs to do many things that are more important than taking care of her father and a house."

Connie sat up now and looked at him. Her eyes were swollen, and John handed his handkerchief to her. She rubbed her eyes with it, then rolled it into a tight ball.

"But, Daddy, you don't love her, do you?" She spoke the words in a puzzled tone. "How can you marry someone else when you loved Mother so much?"

John drew a deep breath. "That's very difficult to explain, Connie. You will have to believe me when I say that I loved your mother very, very much."

He took her hands in his; his eyes were shining. "But I do love Paula. I've known her all my life, and I do love her, Connie. And she is very fond of you and Denise."

Connie's eyes were veiled. "But she'll be our *stepmother,* and you know how they are."

"No," John answered, "I *don't* know how *they* are. And you've been reading too many fairy tales. We'll be a family again."

"When?" Connie asked faintly.

"As soon as possible."

Connie looked at her father closely; then with a resigned

note in her voice she said, "All right, Daddy. I'll never be happy again, but it's okay."

"On the contrary, you'll be very happy again," John told her. "Now come down and have your breakfast. I'll drive you to school; it's too late for the bus."

When she came down, Denise greeted her with bantering impatience. "Hurry, Connie, we'll be late. Why are you such a baby anyhow?"

CHAPTER 10

Do you, John Adams, take Paula Russell, here present, to be your lawful wedded wife; to love, honor, and cherish . . . until death you do part? Then declare so by saying, 'I do.' "

John's answer as he looked at the woman beside him was a clear, decisive, "I do."

"Do you, Paula Russell, take John Adams. . . . then declare so by saying, 'I do.' "

Paula's eyes were misty. She and John could have been alone in the world when she gave her reply with a firm, "I do."

"I now pronounce you man and wife."

The church was silent, listening. This house of God had witnessed the childhood, youth, and maturity of these two now united in wedlock. The late afternoon sun intensified the stained-glass windows above the altar, giving emphasis to the outline of the Good Shepherd. Through the open windows the fresh fragrance of early spring drifted in and mingled with the soft melodies from the organ in the balcony.

Sympathizing with Connie's dismay, they had waited until after the anniversary of Amy's death before being married.

Paula had decided against a veil. Instead, she wore a sheer wool suit, the green of budding lilacs. The soft veil on her small, flower-covered hat only partially covered her glistening auburn hair.

The radiant love shining in their eyes as they turned to walk up the long aisle caused a hush to fall upon the friends and relatives gathered for the ceremony.

The reception at the country club was small and intimate. Hand-in-hand John and Paula accepted best wishes, congratulations, and comments of—"We're so happy for you—Now you're a family again. It's just right."

Connie stood a little to one side and listened. When a well-wisher said to her, "Now you have a mother again," she answered, "You mean we have a *stepmother*, don't you?"

Immediately after John and Paula had left the church, Denise had run up to them and hugged Paula. Connie, however, had remained in the background, her eyes downcast; neither John nor Paula confronted her with more than a warm smile.

Mrs. Russell and Mrs. Adams were beaming in their happiness.

"We won't be gone long," Paula told her mother after the reception, when she and John were ready to leave for their honeymoon. "We're just driving to Chicago for a few days. Later on in the summer we're all going to northern Minnesota for a few weeks."

"Connie and Denise also?" Mrs. Adams asked.

"Yes, we thought they'd like it," Paula answered.

"I should think they'd be delighted," Mrs. Russell replied.

The girls were already at home where Mrs. Adams would stay with them until John and Paula returned.

"God's blessing on you two," Mrs. Russell whispered as they drove away.

Mr. and Mrs. John Adams had four rapturous days in Chicago. Physical communion is no less intense in the flower of maturity than in the budding blossom of youth. Indeed, with its widened horizon of understanding, adult love has the potential for complete and lasting happiness.

If John ever remembered his first honeymoon, it was only to recall his diffident aproach to married life, his feelings of timidity in the adult world. Now, with confident poise, and secure in their love, they entered joyously into the new, abundant life.

Before leaving for home, they purchased gifts for Connie and Denise. Paula found the exquisite figurines which had enchanted her at Christmas time.

"Look, John! I wanted to buy these for the girls last year but was afraid to."

They were adorable, sweet, saucy cherubs with harps, violins, flutes, and pipes.

John was delighted. "Let's buy the entire set," he suggested. "They'll love them."

Spring was flirting with summer when they drove home. Chestnut trees nodded their white plumes in the warm sun. Fat, puffy robins strutted across lawns, halting occasionally to cock their heads to one side, as if listening to the unfortunate worm wriggling underneath. Fields were fresh and green. A gangly young colt tried out his long legs in a pasture strewn with bouquets of yellow dandelions. The world was sunny, clean, and new again.

Paula, aware of every shade of changing green in the

trees, of the beauty of spring in each flower and blade of grass, said, "Can't you feel it all in your very bones?"

John's voice was soft. "And can't you almost taste the fragrance in the air? Remember the odor of petunias on a warm summer night?"

Paula smiled through tears and knew that her waiting, listening days were over. Yet a vague apprehension lingered in the back of her mind.

"Do you think Connie will ever forgive me for marrying you?" she asked when they were near home.

"Paula!" John remonstrated. "What do you mean? Forgive?"

"I'm sure you felt it, too."

John was thoughtful for a moment. "Yes, I sensed her faint disapproval, but it's of me more than of you. She's a very loyal person. When she realizes how good it will be to have you in the house, she'll be all right."

"I hope so, I do love them both."

Nevertheless, her fingers played nervously with her wedding ring. The immediate future of intimate family life under the watchful eyes of two young ladies—one distinctly wary of her presence—filled her with mixed emotions. However, the brightly shining windows, bathed with mellow lamplight, warmed and welcomed her.

Denise spied the car in the driveway and came running to them crying out, "They're here! They're here!"

John swept her into his arms. "How's my girl?"

"We've been waiting for you, Daddy, for you and Paula," she said happily.

"Hi," Connie greeted them quietly and submitted to a kiss from John. For Paula she managed a slight smile.

Mrs. Adams held them both in her arms. "It's good to have you home, my dears."

Susie came running to rub her head on Paula's ankle and

purr loudly. Paula picked her up. "We're together again, old girl, aren't we?" she said.

Denise rescued Paula from her rising wave of shyness in this first evening at home, when she, in matter-of-fact manner, exclaimed, "I'll carry your things upstairs." And promptly she gathered up Paula's small overnight bag to deposit it unhesitatingly on the large double bed in John's room.

"I put fresh towels out for you, too," she told Paula who had followed her up the stairs.

"Thank you, Denise," Paula answered. "We brought something for you and Connie."

"Something nice?" Denise asked eagerly.

"You'll see," Paula laughed. "I hope you'll like it."

Denise ran down the stairs hurriedly. "Connie," she called, "Daddy and Paula brought something for us."

"Oh?" Connie's eyes lit up momentarily.

John had already unwrapped the figurines and now placed them in formation on the piano. Six fragile, appealing, little musicians, waiting only for a signal to begin their celestial harmony! Both girls gazed at the little cherubs for a minute, then Denise said, "They're beautiful! Connie, look, aren't they like the ones Mother wanted us to have and we couldn't find any more? Oh, I love them. Thank you." And she ran from Paula to John with a kiss.

Connie held one in her hand and examined it carefully. Then she put it down gently, and rearranged the group to suit her taste. She thanked Paula and John and said, "Yes, Mother wanted us to have them. I wish—I wish," she stammered and turned and ran to the kitchen.

Crestfallen, Paula looked at John and whispered, "Did I do wrong?"

John smiled at her and with a slight gesture of his head indicated that she remain silent.

"Let's take Grandma Adams home," he suggested. "And we'll see your mother, Paula."

"I wanted to call her," Paula said, "but this is better."

"Aren't you coming, too, Contance?" John called.

"I really have a lot of homework to do," Connie replied. "And Denise has some, too."

"Do you, hon?" John asked Denise.

"Yes," Denise said unhappily, making a face, "I do. Miss Erickson piles it on." And reluctantly she added, "I better stay here with Connie."

"Maybe you better," John agreed. "We won't be gone long."

The three of them were silent in the car. Finally Mrs. Adams said, "Don't feel badly about Connie. She's trying, but at her age loyalty to the memory of her mother is an important obligation."

"That's just it, Mother," John said. "She has this mistaken sense of loyalty; and she's building a wall around herself. She's a romantic teen-ager, and she must find out what's important and what isn't."

Paula listened attentively, then told them, "I'm trying to put myself in her place, at her age. You know I think I would have acted the same way. To have accepted another woman in my mother's house would have been treachery. It's going to take a lot of understanding and patience to win her confidence and love."

"And, darling," John told his wife, "there's no doubt in my mind whatever. I know that you'll win her over. I'm just grateful for Denise. She was a happy, outgoing child even at six months of age. When Connie was serious, Denise was laughing. And she was always daddy's girl."

Mrs. Russell's eyes lit up and she smiled broadly. "Welcome home, you two! You look wonderful!"

John and Paula laughed. "We feel wonderful," they said.

"Have a cup of coffee with me," she suggested. "And some leftover wedding cake. Mr. Ellison, from the club, brought it after you left."

"Tastes better than it did on Saturday," John said. "I was so excited that I didn't know what I was eating."

"You, too?" Paula jested.

The next morning after John and the girls were gone, and Paula was alone in her newly acquired home, she stayed at the cheerful breakfast table for many minutes. Her eyes were watching the birds in the lovely shaded yard, but her heart was appealing to God for help in this task she had so gladly taken upon herself.

She knew there would be problems of her own to overcome. This house, with its characteristics, details, furnishings, had, after all, been planned and executed largely by Amy. In fact, everything in it, including John and the girls, had been Amy's possessions.

I'm the alien, she thought. She had experienced some extremely bad moments last night. In the shelter of John's arms she had allowed Amy's face to appear before her. Every ounce of practical reasoning had to be mustered to calm her troubled heart. *I can see Connie's point,* she now thought, *and like Connie, I will have to live with it. I love John; with all my heart and soul I love him.*

Resting her elbows on the table, she folded her hands under her chin as her eyes examined the back yard. A huge old elm tree near the garage shaded the back door. The tulips edging the lawn were through blooming. Their yellow leaves would have to be trimmed soon. The lilacs at the far end of the lot were already showing colors. Soon their sweet fragrance would drift across to the kitchen window.

In front of the lilacs the peonies were beginning to bud. *Wonder what color they will be,* she thought. Under the huge elm tree a grouping of day lilies and iris caught her eye. *I can put some begonias there,* she decided.

Suddenly refreshing relief lifted her spirit. *It's so lovely, so beautiful. Thank you, Amy. Thank you for everything.* She knew where to begin—with the breakfast dishes. One thing at a time. Each day would bring a new problem and its solution. Each succeeding day, each necessary task would help to identify with the house and the children. Time and the grace of God would surely erase all difficulties, and would soften Connie's heart.

Paula was grateful for the remaining weeks of school. She had opportunity to become acquainted with the house and details connected with her new position as homemaker.

She renewed old friendships in the supermarket, at the cleaners, in the drugstore. It amazed her to realize how much the warmth of these greetings encouraged her and strengthened her conviction in the rightness of her marriage.

"It's good to see you, Paula—John is looking so well—How good for the girls to have you there," were comments heard again and again.

A beautiful, melodious note wound itself around her heart, almost smothering the shadowy interior which held the faint anxiety of Connie's rejection. Connie, who was dutifully obedient, meticulously polite, nevertheless, walked within a restraining wall. Her emotions were hidden behind carefully screened eyes. With stoic submission she agreed to the open piano when Denise asked to resume her lessons. However, she refused to join in the duets the sisters at one time had delighted to perform.

"We'll just ignore her supposed lack of feeling," John said. "To dwell on it will only increase her hostility."

Plans were made for the Minnesota vacation after school.

"Are we going back to Tamarack, Daddy?" Denise asked when she saw the road maps spread out on the kitchen table.

"Would you like to?" John asked. And turning to Connie, he asked her, "How about it? Would you like to go to the cottage we used to rent in Tamarack? You had some good friends there. Remember?"

Connie hesitated, then asked pointedly, "Without Mother?" And perhaps making an effort to break out of her wall, or remembering past happiness at the lake, she added, "Yes, let's go there. I hope the Gruners are there, too."

"How about Paula?" Denise asked. "Where does she want to go?"

"We talked about this sometime ago, and she's much in favor of it," John told the girls.

"What am I in favor of?" Paula asked, coming into the kitchen.

"The lake, Paula, Lake Tamarack," Denise explained excitedly. "We're going next week, you know."

"That's right. Next week by this time we'll be there," Paula answered.

"Do you swim?" Denise asked.

"A little," Paula replied. "Your father and I took lessons when we were only about eight years old. Remember, John?"

John smiled at her. "I remember." Then nodding his head, he added, "We sure did many things together, didn't we?"

"What about Susie?" Denise asked anxiously.

"She could stay with Mother Russell," John suggested. "She's been there before and is used to it."

When they left for Minnesota, Connie seemed to have relented somewhat and was in a happy mood. The weather had been good this year, and the rich farmlands through Wisconsin and Minnesota were covered with heavy, strong stalks of corn and waving fields of grain and hay.

The cottage welcomed them. Tall, swaying elms and old pines shaded the lemon yellow building. Large and comfortable, it faced the lake shimmering in the warm sun. John inspected the boat left by the owner and rejoiced when the motor started easily.

Mrs. Gruner, a blond viking, their neighbor for many years, came to welcome John.

"Hello," she called out. "We missed you last year."

John walked over to her. "We—we couldn't come last year." He stammered a little.

Mrs. Gruner was puzzled. "What's the matter, John? Did something happen?" she asked with concern in her voice.

John spoke quietly. "Amy—she died a year ago this spring, just before Easter."

Mrs. Gruner's voice trembled. "Oh, John, I'm sorry. We didn't know. But, but, what? Who?" she flushed. "I saw you unpack the car."

John looked at her steadily. "Paula and I were married early in May." And, as though to defend the act, he added, "We've known each other since we were children."

"Why, I think that's good. Man is not meant to be alone. And the girls need someone, too."

She looked past John's head to the porch where Paula stood. John turned and saw her.

"Paula," he called, "come here. I want you to meet our neighbor."

The two women studied each other. Paula's eyes were warmly appealing. Mrs. Gruner's smile welcomed her as she stretched out her hand to clasp Paula's.

"John told me," she said artlessly. "Life goes on. You're very happy; I can see that. I'm glad he has you."

110

John's arm was around Paula's waist. Her voice was bright with relief. "Thank you, Mrs. Gruner. We'll be seeing much of you, I hope."

"That you will," Mrs. Gruner laughed heartily. "Don't forget your girls and our Matthew and Ellen are good friends. By the way, where are the girls?"

"They're getting their beds in order," Paula answered. "How old are your children?"

"Matthew is already seventeen, and Ellen is fifteen," Mrs. Gruner replied. "They're gone for some groceries right now."

"And Connie was fifteen in February," John marveled.

"Well," Mrs. Gruner said briskly, "I must get back. Erik still goes to work in Alexandria every morning and comes home in the evening. We'll see you soon. I'll tell Erik," she added with a smile.

Sleep was forgotten in the dewy freshness of the next morning. Birds were flying low, dipping insects; here and there a fish broke the glassy surface of the water and caused ripple upon ripple to fan out gently to the shore. A lone fisherman sat in his boat, half-hidden in the reeds, slouchy hat shading his eyes. The slight breeze ruffling the curtains was cool and pleasant.

"I hope you like fish," John said, "because I'm going fishing; and there are an awful lot of good walleyes in that lake."

Paula laughed and raised her right arm in a mock vow.

"I promise to cook every fish you catch, in any way you choose."

Connie and Denise were in the water for an early dip. Matthew and Ellen Gruner joined them, and their ear-piercing, gleeful shouts brought smiles to John and Paula.

"It was good for all of us to come," Paula said. "Look at them."

Connie, her dark hair falling across her face, was running, falling, splashing with the rest of them.

Matthew, blond as his mother, with laughing blue eyes and the strength of a young animal, met the watery challenge of the three girls with ease. Ellen, his equally blond and blue-eyed sister, was a lovable, chattering magpie.

"Connie's growing up, isn't she?" John said, observing his daughter's delicately molded body. "I suppose the boys will be coming around soon."

"Yes," Paula agreed. "I'm surprised they haven't already been here."

"I suppose she's been too preoccupied with her mother's death to encourage attention from anyone."

Denise almost bounced in the water. Her childish voice was high-pitched with excitement.

"They'll be brown water babies by the time we leave," Paula said contentedly.

The days slipped by rapidly. The Gruners, Dorothy and Erik, who was a match for his wife in size, were good neighbors, always ready for an evening's visit, but never intruding on privacy. The children were together constantly: swimming, boating, walking, or just stretched out lazily in the hot sun on the equally hot sand. In a few days their bodies began to take on a warm, pinkish brown color.

Paula rejoiced in the feeling of friendliness on Connie's part. She did not yet allow an embrace or run into Paula's arms as Denise did. However, her glance had lost the cold, distant look of a few weeks ago.

Paula was happy, in spite of the slight uneasiness she experienced. The Adams and the Gruners were watching the twilight and sunset change the colors of the lake from blue to rose to silver. Sounds of music and laughter came across the water from the yacht club. A motorboat, towing a graceful water-skier, broke the calm, silvery surface of the lake. In the already shadowy distance, the ghostly, lonely cry of a loon rose and fell.

Suddenly Paula thought, *It's so beautiful, I'm going to cry.* A wave of dizziness was overwhelming her. She was grateful for the deepening twilight. In a few moments it passed, but left a strange, mysterious feeling of unexpected happiness, mingled with anxiety. *What's wrong with me?* she thought. *Must have been out in the sun too long this afternoon.* They had gone for a long boat ride, exploring the shore and hidden coves of the entire lake.

By the time the Gruners left, she felt fine.

"I'm going to the club house in the morning to call the office," John said. "Anything we still need?"

"No," Paula answered. "We're leaving day after tomorrow, aren't we?"

"Yes, but that's already longer than the two weeks we originally planned to stay away. That's why I better call."

The morning sun was especially bright—perhaps in contrast to the mountainous clouds on the northwestern horizon.

"We've had such good weather these past days! I hope the record won't be broken today," John said as he saw the clouds. "While I'm out, I'm going to drive the twenty miles to Alexandria and see one of our customers there. Then we can go right through tomorrow."

Glancing up at the clouds again, he said, "The girls ought to stay off the lake today. The wind can churn that water into a boiling kettle in a few minutes."

"I'll tell them," Paula promised. She leaned in the car window to kiss him. "Come back safely."

In an hour Paula knew they were in for a storm. Looking out, she saw Matthew and Connie push the boat into the water. She ran to the porch and called out, "Connie, do you think you ought to go out on the lake? Look at the storm coming up."

Connie turned to look at her. "We're just crossing over to the club house," she said.

"I think it would be wiser to stay here," Paula suggested.

At the same time Dorothy Gruner called to her son, "Matt, get that boat high onto the beach. We're in for a bad one."

Matthew and Connie exchanged a few words.

"Take the motor off," Mrs. Gruner ordered, "And off the Adams' boat also."

"Okay, Mom," Matthew replied. "It won't be here for a while, though. Can't we go for a Coke first?"

"Not as far as I'm concerned," Mrs. Gruner called, "but ask Paula."

Paula had hoped the decision would not be hers. But remembering John's words about the wind on the water, she said, "No, Connie. You better stay here. Your father does not want you on the lake in a storm."

Connie's answer was a sullen, "All right," as she helped Matthew pull the boat out of the water and watched him carry the motors into the shelter of the boathouse.

Paula was meant to hear a bitter, "She's not even my mother," as Connie turned to walk to the cottage.

"I'm sorry," Paula began when she saw the gloomy expression on her stepdaughter's face. "Your father gave instructions that you were to stay off the lake in stormy weather."

Connie mumbled some words about "You can't boss me around," and walked to her room with hostile eyes.

In a short while low, deep, growling thunder could be heard, even though the air was breathlessly, deceptively quiet. The lake changed to a dull gray as the wind began to blow. Suddenly, with a flash of lightning and a deafening roll of thunder, the storm lashed at the cottage. Denise had closed all the windows and now stood near Paula.

"I don't like it when it's so noisy," she cried out.

"It's all right, dear," Paula said as she hugged Denise's shoulder. "We're all right. I hope your daddy isn't driving in it."

The wind was a vicious, living thing—tearing, scratching, pulling, breaking wherever possible. Muddy water, thick with debris, was thrown across the wooden pier and up to the top of the beach. Paula hoped the boats were tied securely.

When a tree limb fell onto the roof with a crash, Connie came out of her room and sat down in a chair far removed from the windows.

As quickly as it had come, the storm blew over. It would be several days, however, before the roiled water of the lake would be clear again and clean enough for swimming.

John drove in an hour later. "Is everybody all right?" he inquired immediately.

"Oh, Daddy," Denise cried, "it was terrible. Where were you?"

"I was in Mr. Hansen's office. It was raining, but not too hard. The nearer I got to Tamarack, the more I realized it must have been pretty bad here. Trees are down, a haystack was blown apart, and grain is flattened in the fields."

Paula smiled her relief at his safety. "I'm glad you were not on the road."

"Connie okay?" John was looking around for her.

"Yes," Paula replied quickly. "Yes, she's fine. She just went to her room."

John seemed dubious. "What happened? She wasn't out on the lake, was she?"

With childish frankness, Denise interrupted, "No, she wasn't, Daddy. She and Matt wanted to go for a Coke just before the storm, but Paula wouldn't let her—and now she's mad."

"She's all right, John," Paula insisted. Her voice was calm.

Connie came in casually. "Hi, Daddy. Were you caught in the storm?"

John looked closely at her. "No, I wasn't. Denise says you're mad because Paula told you to stay home."

"Oh," she shrugged her shoulders indifferently, "we could have been back before the storm broke."

"Nevertheless, I told Paula not to allow you on the lake, and you have no reason to be angry."

"Oh, Daddy," she protested haughtily, "I'm not a child any more, that I must be told what I can or cannot do."

"If you behave like a child, then you must be treated like one. It's as simple as that," John enlightened her.

"All right," she agreed somberly, but her eyes avoided Paula's.

Paula's heart sank. *We're back where we started,* she reflected. *I've committed the unforgivable sin of becoming a stepmother, and she'll never let me forget it.*

The Gruners helped John and Paula pack in the morning while the children had a last boat ride.

"It's all right for them to go out now," Dorothy Gruner remarked, "but yesterday—" She shook her head. "Sometimes I think you have to sit on them, literally, before they know you mean it for their own good."

Paula laughed, but her voice had an earnest note in it.

"I was glad you backed me up yesterday," she said.

It helped to know that it wasn't only stepmothers who had occasional problems.

CHAPTER 11

THE SUMMER WAS HOT and humid. Paula worked in her garden and beads of perspiration formed on her brow. She went inside and felt the room reeling before her eyes; this time the experience was accompanied by a faint nausea. An elusive thought, coming from a great distance, knocked at her consciousness. She was afraid to open the door to it just yet, but kept it hidden in a far corner of her heart. It refused to remain there, however, and drifted back again and again, in a dreamlike quality.

When she lifted her head one morning and the window zigzagged, she knew without a shred of doubt, that now she could open the door wide and enjoy the sweet promise of the dream. For the time being it was her secret and hers alone. "I'm going to have a baby," she whispered to herself. "John's child!" Her eyes became pools of deep blue; her skin took on a rosy hue. Happiness radiated from her as warmth from the sun.

The girls were back in school, John was at the office, and Paula had the day to herself. She drove in to see Dr. Parker.

"It's true all right," he told her. "I'd say about the middle of March or so. You should have come sooner, you know. How do you feel?"

Paula beamed at him. "Like a million dollars, doctor."

He looked at her over the top of his glasses and smiled.

"Happiness is the very best medicine. I'm sure that will be all you'll need for this pregnancy. Come back in a month."

That night before turning out the light, John looked closely at his wife.

"You know, Paula, you're growing more beautiful every day. You're positively shining."

She couldn't keep the secret from him any longer.

"Thank you. You know why?" She smiled brilliantly. "You're going to have a son."

John's jaw dropped. He looked at her with wide eyes as she came into his arms. With tenderness reserved only for those deeply in love, he held her close to him and whispered, "Paula. Oh my dear. Are you sure?"

"Yes. I saw Dr. Parker today."

"When?" John's voice was husky with emotion.

"The middle of March, Dr. Parker said. And don't ask me how I know that it will be a son. I just know."

John chuckled. "Womanly intuition, I suppose."

"Call it what you will—you'll have a son."

John was thinking out loud. "A child in the house again! How good it will be. When do we tell the girls?"

"Let's wait until everybody is here for Thanksgiving," Paula suggested.

"Fine," John agreed. "But you'll probably need to sew some buttons back on my shirt. I'm so proud they'll pop off."

"I'll be happy to," Paula promised smilingly.

After a clear, golden autumn, a cold, wet wind gathered the leaves into mounds against the fences and then spread them over the garden. The rain bedded them down to protect the beauty of spring waiting underneath.

Paula was happy despite Connie's continued coolness toward her. Connie's behavior was one of tolerance, broken a little when Paula played her records. She came to sit in the living room with them then. But she refused to touch the records or the piano. She was extremely courteous, instantly obedient—a perfect stranger. She seemed such a miserable child. Paula longed to comfort her, to place her hand on Connie's hair when she saw her deeply engrossed in home-work—looking lonely and exposed. She wanted to assure Connie of their love, but a glance from those aloof eyes checked her impulse immediately. The wall was rebuilt, higher and stronger than ever.

Thanksgiving Day was crisp and quiet. Mrs. Adams and Mrs. Russell were willing helpers in the preparation of the dinner. Denise's light, insistent chatter was frosting on the serious conversation underneath. Connie's smile, although slight, was at least an attempt, and Paula was gratified. Dessert of pecan pie and coffee was still on the table when John remarked, "Well, next year at this time we'll have another one around the table."

Paula felt her cheeks flush. All eyes turned toward John. It took a few seconds for the meaning to penetrate. Then Mrs. Russell's and Mrs. Adams' face broke out in happy smiles. However, before either could say a word, Connie in a pretended fit of coughing and choking, arose stiffly and looked at her father with mockery in her eyes.

"Father!" Her voice was steely. "You'll be the laughingstock of the town!" Scornfully, she added, "At your age!"

John's face was white. His eyes matched hers in steel,

and his words were equally sharp. "That's enough from you, young lady. Go to your room."

Connie opened her lips to say something, but seeing the look in her father's eyes, she ran from the room.

Denise was bewildered. She strained to hear and understand every word. When the reason for all the commotion finally dawned upon her, she squealed with joy.

"Daddy, Paula—you mean we're going to have a baby? Really? Is that who's going to be here next year?"

"That's right, doll," John declared. His eyes wandered toward the stairs. "I must talk to her," he said.

"Now?" Paula asked fearfully.

"Yes. She must be staightened out. This has gone far enough."

"You won't hurt her, Daddy, will you?" Denise asked. "She cries enough as it is."

John turned sharply to Denise. "What do you mean, 'cries enough'?" he asked.

"I often hear her crying at night," Denise answered. "She thinks I'm asleep, but I can hear her."

John looked at them all. "I *must* talk to her, now more than ever."

He strode up the stairs and opened the door without knocking.

Connie was slumped down in a chair in front of her mother's portrait, silent and dry-eyed. When John entered, she turned her back to him. He felt helpless.

"Connie," he spoke softly now. "What are we going to do? We can't go on this way. Haven't you beaten your head against the wall long enough? Can't you relent a little? Aren't you ready for some happiness soon?"

She refused to look at him.

"Why do you persist in this childish behavior?" he asked.

She turned to him dejectedly. "Daddy, I'm only thinking of you, feeling sorry for you. People will laugh at you when they know that you are going to be a father again. And what about me? I'm going to be sixteen, and we'll have a baby in the house. They feel sorry for me as it is because I have a stepmother."

She began to cry softly.

"Is that it?" John asked gently. "What a mistaken idea you have."

He placed his hand on her cheek and held it there.

"Connie, you may be going on sixteen, but you're still a child. All I can say now is that you will have to find your own answer when people feel sorry for you. As for me— forget it. I am, and will be, one of the proudest, happiest fathers in town."

Despite Connie's faintly cynical expression, Paula kept her inner glow. She was "at home" now. She knew the hairline crack in the dining room wall, the exact board in the basement stairs that squeaked, how to open the kitchen window when it stuck; she was no longer an alien.

She was contributing something to the family, and whether or not Connie approved, the contribution would become a part of them all. They would be a united group—of this she was sure.

She understood Connie's continued loyalty to Amy's memory. Yet several times, when Denise threw her arms around Paula, Connie's eyes had a fleeting look of gentleness, almost of yearning. It was in these moments that Paula's heart beat faster and she caught her breath.

"Someday," she told John, "the wall will crack and then crumble. We must love her very much and be patient."

As the crisp December days followed, Paula again filled

the stereo with Christmas music. She felt the familiar, peculiar melting away of tension. Even Susie seemed to find a special delight in the sweet strains. She purred her pleasure at Paula's feet.

"You've been here longer than I, haven't you?" Paula asked her old friend. "You were accepted immediately. Wish I'd be."

The late afternoon sun warmed the pot of hyacinths on the window sill in the dining room. The satisfying, homely smell of a casserole in the oven and an apple pie cooling on the shelf drifted through the house. The small life within Paula stirred and made itself known from time to time. A tremendous surge of tenderness washed over her.

"You're not forgetting the plant Christmas party, are you?" John asked later in the evening.

"To be truthful, I did forget. When is it?"

"We're doing it differently this year," John stated. "It's going to be an open house affair—a week from Saturday afternoon. The entire family is invited. We have a few new people, and this will give them a chance to meet the rest of the gang."

"Sounds like a good idea." Paula agreed.

"Speaking of Christmas," she continued, "what shall we give the girls?"

"I was thinking about a portable color TV for their room."

Paula considered the suggestion. "That's good, but wouldn't it tend to keep Connie away from us even more? What about new outfits for them? They might like new dresses for the party."

"Of course, you're right. Connie has picked her own for a few years, but Denise still needs some help."

"I'll go with her," Paula promised.

Christmas preparations have a way of absorbing human weaknesses and transforming them into love and peace. Paula was happier than she had been for a long time. The house spelled CHRISTMAS from top to bottom. Jars of cookies were stored in the cool basement. Fruit cake was ripening in an old copper wash boiler from her mother's basement. Mrs. Adams brought more cookies and candy.

Although Christmas was still a week away, soft candlelight glowed in the windows, and Paula's beloved crèche was set up on a corner table. Only the tree was lacking, and that would be trimmed in a few days, when the girls were home for the holidays.

Paula felt certain that Connie had at last forgiven her. The three of them, Paula and the girls, had gone shopping together and found a heavenly blue dress for Denise. It made her look like a princess. Connie found well-cut, bright red velveteen which set off her dark beauty.

For John they found a wine-colored woolen robe. Grandmother Adams and Mother Russell were remembered with the softest of soft sweaters. And Susie would have a new ribbon for her "anniversary," as Denise called it.

Driving through holiday traffic on the way home, Connie watched Paula handle the Mustang and remarked, "When I'm sixteen, I want to drive."

"Why not?" Paula asked. "Do you have a driver's training course in school? Perhaps you should enroll after Christmas."

"Would Daddy let me?" Connie asked. "He doesn't like me very much these days."

"Connie!" Denise cried out. "You're being silly. A daddy never stops liking—he can't—he's our daddy."

Paula felt a tear in her eye.

"She's right, Connie, you know that. Ask him—he'll understand."

"I will," Connie's voice was happy. And again Paula felt that now, surely, everything would be all right.

The large recreation room at John's plant had a huge tree in one corner and several small artificial trees on a long table at one end of the room. The table was crowded with dainty sandwiches, relishes, cookies, fruitcakes, and gifts for everyone. A piano was kept busy by different groups of carolers.

Again Paula met old acquaintances, some older, and a few younger. The three newest employees were strangers to her. She watched with pride as every employee greeted John. He had a special word for each one. They were a loyal group, working for and with each other in mutual respect and understanding.

Connie is a born hostess, Paula decided, observing her at the table where she was serving and helping the caterers. Her hair was held in place with a wide band of ribbon; her soft lips were smiling.

"Daddy," she asked, "do you have a large tray in the lunchroom? These sandwich plates are stacked too full."

"Yes, I'll get one," John said. At that moment, however, one of the salesmen stopped him and asked advice about a problem.

"Just a moment," he told the salesman. Then to Connie he said, "Go into the kitchen, and way to the back, in the sort of pantry or closet, there's a large tray on the back of the door."

"I'll find it," Connie answered and went to look for it.

The kitchen contained supplies for coffee breaks, where employees could warm lunches when they wished. The closet was around the corner, hidden from the rest of the room. It was necessary to close the door to find the tray. Connie's hand was on the knob ready to open the door again, when she heard voices in the kitchen.

"Is that the new Mrs. Adams?" a woman asked.

"You mean the red-haired, pregnant one?" the other answered by asking another question.

Had her life depended upon it, Connie could not have opened the door.

"That's the one. From what I've heard since I came here, they were childhood sweethearts and he jilted her."

"Well, she's got him now—on the rebound, I suppose. And to make sure she keeps him, she's got herself pregnant as soon as possible."

Connie's face was flaming.

"Funny she never married. Guess she lived *alone*." The word was given a doubtful meaning by inflection.

"She lost no time in going after him when his wife died. Poor kids—having to put up with a *stepmother*."

The emphasis on the last word was not lost on Connie.

They obviously had gotten what they came for—their voices faded away.

Connie's heart fell as a heavy rock falls into the depths of murky water. Her hands were cold and moist. She shivered.

"Daddy, Daddy," she whispered. "Why did you do it?"

Slowly she opened the door and went back to the table.

John saw her white face and asked, "Are you ill, Connie? What's wrong?"

She looked at him with blank, withdrawn eyes. "I'm all right, Daddy, I found the tray."

Her hands moved; she spoke occasionally, yet as one in a dream. Her ears closed to all sounds except the women's voices in the kitchen. She didn't know them and didn't want to know them; she hated them; she truly felt ill.

The guests were leaving. The caterers were gathering up their belongings.

125

"What's wrong with Connie?" Denise asked her father, detaching herself from the group of youngsters who were on their way out. "She walks around like a zombie."

John was concerned. "I don't know, hon. She's not feeling well. We'll be leaving soon; get your things."

"What happened?" Paula asked.

"Believe me, Paula, I don't know." John was mystified. "I sent her to the kitchen for a tray; when she returned, she seemed ill, but she told me she was fine."

Paula went to Connie who was standing near the door. When she placed her hand on Connie's arm, it was pulled away abruptly.

"Is anything wrong?" Paula asked gently.

Connie cast a look of distrust at her stepmother and said, "Don't touch me. Leave me alone."

In the car she sat frozen, stiff with resistance. Paula thought, *I'll ignore her. This can't go on. We can't gauge our conversation and actions to her moods. Whatever happened in the kitchen we'll never know.*

Aloud she asked, "John, who were the two inseparable women?"

"You must mean Sylvia Hurtience and Sophie Reems. They're two of the newer employees. Why?"

"Oh—they seemed so superficially concerned about my health. Kept asking questions and giving advice. Somehow I had a feeling of dislike for them."

"They do their work well, but they do like to gossip," John said.

Connie stared silently out the window.

John stopped the car at the side entrance and said, "I'll let you out here and put the car in tonight. It looks like snow. Connie, will you open the garage door, please?"

Connie lifted the overhead door and allowed it to ascend

126

rapidly. A streak of white fur swept past her.

"Susie!" Denise cried. "Were you out all this time?" She cradled the cat in her arms. "You scared her, Connie. She likes to crawl up on that rafter above the door."

"She's all right out here," John said. "That's why I made the small swinging door at the bottom of the large one, so she can go in and out anytime she wants."

"You look very tired, dear," John said to Paula in the privacy of their room before retiring.

"I am a little tired," Paula answered, "but that's not my worry."

"You're disturbed about Connie again. I am, too," John told her. "She was almost cheerful before going to the kitchen, and seemed frightened and ill when she returned."

"Has she spoken to you about taking the driver's training course after the new year?" Paula asked.

"No," John's voice raised in surprise.

"She wants to take lessons after her sixteenth birthday, and I suggested the course. Also, that she, herself, speak to you."

"Of course I'll give my permission. It will give her something to think about."

In the morning several inches of soft snow had fallen. The wind from the east was soaked with moisture from Lake Michigan.

"I suppose it's unChristian to suggest it," John said "but don't you think you better miss church services this morning? It's wet and slippery underneath that snow."

Paula smiled at him. "And I'm sort of clumsy now. You're right; I'll stay home."

Denise came down the stairs ready for church.

"Isn't Connie coming?" her father asked.

"She went back to bed after breakfast. Said she's not feeling well."

"You go on," Paula urged them. "I'll look in on her. She's probably coming down with a cold."

After clearing the breakfast dishes away, she went to see about Connie. The door was slightly ajar. She rapped gently and entered at the same time. Connie was in bed and turned quickly when she heard Paula. A fleeting look of welcome showed in her eyes before she dropped them in unfriendliness.

"I thought you were all in church," she said dryly.

"Your father thought I better stay home today. Are you coming down with a cold? Can I bring you something?"

Connie turned her head away and said indifferently, "Don't bother. I'm all right. It's just the sniffles."

Paula lingered in the room. She straightened Denise's bed, hung pajamas in the closet, and shook out a wrinkle in the drapes.

Sitting down in a chair near the bed, she said, "Let's get our differences cleared up once and for all, Connie. Is it impossible for you to forgive me for being your stepmother? Has it really been so bad these months?"

Connie refused to answer. She stared at the ceiling, twisting a strand of her hair with an index finger.

"You're making it very unpleasant for your father," Paula continued.

"You're doing that." Connie flung the words at her. "It wasn't enough that you married him; now you're making people laugh at him because—because of the baby."

It was difficult for Paula to keep her voice under control. She waited a moment, then said, "I'm sorry for you, Connie. You're so mistaken. Someday you'll understand, but right now I suppose there is nothing I can say to you, except that you are wrong. People are not laughing at him—they're happy for him."

"I don't believe that," Connie retorted sharply. "Just

128

leave me alone. I won't bother you, and you don't bother about me."

Paula got up slowly. It was becoming uncomfortable to get up out of an easy chair.

"Very well. But remember, this baby will belong to you and Denise too—even if only as a half-brother or sister."

She went back to the breakfast table. For the first time since her marriage, she remembered Tony's words: "She's jealous. Once a girl her age takes mother's place, it's not easy to dislodge her."

Dear God, Paula wondered, *what will happen? How can I help her?* She rested her forehead on her folded hands and tried to think of a solution to the problem. A swift movement in her side returned her to the present, and she realized there was no set path to take. There was no easy way out. If Connie persisted in her stubborn refusal to accept her, it would simply have to be endured.

There was a small ray of hope, however—the girl's attachment to Susie. As long as she was capable of giving love to anything, Paula felt there was promise of a change.

Christmas day was over. The day meant for joyous outpouring of happiness, for merrymaking and family solidity had been a mockery for Paula. Pretense was foreign to her nature, and it was extremely difficult for her to hide behind a facade of harmony while her heart was troubled.

Dinner had been at Mrs. Adams' house. A small tree was charmingly decorated. Denise's light-hearted, running comments on any topic that entered her mind focused attention on her and made Connie's lack of conversation inconspicuous.

Now, at home, John looked around the room contentedly. The lights on the tree were twinkling like stars, and the odor of fresh pine was pleasant.

"Do you know, Paula," he reminisced, "that a year ago tonight I sat here for a long time, thinking of you? Remember you almost fell while we were walking, and I caught you?" He smiled. "That's when I woke up."

They were watching the flames in the fireplace, listening to Christmas music. Paula placed her hand on his arm.

"John, have you ever regretted it?" she asked gravely, looking up at him.

"Regretted it! Darling!" He shook her gently. "Never, never. I should ask you that question. With Connie's behavior toward you, I am sure there have been times when you wondered about it."

"For me it has always been right," Paula answered. "And I believe for you, too. However, I do pray that Connie will someday understand and accept me."

"You can't spank a young lady," John said, "but I've been tempted several times. By the way," he continued, "she asked about the training course. I told her to go ahead."

"Are you picking up the girls after their church doings?"

"No," John said. "A boy, Gary Zimmer, is bringing them home."

"Well!" Paula exclaimed. "Really? That's good. An interest in someone else may divert her attention from me."

In an hour or so they heard a car in the driveway and loud, merry voices.

"Oh, we had such a good time," Denise cried out happily when the two girls entered. "Gary brought us home, and he's got a whole car-full yet to go. May we go again on New Year's Eve? May we, please?"

John laughed. "Wait a minute; you're going too fast. Go where?"

"We all decided to have another party at church then," Connie volunteered. "The assistant pastor and his wife offered to chaperone."

"Well, then I guess you better be there," John told them. *Will Connie ever look at me with such an open, direct gaze?* Paula wondered.

The short days of Christmas week were shortened even more by the gray, solid clouds that hid the sun. The damp, bone-chilling wind kept Paula at home.

"You looked sort of tuckered out at Aggie's," her mother said over the phone.

"I feel fine. Christmas tires the best of us, doesn't it?"

"I suppose so," Mrs. Russell replied, and added, "Soon it will be a year since your father's death."

"Yes, Mother. We were talking about it last night. May we spend New Year's Eve with you?"

"Please do," Mrs. Russell replied eagerly. "I'll ask Aggie over, too."

"Good. We'll pick you up for church services first and then stay with you until the girls get through with their party."

"We didn't trim your outdoor tree this year," John apologized New Year's Eve.

"That's all right, John," Mrs. Russell assured him. "But somehow it didn't seem to matter."

"Next year you'll feel better," Mrs. Adams comforted her old friend, "when we have a grandson in the house."

John laughed at them. "If all of you feel that way, it must be a son. You'd never forgive Paula if it were not."

"Oh—I feel the same way," Paula said. "You're out-guessed, by womanly intuition."

Snow was falling heavily at midnight, and the sound of the many bells and whistles was muffled and far away. John and Paula stood on the front porch and listened as the door of eternity closed on the old year and a new, unmarked one came forth.

"A happy, blessed New Year to you, my dear wife," John said as he drew her close in his arms and their lips met.

In a few moments the bells ceased their clamor and the new year was on its way.

"Let's pick up the girls and go home," John suggested. "It's pretty late, you know, for a woman in your condition to be out."

The party in the church parlors was over; young people with whistles, horns, balloons, and noisemakers were tumbling out of the building.

Denise giggled halfway home. "This is about the best New Year's party I've ever been to!" she exclaimed.

"Silly!" Connie told her. "It's the *first* one you've ever been to."

The streets were full of cars until they entered their street at the edge of town.

"How come we haven't seen any light in the Hargrove house for a while?" Denise was still talking.

"Don't you remember?" John reminded her. "They leave for Florida two weeks before Christmas and usually return near Easter time—depending upon the weather up here."

"That means we're really far out and by ourselves, doesn't it?" Paula asked.

"I guess so," John answered. "Are you afraid to be out here?"

"No—never," Paula replied. "I love the country."

CHAPTER 12

IN THE WEEKS FOLLOWING, Paula realized the meaning of Connie's "I won't bother you." It was as though an invisible curtain hung between them. Connie avoided her whenever possible. She was courteous to John, cuddled Susie, and completed her homework diligently. However, no remark was ever addressed to Paula directly. She felt the rejection keenly and could only hope in the future.

It was bitter cold; the thermometer slid to ten, then twelve below zero. The snow crunched underneath the tires. The sharp, bright light of the full moon caught the whirling snow showers and turned them into minute diamonds which glistened and danced on the edges of the snowdrifts.

And yet, Paula thought, *January is a beginning again. The earth, which for months has been on a downward path to darkness, away from the sun, inches its way back to light. And however sharp the crack of a frozen limb on an old tree, however bone-penetrating the cold, the promise of spring is in the background. There comes a day when the icicles grow on the south slope of the roof, and another when the warmth of the sun loosens their hold and they shatter on the walk below.*

By the end of January, seed catalogs were found in the mailboxes, and greenhouses were preparing and hoping for an early spring rush.

The first robin was there, Paula noticed, pecking away at a frozen apple on the old tree near the street and scolding at his foolish early arrival. Chickadees were half-buried in the snow, looking for crumbs spread out for them. With the increasing daylight, it seemed their chirps became louder and merrier.

There would be more shivering cold weather, more snow, Paula knew, but somehow the thought was not frightening. Life was on its upward swing again—to light and warmth and growth.

She was content to remain at home during the blustery days of January and February. Her movements were slowed down, and occasionally she felt short of breath.

The girls had gone to a Valentine party. The house was quiet. Susie was asleep on the rug at their feet.

"What did Dr. Parker say today?" John asked.

"According to him, it will be about the middle of March."

John looked up from his paper. "The middle of March! I've got to be in Chicago at the plastics convention on the seventh or eighth."

"That's a week earlier," Paula said. "Let's not worry about it now. And Chicago isn't so far away."

"Maybe I can send one of the salemen," John said, narrowing his eyes in thought. "But I really ought to be there myself."

"Don't worry, dear. That's almost a month away, and you'll be back."

"I'm going to think about it just the same," John replied. "Oh, by the way, do you remember those two chattering, gossipy women at the Christmas party?"

"Yes, I do. What about them?"

"They were fired last week."

"You said they did their work rather well."

"They did, that's true," John replied, "but the entire office force was disrupted by their sly gossip. Latest rumor they started was about an employee of ours, a young widow. Her husband was killed in Vietnam a year ago; she has a three-year-old son. Two weeks ago she dated one of our salesmen and asked him to come in for a few minutes. Their vicious tongues really tore her to pieces."

"How horrible!" Paula was shocked. "John, is it possible that they said something to Connie at the party?"

"I hope not," John answered, with a frown, "but it's possible. Shall I ask her about it?"

"I wonder if that would be wise. Perhaps when she knows they're gone, which she will in time, and why, she'll figure it out for herself."

"That's probably best," John agreed.

"She'll be sixteen on Saturday. What shall we give her for her important birthday?" Paula asked. "I wish we could have planned a party."

"Next year," John said. "She's been wanting a transistor radio. I'll find one for her."

Paula's eyes lit up. "John, why don't you take her out for dinner? She'd be delighted."

"Just the two of us?" John thought about it and nodded his head. "Why not? I'll ask her."

"Must you call for them after the party tonight?"

"No. Connie said Gary Zimmer would bring them home."

"He's the young man who brought them home from the Christmas party, isn't he?"

"Yes, he is," John replied, wondering a little.

"I don't remember the Zimmers."

"No, you couldn't. They came from somewhere in Iowa about three or four years ago."

They heard a car at the side entrance, and in a minute Denise ran in. "Hi!" she called loudly. "We're home."

"So we hear," John laughed. "Where's your sister?"

"She's coming. She and Gary are talking about her birthday."

Paula and John exchanged glances.

Denise came to Paula and affectionately laid her cheek against her stepmother's. "Feel how cold," she said.

Paula kissed the cheek and said, "You smell of fresh air."

When Connie came in a short time later, her eyes were shining.

"Daddy," she said eagerly, ignoring Paula, "Gary asked me to go out with him on my birthday."

"Oh?" John smiled at his sparkling daugher. "I wanted to ask you to have dinner with me that night."

She looked at him in surprised delight, disbelievingly, and said, "You're joking, Daddy." Then, stealing a quick glance at Paula, she added, in a spirit of defiance, "I'd love to. We could have an early dinner and be back by seven-thirty, when Gary will pick me up."

"Good," John replied. "We'll have dinner at six at the club."

A slightly puzzled expression appeared on Connie's face. Again she cast a quick look at Paula. Then turning toward the stairs she called back, "I'll be ready."

Paula wondered about the studied look. "Do you suppose she expected me to object?" she asked John.

"I don't know," he replied, "but," he added in a whisper, "I'm grateful to Gary for asking her out."

136

Every girl's sixteenth birthday should be a special occasion, Paula reasoned the next day. *It's not just any ordinary birthday, but the sixteenth one. You're definitely out of your childhood years; you're a young woman. You're not completely mature, but that delicious year when you giggle a lot and weep easily. You carry the sufferings of the universe on your soul one minute, and the next abandon them to the adult world—and go on your way rejoicing.*

Although Connie pretended indifference, as befits a young lady with the attention of two men in her life in one day, she could not conceal her inner excitement. Several times she was on the brink of speaking to Paula—confiding in her. Once she caught herself just in time; her lips were already open, forming a question—*Shall I wear my hair up or down?*

It is difficult to shut even one person out of your life when happiness enters, and Connie was happy today. Paula had baked a gloriously large birthday cake. Both Grandmother Adams and Mother Russell were there for lunch. Beautifully wrapped gifts were piled on the coffee table in the living room—sweaters, pajamas, slippers, lipsticks, and the transitor radio.

Looking at her, Paula thought, *What a lovely young girl she is, with her father's hair and eyes and her mother's charm.* How deeply she longed for a glance of recognition from those dark eyes. Just once Connie had looked at her, fleetingly, to utter a self-conscious "Thank you for the sweater," but that was all. Denise's affection was the fire at which Paula warmed her heart.

Promptly at six o'clock John escorted the birthday child in to dinner. Connie's cheeks were burning with excitement. Afer long deliberation, she had decided against wearing her hair up; instead it was held in place with a velvet ribbon. However, it was the light in her eyes and the curve of her soft cheek, the grace of her walk, that brought forth low, admiring whistles from John's friends.

"Daddy," she said blissfully on the way home, "this was the very best birthday present you ever gave me."

"I can't remember when I've been so pleased to give you a present," John told his daughter. "You're quite a young lady now. I am proud of you."

And a few moments later he added, "Paula was sure you'd be delighted."

Immediately Connie froze beside him. She drew her breath in sharply. "You mean it was *her idea,* not yours?" she cried.

"Well, well," John stammered a little.

"Was it, Daddy?" Connie demanded.

"Originally, yes," John admitted. "It was Paula's idea. But I immediately thought how happy I'd be to take you."

"Never mind," her voice was flat and lifeless. "Don't say any more. You did it only because *she* asked you to, not because of me or my birthday."

John was astounded. "Connie, stop it," he said sternly. "It was because Paula wanted you to have a birthday to remember that she suggested it. When will you realize that she loves you?"

Connie sat erect and lonely, her eyes straight ahead.

"Loves me!" she mocked. "She's my *stepmother.* How can she love me?"

"For a supposedly bright young woman, you're very childish," John couldn't help observing. "Why can't a stepmother love a child? Paula loves you. You are deliberately seeking misery."

When they reached home, Gary's car was already there.

"I'm not going out with Gary," Connie said in a cold, stubborn tone of finalty.

John's temper flared. He stopped the car and looked at her.

"Now see here. You are not going to take your immature attitude out on Gary. You're going to behave like the young woman you are. It's time you respected the feelings of others."

Connie's eyes opened wide as she listened to her father. She started to say something, but clapped her hand over her lips to stifle the retort. Her eyes fell.

"Okay, Daddy," she said, near to tears. "I'll go with him. Let's go in."

Just before entering, Connie stopped briefly, and John saw the growing young woman emerge again. She straightened her shoulders and ran her fingers underneath her hair, fluffing it out with a toss of her head. Then she placed a smile on her lips and walked in.

"Hi, Gary," she called out as she ran up the stairs. "I'll be down in a second."

"Did you have a good time?" Denise called after her.

The reply was lost in the closing of the bathroom door.

John shook hands with Gary. "Sit down," he urged the young man.

"Gary has been telling us about the cold winters in Iowa," Paula remarked.

She liked this tall, broad-shouldered young man. His easy manner was natural. His blue eyes behind horn-rimmed glasses were clear and warm. His red hair was worn in the style of the high school crowd—short and well contoured. Freckles peppered his face, and a stainless steel tooth glistened when he smiled.

"Tell them how you got your tooth, Gary," Denise giggled.

"Denise!" John scolded.

"Oh, that's all right, Mr. Adams," Gary laughed. "I

don't mind. I'll tell you. After a heavy snowfall five years ago, some of the fellows made a slide over a picket fence in our back yard. Well—my pants caught on the fence, and I fell on my face on the concrete walk and broke my tooth.

"The dentist thought it was better to put this one in until I'm through high school because of football roughhouse and so on."

"That's too bad," Paula commented sadly.

"It doesn't bother me, Mrs. Adams," Gary told her. "Mom was upset at first, but," he smiled and shrugged his shoulders, "it's there, and that's that."

"You know what the girls do?" Denise asked with twinkling eyes. "Gary shines his tooth with a handkerchief and the girls use it as a mirror."

Connie came down during the laughter and joined in.

"That's why he's so popular," she teased.

"Have a good time," John told them when they left.

"Thank you, Mr. Adams, we will," Gary assured him as they ran to the car hand-in-hand.

As soon as the door closed, Denise bombarded John with questions. "Did she have a good time, Daddy? What did you eat? Will you take me to dinner when I'm sixteen?"

"Whoa—whoa," John laughed at her. "I think she had a good time; we had steak; and *yes*, I'll take you to dinner on your sixteenth birthday—which won't be for a few years yet!"

He grabbed her in a tight embrace and kissed her soundly. Denise squealed for joy.

Paula watched them with a catch in her throat. *This is my family,* she thought, *my home.*

CHAPTER 13

IN THE CLOSING WEEKS of pregnancy Paula discovered that being blessed with good health does not necessarily alleviate discomfort.

"I feel like a barrel," she told John. "If I ever fall, I'm sure I'd roll."

The baby was extremely active, and she often felt the thrust of a small heel in her side, pushing outward.

"He'll be early," Mrs. Russell predicted. "All that action means something."

"Anytime he's ready," Paula decided, "I am."

The first week of March brought unseasonable warmth for a few days; the snow turned into slush during the day and thin, brittle ice at night.

"Do you think I should go to Chicago tomorrow?" John asked. "I'm worried about you."

Paula reassured her husband. "Of course you should go. He's not due for at least another week—or two. And you'll

141

be home again by Saturday. What can happen? We'll be fine.''

"All right, but I'll leave telephone numbers where you can reach me any time. And if you even think you'll need me, be sure to call right away. I can be home in about two hours.''

By Thursday morning the wind had shifted from the south to the east and was heavy with the fishy smell of Lake Michigan. Sea gulls were far inland on open patches of muddy fields.

"We'll probably have snow by nightfall," John stated. "Girls, be sure to ride the bus home from school; Paula will not be able to pick you up.''

"We'll be all right," Denise told him. "Don't worry, Daddy. I'll take care of Paula, too.''

"Thank you, darling" he replied. "I know you will.''

John kissed his wife and held her close. "'By dear, but I still feel I ought to stay home.''

"Nonsense," Paula chided. "You know you should be there—and really, we will be all right. See you Saturday. Have a good time," she added mischievously.

"I'll phone after six," he called to her from the car.

By noon the wind had become more than a breeze. Dark, massive clouds hung low. Instead of snow, a cold rain was blown about fitfully.

Paula was relieved when she saw the girls coming in the door.

The rain was now driven by sudden, strong gusts of wind. It rattled on the windows like handsful of small gravel stones. The yard was strewn with debris—dried twigs broken off the large, ancient elm.

"It's miserable out there," Denise stated. They could hear the wind shriek and howl as they watched TV.

When John called at six-thirty, the connection was bad,

but Paula assured him everything was fine. "We're all home; we're warm and comfortable, and I feel fine. Don't worry."

"According to weather reports it will be a bit better by tomorrow afternoon, but rain and sleet are predicted," John said.

"We'll listen for school news," Paula told him. "Maybe we'll all be here for the whole day."

The thought of being weather-bound brought a feeling of adventure. "Yippee!" Denise cried. "Maybe school will be closed."

Connie repudiated the probability. "They don't close the schools just because of rain," she advised her sister.

Susie went to the door, begging to be let out.

"Oh, Susie," Denise wailed. "Now? In this weather? Must I let her out, Paula?"

Paula smiled at Denise's reluctance. "Susie knows best, I guess. She'll be all right. She can always scoot into the garage."

When Denise opened the door, Susie drew back a little, then dashed out quickly.

From the TV came the latest weather report. "Wind has now reached gale force—gusts up to fifty miles an hour. Forecast: Continued rain, possibly sleet, ending by noon tomorrow. Diminishing winds."

Gleefully Denise exclaimed, "I just know that school will be closed. Hurray!"

The wind tore at the corner of the house like some living, angry monster. Occasionally the lights flickered, and Paula thought, *If the power goes off, we'll be in trouble.*

Connie turned on the garage light and looked out. Susie's small door was swinging wildly. A sudden, powerful blast of wind tore and twisted the old elm near the garage. A large limb snapped with a loud report and slammed down on the concrete. Susie, terror-stricken, leaped for her door—but not fast enough. The jagged end of the heavy limb bounced into the air, then fell and struck her, pinning her tight to the driveway. She gave an unearthly shriek of pain and fear, struggled for a moment, then lay still.

Connie screamed, and heedless of the rain, ran out the door. Frantically she lifted and pulled at the fallen branch. Paula and Denise followed her. The wind and the rain plastered their clothing to their bodies; their hair was drenched in a few seconds and hung in strands.

"She's dead, she's dead!" Connie screamed above the wind.

Denise cried out. "No, no! You and Paula lift the branch, and I'll take her out."

Paula and Connie strained every muscle and managed to raise the branch high enough for Denise to slip Susie out. Connie took the limp body and ran into the house with it.

Denise took Paula's hand. At the bottom of the steps Paula tripped on a small broken piece of the tree and stumbled forward. Denise tightened her hold and kept her from falling.

Connie was on the kitchen floor, cradling Susie's quiet body.

"Is she, is she . . ." Denise asked, not being able to say the dreaded word.

Pools of water were forming on the floor and Paula shivered.

"We must get out of these wet clothes," she said softly, "or we'll all get pneumonia."

Suddenly Connie jumped to her feet. "Get out of these wet clothes," she mimicked Paula. "How can you be so heartless? You killed her. You told Denise to let her out. I hate you! I hate you!"

Her voice became louder; her eyes blazed at Paula.

"First you gave Susie to us so we wouldn't notice you taking our daddy from us. Then when you have him, you kill her because she loves us more than you."

She was sobbing hysterically now. "Why didn't you leave us alone? I hate you. Why don't you go away?" And she ran from the room, dripping water up the stairs.

Paula stood, as though nailed to the floor. Connie's words dug deeper and deeper into her heart. She was numb, frozen by the chill and hatred in her stepdaughter's eyes and words.

O Lord, she thought, *does she hate me that much? What shall I do?*

Denise, stunned by Connie's outburst, began to cry. She came to Paula and took her hand to lead her to a chair. Then embracing her impulsively, she cried, "No, Paula, no. She can't hate you, she can't. She knows it was an accident."

"Thank God for you, my dear," Paula said. With trembling hands she wiped the tears from the small face.

They looked at Susie, lying where Connie had left her. Paula lifted the lifeless pet and gently stroked the wet coat.

"Poor old girl—poor Susie. You were such a good friend for so long. You knew I wouldn't hurt you."

"What shall we do with her?" Denise asked tearfully.

Paula was shaking with cold. "Let's leave her on the rug for tonight. Right now we must get out of these soaking wet clothes. Run along and change, dear. I'll be there right away. And ask Connie to change, too."

Gently she placed Susie's body near the door. Before turning off the light, she walked back and carefully covered her old friend with a corner of the rug.

Connie was already in bed—face to the wall, silent.

"I know you're not asleep," Denise told her after switching on the lamp. "You should be ashamed of yourself—you know very well that it was not Paula's fault."

Connie refused to make a sound.

145

Paula found a pair of John's flannel pajamas and turned the switch for the electric blanket to High. She was uneasy. The warm shower had been pleasant; she was comfortable enough, yet she felt a hint of an ache far down in her back. Sleep would not come. She stared at the ceiling. Connie's eyes mocked her; the sound of her voice still echoed in her ears. Misgivings assailed her. *Will she hate her brother or sister as she hates me? Will bitterness and discord bring misery and heartbreak where we expected such great happiness? Is it, after all, impossible to be a good stepmother? Oh, John,* she pleaded, *what can I do?*

Tears came easily. Reaching out for a tissue on the table, she felt a sharp, knifelike pain in her back. A low cry escaped her, as she almost doubled over, and a terrifying thought came to her. Her hands were wet with perspiration. *It can't be,* she thought, *it can't. It's too soon. I'll lie real quiet. It's only a backache. Maybe I lifted too hard on that branch, or wrenched something when I stumbled.*

When no additional stab of pain occurred after fifteen minutes, she felt relieved and attempted to sleep. How she longed to be able to turn onto her side, but that would have to wait a few weeks. The only fairly comfortably position now was flat on her back.

She was dozing off when a sudden attack came again. She held her breath and clenched her teeth. In a few moments the pain subsided, but the truth was there.

Dear God, she prayed, *what am I going to do? This is it, I'm sure, and I better do something quick before it's too late.* She dressed as rapidly as possible . . . *I'll have to call a cab immediately,* she decided.

Denise heard her movements and came to the door, rubbing her eyes. "Can't you sleep, Paula? I can't, either."

Another twist in her back caused Paula to hang onto a chair.

"What's wrong?" Denise cried. "Are you all right?"

"The baby's coming, Denise," she said when the spasm was over. "I've got to call a cab right away. Will you please find the number for me?"

Denise was wide-awake. She grabbed the phone book in the upstairs hall and paged feverishly. "Here, the Red Checker, 753-3880."

"Dial it, please. I'll talk to them."

Denise dialed and waited, a puzzled look on her face.

"It's not ringing, Paula," she said, "I can't hear anything at all."

"Try again, Denise. Maybe you dialed the wrong number."

Denise dialed again, carefully. Then shook her head.

"No, Paula. It's not working."

Paula gripped the back of the chair. "Denise—Oh, no! The storm—the wires must be down. Perhaps when the branch broke. What are we going to do?"

"I could run to the Hargroves," Denise offered.

Paula shook her head. "They're not back from Florida. Remember? No, I'll have to drive myself to the hospital."

"No, you can't," Denise objected. "Please, Paula, you can't go by yourself."

"You're right," Paula agreed. "I can't go by myself. Connie will have to drive."

She flicked on the light in the girls' room. Connie showed no sign of being awake.

Firmly Paula placed her hand on the girl's arm and spoke to her, "Connie, I know you hate me. But right now we can't think of that. The baby is coming, and you will have to drive me to the hospital. There is no other way. The phone is out of order."

She drew her breath in and held it until another pain receded.

147

With her face still to the wall, Connie answered, "You know I've had only three lessons. I can't do it."

"There is no other way," Paula said. "You must help me."

Abruptly Connie turned to face Paula. "I won't do it," she said sharply.

Paula looked at Connie sternly and said, "For your father's sake, and for the sake of the love he now has for you, you will drive me to the hospital. How you feel about me doesn't matter in the least right now. You can hate me all you want. But we must think of the baby."

Connie stared at Paula for a few seconds; then stubborn refusal surrendered to the look in her stepmother's eyes. Without a word she got out of bed and began to dress hurriedly.

"I can't back it out of the garage," she said when they were ready to leave the house.

"I'll help you," Paula told her. "Maybe I can back it out at least a little, and then you can continue."

The wind was blowing hard, although not in the angry gusts of an hour ago. But it was still raining and turning colder.

Another sharp pain harrowed Paula; this time her entire body seemed involved. She pushed against the door and clenched her fists as tightly as possible. When it decreased, she said, "Now, let's go quickly."

Connie gave her a searching look; Denise took her arm and helped her to the car.

"We better take the anti-frost spray with us," Paula advised.

As quickly as her movements allowed, Paula started the car and was able to back it into the street. Then she slid away from the wheel.

Connie went around the car and got in. "I can't," she

148

wailed. "I can't. I'm afraid. I've driven a car only three times."

"Yes, you can; you must," Paula insisted. "You know the basics. We'll take it as slowly as possible."

The quiet strength in Paula's voice urged her on. She followed instructions carefully. The initial start was an abrupt one, and the car lurched forward. However, with Paula's suggestions and directions, Connie gained confidence.

"Take the cutoff onto Seventh Street," Paula said.

She pushed her feet down hard on the floorboard when another pain came. There was no doubt whatever by now. She knew it was necessary to get to the hospital quickly.

The windshield was beginning to freeze over, and the wipers would not clean it. "I can't see," Connie cried.

"Stop," Paula ordered. "Denise please take the anti-frost and spray the entire windshield."

It helped considerably, and Connie was doing nicely. Paula gripped the edge of the seat tightly and bit her lips to hold back a cry.

Seventh Street was straight; traffic was nonexistent at midnight. The rain continued, freezing as it fell.

"Don't even stop for stop signs. If there's no one coming," Paula urged, "just keep going."

"There's a tree in the way up ahead," Connie cried.

Quickly Paula appraised the situation. "You can squeeze by on the left side," she said. "Just keep going—don't let the motor stop."

"I'm afraid," Connie wailed. "I'll hit the curb on the other side."

"No, I don't think so," Paula encouraged her. "Just keep on. You're doing well. Only three more blocks."

It was urgent now; the pains were coming at regular and close intervals.

Connie headed the Mustang over to the left. The tires scraped on the curb, the branches of the tree scraped the side of the car; but she made it.

"Good girl," Paula praised her. "You're all right."

Denise, on the edge of the back seat, let out her breath.

"You can too drive," she told Connie, proudly.

However, attempting the curve onto the slight grade at the hospital entrance, Connie pulled the wheel too sharply to the right, then, sensing her error, she turned quickly to the left. By now the streets were becoming an icy glaze, and she lost control of the car. The front wheels went over the curb and into a large, bare shrub. They stopped with a jolt, and Paula moaned. She bent over and cried out, "Denise, run in and tell anyone in the office that it's an emergency. Run! Run!"

Denise was out of the car before Paula stopped talking.

In a few minutes they were inside. Paula sat in a wheelchair, again tortured by a spasm of pain. Perspiration covered her brow; she was breathing heavily.

"Connie," she called, "call your father. You know where to reach him." Her eyes implored Connie's help.

Connie nodded her head—and in one, sudden movement she was kneeling near Paula.

Tears streamed down her cheeks; her hands gripped the wheelchair. "Paula, Paula," she sobbed. "Please don't die! I'm sorry. I don't hate you, I don't. I didn't mean all those horrible things I said."

The wall had finally tumbled and was crumbling away.

Despite Paula's pain and discomfort, she put her arms around the weeping girl, and with her own eyes filled with tears, said to her. "I won't die, dear. Certainly not now. Thank you—thank you for getting us here. Call your daddy now. Your brother can't wait much longer."

In Chicago, John was frantic. The sleet storm was worse

there than farther to the west. The details were unimportant to him now; all that mattered was that Paula was in the hospital, and he was not there with her.

"Call the floor nurse," he ordered Connie when she phoned him.

Miss Burns assured him that everything was being done for Paula; she was already in the labor room.

"Let me call you the moment the baby is here," she suggested quietly, in her controlled voice.

"Yes, please do that," he pleaded, and turned away from the phone with a prayer, *Oh, God, take care of her.*

A panicky, wild two hours later the phone rang in his room.

"'Daddy,'" Connie cried out to him, joyfully, "we have a baby brother. Oh, he's so tiny."

"How's Paula?" was John's first concern.

"She's fine, Daddy, just fine. She's sleeping now, but Miss Burns said for you not to worry; everything's all right."

"Thank God!" John said fervently. "I'll be there just as soon as I can. The street crews are already working."

The wind had quieted down to a breeze; the sleet was now light and mixed with snow. It was turning much colder. The highways were slick, but sanding crews were busy, and John drove on. He reached the hospital in time to see Paula's Mustang being pulled out of the bare bridal wreath shrub.

Grace DenBoer was at the switchboard. "Good morning, John," she greeted him cheerfully, "and congratulations!"

"Thank you, Grace," John answered, "but how, and where, is my wife?"

"She's in 503 and feeling fine. Waiting for you."

John was already on his way.

EPILOGUE

AT HOME, A WEEK later, Connie and Denise stood near their brother's crib.

"His fingernails look like tiny, pink pearls," Denise said softly.

"And just think," Grandmother Adams said with twinkling eyes, "those pink pearls will be covered with grease and mud someday, like his father's have been. Even looks like his daddy."

Just then a smile flickered across the baby's face.

"He's still playing with the angels," Mrs. Russell reflected.

John and Paula smiled at each other.

Both girls looked up, and Connie said, "When he grows up, he'll call you 'Mother,' won't he?"

"Yes, he will," Paula answered.

"Well, won't it be confusing to him," Denise asked, "if we call you 'Paula' and he calls you 'Mother'?"

"We'll have to explain it to him," John said.

Connie hesitated a second, then said, "We've been thinking about it. Wouldn't it be simpler if we also called you 'Mother'?"

Paula's heart skipped a beat, then pounded in her ears.

Joyously, with tears and laughter, she opened her arms to her family, as she whispered, "Thank You, Lord, thank You."

FOUNTAIN OF LOVE

Lydia Heermann

To my husband, Dexter Daniels, Jr., my source of never-ending love

—VSD

and

For those who cared enough during the dark days to light up my life with love and joy

—PEK

"For there is in every creature a fountain of life which, if not choked back by stones and other dead rubbish, will create a fresh atmosphere, and bring to life fresh beauty."

Margaret Fuller (Ossoli)
1810–1850

CHAPTER 1

THROUGH A BRIDAL-VEIL MIST, the silver Mercedes sped into the night—the laughing couple inside oblivious to the danger looming just around the next bend in the freeway. Suddenly—out of nowhere—jackknifed across the rainslick road—was a huge fuel tanker, forming a solid, immovable object. The mist lifted momentarily as the driver of the silver sports car looked on in horror. There was a squeal of brakes and a frantic turn of the wheel before impact. A split second later, both vehicles were engulfed in flames . . .

"No! No! Stop! Please stop!" Joy Lawrence screamed, her fists clenched, tears raining down her cheeks. Her eyes flew open as she pulled herself to a sitting position in bed, her slim body beneath the delicate fabric of her nightgown damp with perspiration.

The ribbon of moonlight filtering through her bedroom window told Joy it was still nighttime. Over two hundred and fifty nights since the accident. At least a hundred nightmares as cruelly vivid as this one.

9

"Stop it! Stop it!" she shrieked. But there was no one to hear her except Granny, her calico cat, who was deep in her mice-and-cream dream world. The outburst shattered the last remnants of Joy's terror. She lay spent in the gray shadows of the pre-dawn, afraid that the nightmare would recur if she went back to sleep. She threw the covers aside and stepped from her bed, hours before her sleep was satisfied.

She flipped on her bedside lamp. Restless and distraught, Joy's eyes darted around the room. The familiarity of her surroundings temporarily comforted her.

As one of Atlanta's leading dress designers, Joy had decorated her small, five-room cottage with a romantic flavor—reminiscent of English countryside hospitality. A plush, mauve carpet covered the floors throughout the house, providing a soft backdrop for both the muted tones and startling decorator colors she had chosen.

Joy's bed, her own original design, had been featured in *House and Garden* magazine. She had worked with a master craftsman to create the look of a window box of flowering violets. The base of the bed was made of wood and stained with a black matte finish. The open, ruffled canopy was a veritable garden of hand-stitched purple violets. The soft curtains were drawn back with pull-cord streamers of pastel green silk to simulate the stems of the violets. She had appliqued garlands of violets on the bedlinens.

A petit point picture in lavender yarn on a creamy background carried out the delicate floral motif with the embroidered words: "Forget-me-not, the bluebell, and that Queen of Secrecy, the violet . . ." Keats.

Nestled in the corner of the studio bedroom was Joy's oversized working table of pristine white flagstone, providing an interesting background for living things—a brass urn of feathery ferns. Shimmering fabric samples and sketches

10

of party clothes for her clients were strewn over the surface of the desk. The list of those who engaged Joy's services to design their clothes read like the *Who's Who* of Atlanta.

Joy pulled her parfait pink robe around her shoulders and sat down at her worktable. Perhaps an hour or two of hard work would dispel the memory of the terrible dream. She fingered the drawings of two of the gowns she had recently designed for the leading social event of the year—the Piedmont Hospital Ball. The gowns had been designed for two of her favorite customers, Mrs. Lenora Hewett and Colonel Carr's wife, Helen.

She looked with decided approval at the Hewett design. She had used scarlet satin, richly embellished with exotic Persian flowers. Mrs. Hewett left all the details of style and color up to Joy. Her only request was that the gown and her walking cane must match. Joy had chosen a rich walnut stick and had taken it to Monsieur Berlien at the Berlien Jewelers on the Park. Monsieur had studded the walking cane with rubies. The total effect of the ensemble defied description.

Mrs. Hewett's breath had caught in mid-air at the first sight of her ensemble. She didn't speak for a few moments and then she exclaimed, "Joy Lawrence, you are a genius! You have the creativity of your mother, and the class of Coco Chanel, Dior, and Schiaparelli all rolled into one gorgeous lady!" Joy had delighted in her friend's satisfaction.

Mrs. Carr's ball gown was, of course, very different. Each of Joy's designs was unique—never duplicating a single feature of another design. She smiled now as she recalled Helen's reaction the first time she saw the sketch for her gown. In lady-like fashion, she had nearly exploded! "Joy, I didn't think I had to tell you after all these years . . . you know my gowns are always to be white, beige, or

11

cream. My goodness, that does not anymore look like me than . . ."

"Now, now, Mrs. Carr. You are under no obligation to accept these drawings or my ideas. I just thought with your divine figure, your peach-blossom complexion, and the dancing lights in your strawberry-blonde hair, it was high time you selected something not resembling a lady quail," Joy retorted as light-heartedly as possible.

Mrs. Carr was a bit taken aback by Joy's reply and decided to trust the expertise of the young designer. The gown was of glorious silk gazar, as deeply and mysteriously purple as a precious amethyst. The low-backed silhouette gave it an air of tender femininity, embraced by an orchid capelet. On the day after the creation was delivered to the Carr home, a note came to The Boutique from Colonel Carr by special messenger. It read simply: "Helen's gown —pure ecstasy!"

Usually Joy could lose herself for hours in the dreamy images of her drawings, but not tonight. Normally her cottage was a secure haven. Tonight she felt as though the walls were closing in on her, suffocating her.

Perhaps a few deep breaths of the crisp night air would balance her teetering emotions. Joy removed the bolt lock on the sliding-glass doors which disappeared between the bedroom and the trellised area opening into a mini-porch. She stepped out barefooted and inhaled the chilly March air. Exhale . . . inhale . . . exhale. She felt calmer, more relaxed. She went back into her bedroom and locked the doors. Suddenly the nightmarish fear swept over her again and she felt she had to get out of the room . . . out of the house.

She grabbed a pair of white, wrinkled slacks and a multi-striped blouse that was thrown over the chair. Quickly she slipped into her tennis shoes without even bothering to tie

12

the laces. She scooped the cat out of her warm basket and dashed out to her car. Granny curled up in the seat beside her mistress and went right back to sleep. Joy turned the ignition key and her red Mustang convertible began to hum as she shoved it into reverse and backed recklessly out of her open garage. A fast drive with her windows down might help her to forget. At least, perhaps it would steady her rapid pulse and lift the depression that had crushed down upon her.

I'm losing my mind, Joy thought. *Otherwise why would I be driving sixty miles an hour at four o'clock in the morning—going nowhere!*

Even at that hour the city of Atlanta was teeming with life. She careened around the corner of Peachtree Street and flipped off her automatic cruise control. Her car coasted back to the acceptable speed limit. The spectacular Hyatt Regency with its glass tower addition loomed ahead. Her spirits were buoyed briefly as she thought of the exotic birds and the glass elevators in the atrium-lobby. But the uplift in Joy's mood was short-lived.

"Am I crazy? What is happening to me?" she cried out in desperation. But there was not a sound except the steady breathing of the cat.

Now as she drove through the streets of Atlanta lined with darkened houses, she wondered how any of the population could be sleeping peacefully. The city sounds of the early morning—the clatter of milk and produce trucks, garbage vehicles, mail carts, a few tipsy party-goers singing as they toddled down the sidewalks—only added to her restlessness.

Slowly Joy began to reconstruct in her mind the events of the previous evening. What had she done to trigger the nightmare? She had taken a languorous bubble bath and settled down with a romantic novel, *Cherry Blossom Prin-*

13

cess, by her friend Marjorie Holmes. On page 124 she had read, "Little girls your age should be in bed." She smiled to herself and marked the page so that she could pick up where she had stopped reading. She was no little girl, but the advice was applicable to big girls as well.

That was the last thing she remembered before falling asleep. And now here she was, too tired and confused to think clearly. She turned on the radio to see if some early morning music would calm her nerves, then reached over to rub her pet's soft fur.

Joy had found Granny the day she moved into her cottage. The cottage had originally belonged to Joy's parents and was nestled in a secluded corner on the grounds of the estate. Faire and Townsend Lawrence had intended it to be used as a recreation house, but it seemed an equally delightful spot for the grandparents when they came for a visit. Thereafter the small cottage was called "Granny's flat." That's why, on the night Joy had found the half-starved calico cat in the shrubbery, the name had stuck. And when she noticed the cat's unusual eyes—one, a brilliant blue; the other, as yellow as topaz—she knew Granny had found a home. "Why, you belong here with me!" Joy had exclaimed. "Topaz is my birthstone, and you are certainly the best birthday present I've ever received."

Not only did Granny provide her with companionship, but often with excuses. Joy smiled to herself as she thought of the number of times young men had telephoned her for a date, and she had explained coyly, "Sorry, but I have to stay home with Granny tonight." She always hoped they would never discover that Granny was not an adorable little old lady, but rather a peculiar, odd-eye calico cat. Granny returned Joy's pamperings with her own brand of love— purrs and soft, furry rubs against Joy's ankles.

The night ride for cat and mistress had been going on for

more than an hour when Joy noticed that the gas gauge was registering almost empty. Nearing the Druid Hills section of Atlanta, she decided the wisest thing to do was to stop at The Boutique and wait until morning. She made two right turns and parked her Mustang under the porte-cochere. The cat peeked up over the window to see what was happening, then curled up and promptly went back to sleep.

Joy squinted in the semi-darkness. The March sky was beginning to lighten a bit with splashes of gray and pink stripes. The dove-colored pre-dawn matched Joy's mood. She continued to study the shoppe, a wedding present from her father to her mother. She had made few changes since she had become the proprietor.

Will I ever stop missing them? she thought. They had given such permanence and substance to her life. Somehow they had implanted their strong Christian beliefs in her heart from the time she was old enough to understand. They had guided her without dictating, and this had allowed her to grow in her faith as she had grown physically. "I wonder if I ever told them enough how much I appreciated them?" she spoke aloud. "I'm a lucky woman—wonderful parents, this beautiful shoppe, the best clients in Atlanta, and my friend Ellen to help me run it. Well, if I'm so blessed, then what's the matter with me? Why am I behaving like some kind of immature brat?"

Joy picked up her cat, cradled her lovingly in her arms and made her way to the nearest side door. She unlocked the door and turned off the alarm system to prevent setting it off as she entered. The serenity of the posh interior was in direct contrast to the seething emotions inside her.

She put the snoozing cat on a nearby footstool and then sat down at her desk. She ran her fingers through her tangled hair. Her emotions were still ricocheting off her rib cage and into the pit of her stomach like a pair of racquet balls. She

15

was not accustomed to wasting time. But she had no interest in doing anything that required effort. She rested her arm on the desk and laid her head down to wait for Ellen. Sleep took over for at least a moment.

CHAPTER 2

ELLEN TURNER COULDN'T shake the uneasy feeling that had hovered over her since the wee hours of the morning. In all of her fifty-two years she had never felt so disturbed, although she could not think of a proper reason. Her breathing reflected her nervousness as she hummed short snatches of familiar tunes. Her stride was long for her petite frame, which she kept firm and lithe with regular exercise. She raced along at almost a jogging tempo.

Gray shadows played through the giant oaks that lined the boulevard. The sun, struggling to peek through, rested its first beams on the oversized azalea bushes and dogwood trees. Atlanta had always been Ellen's home. Though she had looked at these same trees, these same bushes, these same shops every morning for as long as she could remember, she had never tired of them.

She tried to think of little things—like the letters she must mail, the fur boots in the window of Rich's, the milk she needed to pick up after work. But the wary feeling that sat now on her shoulders crowded out her thoughts.

Click—click—click. The sound of her boot heels was all Ellen could hear, along with the muffled sound of early morning traffic. The leftovers of winter in the form of a chilly frost had turned the Georgia clay to iron. The sidewalks were merely a thin, piecrust topping for the hardened soil.

She stopped at the corner stand to purchase her usual newspaper from old Mr. Johnson. The date on the paper read: Tuesday, March 1.

"Good morning, Mrs. Turner."

"Good morning to you, Mr. Johnson."

"Ma'am, it seems like you and I are the only folks up early this morning. When it's nippy, folks hate to roll out of bed," he chuckled good-naturedly.

"I don't blame them a bit. But I like to get to The Boutique early and tidy things up before Miss Lawrence arrives at noon," replied Ellen.

"Noon! Folks waste the best part of the day when they lazy around until noon."

Ellen searched in her purse for some coins.

"Lazy? Well, if there is one thing Joy Lawrence isn't, it's lazy," Ellen retorted. "She's just like her mother. She gets up before the sun. Then she does some of her dress-designing in the quiet of her home before she comes to the shoppe. No, Mr. Johnson, Joy doesn't have a lazy bone in her body."

"Oh, no ma'am, I didn't mean Miss Joy was lazy. Never was finer folks in this world than the Lawrences. Mr. Townsend was the kindest, most generous man I ever met. Sometimes he'd buy a paper and tip me a five-spot. I'll always remember the day they had that terrible automobile accident. When I heard about it, I cried. I had lost a good friend—me, just a nobody and him a mighty big man. But he called me 'friend.' When my wife was sick, well, he sent his doctor to see her. She'd have been dead if it hadn't been for Mr. Townsend.

"Rich? Sure they was. But they was never ones to flaunt it or brag. Seems like they had more fun helping other folks with their money than they did spending it on themselves. Beatenes' thing I ever run across. Nope, there aren't many folks around like the Lawrences. Too bad, too."

Ellen hoped the old man's chatter would soon come to a stop. Memories were hard for Ellen. But no such luck. Mr. Johnson took a deep breath to choke back the tears in his quivering voice.

"Yessirree, I remember it like it was yesterday. And it's been pretty nearly a year. The newspaper called him a 'self-made financial wizard.' And Mrs. Lawrence, she was as pretty as a picture. The newspaper said her name was Faire—Faire Lawrence. Well, her mama sure named her right. Sure is nice you and Miss Joy kept Mrs. Lawrence's dress shoppe. I know she's looking down mighty proud."

One thing about Mr. Johnson, he surely was a "talker." Ellen was having trouble finding her coins through the tears that had brimmed over when the old man began to talk about Townsend and Faire Lawrence. She found her money, counted it out, picked up a newspaper, and put it in her carry-all bag.

The traffic light signaled "Walk" and she hastened to cross the street. The conversation with Mr. Johnson had done nothing to perk up her spirits. She had tried for the sake of herself and Joy not to dwell on the deaths of her friends. Ellen had plunged into a therapeutic frenzy of work. She had become Joy's surrogate mother, her best friend, her business partner.

"If I had been fortunate enough to have a daughter of my own, I would not love her any more than I do that girl," she muttered as she walked.

And so, Joy and Ellen—one, young and vivacious; one, middle-aged and lonely—reached out to each other in their mutual loss. Sharing their grief somehow made it more bearable.

Ellen rounded the corner leading to The Boutique. *Where have all the years gone?* She continued her reminiscing as she hurried along. She smiled to herself. She had to admit that she was comfortable and pleased with her life.

Joy and The Boutique are my life now, she mused.

Ellen's thoughts were still skittering about when the shoppe came into view. Old oaks formed an umbrella over the green-and-white canopy that led from the street to the heavy, walnut door of the salon. A small, bronze plate read simply, "The Boutique."

Ellen put her key in the lock at the same moment she spotted Joy's Mustang in the carport. Her spirits soared like sunshine. She could hardly wait to tell Joy about the new orders they had already received since the weekend ball. Their work calendar rotated around three major Atlanta social events: the prestigious Piedmont Hospital Ball held annually on the last Friday in January, at the Piedmont Driving Club; the Crawford W. Long Hospital Benefit Ball, held at the Cherokee Town Club in February; and the late summer Debutante Ball.

She turned her key and stepped onto the plush, pink Oriental rug. The rug unified the rooms of the salon with a muted variant of the luscious color. A love seat with deep cushions of rose velvet added to the elegance. A scroll-topped armoire dominated the entry, and an antique cherry cabinet displayed an assortment of miniature porcelains, among them Joy's favorite—the Boehm pink perfection camellia.

"It's me!" Ellen called cheerily. There was no reply, but the faint scent of Joy's perfume permeated the rooms.

"It's me, dear. I'm going to open the draperies and I'll be right there."

Still there was no reply. It was nothing more than an unsteady sensation. But Ellen didn't like it.

The sounds of silence were eerie. She could have heard a pin drop, a page turn, a muffled sigh. But there was nothing. Ellen quickly turned on the lights. She forgot all about opening the draperies as she hurried to the back of the shoppe.

Her breath almost stopped. Joy was slumped over her desk, her shoulders shaking with inaudible sobs.

Ellen's eyes widened in disbelief. Feverishly she unbuttoned her blue coat, kicked her sturdy walking boots to one side, and rushed over to Joy.

"What is it, dear?" she asked.

Joy, always immaculately groomed, was a mess. She was as pale as alabaster. Her eyelids were swollen as she looked up at her friend. Large, unchecked tears came in floods down her cheeks and soaked her rumpled blouse. She looked as if she had slept in her clothes.

"I—I don't know, Ellen! I feel crazy . . . almost like I'm having a nervous breakdown. I'm coming apart inside!" The buzz saw whining in her head was so loud that she was surprised Ellen couldn't hear it.

Ellen waited, not interrupting to calm the sobs that came now in huge gulps. When the crying subsided, she said quietly, "You are not having a nervous breakdown. You are not crazy. You are not coming apart. Joy Lawrence, you are just exhausted, bone-weary, fatigued," she emphasized. "You haven't done anything but work, work, work these past nine months. You haven't taken off one single holiday. Now, young lady, work is the best antidote for grief that I know anything about. But *overwork* is another thing. You are killing yourself."

21

The younger woman snuffled, blew her nose, and began to pour out her heart to her friend. "I had another of those awful nightmares, Ellen. I saw Mother and Daddy's car burst into flames when it struck the tanker, and no one could get them out! It was as clear as if I had been there and had seen it myself!"

Ellen was familiar with Joy's nightmares. She had spent more than one night comforting her young friend—hearing her out as she poured out her grief—preparing warm milk so that she could slip into dreamless sleep.

"What can I do to help?" Ellen coaxed.

"Nothing. I have to get myself together. No one can do it for me. I pray, but God seems so far away. Sometimes I think He's left me, too."

"Of course He hasn't! Joy, God is with you all the time. He was there last night. He is here now. You just *feel* far from Him because your mind and body are exhausted. He will never leave you and, when you get through this terrible ordeal, you will feel even closer to Him than before. I know you find that hard to believe now, but it will happen. Just remember that," she explained to Joy softly.

There was silence for what seemed like a very long time. Joy was the first to speak. Her voice quavered.

"I've had a long night to think about things—a lot of things. I need to get away for a while. What would you say if I took off a few days, maybe a couple of weeks. I hate myself. I don't feel like designing another gown. I even dread coming to The Boutique some days. Does any of this make sense?"

"Perfectly good sense!" Ellen affirmed. "I say *go*. What you need is a good dose of sunshine, sand, and sea. Don't worry about me. Granny and I will take care of everything. And for goodness' sakes, don't worry about this shoppe!"

Joy felt tiny fingers of relief creep up her spine, soothing taut nerves and muscles. Having made the decision, she was already beginning to feel better. She stood up suddenly. As she did, she caught her own reflection in the full-length mirror. she could not believe what she saw—raggedy lines across her salty, stained face; hair that had been combed with her fingers; wrinkled clothes.

"Is this really me?" she gasped.

Ellen laughed. "I'm afraid so. While you put yourself back together, I'll fix you a strong cup of coffee and a croissant. The society section of the paper should have the pictures of the Ball. Why don't you check?" Ellen put down the newspaper and disappeared into the kitchenette.

As Joy read the society news, noting with satisfaction the accuracy of the reporter's descriptions of the gowns, Ellen poured the coffee into a delicate Lenox china cup. She buttered the croissant and added a generous dollop of orange marmalade. She smiled at Joy. "I'm making your reservations this very morning."

"Where am I going?" Joy giggled.

"To Boca Raton, Florida, my dear. When you were just a little girl and visited there with your family, you would say, 'I love this place better than anywhere in the world. If I ever run away, you can find me in Boca Raton.' Now you are a big girl, and I say run away to Boca Raton!" Ellen threw her head back and laughed. Her laughter, like the tinkle of silver bells, was so like her mother's that Joy felt a momentary pang of nostalgia.

"It sounds perfect!" she said. "To tell you the truth, I'm glad I don't have to make another decision. My brain is as full of cobwebs as my hair is full of tangles," Joy called back over her shoulder as she went into the bathroom to freshen up. She could remember with fondness the Cloister—pink stucco, the soft glow of candlelight falling on old damask, warm hospitality.

She was in better spirits, though she didn't look a great deal better. Mechanically Joy tended to some paperwork at her desk. *Maybe tomorrow a new life will begin for Joy Lawrence,* she fantasized. *Off with the old me and on with the new.*

Tuesday was always a slow day in the shoppe. Both of the women welcomed the inactivity. Ellen answered the telephone, talked to a few customers who wandered in, and made Joy's airline reservations for the following morning. And as if in confirmation of her plans, there was a cancellation at the Cloister. Joy's room was in the west wing of the elegant, old hotel. So far, so good.

By five o'clock, they were already getting into the Mustang, with Ellen holding Granny. They drove home in silence. Both women were worn out from the strain of the day. They looked forward to hot showers and an early bedtime.

Joy was grateful for Ellen's company. Maybe she would be spared another nightmare tonight. At least she wouldn't feel the aching loneliness.

Joy's home was only a short drive from The Boutique and little more than fifteen minutes from the bustling center of Atlanta. The cottage, at the end of a tranquil, dogwood-lined lane, had an aura of romantic legend about it. Squirrels darted from tree to tree in an apparent 'welcome home' gesture. The cottage shone brightly since, in her hasty early-morning departure, Joy had forgotten to turn out the lights.

Ellen was as familiar with Joy's home as she was her own. She kept a nightgown, toothbrush, a set of electric curlers, and a complete change of clothes there. They came in handy when the two worked late, the weather was too bad to take the bus to the suburbs, or an emergency arose.

"Dear, why don't you go take a leisurely shower and put on your gorgeous panne velvet caftan with the rose, mint, and champagne stripes," Ellen suggested. "You always feel better when you wear it. I'll put linens on the sofa bed."

As she went into the living room, Ellen remembered how surprised she had been the first time she saw it after Joy's redecorating spree. With the mauve carpet, she had chosen as the predominant color a rich aubergine. Joy called it an "eggplant purple."

Noting her friend's expression, Joy had quickly said, "Before you say one single word, Ellen, let me show you how this shade looks at night in my magical world of candlepower!" Joy had always loved candlelight. She loved to eat by it, entertain by it and, as a little girl, she had insisted on having her own bedside candle to light each night.

Groupings of candles dominated the room now—short ones; chunky ones; tall, skinny tapers. There were so many that, when lighted, they almost matched the lamps with their luminosity. Depending on the natural, artificial, or candlelight, the aubergine changed dramatically. The effect was breathtakingly beautiful.

"One reason you are the best couturière in the business is your sensitivity to color," Ellen had congratulated Joy on her choice of the unusual combination.

As the older woman made the bed, Joy got her luggage out of the foyer closet. She decided on one large suitcase, a cosmetic carrier, and her airplane-weight hanging bag. Then she began to select her clothes for the trip, being careful to place sheets of crisp, scented tissue paper between her garments.

"I'm getting hungry," Ellen remarked. "How about one of your favorite Turner omelets oozing with cheese, a green salad, and a cup of tea?"

"Perfect!" Joy exclaimed. "You always know what I want even before I do."

She welcomed the few moments alone to pack, making mental notes of the accessories she would need. *That's another nice thing about Ellen. She senses when I need her and when I need to be alone,* Joy thought. What should she wear on the plane? Boca Raton would be so much warmer than Atlanta. She was quick to decide on a tailored two-piece dress in teal blue, with shutter tucking, soft, inverted pleats, and a crisp tuxedo collar, with a kicky, black bow tie at the neckline. She chose a white mohair coat to carry on the plane and sling-back lizard sandals. She carefully attached her tiny, crystal cat pin with its topaz eye and 14-karat gold trim to the left shoulder of the bodice. The pin had been a gift from Ellen on her twenty-first birthday.

Joy's melancholy mood was still hanging heavy when she reached into her closet and accidentally brushed against the peach silk garment bag made especially for "the dress." She remembered with elation the circumstances behind the creation of this gown. She lifted the cover and, even though she had been the designer, she admired the work as if it had been done by someone else. Now her thoughts wandered back to the day in the shoppe when a flinty, old dowager had asked Joy, "Are you anywhere near the designer your mother was?"

When she had left without placing an order, Joy had said to Ellen, "There will never be another designer like Mother. You know that. After all, you and Mother were friends all of your lives, Ellen. She was able to create in each of her clients the joy of feeling feminine—to be pretty, desirable, and ladylike all at the same time. But I can't let *her* designs be *my* designs. I have some ideas of my own, and it's high time I expressed them!"

Ellen had not said a word. She had been waiting for the

26

moment when Joy would begin to assert her individuality. She knew, too, that if one human effort could help her young friend overcome her grief, it would be work.

Joy remembered how she had begun to sketch. She would make line drawings, then tear them up in frustration. For a while there was nothing but huge wads of paper cluttering her desk. But at least it was a beginning—both to get a hold on her own life and to breathe a fresh spirit into The Boutique.

"I know what I'll do!" Joy had exclaimed, on the verge of an inspiration. "I'll tell John I want to go to the Piedmont Hospital Ball this year—wearing an original design!"

"Good idea!" Ellen had replied. "*This* will be a first. For once, you won't just be there as 'window dressing' for *him.*" Ellen's poor opinion of Joy's fiancé was obvious with every word.

"About John—" Ellen had continued, "do you really think the two of you share the same goals—the same beliefs? You love children, but John is too busy climbing the ladder to success to be much of a father, it seems to me. And what about his faith? Is he a believer like you—or is he drifting? Joy, have you ever considered all of these things —or are you just grasping for someone to hold onto since your mother and father died?"

The words, spoken in love, had stung nevertheless. Joy had paused, sensing that her friend was telling the truth— truth that Joy was not ready to hear. At the moment she had chosen to ignore the reference to John.

"Today I will design the most beautiful gown in the world," she bubbled. "There will never again be anything like this one. My reputation and yours, Ellen, rests on the reaction to this gown."

Sitting on the side of her bed, Joy still believed that the gown was one of the prettiest she had ever seen.

Black. I'm glad that I made the skirt of rich, black velvet.

27

Black is a color with intense impact—it says you are expecting things to happen. How true that was when I wore it! She laughed aloud. Her thoughts continued. She had decided on the decoration for the bodice from a delicate bone china hairpin tray that her grandmother had given her. A cloisonné butterfly decorated the tray. When she had turned it over, tiny letters on the back spelled out, "Painted Lady." And that was what she had called the design for the gown.

She had chosen sheer, Parisian silk mesh, nearly invisible to the naked eye, for the bodice. And then with an artist's eye, she had begun to work, tracing in chalk on the silk mesh a twelve-by-twelve-inch butterfly. She measured and pinned the pattern to the bodice. From wingtip to wingtip, it spanned the entire front of the gown. Each section of the wings was sewn with a single hue of tiny crystals. Divisions of flaming orange, rich purple, sunflower yellow, hot crimson, sky blue, and parrot green crystals transformed the butterfly design into a fantasy. Joy had then used tiny whispers of 14-karat gold thread to form the antennae of the butterfly. She had slipped the bodice over her head and made sure that it fit perfectly her curvaceous figure. Then she took the almost invisible strands of silk and sprinkled tiny, black onyx beads as minute as grains of pepper on the silk mesh, following the lines of her body, giving an air of provocative mystery.

When Ellen had seen the gown for the first time, she had gasped in utter disbelief at its beauty. Joy was completely satisfied with the finished project.

She had worn the gown only once. But once was enough. Atlanta socialites were still talking about it. When she had arrived at the Piedmont Driving Club with John, all eyes had turned in her direction. She could hear the "ooohs" and "aaahs" as she spoke to one friend and then another. Her

28

reputation as a designer had been firmly established that night.

No, she would not take "The Painted Lady" gown with her to Boca Raton. It was not the kind of dress in which one dined alone. But she reveled in the happiness it had once brought to her. She was caressing the gown when her thoughts were interrupted by Ellen's cheerful voice, "Soup's on!"

Joy zipped the garment bag around the gown and joined her friend for supper.

After supper, Joy hugged the older woman impulsively. "I really don't know what I would do without you, Ellen," she said. "Sometimes I miss Mother and Daddy so horribly. It seems that, when they left, they took all the brightness out of my life—all, that is, except for you."

Ellen reached over and patted Joy's hand.

"As they used to tell me," Joy sighed. "Christians shouldn't accumulate their treasures on this earth. Well, I have been richly blessed with material things—but my *real* treasures are surely in heaven now."

Ellen sighed. "Joy, dear, Townsend and Faire would be the last to want you to feel that their love was your only real treasure. Pardon an old lady's preachments, but I think Jesus was talking about His love and the deep joy that one finds in Him whatever the circumstances. I happen to know that you were named for that eternal kind of love—your parents' most priceless possession."

"Oh, Ellen!" Joy choked back the sobs. "Will I ever really feel it again? I know God's promises are true—that only His grace is sufficient—not beautiful gowns, or charming cottages, or even dear friends like you—but He seems so distant, so remote. There is an empty place in my heart—as if it had no home. I'm afraid, Ellen, that right now my feelings don't match my name."

"Then it's fortunate, isn't it, that we don't have to rely on our feelings. Just keep believing, Joy. Just keep believing."

They sat for a moment in companionable silence— Ellen's worn Bible open to her favorite passage—and read together the familiar words that had sustained her through her widowhood and the death of two infant children: "Come to me, all you who are weary and burdened, and I will give you rest. Take my yoke upon you and learn from me; for I am gentle and humble in heart: and you will find rest for your souls."

Before Joy went to sleep, Ellen slipped the Bible into an open suitcase, beneath the scented tissue. It seemed only right that Joy should carry with her this divine Love Letter as she was setting out to put back together the slivers of her broken world.

Morning dawned bright and clear. Both women had slept well and felt refreshed. They ate a quick breakfast and tended to some last-minute details before leaving for the airport. Joy checked the contents of her suitcase, adding her make-up kit. Ellen made up the sofa bed, placed Granny's wicker bed in the Mustang, and carried along some extra cans of cat food. She would drop Joy off at the terminal on her way to The Boutique.

The cat remained unruffled throughout the proceedings; she was as much at home in Ellen's apartment as she was in her own cottage. Granny was then put in her bed on the back seat of the car, the luggage was stowed in the trunk, and Ellen and Joy climbed into the Mustang.

There was a minimum of confusion at the busy Atlanta airport as Ellen drove up to the loading zone. The porters were quick to unload the luggage and check Joy's tickets. Joy hugged her friend, patted Granny, and entered the sliding-glass doors opening into the noisy terminal.

Ellen watched her walk away. *Please, dear Lord, help Joy find You again. She feels so lost and lonely. Show her that she is always surrounded by Your love. And, Lord, please bring back that joyful spirit. I miss the happy girl I knew . . .''*

Her whispered prayer was interrupted by the honking of horns as other passengers rushed to catch planes. Granny whimpered. Ellen accelerated the sporty little car and shot out into the flowing traffic leading from the airport.

CHAPTER 3

THE WARMTH OF THE Florida sunshine and the soft sea breeze performed their magic to produce a slightly more relaxed expression on Joy's face as she waited for the driver to put her luggage into the limousine. She stood facing the breeze, closed her eyes, and breathed deeply.

The beautifully tailored mohair coat that had only hours before felt perfectly comfortable in the brisk air of early-morning Atlanta was now entirely too warm. As she removed the coat, she smoothed the skirt of her teal blue dress. Her shoulder-length hair, dark honey-blond with highlights of pale wheat, glistened in the sun. Even here in Palm Beach where the "beautiful people" congregated, she was striking. To the casual observer, she appeared to be a self-assured and confident young woman. Nothing could have been further from the truth.

Inclement weather at the point of origin had delayed the plane's departure from Hartsfield International, and she had arrived two hours later than anticipated. She was eager to get to the Boca Raton Hotel and Club for a much-needed respite from her problems. She felt they were becoming almost insurmountable. Surely two weeks of solitude in this tropical setting would help her put things into perspective, and she could again function as a happy and productive woman.

Glancing once more at the driver, she realized that he was loading some rich leather luggage into the limo beside hers. It had a distinctly masculine look. The last thing she needed now was to share the ride to the hotel, especially with a man. As far as she was concerned, she wanted to have as little contact with men as possible. Her recent broken engagement to John was still as painful as an open wound. All she wanted now was solitude.

"If I'm riding with *you*, then this trip has definite possibilities." The man's voice startled her.

Turning abruptly, she found herself looking into brown eyes, flecked with gold. They were accentuated by heavy, dark eyebrows, and emphasized by tiny laugh lines creased in a friendly grin. For a long moment she took in no other detail of the man's appearance—just those eyes. Realizing that she was staring, she turned away as he said, "I'm Brett McCort, and you are . . . ?"

Her rotten mood was no reason to forget her manners, she thought, but at this moment she wanted to rebel. She bit back a curt reply, and said, "Joy Lawrence."

"Well, Joy Lawrence, I'm looking forward to knowing you better."

"Don't count on it." Forget the good manners! She wanted to let him know that she needed neither conversation nor companionship. She just wanted to be alone. Why couldn't Greta Garbo have been riding with her instead. *She* would have understood.

Brett gave her a slightly crooked smile that appeared to be a challenge but said nothing. He turned toward her, studying the interesting planes of her face—the perfect symmetry of her features.

Joy sat stiffly erect and stared straight ahead as they pulled away from the airport and headed toward the interstate highway. Her life had crumbled in such a short time, she thought.

It had been only nine months since both of her parents had been killed in a tragic automobile accident on another interstate highway as they were returning home to Atlanta. Joy had been devastated. This tragedy combined with the death of her older brother, Bill, in Vietnam left her completely alone.

Memories ravaged her thoughts like a storm-tossed sea. The painful emotions they evoked were made bearable only because there had been so much love in the family. She recalled how Bill had teased her. "The day they brought you home from the hospital—a tiny, six-pound bundle wrapped in a soft-as-down blanket, Dad told me to climb up on the sofa and stretch out my arms. I was shaking so hard I almost gave you the colic, but you smiled up at me. Then Dad said, 'Billy, little Joy is yours to love and help care for.' It never occurred to me that there were nurses, maids, and two adoring parents looking out after both of us. You were always my private 'charge.' And you know what, sweetheart? I have never stopped feeling you're something very special!"

Now there was no other human being to whom Joy felt special—except, perhaps, to Ellen. When she had turned to John, her fiancé, for help in sorting out the tangle of legal problems arising from the probate of the wills, she had discovered how immature, unfeeling, and unreliable he really was. It was then that she had returned his ring and cancelled all plans for their wedding.

Startled from her reflections, she heard Brett say,

"Someone as beautiful as you shouldn't frown so much. Didn't your mother tell you that your face might freeze like that?"

She turned and with a tired little smile said, "I'm afraid my thoughts weren't happy ones. And I think my face has already frozen like this."

"Then I want to be around for the spring thaw! Anything a stranger could do to help a lady in distress?"

"Thank you, but I really came here to get away for a while. I—I just want to be alone." She didn't mean to be unkind, but the man was so persistent!

He was silent only a short time before beginning another line of questioning. "Are you from Atlanta?"

"Yes—Buckhead."

"Lovely place—I have an apartment near there . . . I'll bet your tyrannical boss sent you down on business, and you're fuming because you won't have time to hit the beaches!" He grinned in triumph.

The man wouldn't give up! "I don't have a boss," she responded coolly.

"Aha! Then *you're* the tyrannical boss—and you're regretting your decision to leave and let someone else mind the store."

"Wrong again!" This time Joy could not restrain a slight smile.

He threw up his hands. "I give up!"

The expression of dismay on his face was so appealing that Joy relented and told him a little more about herself. "I own a small boutique and design a line of clothes that is sold there."

"Ah, I should have known. You really know your colors. The dress you are wearing makes your eyes sparkle like aquamarines."

His approving look did not stop with her eyes, but

traveled down her trim figure, over her shapely legs and to her toes peeking from the sleek, sling-back sandals.

Joy tensed noticeably. She felt the color rush to her cheeks. His attitude was becoming entirely too personal. She turned and looked out the window, putting an end to further conversation.

Before she realized it they had turned onto El Camino Real. It was just as she had remembered. Some of the royal palms had been replaced, but a few remained near the circle. When she was a small girl, she had pretended that the tall palms lining the sides of the wide boulevard were giant soldiers standing at attention while she, the princess in her golden carriage, rode by, waving to the people she passed. How simple and uncomplicated those childhood days had been. Could anyone ever recapture that same happy feeling? How she wished it were possible!

Brett broke the silence. "A quarter for your thoughts."

"Has inflation raised the cost of thoughts *that* much?" Joy smiled in spite of herself.

"Only for special thoughts," he answered. "And anything that could bring a smile like that would be worth a quarter."

"I was just remembering some childhood fantasies I had when I vacationed here with my parents. I used to pretend that I was a princess in a golden carriage riding down this same street." She glanced at him hesitantly, hoping he wouldn't make fun of her.

His expression softened as he said, "I don't find it hard to picture you as a princess. In fact, you seem to fit the part quite well."

The limousine swung off the circle into the palm-lined main entrance to the Cloister. The exit and entrance drives were divided by a wide median, planted with exotic flowers so beautiful that one passing glimpse was never enough.

"Oh, there's Pan!" Joy exclaimed, her face alight with pleasure for the first time since the trip had begun.

Brett, pleased to see her happy expression, urged her to continue. "Who's Pan?" he asked.

"The statue there between the two sets of wrought-iron gates. Don't you know your Greek mythology?"

"No, but you could give me a brief lesson."

She was not sure whether he was teasing her, but she launched forth. "Pan was the god of pastures, forests, and flocks. Various stories are related to Pan. One of them tells that the nymph, Syrinx, fled from him and was transformed into a bed of reeds, whereupon Pan took reeds of unequal length and invented the shepherd's pipe. He challenged Apollo, god of music, to a musical contest. Apollo won and poor Pan had his ears changed to those of an ass for objecting to the decision. When Tiberius was the Roman emperor, it was said that passengers of a ship thought they heard a voice shouting that Pan was dead. The early Christians believed this story was a reference to Christ's birth and an indication that a new era was beginning."

"That's much more interesting than any history lesson I was ever taught," he commented sincerely. "With you as my teacher, chances are that I could improve my limited education."

"From the looks of things, you seem to be quite successful at whatever it is you do. So you must have more than a limited education." She allowed herself to eye him appraisingly.

"Well, I graduated from Auburn University with a degree in architecture, but I majored in football. To tell the truth, I just studied what was necessary to get my degree. Lately I have regretted not having read anything much but professional journals and an occasional Robert Ludlum thriller."

37

Engrossed in conversation, neither realized that the car had stopped and the uniformed doorman was opening the door for Joy. As she started to step out, she turned and gave Brett a goodbye smile.

"You can't get rid of me that easily," he grinned. "I'm staying right here at the Cloister. You thought I'd be staying at the Tower or the Beach Club, right?"

"Right," she admitted.

"Princess, you don't own the copyright on memories. My folks brought me here when I was a child, too, and I enjoy coming back whenever I'm in the area. And besides, when I get home, my mother will insist on knowing about all the changes and the interesting people I've met. You're the most interesting to date!"

He put his hand firmly on Joy's elbow and steered her through the doors into the spacious lobby. As she looked to her left and then to her right, she recognized the ornate ceilings, chandeliers, and arches of all descriptions that had brought world renown to the grand old hotel. A myriad of graceful fishtail palms, green plants, and colorful floral arrangements were a delight to the eyes. All of these and the lovely furnishings gathered from around the world combined to make a truly elegant entrance. It seemed to Joy that she had stepped back in time to the early part of the century. She felt very much at home. Her mother had probably been right when she had said that Joy belonged to 'an earlier time.'

Brett stood patiently watching as she took in every detail, trying to etch each of them indelibly into her mind. Reluctantly she moved toward the registration desk. The clerk smiled at her and told her that Peter, the bellman, would take care of her luggage and show her to her room. He also offered her some brochures that would help her find her way around the huge complex. She flipped through the booklets, admiring photographs of the twenty-six story Tower that loomed beside the Cloister and the Boca Beach Club, which had been built since her last visit.

While Peter was getting her room key from the desk clerk, she told Brett goodbye. Then she followed the pleasant young man who was carrying her luggage to the elevator. As she stepped into the elevator, she heard another bellman call to Peter to hold the door. Brett was following close behind, an impish look in his eye.

When they stopped at the third floor, she realized that he was getting off with her. Had he arranged this? Hadn't she tried to make it clear that she wanted to spend this time completely alone? The relaxed feeling she had begun to enjoy during the latter part of their ride was rapidly dissolving into irritation. She resolved to avoid further contact with him.

As she followed the bellman into her room, she heard Brett's voice call light-heartedly, "Princess, would you believe my room is just next door to yours?"

"Oh, no!" she groaned. Well, that was par for the course. Everything she had attempted lately had gone awry. Why should things change now?

Closing the door, she turned to savor the beauty of the room. Outside, amid all the tropical trees, stood the majestic, old Banyan tree, its leaves glistening in the sun. The rest of the room was just as she had remembered it, but with Brett next door, she felt that she would find it hard to relax. Why did he have to come here—and now—of all times?

Joy kicked off her shoes, slipped out of her dress, and donned an azalea-pink jump suit, trimmed with narrow bands of spring green. She walked to the window and looked at "her" Banyan tree and the golf course on which it stood. It seemed incredible that everything could be so green and spring-like here, when only a few short hours

39

away by plane, the trees were bare, and snow and ice covered the ground. Oh, just to be able to relax in this beautiful place, with no schedules to meet, would be heavenly, she thought. She decided to stretch out on the bed to rest for just a few minutes. Then she would take advantage of that fabulous swimming pool.

The insistent ringing of the phone reached Joy's sleep-drugged brain, and she stirred. Where was she? The room was dark, and she was completely disoriented. At last her eyes became accustomed to the semi-darkness. She turned on the bedside lamp and reached for the phone.

"Hello," she murmured groggily.

"Hi, Joy. Are you ready for dinner?" Brett's voice sounded cheerful and expectant.

Joy grimaced. "I didn't know that we had any plans for dinner, and besides, you waked me!"

"Sorry about that. I bet the frown lines are very deep now. I can almost see them through the phone. But you do have to eat, don't you? I know you didn't have any lunch, because the flight was delayed. Come on now—smile just a little and tell me you will have dinner with me. Why should both of us eat alone?"

"Okay, okay," she quickly replied. She knew he would persist until she gave in. Maybe she could nip this little relationship in the bud before it got completely out of hand.

"Great! Can you be ready in about thirty minutes? And will the 'Court of Four Lions' be all right? It's quiet and casual there—the perfect place to unwind." His voice clearly showed his desire to please.

"Fine," she agreed. I'll be ready in half an hour." She stared at the telephone. If Brett hadn't asked her to dinner, she probably would have either skipped the meal entirely or just picked at her food. With all she had to accomplish in the next two weeks, she didn't need to miss any meals. She had already lost entirely too much weight. Not only were her clothes too large, but her face had become almost gaunt. Yes, she would have this one dinner with him, and then she could spend the rest of her visit alone, as she had intended.

After a quick shower, she went to the huge walk-in closet and looked around approvingly. What a pleasure it was to have room in which to hang an entire season's wardrobe without pushing and shoving hangers back and forth. At the end of the closet was a chest, large enough to accommodate everything from hats to shoes. Joy decided that, when she built a house, she would include a closet like this one. Glancing through her dresses and suits, she selected a ribbon knit skirt and a matching long-sleeved pullover with a flipped-up collar, scalloped along the edge. The hyacinth blue emphasized her eyes that now sparkled under long, curling lashes.

She reached into her small, brocade jewelry roll and lovingly removed an unusual gold locket which had belonged to her maternal grandmother. On the oval face was etched a single delicate rose. Each petal of the rose had been embedded with bits of "rose gold," which had been very popular in her grandmother's time. She opened the locket and studied pictures of her grandparents, looking very solemn, as was the custom for portraits in their day. She carefully fastened the clasp, letting the locket rest just in the curve between her firm, small breasts. The pale blue of her pullover sweater was the perfect backdrop for this treasured keepsake. Only small gold hoops at her ears were needed to complete her outfit.

She checked her make-up once more and ran a comb lightly through her softly waving, shoulder-length hair. Smiling at her reflection in the mirror, she was aware that

41

she already evidenced the refreshing sleep and change of scene. Her spirits lifted.

Promptly at eight-thirty there was a knock on her door. When she opened it and saw Brett standing there, she was startled by his rugged good looks. She had paid little attention to him during the ride from the airport. Now as he stood there smiling, her heart skipped a beat. Quickly she turned to reach for her clutch bag, hoping that her approving glance had not been too obvious.

Brett was the first to speak. "Well! You look as if the nap revived your sagging spirits."

"Yes. I can't remember when I've been able to take a five-hour nap. It was pure luxury," she replied, suddenly realizing that her sleep had been untroubled and—dreamless.

The restaurant was almost completely surrounded by windows overlooking the golf course, now dark and deserted for the day. Brett seemed to belong in a setting like this, she thought. Exposed wooden beams and a massive, but artistic, wooden lighting arrangement in the center gave the room a feeling of an English hunt club. The maitre d' pulled out a comfortable leather-covered chair for Joy as Brett seated himself to her right.

Joy glanced at him appreciatively, noting his neatly tailored navy blazer, pale blue shirt, and khaki slacks. His designer tie showed his excellent taste in clothes. But it was his tanned face, framed by the thick, wavy, dark hair—and his penetrating eyes—that would turn any woman's head.

When Brett asked if he might see a wine list, Joy murmured that Perrier water would be fine. The waiter took the order and departed.

"Well, Princess, we have one more thing in common. I

don't drink either. Guess it's because I really did try to stay in training when I played football at Auburn—or my strict upbringing. My conscience bothered me even if the coaches didn't know when I broke training," Brett confessed.

This was the second time Brett had mentioned his family, Joy observed. Strange how one's background continued to affect every experience of life—even into adulthood. Joy glanced down at the heavy pewter service plates and the usual seven pieces of flatware on the table in front of her. She remembered how her mother had taught her to start with the piece of silver that was on the outside and work toward the plate. It had been so simple after it was explained, but it had been an awesome decision for a small girl.

When the waiter returned with the Perrier water and had taken their dinner orders, Brett turned to Joy and said, "You're smiling to yourself again."

"Yes, I was just thinking what a powerful impression, either good or bad, parents can make on a small child. I was very fortunate to have had two who really cared. . . . Tell me about your family," she said quickly, before Brett could question her.

"My parents live in Atlanta. I have a brother, Scott, who is two years younger than I. He is connected with an insurance firm in Atlanta. My 'little sister,' Laura, is twenty-four and works for a television station there. None of the three of us is married. Mom and Dad think they will *never* have any grandchildren. Apparently they made home so pleasant for us that we all wanted to stay as long as possible. I moved out two years ago at the ripe old age of thirty and got an apartment closer to my office. But Scott and Laura show no signs of cutting the apron strings," he chuckled.

"I can't help but envy you. It would be so wonderful to have a family like yours. You must have had some happy times together."

Brett looked at her quizzically. He wasn't sure if he should ask about her family because such a wistful expression crossed her face when she mentioned them. But without asking, he would never know, so he plunged ahead, "And how about your family?"

Joy winced. It was still so hard to talk about them. "My only brother was killed in Vietnam and both of my parents died in an automobile accident nine months ago." Surely he would not probe further.

Brett watched as her eyes misted and the worry lines appeared once again on her forehead, and wisely refrained from further questions. He smiled sympathetically and said, "Well, I have enough family to spare. Why don't you share mine?"

He was trying so hard to make her feel better. She was touched.

"How do we work out the custody arrangement?" she asked. "Do I get your mom and dad or Scott and Laura?"

With the tension eased, he smiled. The creases that were almost elongated dimples on either side of his mouth deepened, and the laugh lines beside his eyes grew more pronounced. Joy wondered why she had never noticed the deep cleft in his chin. *He has a nice face,* she thought.

"This summer you will have to go with us to our house on Lake Allatoona. We always have a terrific time there. Do you water ski?" he asked.

"I can manage a short distance on two skis, but that's about all. I do like to swim and sail, though."

"With all the McCorts teaching you, it won't be long until you'll be ready for competition at Callaway Gardens," he assured her.

Joy's laughter bubbled forth at the absurd idea. She was startled. How long had it been since she had heard herself laugh?

Brett watched as Joy devoured the last bite of her shrimp, scallop, and mushroom kabobs. How could one small woman consume such enormous amounts of food? She had started her meal with steamed cherrystone clams, followed by soup with large pieces of pita bread that had been dipped in butter, sprinkled with garlic salt and parsley, and broiled lightly. Very little of the mound of spinach salad remained, and now she appeared to be thoroughly enjoying the last tidbit of artichoke with hollandaise sauce.

Brett looked at her now contented face and laughed heartily. "Young lady, I may just have to rent a golf cart to drive you back to your room. You surely can't walk after downing such a meal. And you still have room for *dessert*. Incredible!"

CHAPTER 4

SLOWLY, VERY SLOWLY, Joy opened her eyes. She yawned and stretched languidly, savoring every moment. How long had it been since she had been able to sleep as late as she wanted? Outside, the world was dewy-fresh.

Suddenly a brilliant flash of scarlet caught her eye. She jumped out of bed and rushed to the window. There, sitting on a branch almost close enough for her to touch, was a cardinal. His plumage, so unbelievably red, was in startling contrast to the shiny, dark green leaves of the tree. Joy watched him, entranced with the colors. Maybe, just maybe, she would sketch a dress this morning—emerald green silk with a mandarin collar, accented by vermillion red piping and frog closings—an Oriental design. Yes, that would be striking, she decided. The cardinal, sensing that he was being observed, darted away. Joy's breath caught in her throat. It was almost as if God had sent the bird as a harbinger of hope.

Her adrenalin had begun to flow. She showered quickly and donned a cornflower blue wrap skirt, appliqued with white eyelet butterflies and a matching tee top. She added just a touch of lipstick and blush to her already glowing face, then grabbed her sketch pad and shoulder bag, and hurried downstairs to breakfast.

She stepped off the elevator and rushed into the lobby. Quite a distance away she noticed a familiar figure. That couldn't be Brett! He had been immaculately dressed each time she had seen him, yet there he was wearing a bush jacket, khaki pants, and boots—of all things. Under one arm he was carrying rolls and rolls of paper that appeared to be blueprints. Strange, she thought. She had never asked him why he had come to Boca Raton. Where was he going? His appearance was so out of character with the elegance of the surroundings that she cringed as if she had just heard chalk scraped across a blackboard.

As Brett strode toward the glass entrance, he glanced over his shoulder and saw Joy staring at him in disbelief. His eyes crinkled as a slow smile formed on his lips. He turned and walked toward her.

"What's wrong, Joy? Did you think that I had turned into a 'rambling wreck from Georgia Tech'? I'm a War Eagle from Auburn, remember?" he teased, enjoying her noticeable attempt to mask her disapproval.

"Uh . . . uh . . ." Joy stuttered. "I'm sorry. Please forgive me. I hardly recognized you. You must admit you do look a little different in that outfit."

"These are my 'work clothes'," he explained.

"You told me you studied architecture," she said hesitantly. "I thought architects sat in offices and designed buildings and bridges and things like that?"

"Yes, ma'am, they do," he exaggerated his Southern drawl, "but they also have to see that those things are built the way they're designed. And it's mighty hard to climb over concrete blocks and piles of steel when you're wearing a three-piece suit and wing-tip shoes."

Joy blushed. Who was she to judge someone by appearances? She certainly had been taught never to do that. Yet she was guilty, and he had been aware of it. A wave of regret swept over her.

"Will you have dinner with me tonight?" he inquired.

In anticipation of just such a moment, Joy had carefully rehearsed all the things she would say to Brett that would discourage further overtures on his part. She had almost let herself become involved again, and that would have been a mistake. However, none of those tactful speeches came to mind now that she needed them.

After what seemed to be an interminable pause, she answered, "Brett, thank you, but I can't. As I told you, I came to Boca for one reason—to be alone and to sort out some personal problems. I really do need some time to be by myself."

His face clouded. "You don't want to be seen with such a disreputable character, right?"

"I didn't mean that at all. And I don't want to hurt your feelings. I told you the truth. I came here for solitude. If I can get to know myself, then I will have something to offer others. Honestly, since my world came apart, I'm not sure who I really am. I just need some time." She could see by his expression that he was offended. "Please believe me," she added.

"Okay, Joy, have it your way. But I don't give up easily. You can bet your last dollar on that!" He turned on his heel and stalked out the front door to his rented Grand Prix, parked under one of the porte-cocheres.

Joy watched the silver automobile until it disappeared. She trudged into the dining room. Her appetite had disappeared and the exuberance of a few moments before had turned into a gloomy, gray blob which engulfed her like a fog.

She pushed the golden brown pieces of French toast and crisp bacon around on her plate, her fork making random designs in the thick maple syrup. Joy was more convinced than ever that she should never become attached to anyone again, much less fall in love. All the important people in her life had either died, or she had been parted from them under unhappy circumstances. The pain of loss was not worth the risk. No question about it! She would just have to stay out of Brett's way. She had begun to like him and, if their relationship continued, one of them would surely get hurt.

Sketch pad in hand, Joy walked out the front entrance into the courtyard. Flowers bloomed in such dazzling profusion that her eyes were unable to absorb their brilliance. The riotous color was a shock to her entire system. She needed peace and tranquillity.

Then she remembered the Banyan tree. That was the perfect spot. As she walked through the courtyard and around the side of the building, she passed a couple strolling hand-in-hand on the pathway. A radiant girl gazed back at the Cloister, enraptured with its grandeur. "I love the color of the hotel. What shade would you call it? Conch-shell pink? No, that's too coral. I know, Picasso pink. That's it," she babbled excitedly. "It is just the shade of pink Picasso would use in one of his paintings. And the red-tiled roof is just perfect. No Spanish-style building would be complete without real red tiles."

Her companion nodded. "The hotel would be right at home on the Mediterranean coast, among all of those old villas. Are you really happy that we came here for our honeymoon—instead of taking the Caribbean cruise?"

The girl smiled up into his face, "Of course, I'm happy! I feel as if I've stepped back in time—as if I were in Spain itself. But I would be happy anywhere with you."

Joy watched as the young man put his arm around his new

wife's waist. Slowly they walked away, caught up in their own special feelings. It must be wonderful, she mused, to love someone as much as that young couple apparently loved each other. She shook her head trying to clear her thoughts. *Stop it, Joy! This tropical setting has gone to your head. Get on with your business. And your business is not a romantic adventure. It is dress designing and resting your brain!*

The honeymoon couple's conversation had rekindled her interest in the Cloister. She was aware that most old Spanish buildings were entered through a courtyard; this was no exception. Turning slowly, she looked at the pair of L-shaped wings that extended from each end of the main part of the building and almost surrounded the courtyard. Only the gatehouse where Pan stood playing the pipes and two sets of wrought-iron gates were needed to complete the enclosure.

Joy walked to the center of the courtyard and sat on one of the colorful tile benches that faced the magnificent fountain. She knew that Ponce de Leon had come to Florida presumably to find the "Fountain of Youth." Though he had failed, perhaps she could find the Fountain of Life—a renewal of heart and purpose that seemed to elude her grasp.

In the center of the fountain was a statue of a lightly draped woman standing on a round pedestal supported by tall columns. Wasn't she called the "Lady of Boca"? Joy tried to remember. Looking upward, she saw that the woman's mouth turned upward slightly, almost in a Mona Lisa smile, and she held her head high and proud. Joy wondered just what the model had been thinking when she posed for the sculptor to fashion this extraordinary figure. She must have had a secret that even the artist could not guess. Near the base of the fountain, water spurted from the mouth of gargoyles. The decorative tiles which lined the base seemed to glow as brightly as the tropical blossoms. And all around Joy were citrus trees laden with their golden fruit, just begging to be plucked.

Then she glanced up at the front of the magnificent hotel. Twin towers rose on either end, and windows of all sizes and shapes added softness to the pink facade. Soaring arches made of coral rock and draped with cerise bougainvillea formed double porte-cocheres at the front entrance. Yes, Joy thought, this sight would charm even the weariest traveler.

She strolled through the open gates and turned to follow the pathway that paralleled the wing of the building. Just ahead lay one of the golf courses. Its greens were lush and velvety. The sand traps looked like bowls of sugar with several scoops removed. And the colorful, sometimes outlandish, attire of the many golfers was the only thing marring the verdant ribbon stretching into the distance.

I wonder if Brett plays golf, Joy thought. What made him slip into her thoughts again? She scolded herself. She must stop thinking about him. There were more important matters to resolve without complicating things. Hadn't she just gotten out of one unhappy love affair? She definitely didn't need to plunge headlong into another.

Jogging her thoughts back to her surroundings, she noticed all the exotic trees and plants near the walkway. Pausing to read the plaques identifying the trees, she noted the giant bamboo from Ceylon, a monkey puzzle tree from Australia, a shaving brush tree from South America, a date palm from Arabia, and a lady palm from central Asia. *This is almost a United Nations of trees and plants,* Joy mused. Resolving to come back another time to enjoy the rare shrubs and flowers, she walked resolutely toward the huge Banyan tree.

This tree had fascinated her for such a long time. She

remembered her father telling her, "In India the Banyan trees grow to well over one-thousand feet around and up to eighty-five feet tall. Those long strands hanging down are aerial roots that grow to the earth. They give additional support to the evergreen tree as it grows larger in circumference, since the main trunk would not be able to support such a massive top."

This tree might not be as large as the ones her father had described, but it was very special to Joy. It was strong and sturdy. Heavy winds might break a few branches, but the tree staunchly survived. And the roots reaching down from the branches reminded her of a strong arm stretching to comfort a child. Its large, leathery leaves shed the rain and provided refuge in a storm.

Then she remembered that her father had also said, "This indomitable old tree has some of man's best characteristics. When you are a young lady, you should keep the message of the tree foremost in your mind. It will guide you in choosing your husband, my child." Then he had chuckled softly.

How strange, Joy thought. Daddy had compared this tree to a man. She was beginning to understand what he had meant. It was the reason she loved this old tree. The tree possessed the same qualities she admired in a man: sturdiness, strength, support, protection, compassion, and unbending faith. The frown lines appeared in her forehead. Did such a man exist?

She sat down on a bench, took her artist's pencil and began a sketch of the dress that she had pictured so clearly earlier in the morning. It refused to come to life. The difficulty in transferring her thoughts to paper still plagued her.

Tossing her materials aside, she walked over to the tree, lowered herself slowly to the grass, and leaned back against its huge trunk. The soft, green canopy formed by the tree's branches gave her a feeling of peaceful seclusion. She felt isolated from all of the noise and activity of other guests nearby. She struggled to relax. Her problems had not disappeared, but for the present she would try to enjoy this unique hideaway. She longed for a short interlude of inner calm.

The water in the pool looked particularly inviting that afternoon. Selecting a lounge chair slightly removed from the other sunbathers, Joy removed the skirt that matched her maillot. Her swimsuit, in watercolor stripes of aqua, blue, and lavender, accentuated her trim figure. Not wanting to wait a minute longer to feel the soothing coolness of the water on her skin, she walked to the diving board, paused for a moment, then plunged into the pool. She swam the full length without surfacing. Reveling in the sensation of the cool water, she swam lap after lap until she was exhausted.

Lifting herself to sit on the side of the pool, Joy gasped, trying to catch her breath after the strenuous exertion. She was definitely out of shape and would have to gradually work up to that kind of pace. As she watched the other swimmers, she heard a familiar voice. Turning around, she noticed an attractive dark-haired woman sitting just behind her.

"Joy, is that really you?" the young woman squealed.

Recognizing a friend from Atlanta, Joy exclaimed, "Marianna, how wonderful to see you here!" She rose quickly, hurried over to her friend, and kissed her lightly on the cheek.

"Do we have to come all the way to Florida to get together? It's been months! What have you been doing with yourself?" Marianna McAlister bubbled.

Joy dropped into a chair beside her and smiled at her exuberant friend. "I really am sorry that I haven't called you. So many things happened all at once that I had little time to keep in touch with my friends."

"I know it's been dreadful since you lost your parents. But tell me about the wedding. When are you and John getting married?"

Joy's face clouded as she answered, "The wedding's off. I gave John his ring back and cancelled all the wedding plans. But it's for the best. Our marriage would never have worked."

Marianna's voice reflected the pain she saw in Joy's eyes. "I'm so sorry. This has been a difficult year for you. But, Joy, I can't honestly say I'm sorry that you aren't marrying John. He gave Dan and me an uncomfortable feeling when we were with him. He apparently didn't like any of your friends, from what I hear."

"I'm afraid you're right. Unfortunately I didn't realize that until later. We were spending less and less time with my friends and more with the people who could help him climb the social and professional ladder."

"How sad," Marianna sympathized.

"Even sadder is the fact that John didn't mind using others to get there. I was one of those people. Our value systems were at complete odds. Isn't it strange that you can't see those things when they are happening to you?" Joy sighed and frowned slightly.

"But what finally brought you to your senses?"

"Well, after Mother and Dad died, Mother's boutique was dropped in my lap, and I had to make all the decisions about running it. Trying to get all of the legal problems concerning the wills and property straightened out kept me so busy that I could hardly breathe. But John expected me to continue to attend every social function with him as if nothing had happened. His wishes and needs always came first. I'm just very glad I found out how insensitive he is before we were married," Joy confided.

Marianna nodded. "Honey, don't you worry. There are a lot of nice men out there who would jump at the chance to make you happy."

"I don't need that just now. All I need is time to get my world back together. It's in as many pieces as Humpty Dumpty after his fall. That's why I came down here—to try to put things in perspective. But enough about me. What have you been up to these days?" Joy asked.

Marianna laughed. "Oh, the usual glamorous routine of the ordinary housewife and mother—washing diapers, chasing a toddler, cleaning house, cooking . . ."

"I envy you," Joy stated truthfully.

"You're kidding me!" Marianna looked incredulous. "You have your designing. You travel to exciting places to buy the latest fashions for the boutique. You lead a really exciting life. And with your looks, you couldn't possibly envy *me*."

"You just may be one of the luckiest women alive, Marianna. Dan thinks you are the most wonderful wife in the world. He would do anything to make you happy. And Amy is a healthy, adorable little cherub. You have a lovely home. You are surrounded by love and security. You have everything that is really important. Don't you know that?" Joy asked pointedly.

"Yes, I suppose so. I know Dan loves me and Amy is so precious. Sometimes, though, I feel that my mental capacity is limited to bedtime stories, and my working skills are one level above scrubbing floors," Marianna smiled. "All of us 'nonworking' mothers are barraged from all sides about getting out and 'living up to our potential.' We tend to have terrible guilt complexes."

"What you are doing is just as important as what any so-called working woman is doing, maybe even more important. You can be sure Amy will profit from the time you are spending with her. And just think of all the things you do to make Dan happy. You are always there to support him. Your job doesn't conflict with his. Taking care of those you love certainly has to be an important career . . . Speaking of Dan, is he here with you?" Joy asked.

"Yes, he had to come down on business, so we left Amy with Grandma and took a few days off. But he has business meetings all day, so you and I will have to get together and catch up on old times. How would you like to have lunch with me tomorrow? Maybe we could go shopping at Royal Palm Plaza later."

Joy knew that a few hours with this relaxed and uncomplicated friend would be good for her. "Perfect! Where shall we meet—and when?"

"Will noon at the east end of the lobby be all right?"

"It will suit me fine. See you then." Joy smiled at Marianna and turned to retrieve her cover-up and beach bag before starting to her room. It had been good to see Marianna again. She had been one of her best friends for years. They had been college roommates, and Joy had been a bridesmaid in Marianna and Dan's wedding. She had missed her friends. Well, that was one problem she could begin to remedy right away.

Hoping to avoid seeing Brett, Joy ordered room service that evening. Almost before she had time to slip on a caftan, there was a knock at the door and a waiter appeared. Room service at the Cloister had always been prompt. The food was not only good, but it was served with a flair rarely found in today's fast-paced society.

Joy sat down to the linen-covered table and studied the one perfect pink rose in a crystal vase. The china and silver were arranged as if for a formal dinner in someone's home. These were the things she had remembered and loved about the Cloister. The management and staff had maintained the traditional formality she enjoyed so much. It gave guests the feeling that they were *dining,* not merely *eating.*

After a leisurely meal, Joy picked up a book she had purchased at the airport before she left Atlanta. Propping herself up in bed, she began to read. She had read only a few pages when the phone rang. Wishing that she could just ignore it, she let it ring several times. Perhaps there was an emergency at the shoppe. She picked it up reluctantly.

"Are you hiding from me?" Brett's voice was playful.

"Oh, it's you," Joy said with slight annoyance.

"Who were you expecting—Robert Redford?" he laughed.

"Frankly, I was hoping I wouldn't hear from anyone. I was just enjoying a quiet evening in my room."

"So . . . you ARE going to become a hermit while you are here."

Joy sighed, "No, not really, but I do want to have some time alone. Why should that bother you?"

"It bothers me because *you* bother me, that's why. I told you this morning that I don't give up very easily when I know what I want," Brett stated emphatically.

"You are one of those people who will do anything to get what he wants, regardless of whom he hurts, aren't you? Well, I've just had one unhappy experience with that kind of man, and I have no desire to become entangled again." Joy's voice held an edge of uncharacteristic harshness.

"Hold it just a minute! I think you misunderstood me. The last thing I want to do is to hurt you. You are the kind of woman I would do anything to *please.* What I meant was

57

that you are a very attractive and desirable woman, and I'd like to have a chance to get to know you better. I don't intend to beat down that wall you have built around yourself. But I would like very much to persuade you to open the door. Maybe we could be friends, at least,'' Brett said.

''All right, so I misjudged you. Maybe I'm a little on the defensive when it comes to men right now . . . By the way, how did your work go today?'' Joy asked, wanting to change the subject.

''Oh, pretty good. In the condo we're building south of Deerfield Beach, there are some materials that don't come up to 'specs' and those will have to be replaced. That always slows down the entire project.''

Joy interrupted, '''Specs?'''

''Oh, that's just slang for 'specifications.' You see, there are pages and pages of them that describe the type and quality of all materials we have specified to be used in building the condominium. I work with the engineers and contractor in checking to be sure that everything is up to par. Inferior quality in either workmanship or materials could cause big problems later. A group of local engineers is helping to supervise the construction. Frank and Sam have been a big help in bringing me up-to-date,'' Brett continued.

''I assumed you had been working on this building from the beginning.''

''No, this is a new project for me. One of my partners, Pete Jennings, was originally assigned to the job, but he reinjured a knee that had been hurt when he played football. So he's in the hospital, and I'm filling in until he's up and around again,'' he explained.

''That's too bad,'' Joy murmured. ''How long will he be in the hospital?''

''Nobody knows. It just depends on how fast he mends.

So my plans are very indefinite," Brett replied. "Tomorrow we hope to get things moving again. Every day lost is very costly, especially with current prices. But enough about me. When do you think you will be setting your foot out the door so that I can see you again?" he asked.

"I met an old friend from home at the pool today, and we plan to have lunch together tomorrow," Joy said, hoping to erase the "hermit" image from his mind.

"So, you can go out with other men, but I'm a 'no-no.' Is that how it is?" His voice held a cutting edge.

Joy tried to stifle a slight chuckle. "As a matter of fact, the friend is a lady—my college roommate. We haven't seen each other for quite a while. She asked me to have lunch with her, and then we plan to go shopping."

"Good. Just so long as it isn't with a long-lost lover," he stated firmly. "I would be jealous, you know."

She laughed again. "You're impossible. You hardly know me."

"Joy, time is irrelevant when you see someone very special. I just want you to know I'm staking my claim on you now."

Her voice grew serious. "Brett, please don't rush me."

"Okay, but I want you to know that I'm waiting, not very patiently, but I'm waiting. Have a good day tomorrow and I'll be in touch."

"Thanks . . . and good night," Joy replied and replaced the phone. She had enjoyed talking with him. There was something about him that attracted her like a sliver of steel to a magnet—even against her will. She would have to keep a tight rein on her feelings.

She picked up the book once more and tried to concentrate. The characters had already become jumbled in her mind, and she was forced to reread several pages to refresh her memory. Only a few moments later the book dropped from her hand as her body jerked involuntarily in the first stages of sleep. She roused enough to put the book on the bedside table and to turn off the lamp. She snuggled down into the warm, comfortable bed and almost instantly she was sleeping peacefully.

CHAPTER 5

YESTERDAY'S SUN HAD brought a healthy glow to Joy's cheeks, she noted with satisfaction as she glanced into the mirror. And today she had chosen one of her favorite dresses to wear to lunch. The wood block print of seashells showed coral against white on the overblouse, and reversed to white on coral in the cluster-pleated skirt. The silky polyester fabric caressed her legs when she walked. It was one of those dresses that made her feel especially good whenever she wore it.

Joy walked jauntily through the lobby. She stopped when she spotted the bell captain at the desk beside the entrance. "Domenick, it's so good to see you," she said happily as she walked toward him.

The man's face broke into a warm smile of recognition. "Miss Lawrence, it is good to have you back with us!"

They shook hands enthusiastically as Joy spoke. "However did you manage to remember my name after six years?"

"Miss Lawrence, it's good to have you back with us!" children. It's always good to see how much they grow between visits. But you have only grown more beautiful. I remember, when you visited with us, you would come down almost every day to get a bike and go for a ride." Domenick's soft voice brought back a flood of memories.

"I surely did," she recalled. "You've seen so many of us kids grow up and come back, haven't you?"

"In thirty years, I am now seeing many of those children bringing their little ones back." His eyes sparkled as he spoke.

"Well, I have no children, but I hope you will be here when I *do*! I'm meeting a friend for lunch now, but I'll see you again before I leave."

"Stop by, and I'll have a bike for you," he promised.

"I haven't ridden in years. You might have to use some first aid if I tried."

They both laughed at her joke as she turned away and walked toward the end of the lobby. Joy thought that, for Domenick, it must be almost like a family reunion when he welcomed former guests after several years' absence. He was a precious link with the past.

Joy settled herself in one of the chairs and admired the Mediterranean furniture. Much of it had been imported from Europe when Addison Mizner built the Cloister in the 1920's. He certainly had left his imprint on this part of the state, she thought. He had even created Worth Avenue in Palm Beach, using the same Spanish-inspired style. The arches and tiles were just as prevalent in Palm Beach as here in Boca.

She glanced at her watch for the third time. Joy was always prompt. In fact, she often arrived well ahead of an appointment so that she would not keep anyone waiting.

Marianna, her dark hair waving softly around her pert face, walked rapidly across the lobby. She was a very attractive woman, Joy thought. Her gray-green eyes sparkled when she talked, and her face was constantly changing to reflect her mood or the feelings of those around her. She was wearing a smart vanilla suit with a jade green blouse. As Joy watched her approach, she decided that Marianna was certainly anything *but* the uninteresting housewife she had described.

"You knew, of course, that I would be late, didn't you?" Marianna's face was transformed by her happy smile.

"That thought had crossed my mind, but people do change, you know. I didn't want to take a chance just in case you had."

"Nope, not me. If I ever showed up on time, everyone would fall over in a dead faint!"

Both of them laughed heartily, remembering all the times that Joy had waited for her friend during the years they had known each other. It was good to be together again after such a long time. And to discover that some things *never* change—a reassuring thought.

Because neither of the women was very hungry, they took the limousine to the Royal Palm Plaza for a sandwich at the ice cream parlor. From the window of the plush automobile, Joy noticed that several changes had been made since her last visit. Suddenly her breath caught in her throat as the vehicle pulled to a stop at a traffic light. There, across the street in front of a coffee shop, was Brett! He was listening intently as a striking blonde talked animatedly. *Who is she?* Joy wondered. Brett McCort certainly did get around, didn't he? Oh well, why let a man spoil her day? She would forget all about him, she resolved, but was grateful when the limo made a right turn, obscuring her view of the attractive couple.

When Joy and Marianna entered the ice cream parlor, the hostess seated them at a small table next to the large front window which afforded them a view of part of the plaza and the shoppers as they passed. As this was the peak of the tourist season in South Florida, the small restaurant was filled to capacity. People of all ages, in a holiday mood, were sating their hunger. Joy was amazed at the number of children. She had expected to see mostly retirees.

"Where do you want to go when we finish eating?" Joy asked.

"You know me—wife and mother first. I'd like to do some shopping for Amy. She is growing out of her clothes as fast as I can buy them. Oh, but if that would be boring for you . . ." Marianna paused, her smooth brow furrowed with concern, "we could do something else."

"No, really, I would enjoy browsing in a children's shop for a change. Let's get a pamphlet that shows the location of all the stores, and we'll find one for children," Joy suggested.

The hostess was happy to provide a directory and, while they ate, the two young women pondered the directions to the more than eighty-five shops, restaurants, and offices in the "Pink Plaza."

"Aren't the names of the shops delightful!" Marianna exclaimed. "Listen to these: "The Gazebo, Snappy Turtle, The Tree House, Cricket Shop, and, how about this one, The Pink Pony! Wouldn't you just love to check them all out?" Shaking her head, she concluded, "It would take us a week to do this place justice. I had no idea it was so large. But if we don't get started, we'll never even make a dent!"

After finishing lunch they walked out into the warm sunshine. Clusters of buildings, all designed in the same unique style as the Cloister, surrounded them. The pink buildings, arched walkways, red-tiled roofs, and landscaping were as magnificent as that at the hotel. Bougainvillea, with its bright fuchsia flowers, draped over arches and walkways. Many different varieties of palms dotted the courtyards and gardens adjacent to the buildings. Wrought-iron grillwork added a decorative effect to the stairways and entrances. Fountains abounded in the gardens. Hibiscus, oleanders, poinsettias, snapdragons, and calendulas splashed their colors lavishly on the canvas of green and pink.

Eventually they located a children's store, and as Marianna shopped for Amy, Joy examined the tiny baby dresses. She picked up one and held the soft fabric to her cheek, allowing her thoughts to wander. She had always loved children and had even played with her dolls until she was well past the age when most little girls discarded them. With a deep, almost despairing sigh, Joy folded the tiny garment and put it back on the counter. *Enough wishful thinking,* she told herself. *Babies have to have fathers, and I don't plan to get married any time soon.* She turned away to inspect the appliqued pillows.

"Come see what I've found for Amy," Marianna called. "These should keep her clothed for a few months. The way she's growing, she'll be into another size soon. She's a real McAlister, like her daddy, but she is growing *up* and he is growing in another direction," she laughed. "Where do we go now?"

Joy thought for a moment, then answered, "There is a gift shop I particularly like—the Chambered Nautilus. Would you like to look around there?"

"Oh, yes! It would be heavenly to browse through china and crystal without having Amy's little hands reaching for everything in sight."

The seventeen buildings of the Plaza were all sizes and shapes. Some were set at angles to the others so that even the unusual-shaped spaces formed between them provided areas of cultivation for lush foliage and fragrant blossoms. The two women stopped several times and checked the little map to make sure they were headed in the right direction.

They emerged from one of the triangular gardens into a very large area that was almost like a small park. There, in the corner of one of the buildings, was the gift shop. Marianna looked at the name of the store and paused. "I know this is a stupid question, but what is a chambered nautilus? It sounds like something from thousands of leagues under the sea!"

Joy grinned. "Don't worry, I had to ask, too. It's the name of a mollusk with a coiled and partitioned shell, lined with a pearly layer. That's a sketch of one." She pointed to the sign over the store.

As they entered, they were warmly greeted by a lovely, dark-haired woman who introduced herself as Mrs. Josephs and told them to feel free to browse as long as they wished. Marianna gravitated to the porcelain. She carefully examined an unglazed, perfect replica of a magnolia blossom made by Lefton. She was entranced by its beauty. The single delicate bloom would add the special touch she needed on her hand-carved mahogany table, and would be right at home in Atlanta, she decided.

Then Marianna noticed a highly glazed Capodimonte bowl filled with exquisitely realistic flowers. There were anemones, lavender-blue cup flowers, full-blown roses in shades of pink and yellow, and exquisite white daffodils with yellow throats and a touch of orange outlining the trumpets. She could just picture the bowl of porcelain flowers in the center of her dining room table. She picked it up and carried it to the smiling lady who had greeted them.

"I'm going to start a family heirloom myself," she said, "like those that have been handed down to me." While Marianna's purchases were being carefully wrapped and boxed, she wandered into another area of the store.

Meanwhile Joy had been standing in a room displaying every kind of Oriental treasure imaginable. Her gaze fell on an exquisite ming tree. It was breathtaking! The gnarled trunk and branches were shaped from fine strands of metal that had been twisted into a replica of an ancient, windblown tree. The leaves appeared to be coated with a dusting of priceless jewels. Perry Marshall had guided the skilled enamelists from Bovano in fusing glass crystals to copper, using the ancient techniques of cloisonné enameling. *Oh!* Joy thought. *Wouldn't I just love to have that piece in my home?*

Reluctantly she turned her attention to the other items— delicate, handpainted fans and embroidered wall hangings. She knew that one who had never done handwork could not possibly appreciate the time and patience required to create such works of art. Again Joy was grateful for her heritage —a family who encouraged learning such skills and creating things of beauty.

She was remembering how her grandmother had first taught her to embroider when she caught a glimpse of a display of handcrafted objects from China. There were elegant birds with enameled, filigreed wings. But before she could inspect them further, she noticed a vase nestled in a silk-lined, silk-covered box. It appeared to have been made from a gossamer web, spun from delicate strands of sterling silver. The vase was magnificent, she thought, but it was the card beside it that intrigued Joy. The message on the card read: *Cherry blossom. Offering the strength to endure the winter, the cherry blossom reveals beauty and warmth even at the worst of times.*

Joy turned to Mrs. Josephs and asked, "Where did you manage to find these indescribable treasures?"

A happy smile lighted the shop owner's face as she replied, "Oh, you like my favorites! This is an exclusive SuHai collection done by the artisans of Chengtu, China. Each filigreed vase is handmade and is numbered in a limited

67

edition series. I'm very pleased to have this collection. The designs are said to bestow on the owner harmony in life."

"I must have that vase. This has been the 'winter of my life,' and the message of the cherry blossom speaks to my heart."

Noticeably puzzled, Mrs. Josephs carefully packaged Joy's purchase. The striking young woman showed no trace of sadness. What could be hidden behind that lovely face that would disturb her so?

Joy walked back to look at the ming tree once more before she left. Tomorrow she would have to try again to sketch the emerald green-and-red dress. Seeing these lovely things had fueled her resolve to try again.

After leaving the gift shop, Joy and Marianna wandered through several other stores, their eyes feasting on a banquet of unique items. Marianna suddenly remembered that she needed to buy a birthday card to send to her brother. They located a card shop and, while Marianna made her selection, Joy read some of the humorous cards that were becoming very popular. She discovered that she was chuckling to herself and called Marianna to share some of the fun. The two of them lost all track of time as they giggled like small girls over the clever verses.

"It has been a long time since I have had such fun!" Joy said.

"Do you realize what time it is?" Marianna asked in amazement, as she checked her watch. "Dan is probably already back at the hotel, wondering where I am!"

The two young women hurriedly collected their purchases and went to the place where the limousine would pick them up and take them back to the hotel. On the ride back they chatted excitedly about their afternoon outing. Joy's spirits had lifted considerably, and she felt more like herself than she had in many months.

As they entered the hotel, Marianna asked, "Why don't you have dinner with Dan and me tonight? He said he wanted to be sure to see you while you are here."

Joy was hesitant to accept the invitation, feeling that the couple probably would prefer to dine by themselves. But, at Marianna's insistence, Joy conceded that it would be much nicer to have dinner with friends than to spend a lonely evening. After arranging to meet at eight o'clock, the friends parted to go their separate ways.

A relaxing bubble bath would be much better than a quick shower to ease her tired feet and body, Joy decided. She turned on the tap and slowly added the bath crystals. Immediately the water was transformed into iridescent bubbles of rainbow colors, swirling about in ever-changing patterns. Joy longed for a fabric that would duplicate the kaleidoscopic exhibition.

She slid into the tub, trying not to disturb the bubbles. They floated around her body as she lay in the soothing water, letting her mind flow in random patterns like the colors of the bubbles. The day had been so filled with beauty. She wished that she could infuse some of it into her brain to erase the darkness of the depression she had been experiencing. Things did seem a little brighter, though. Spending the afternoon with Marianna had helped a great deal. And having dinner with her friends would be like old times.

The water had cooled and the bubbles had vanished before Joy's reverie was broken. Hurriedly she reached for a thick, fluffy towel and rubbed her skin until it tingled. Wrapping a soft, fleecy robe closely around her, she walked into the bedroom.

It had been days since she had watched television or read

a paper, so she flipped on the set to a national news broadcast. Settling back in an easy chair, she watched as correspondents narrated tragedies, wars, investigations, and legislative happenings. *Good grief!* Joy thought. *Does the news always have to be bad? Isn't there something happy that deserves media coverage?*

Flipping the dial again, she discovered a channel that continuously broadcast a listing of the activities that were available to guests of the hotel—water skiing, aquaslimnastics, fashion shows, an historical hotel tour, scuba classes, sailing, fishing, golf, tennis, movies.

She glanced at her travel alarm clock, jumped up, and hurriedly began putting on her make-up. Where had the time gone? At least she had always made a habit of laying her clothes out ahead of time. The tissue silk crepe de Chine caressed her body as she slipped the dress over her shoulders. While she tied the soft bow at her neck she studied her reflection in the mirror. What had Brett said about her knowledge of color? Yes, she admitted, the azure blue of the dress did heighten the darker aquamarine of her eyes.

She stepped into strippy sandals and turned once more to the mirror to comb her hair. She was lucky, she thought, that her hair had just enough natural wave that it wasn't necessary to spend valuable time curling it. Usually she could shampoo it, blow it almost dry, and then comb it lightly until it fell into soft waves to her shoulders. She was glad now that she had decided to have the pale wheat highlights added. Her hair had turned much darker over the past year or so, and the lighter strands gave it the sun-streaked look of a teen-ager.

Could she really be twenty-six years old? She should be taking better care of her hair and skin, Joy thought. Now was the time to begin a regimen to delay premature age lines and extra pounds. *Well,* she thought, *while I'm trying to get my head straightened out, I might as well work on my body, too.*

With that resolution Joy picked up the clutch bag that matched her sandals and started for the door. At the last minute she turned, walked to the closet, and selected a soft woolen shawl, woven in shades of blue, turquoise, and lavender. She knew that, even in Florida, the nights could be cool, and she wanted to be ready for whatever the evening held.

CHAPTER 6

W HEN J OY ENTERED the elevator, the operator smiled at her approvingly as she requested the lobby level. Though the elevators were self-operating during certain hours when few people were using them, there was an operator on duty for peak times. This practice was another example of the ways in which the Cloister gave their guests a cherished feeling. Those push-buttons could not smile at you or tell you to have a nice evening as this kind man did when she exited.

Joy made her way across the long lobby which extended from the east wing to the west wing of the hotel. Dan and Marianna McAlister arrived at their meeting place only moments later. Dan stepped over to Joy and gave her a bear hug.

"You look like a million dollars, Joy," he said, as he held her at arm's length. "Tonight must be my lucky night. I'll be having dinner with the two most gorgeous women around."

All three of them laughed. When Marianna hugged her, too, Joy was struck by the fact that she had missed this warm, affectionate touching and hugging that had always been so much a part of her family life and with close friends. John had detested outward displays of emotion—another distinct difference between them. She had no need to grieve over him. Their broken engagement was one of the best things that could have happened to her. Suddenly Joy was *sure* of that, and she felt a heavy weight lifting from deep within.

Putting an arm around each of the women, Dan continued, "Both of you are too pretty to hide in some dark restaurant tonight. How does the Cathedral dining room suit you? Every man in the place will be looking at you and envying me."

Without waiting for an answer, he guided them toward the dining room. As they entered, Joy gave a soft gasp. "I never come here that I'm not overwhelmed with the elegance of this room," she said. "Usually, when you return to a place you remembered from childhood days, it seems smaller and not as impressive. But this is even *more* magnificent than I remembered."

For a moment they stood admiring the lavish decor. Two rows of the famed 14-karat gold-leaf columns supported arches that extended upward to an incredible height. The ornate ceiling had caused many a neck to swivel in wonder. Suspended from the soaring ceiling, immense but delicately lovely golden chandeliers illuminated the dining room. Miniature replicas of these hung along the side walls, shedding a soft light on the diners.

The maitre d' led them to a table near the dance floor and assisted the women into comfortable upholstered chairs. The table, covered with a white damask cloth, was set with service plates in the hotel's unique china, and formal place settings of silver and crystal. Joy remembered how very grown-up she had felt when she had been seated, as a ten-year-old child, with her parents. She had the same feeling now.

One particular memory of that visit would always be vivid in her mind. Her father had been an excellent dancer, and she had always enjoyed watching him dance with her mother. But on that night her father had spoken with the orchestra leader and, when he returned to the table, he bowed, not to her mother, but to Joy! "Young lady, may I have this dance?" he had asked.

With the memory, she could almost feel the blush that had suffused her face that evening. "But, Daddy, I can't dance as well as Mother. I would embarrass you." She had glanced at her mother, who smiled her approval.

"You would never embarrass me, Joy," her father reassured her as he took her hand and led her to the ballroom floor. They reached the floor just as the other dancers stood applauding the last medley. The orchestra leader looked over at her father, smiled, and the strains of "Misty" flowed melodiously over the room. Her father took her hand and led her in a graceful step.

"Joy, I asked them to play that song because I always think of you when I hear it. I wanted it played for our first 'formal' dance together."

"But what is the name of the song, and why does it make you think of me?" the little girl had asked.

"It is sometimes hard to explain why a song reminds you of someone, but I'll try. My first glimpse of you in your mother's arms on the night you were born touched me so deeply that my eyes filled with tears, and I wasn't able to see you clearly. My heart was so full of love for both of you that I wanted to hold on to that moment forever. Later that night, when I got into the car to go home, the first song I heard on the radio was 'Misty.' Since then I've always thought of you when I hear that song—because I first saw

74

you through misty eyes of love. Perhaps you will understand when you are grown and have a child of your own." Her father's eyes had glistened with tears once again as he smiled down at her.

Joy felt a bittersweet happiness. How she missed those two wonderful people. But they had given her beautiful memories and a love that would be with her forever.

"Joy, dear, you aren't crying, are you?" Marianna's concerned voice interrupted her reverie.

"Only a few happy tears," Joy insisted. "I was just thinking of the wonderful times I spent here with my parents."

"Just wanted to be sure you are all right." Marianna reached over and patted Joy's hand.

The waiter had returned with a cooler and a bottle of Perrier. He poured the sparkling mineral water into frosted glasses garnished with slices of lime. Joy sipped her drink slowly, and her face brightened.

"Dan, do you stay in touch with many of the guys we knew in high school?" she asked. "We ought to have a reunion. Everyone is literally scattered all over the world now."

Dan told her about several mutual friends whom he still saw occasionally in business and at social gatherings. Marianna added interesting little anecdotes as they talked. The friendly conversation brought back the closeness the three had once shared.

Suddenly Marianna put her hand to her mouth and gasped. "Dan! I almost forgot! I want to reach Mother on the phone before Amy goes to sleep. Nobody answered when I tried to call earlier. I just have to hear from Amy, or I won't sleep a wink tonight!"

Dan agreed that she would, indeed, be wakeful and, what's more, that she would probably keep *him* awake if she didn't ease her mind about the baby's welfare. He rose to help her from her chair.

"I'll be back in a few minutes. Excuse me, please," she said as she hurried from the dining room to the nearest telephone.

While Marianna was away, Dan and Joy talked animatedly about the past football season. She had always enjoyed football. Her big brother, Bill, and her father had taken her to Little League practice and games, where she had become quite knowledgeable about the sport. She missed those talks. None of the women she knew liked football. Dan laughed and admitted that, in college, the guys had agreed that she was the only girl they could talk to who knew the difference between a defensive tackle and a split end.

"The year you were voted Homecoming Queen must have gone down somewhere in the history of the school. It was the first time a Homecoming Queen ever *watched* the football game!" Dan laughed heartily.

Joy studied his face as they talked. He had a knack for putting others at ease. He was an attractive man with blue-gray eyes and well-groomed, auburn hair. His suntanned face, sprinkled with lines that could have been created only by smiling, would definitely be described as warm and pleasant. Marianna was a lucky woman. She would certainly never tire of seeing that happy face across the breakfast table every morning.

Suddenly his expression grew serious. "Joy, don't turn around just now, but there is a man to your right who is staring daggers through both of us. When you have a chance, glance in that direction and see if you know him."

It was not necessary to see him. She recognized the deep voice asking the waiter about the various entrées. It was Brett! But why would he sit there, glowering? If he had seen her, why didn't he come to the table and speak to her?

Marianna returned, smiling broadly. "Amy is just fine. I spoke with her and she said, 'Mama.' Mother says that she has been an angel."

Dan kissed her lightly on the forehead as he held her chair. He had scarcely taken his seat when he rose again, staring over Joy's shoulder. She turned her head to find Brett at her side. His mood apparently had changed abruptly. He was now smiling and jovial. He spoke to Joy, then extended his hand to Dan.

"Brett McCort," his voice exuded friendliness. What had caused such a change? Joy was puzzled.

With introductions out of the way, Dan asked Brett if he would care to join them for dinner. He failed to see the slight shake of Joy's head as she tried in vain to discourage Dan's invitation. Brett accepted quickly, excusing himself only long enough to make the arrangements with his waiter.

"I had no idea you knew him, Joy. Why do you suppose he was glaring at us? He seems like a nice-enough fellow, though."

"I met him on the limousine ride from the airport in Palm Beach, and I have no idea why he should be acting so strangely. But I'm still trying to decide why the name 'McCort' should sound so familiar to me. It has been bugging me ever since we met." Joy's face wrinkled in thought.

Before they could conclude the conversation, the waiter returned to set a place for Brett. Dan and Joy had delayed their first course while waiting for Marianna to make her call. Now the four of them crunched on the crispy treats from the relish tray, and Joy smiled in anticipation as the waiter placed a bowl of watercress soup in front of her.

"Joy may be small, but you won't believe what she can consume at one sitting," Brett teased.

Then he proceeded to tell the other couple everything that she had eaten the night they had arrived. He embellished the story, making it impossible for Marianna and Dan to eat because they were laughing so heartily.

"Don't think you can shame me into eating less tonight. I intend to enjoy every bite of every course," Joy said in mock defiance. "And I'm even going to have melon sherbet for dessert," she added as the others continued to chuckle.

The dinner conversation flowed in a lively vein. The men discovered that, among their common interests, was the fact that their offices were located in the same area of Atlanta. Not wanting to bore their companions, they refrained from too much talk about business. Brett's natural wit and Dan's carefree banter kept everyone in high spirits.

When they had finished their entrées, Brett turned to Joy. "It's a shame to let all of that good music go to waste. I'm not the best dancer in the world, but would you at least give me a chance?"

Joy smiled in agreement, and he led her to the dance floor. The rhythm of the soft music made it easy to follow Brett, who was a very good dancer despite his modest evaluation. She relaxed in his arms, and they moved gracefully across the shiny floor.

When the music stopped for a moment, Joy asked, "Why in the world were you glaring at Dan before you came over to our table? You made him feel very uncomfortable."

Brett hesitated a moment and then confessed, "Oh, just a fit of jealousy, you might say. You had told me the *old friend* you were meeting today was a woman. Well, when I came into the dining room and found you and Dan making such a cozy, little twosome, I 'saw red.' I hoped to make him uncomfortable enough so that he would make it a short evening. Then I planned to ask you to go for a walk with me. How was I to know he had a wife who just happened to be out of the room when I came in?"

Joy, strangely pleased, continued, "How did you know she was his wife, or that he wasn't really my date?"

"For crying out loud, Joy! He kissed her when he helped her into her chair. Would your date kiss another woman right there in front of you?" He looked at her as if he thought she were a little more than dense.

She giggled, "I'm afraid I didn't notice that little clue, Sherlock."

"Stick with me, Dr. Watson, and we can have some interesting adventures," he smiled and hugged her to him as they continued to dance.

The music of Van Smith and his orchestra was exceptional. The band leader was also the pianist of the group. Unlike many other orchestras that Joy had heard, these musicians seemed to truly enjoy what they were doing.

Mr. Smith smiled and nodded as the dancers moved past and occasionally talked with them as he played the piano. As he finished a medley of songs, Joy and Brett stood directly in front of the band, applauding appreciatively. Smith asked Joy if she had a favorite song. When she shook her head, Brett requested "You Light Up My Life." The pianist smiled and began to play the lovely melody without benefit of sheet music. The rest of the orchestra followed as if they had carefully arranged scores before them.

Brett held Joy a little closer as they danced. A feeling of déja vu swept over her. Long ago she had experienced this same event, when she had danced to the music of a song requested for her by her father. She reacted with a slight shiver.

Brett moved back slightly so that he could look into Joy's astonishingly blue eyes. "You do light up my life, you know. I thought of that song the first time I saw you. Your hair shone so brightly in the sunlight at the airport that it seemed to form a halo around your head. You are the angel I have been needing.''

Joy shivered again at his words. She felt anything but angelic. If he only knew her anguish. Tenderly Brett kissed her lightly on the forehead before escorting her back to their table.

Their dinner ended pleasantly, but not until Joy had finished the last bite of her melon sherbet. Merriment sparkled in Brett's eyes as he pointed to the empty crystal dessert dish.

He turned to the McAlisters and commented, ''What did I tell you? She can eat more than a farmer at harvest time. Her grocery bill must rival the national debt.''

Joy joined in the friendly banter. ''You should see what I can eat when I'm *really* hungry!'' she exclaimed. Laughter erupted once more.

No one was ready for the enjoyable evening to come to an end, but Dan needed an early start the following morning, hoping to wind up his business. He and Marianna excused themselves reluctantly. Brett assured them that he would see Joy safely to her room, and the couples parted in the lobby, with Joy promising Marianna that she would be in touch the following day.

Brett took Joy's hand and they started across the lobby. Suddenly he asked, ''Would your shawl keep you warm enough for a short walk in the courtyard?''

Trying to retain the carefree feeling of the evening, she turned to him and said in a teasing voice, ''I think a walk would be good for me. It will settle my dinner so that I'll have room for a midnight snack.''

They walked arm-in-arm out the front door. Lights played on the fountain and the exotic plants in the court-yard. The citrus trees lining the drive were studded with tiny, white, twinkling lights; and the heavy fruit might have been shining ornaments on a Christmas tree.

"I feel as if I were in another world," Joy whispered, "a world of enchantment."

"Perhaps you are," Brett acknowledged. "I only know that I want to be included in that world." Brett's eyes were probing hers—trying to read there her reaction.

"Please, Brett, don't. You don't know anything about me—nor, I, you." Joy was frightened. "I have so many problems that need to be resolved. Can't we just enjoy spending some time together without any serious involvement? There's no room in my life just now for you—or any other man."

"Sorry, Joy. I guess I came on too strong. But maybe we know each other better than you think." With difficulty he shifted the mood to a lighter vein. "I'm not sure, but I think the 'Lady of Boca' is keeping a secret about us."

They gazed up at the magnificent fountain in the center of the courtyard. The Lady smiled mysteriously.

CHAPTER 7

AT HOME, JOY was an early riser—not wishing to miss a single moment of any day. In Boca, after a few leisurely mornings in which she caught up with her rest, she was back into her well-ordered routine. Today she had dressed in a nautical outfit—white twill pants and a matching middy blouse, accented with navy blue braid and a brilliant red sailor tie. A brisk walk up El Camino Real had increased her growing appetite and had heightened the color in her cheeks. She was among the first to enter the dining room.

Her mouth watered as she stared at the stack of luscious, golden pancakes. The butter melted and mingled with the raspberry syrup to form small rivulets which flowed across her plate toward the strips of crisp, lean bacon. She savored every delectable morsel. With a satisfied sigh she leaned back in her chair and sipped her second cup of coffee.

Brett's arrival in the dining room surprised her for some reason, though she had grown accustomed to his casual attire and the ever-present boots that he wore to work. When he spied her sitting alone, he approached her table.

"So, you ate all of the evidence before I could log the calories, didn't you?" His dark eyes twinkled merrily as he spoke.

"Why do you think I got up at the crack of dawn?" Joy replied in mock indignation. "I need all of my strength today because I plan to get to work."

"I'll let you off the hook this time. But if I promise not to ask what you ate for breakfast, will you sit with me while I eat mine?" he offered a compromise.

"Fine—provided I can have a taste of whatever you order," she teased.

"No way! I'd probably go to work starving if you ever got a fork on my plate!"

Joy enjoyed the free and easy rapport they had established.

"What are you planning to work on today?" Brett asked as he sipped his orange juice.

"I've had an idea for a design ever since my first day in Boca, but I haven't had much luck in getting it down on paper. Maybe today everything will click, and I can finish it."

"Do you enjoy your work, Joy?" he inquired.

"Yes and no. I've always enjoyed designing dresses, but since Mother died, I've had to take over the management of the entire boutique. She used to take me with her on buying trips, but I just went along to see the clothes and accessories. I had no idea how she decided what to buy and how many. She handled all of the business details. I feel so inadequate when it comes to the shoppe's management. It's hard to forget those problems when I try to be creative. My mind is just one, big, gray fog." Joy frowned slightly as she spoke.

"Joy, I'm not a psychologist, but it sounds to me as if you've had so much on your shoulders that you are just depressed—and with good reason. Who wouldn't be after all you have been through? I think you're on the right track with this trip. The sunshine and surroundings are a big change from the cold, rainy weather we were having back home. Just give yourself some time. I wish I could help." Sympathy for the lovely young woman sitting across from him flooded Brett.

"I appreciate that. Really, I do. But it's something that no òne else can do for me. I have to work it out in my own way. You have done a lot by helping me laugh again."

"Happy to be of service, ma'am." Brett exaggerated his own slight Southern drawl, hoping for a smile. This time it worked as Joy's expression slowly changed from a frown into a small but sunny smile.

"Brett, how can anyone be 'down in the dumps' when they are with you?"

"Ah jus' aim to please, honey chile." Once again he was rewarded with a flash of even, white teeth.

Brett glanced at his Rolex. Reluctantly he said, "I hate to leave, but if I sit here enjoying your company much longer, Sam will think that I'm not coming to work today."

"Is the work on the condo going all right?" Joy queried.

"Yeah, it's a little slow, but we are beginning to iron out some of the problems. By the way, I hope to be back here for dinner tonight. Would you and the McAlisters join me for dinner at the Beach Club?" Brett asked casually.

"I really have wanted to go over there. I'll ask Marianna and let you know when you get in this afternoon." Joy felt a glow of anticipation.

"I'll call you as soon as I get back. Hope you can make it," Brett said as he rose to leave. He winked at her and started for the door.

Joy sat at the table for a few more moments, sipping a fresh cup of coffee and letting her thoughts wander. Last night had boosted her spirits considerably. It had been such a long time since she had experienced that kind of relaxed conversation with friends. Brett had become a part of the group as easily as if he had always known them. But what did he want of her? Was she seeing too much of him? Giving him false hope that she might possibly fall in love with him? Was she even capable of loving anyone at this point in her life? And if she could love again, was it worth the pain that always followed the loss of the loved one?

Joy pondered these disturbing questions as her coffee grew cold. No, she would be better off in the long run if she never opened her heart to anyone again. What she needed was a platonic friendship, whatever that indefinable phrase meant. She would have to fight the warmth that was growing more pronounced each time she was near Brett.

Sitting at the lovely antique desk under the two large windows in her room, Joy looked intently at the Banyan tree. She turned to her art pad and sketched a series of long, crisp lines. The emerald green Oriental dress began to take shape. Her pencil moved swiftly and surely. The touches of scarlet, slashing down the dress and around the mandarin collar, like the flash of the cardinal against the Banyan tree, were dramatic and bold. Joy preferred to execute her drawings in color after the lines of the dress had been firmly established. Now, she thought, if she could just find the exact green silk jacquard fabric she pictured so clearly in her mind . . .

Why hadn't she thought of it before? The inspiration came to Joy with sudden clarity. The dress would be a perfect foil for Elayna DuRant's olive complexion, long jet-black hair, and eyes resembling well-polished jade. Joy brightened noticeably. Elayna had just the coloring and figure to wear this floor-length Oriental creation. She would look even more exquisite than usual—her eyes changing from jade to emerald. Elayna would be so pleased! She loved exotic and startling clothes.

Joy wrote Elayna's name at the top of the drawing. Relief flooded her. With one design completed, she had successfully cleared the first hurdle. It was especially rewarding since Elayna had already placed her order for a dress to wear to the Hospital Ball next year. It was a start—a very small start.

The morning passed so rapidly that it was well past noon before Joy realized she had not called Marianna. She had been so engrossed in her work that all other thoughts had been blocked from her mind. Ah, that was a good sign, too. It had been months since she had been able to free her mind for such intense concentration.

Marianna answered the telephone on the first ring.

"I'm so sorry that I didn't call this morning. I got so caught up in my work that the time slipped by before I knew it," Joy apologized.

"Don't worry about it a minute. I've been sitting in the sun trying to get as much tan as possible before going home. Are you planning to work this afternoon, too?"

"No, I'm through for the day," Joy replied. "Things went better than I had hoped and I want to quit while I'm ahead. By the way, I saw Brett in the dining room this morning. He wanted to know if you and Dan would have dinner with us at the Beach Club tonight."

"That sounds like fun! But are you sure the two of you wouldn't like to have dinner alone? You don't need us old married folks as chaperones," Marianna teased.

"I just met the man! I'm certainly not interested in the

least in a romantic entanglement right now.'' Joy wondered if her words were entirely true. ''Will you come? Please.''

''Of course—if you're sure we won't be in the way. What time?''

''About eight, I imagine. But he's going to call me when he gets in, and I'll let you know later.''

''That's fine. What do you plan to wear? I haven't been to the Beach Club yet, so I don't know how they dress for dinner.''

''I haven't either, but we will probably see everything from long formals to short dresses. You'll look great no matter what you wear.''

Marianna chuckled, ''Thanks for the vote of confidence, but you are being partial to an old friend, I'm afraid. Call me after you talk with Brett.''

''I'll do that,'' Joy replied.

She stood up, stretched, and walked into the closet to select her ensemble for the evening. After several rejections, she chose a feather-light dress with soft folds of fabric draped to shape a surplice-style bodice that left her shoulders bare. The short, circular skirt would swirl around her legs as she walked or danced. Its soft, lilac color gave the dress an even more delicate and feminine appearance. Carefully she hung it to one side and placed a pair of high-heeled sandals on the floor below the dress. Her lacy lingerie and evening bag were placed on the .top of the chest-of-drawers. Having dispensed with those details which would save last-minute frustrations, she slipped into a jonquil yellow swimsuit, added a cover-up, and headed for the pool for a well deserved break.

After a strenuous swim, the delicious warmth of the sun further relaxed her aching muscles. Joy stretched and moved into a more comfortable position on the chaise. It wouldn't do to get a sunburn. She stood and raised the back of the lounge chair so that she could watch the activity going on around her. Only moments after she was settled, a hand holding a yellow flower was thrust in front of her. Startled, she turned to find Brett at her side.

"You looked just like a yellow buttercup sitting there. All you lack is a buttercup for your hair." He grinned like a small boy carrying a bouquet of wildflowers.

"You're crazy, do you know that?" Joy laughed. "That's not a buttercup—it's a yellow hibiscus."

"It doesn't matter what it's called—I just thought it would look great tucked behind your ear." He studied her face thoughtfully. "Now which side signifies that you're spoken for?"

"I don't know. Why do you ask?"

"I just wanted to be sure the guys stayed away." He placed the flower carefully over her right ear and tenderly stroked her hair before moving away.

Ignoring the obvious intent of his comment, Joy grinned in spite of herself. "Thank you! Now maybe all those men who have been hanging around all afternoon will disappear," she said, looking around as if to dismiss the invisible admirers. "Now, tell me, how was *your* day?" she asked.

"Great, really great! It got off to such a good start at breakfast that nothing could have possibly gone wrong. Are you game for a race in the pool?"

"I'm afraid not. I swam twenty laps earlier, and I think that's my limit. You go ahead and I'll watch. But please do me a favor. Don't yell, 'Hey look, Mom!' I've heard that at least a dozen times from every kid who has been in the pool," Joy laughed.

He walked to the diving board, stood poised for a moment, then, with a devilish grin, called to Joy, "Hey, look

Mom! No hands!'' He executed a perfect 'cannonball,' tucking his knees to his chest and entering the pool with a wild splash.

Joy's laugh bubbled from deep within. That felt so good, she thought. When was the last time she had really laughed from the very depths of her being? Brett was better than the tranquilizers the doctor had prescribed immediately after her parents' death. With him around, there would be no need for them at all.

She studied his body as he emerged from the pool and walked back to the diving board. He was very well built. An unusually broad chest and shoulders slanted upward to a muscular neck that must have been developed by a great deal of exercise and probably some weight lifting. His navy blue swimsuit revealed a trim waist and hips. Joy noticed with approval his straight, muscular legs. Funny, hadn't it always been the men who admired women's legs? Nevertheless, those were good-looking legs, she insisted silently.

The water clinging to Brett's body caused every muscle to glisten as if covered with oil. Joy became aware of a strange sensation in her chest as she watched him. It was as if a giant hand had squeezed her heart and stopped it for a moment. When it was released, it hammered at twice its normal speed, as if to recapture the missing beats. She gasped. She could never remember having felt this way before. Brett's undeniable attraction was indefinable. He stirred feelings within her that were both delicious and disturbing.

Her eyes were riveted on him. The sunlight playing on his thick, dark hair turned it to red-gold. Heavy brows emphasized the luminous, brown eyes. Unquestionably Brett McCort was a handsome man by any standards. But Joy knew that, beneath the attractive exterior, was also a compassionate and caring person. She had taken note of his thoughtfulness and the sincere desire to bring happiness. She wondered about his religious background. Perhaps, someday, she would have an opportunity to ask him . . .

Joy mentally gave herself a hearty shake. She was appraising the man as if she were a schoolgirl with her first crush. She scolded herself soundly.

A young child brought her back to reality with his cry, "Hey, Mom, watch me!" Joy laughed with delight and relief. Brett had also heard the small voice and was laughing with her as he flopped in exhaustion on the lounge chair next to hers.

"Did Marianna say that she and Dan could join us tonight?"

"Yes, she had been hoping to go to the Beach Club before they left. But they will need to know the time," Joy replied, having at last curbed her runaway emotions.

The two of them agreed that eight o'clock would be best. In deference to Dan's schedule, they decided not to make the evening a late one.

As the sun began to set, there was a sudden chill in the air. Joy shivered as she stepped into her jump suit and zipped it up to her chin.

"I'd better get going. It will take me quite awhile to get my hair unsnarled and presentable for dinner, unless you want me to go looking like this," She pirouetted and posed before him in an exaggerated model's stance.

"You look fine to me, Buttercup, but I don't think the maitre d' would take kindly to your present state," he grinned.

"In that case, I'll see you later." She tossed the words over her shoulder as she walked rapidly past the Tower and back to the Cloister.

Brett watched her until she had disappeared from sight.

She was really quite a woman, he thought. What was it that had mesmerized him after such a short acquaintance? He had known many beautiful, charming, and intelligent women in his time, but there was something about Joy that he couldn't resist. He had thought about it all day. She had made it very clear that she wasn't ready for a romantic relationship. Yet he seemed to be falling in love with her. He wasn't looking for a brief encounter. He wanted to marry her—to take care of her for the rest of her life.

As the sun set over the Cloister, he watched the clouds turn into brilliant pink cotton balls and the sky explode with a myriad of flaming colors. The vivid colors reminded him of this unusual woman who had entered his life so suddenly and had illuminated his being. *Oh Joy, I wish that I could light up your life as you have mine,* he thought.

Finally he rose, hoping to give his whirling thoughts time to rest before he saw her again. He would have to be very careful not to push her. She might run from him like a frightened little rabbit. No, he must bide his time. Only one thing was certain. He fully intended to marry Joy Lawrence. And he was willing to wait—as long as it took.

CHAPTER 8

JOY, BRETT AND THE McAlisters boarded the shuttle bus at the entrance of the Cloister for the short ride to the Boca Beach Club. Brett pointed out the statue of Pan at the entrance to the courtyard and insisted that Joy tell the story of the legendary musician. By the time her tale had ended, they had crossed the Intracoastal Waterway and were approaching Highway, A1A, paralleling the Atlantic.

Joy commented on the number of condominiums that had been built on the beaches of the Gold Coast since her last visit. "They are lovely, but they do block the view of the ocean," she said with a wry look. "I always enjoyed riding on this highway and looking at the ships far out on the horizon. You could tell if the ocean were rough or calm by the number of whitecaps in the distance."

"Hey, lady, don't knock the condos!" Brett objected. "After all, people need a place to live and architects like me need jobs designing them."

"I know, and I can see both sides of the question, but progress does require sacrifices of one kind or another. I guess you can't have your cake and eat it, too. Maybe I am too much of a sentimentalist, but I wish we could hold onto more of the rich traditions of the past.''

Their debate was interrupted as they neared the entrance to the Beach Club. The gateman waved the shuttle through and soon they were alighting from the bus in front of the restaurant. Marianna and Joy immediately spied the shops that lined the walkway leading to the dining room and walked over to look at the window displays.

Dan turned to Brett and said, "You haven't been married, so you haven't learned yet that you never ask a woman to dinner where there are stores nearby unless you have plenty of time. Thank heaven, the shops are closed! Otherwise we probably wouldn't get to eat until midnight! By the way, how did the work go today?''

"Not so good. There has been a delay in the delivery of some materials. So, we're going to have to close down for several days. I'll probably be taking the early flight back to Atlanta in the morning to take care of some things in the office while we're waiting,'' Brett explained.

"Marianna and I will be leaving in the afternoon,'' Dan said. "I have a few more things to finish up at the Gulfstream Bank building in the morning and then we'll head for home. This hasn't been much of a vacation for me, but I'm glad Marianna was able to get away for a few days. With all of the bad weather, she'd been having to stay pretty close to home, and she really needed a change of pace.''

"Did I hear my name mentioned? And what were you saying?'' Marianna asked, as she and Joy returned from their short window-shopping jaunt.

"Honey, how could any comment about you be anything but spectacular?'' Dan teased.

"Better watch it! You'll be back to cold beans and franks

before you know it. There is no chef in *our* kitchen like the ones here,'' Marianna said.

Dan put his arm around his pretty wife, and kissed her soundly. ''Mmm, kisses like that will build up brownie points very quickly,'' she told him as she snuggled against him.

Starting toward the dining room, Brett followed Dan's lead. He put his arm around Joy's waist and bent to give her a kiss. Joy surprised him with a bright smile.

The maitre d' led them to a table overlooking the ocean. The view was superb. Even though it was dark outside, the floodlights picked up the whitecaps as they rolled toward the shoreline. There the water quickly lost its frothy topping and flowed rapidly back into the Atlantic, where it was churned once again into a white torrent. The four diners watched in silent awe, pondering the power and beauty of the ocean.

When the captain approached with the oversized menus, he explained how the fish of the day was prepared and gave them additional information about appetizers and entrées. As he left they opened the menus and studied them carefully.

''Do you think they could fix me a good burger and fries?'' Brett asked, without cracking a smile.

''You can't be serious!'' Joy scolded. ''With all of these delicacies on the menu, you want a burger?''

''But, Joy, the menu is printed in French. Remember my 'limited education.' If I ordered, I might get fried grasshopper or something equally nauseating,'' Brett said.

''Don't be silly! Just look at the small print under the French words. It tells you in plain English not only what the item is, but how it is prepared.'' Joy laughed, knowing that he was teasing her again.

Later, Brett listened with pride as Joy placed her order in

what he assumed must be very good French, because the waiter wrote down her selections without question. After the waiter had removed the menus and walked away, he couldn't resist asking, "Did you notice that Joy ordered in French so that I wouldn't know how much she was planning to eat tonight?" The standing joke brought a round of chuckles. Even Joy was amused.

"Do you guys feel a little out-of-place in your conservative business suits?" Marianna changed the subject. I have never seen men wearing such bright outfits in my life. Today, while I was shopping, I saw one man in a yellow jacket and slacks. And his tie looked like a rainbow," she giggled. "But that's not all. There was one wearing a jump suit made from some pink-and-green tropical print. Can you picture that in one of your offices?"

"Hey, no fair! We guys have to break out of our shells occasionally. After all, you girls can wear those bright colors all the time. In these exotic surroundings, even the 'wallflowers' are knockouts!" Dan quipped.

The amiable conversation was interrupted during the meal by appropriate moans and groans as each course was completed and another begun. Joy's plate was watched with interest, to see just what she had ordered. True to her reputation she devoured her appetizer, Nage de Fruit de Mer Florentine, which, she explained, was a combination of oysters, mussels, and clams on spinach, topped with a white wine sauce. This was followed by a salad and cream-of-asparagus soup.

"Don't you think you had better dance off some of those calories before your entrée comes?" Brett asked as he rose, taking for granted that she would welcome a short respite.

"Delighted, sir!" she replied.

Joy smiled at Brett as they walked toward the parquet dance floor. She admired the way he moved—casually, but with dignity. And he did look very dignified tonight, she thought, in a heather brown suit, white-on-white striped shirt, and an amber silk Rooster tie. Then her heart began to hammer, and a knot formed in her throat. In spite of her best intentions, she could not control the attraction she felt for him.

The orchestra that was playing at the Cabana dining room was excellent. Brett took Joy's hand and whirled her into an intricate dance step. Then he held her lightly while they savored the music.

What a delicious feeling it was to be held like this, she reflected. John had been so undemonstrative, using affection only to further his interests. Joy doubted that they would ever have had a compatible and loving relationship. Well, thank goodness, he was out of her life forever. She pitied the poor girl who would take her place in John's life.

She cast a quick glance at Brett. What was it about this man that she found so hard to resist in spite of her determination not to yield to her emotions. Brett took her hand and placed it on his other shoulder. With his right arm still holding her tightly, he outlined the contours of Joy's face with his free hand. The touch of his fingers on her face sent lightning bolts of excitement down her spine.

She closed her eyes and listened in silence as the band began to play "their song." Her life had been undeniably brightened by this man who was a stranger until only a few, short days ago. She wished that time could stand still and she could hold onto the delicious feelings that enveloped her.

The fragrance of Brett's cologne wafted about her in a most sensual way. She knew that it was sandalwood, but there was something different—perhaps a blend of the essence itself and the unique chemical reaction of Brett's body. The aroma clung to her, awakening dormant sensations she had refused to acknowledge until now.

Time had passed so quickly that the orchestra had stopped for a break before Joy was aware that there was no longer any music. She pulled away from Brett and looked into his eyes. Their shimmering amber flecks were more prominent than ever, and she sensed that he could see into the very depths of her soul—that he could read her thoughts. She must guard her private world very carefully.

"Let's pretend the music hasn't stopped and stay here until the orchestra comes back," Brett whispered.

"I don't think that would be too smart. People would probably think that we were the floor show and start to throw tomatoes at us if we just stood here looking at each other," she said with a grin.

"I suppose you're right . . ." He still held her tightly. "Then how about a walk on the beach after we eat? We can send the chaperones back to the Cloister."

"You are the most determined man I ever met! Have you always gotten everything you wanted?" Joy asked.

"Everything that was worth having," Brett confessed. "I had to work hard for all of the good things, but they are important enough to me that I didn't mind the hard work. Now, don't change the subject. Will you go for a walk with me?"

"Your powers of persuasion are too much for me. I give up," Joy said.

"Hey, I like the sound of that!" Brett said brightly, but his smile faded as he saw her reproachful look.

"Don't get me wrong," he continued quickly. "I only meant that I'm glad you agreed to the walk. No ulterior motives intended, I assure you."

Hand-in-hand, they strolled toward their table, admiring the triple-tiered atrium design of the room. The waning moon could be seen through the skylights and banks of windows that were built into the ultra-modern building.

Verdant runners from hundreds of philodendron plants cascaded like waterfalls from one of the levels that soared above them. Palms and tropical greenery were placed at strategic points throughout the room to break the stark white expanse of the room. Joy loved the plants and the view afforded by the extensive use of glass. Brett, particularly, was appreciative of the unusual architectural design.

"Isn't it strange that everyone in this room would probably describe this place differently?" Joy mused.

"The old saying that beauty is in the eye of the beholder applies to things as well as to people, Joy. Now, I like the appearance of this structure, but I know you really don't care for modern architecture. You probably think of it as just another obstacle to the beauty of nature, just like you feel about the condos on the beach." Brett summarized their differing views.

"Let's not start on that again. No one has been able to solve that problem yet, and I don't think that we will be able to solve it tonight." Joy ended any further conversation which might spoil the warmth she felt toward this man who was becoming so important to her.

The remainder of the meal was accompanied by cheerful conversation and more chuckles as Joy devoured her poached filet of snapper with lobster sauce and vegetables. When the waiter came to take their dessert orders and displayed the luscious desserts from which they could make their selections, Brett turned to Joy.

"And what kind of sherbet will you have?" he asked.

Joy wrinkled her brow in deep thought. Finally she said, "I believe I'll try the raspberry mousse."

The faces of Joy's companions registered utter disbelief! Even with all of the good-natured teasing about her appetite, they could not fathom her ability to eat dessert after such a meal. She proved them wrong shortly when she finished the last bite and then accepted chocolate after-dinner mints. They were all still laughing when they emerged from the restaurant.

"By the time she goes home, she will have gained twenty pounds," Brett grinned.

"Well, frankly, I'm glad to see her eating so well. She looked too thin when I first saw her," Marianna added her opinion.

"Don't worry. When I gain five pounds, I'll cut back," Joy assured them. "After all, I'm the one who has to do the cooking at home. So, I plan to take advantage of the cuisine while I'm here."

Brett turned to the McAlisters and said, "Joy had promised to take a walk on the beach with me. We'll work off a few calories so that she can eat everything she wants tomorrow."

"You two go for your walk. Frankly, I'm bushed and we have to get up early to pack for the trip home tomorrow," Dan said.

"Oh, no! Are you and Marianna really leaving so soon?" Joy moaned in disappointment.

"Yes, I'm afraid so. I just have one or two loose ends to tie up in the morning. Then it's back to the old grind," Dan told her.

Joy hugged him and then turned to Marianna. "You have been a lifesaver to me. I'm so glad that we had this time to renew our friendship."

"It's been wonderful, Joy. Do call when you get home, and we'll go out for lunch," Marianna smiled, unable to resist one last mention of food.

With affectionate embraces all around, the McAlisters boarded the shuttle bus for the ride back to the Cloister. Joy's eyes welled with tears, and her chin began to quiver slightly as she watched her friends drive away. She had just rediscovered an old friend at a time when she needed her most. Now she was leaving and Joy felt a sense of loss.

Brett put a comforting arm around her and studied her face carefully. He thought she looked like a porcelain doll with crystal tears rolling down her face. Sensing that her emotions were very fragile, he tried valiantly to control his own.

Slowly he pulled Joy to him and kissed her tenderly. The gentle kiss began to ease some of her pain, and she found herself responding with a fervor that surprised them both. She clasped her arms about him as if he were a life preserver tossed to a victim of shipwreck. Her eager response kindled his desire. He kissed her deeply and she answered with warmth and longing.

Reluctantly they parted and strolled toward the beach.

CHAPTER 9

JOY QUICKLY FOUND that walking on the beach while wearing high-heeled sandals was not only very difficult but a little ridiculous. Brett supported her as she removed first one and then the other. Taking the sandals, he poked one in each of his coat pockets, then removed his coat and slung it carelessly over his shoulder. With his arm around her slim waist, they began to walk down the beach. Joy's head rested against his strong shoulder.

They ambled along in silence for a short distance, unaware that they were headed in the direction of the Boca Raton Inlet. They soon discovered that their progress had been halted by the span of water which poured into the ocean.

"If we want to go any further south, we'll have to swim across the mouth of the inlet," Joy laughed at her astonished escort.

"I had forgotten that it was so close to the Beach Club. The hotel is surrounded on three sides by water." Brett was chagrined.

Hoping to temper his disappointment, Joy spoke. "They say that this is where Boca Raton got its name. Apparently some seventeenth-century Spanish sailors thought that the mouth of the channel with its sharp pointed rocks resembled the teeth in a rat's mouth. *Boca Raton* means 'mouth of the rat' in English." Joy grinned as he wrinkled his nose in distaste.

"That has to be the most unromantic thing any woman has ever said to a man while strolling along the beach on a beautiful, moonlight night. But I like the Spanish pronunciation the 'locals' use—making 'Raton' rhyme with 'stone.'"

"There are some interesting stories about the harbor, too," Joy continued. "It is said that pirates once hid their ships inside the rocks so that they could dash out and capture vessels carrying gold and treasure, and even beautiful women. I can just picture you as a pirate with a cutlass in your teeth, jumping from one ship to another. You would probably have grabbed the fairest of the damsels and carried her back to your ship. She would have fallen madly in love with you and followed you gladly back to Spain or Portugal!" Joy's imagination ran rampant with images of earlier days.

"Aha, I like the picture you are conjuring up! So, I'm a pirate grabbing a beautiful lady and bodily carrying her away with him, huh? Perhaps . . . like this?" He swept Joy up in his arms and ran with her a few yards up the beach.

"No, Brett! Put me down! That was just make-believe. Put me down!"

"But I want to make all of your fantasies come true, Princess. So I'm going to carry you off to a deserted island and we will live there happily forever and ever." He laughed as she vigorously but vainly tried to escape.

Abandoning her efforts, she was unable to keep from

joining in his laughter. Exhausted from their spirited tussle, Joy began to relax in his arms. He held her easily. She felt no heavier than a child, he thought. As their laughter subsided, Brett bent his head slowly to hers and moved his lips softly over her forehead to her ear. His deep breathing ruffled her hair as it spilled around her shoulders. She wrapped her soft arms around his neck as his lips tenderly sought hers.

Brett showered Joy's face with kisses, his lips lingering at the hollow of her throat where the pulse pounded erratically. Through the soft fabric of his shirt, Joy could feel his heart beating in tempo with her own. He kissed her once again and she sensed his growing desire. Powerless against the fever his kisses ignited in her, she reveled in the exquisite agony.

Uttering a low moan Brett released her decisively, setting her down. As Joy's feet touched the sandy beach, she became conscious that her knees would no longer support her body. Brett held her gently as she spread her shawl and settled on the beach. Then he dropped down to sit beside her. With the moonlight bathing their faces in its soft glow, they watched the relentless pounding of the surf, reflecting their own rising passions.

At last Brett spoke, his voice husky. "Joy, I almost lost control a minute ago, and I love you too much for a casual affair. You're too important to me."

Joy breathed deeply, exhaling in a long sigh of relief. "Thank you, Brett, for caring that much." Her gratitude was intensified by the knowledge that it was he who had regained his composure long enough to halt the rushing tide of emotions that had threatened to sweep them both away.

"Believe me, that was one of the hardest things I've ever had to do. I want you so much, but not like this," he answered. Then seeking an avenue that would relieve some

103

of his pain, he continued, "But don't involve me in any more of your fantasies. I began to pretend that I was the pirate kidnapping you and, suddenly, I was living the part. If I had had a ship, you would have been halfway to the Bahamas by now!"

She laughed in relief, as a sense of normality returned. Joy straightened the soft swirls of her dress and retrieved her shawl which now resembled a beach blanket instead of a couturier's dream.

Brushing the last grains of sand from her dress, Joy opened her evening bag and found a comb to run through her hair. Then she made an attempt to repair her make-up.

"You look great without any of that," Brett smiled fondly as she touched her lips with gloss.

He shook her large shawl vigorously, letting the ocean breeze carry away the last vestige of sand. Then he lovingly wrapped it around her shoulders and pulled her to him for one last embrace before they left the shore. Holding her closely to him, they walked toward the entrance where they would catch the shuttle to the Cloister.

As they rode past the fountain on their return, Brett turned to Joy. "Let's don't end the evening just yet. How about a walk in the courtyard?"

Sharing his reluctance to break the spell of this perfect evening, Joy quickly agreed. They walked slowly, admiring the citrus trees with their tiny, twinkling lights. The colored spotlights focusing on the fountain bathed "The Lady" in a myriad of changing hues, adding dimension and depth to the crystal water spilling forth. The statue stood, proud and serene above them, her secret safe behind her enigmatic smile.

"I love this place," Joy said. "The Garden of Eden itself could not have been more exquisitely beautiful."

"Perhaps this *is* the Garden of Eden. At least you are my

Eve—my lovely little temptress. There are times when you frustrate me, puzzle me, tease me, delight me—but you are worth the risk.''

Brett had seated himself beside Joy on one of the glazed tile benches that were positioned to offer the best view of the fountain. Now he looked into her face. She could feel his eyes, like little fingers of heat, caressing her. She turned toward the source of the warmth, her heart in her throat.

"Joy, you must know how much I love you." He stared intently into her sparkling, aquamarine eyes and pondered how to tell her that he must go to Atlanta the following day. He would miss her as if she were a limb that had been severed from his body. She had become a part of his very being during the few short days he had known her.

Joy found it impossible to speak. Her emotions were at such a peak that she was afraid to chance a reply. Her body began to tingle once more with the memory of Brett's embrace. What had happened to her? She had known this man only a few days; yet, tonight, she had tossed her inhibitions to the wind and succumbed to his passionate kisses. What could she have been thinking to let such a thing happen? She had been so determined that she would not become involved with anyone again. Yet she sat quivering under his steady gaze—his velvety, brown eyes almost hypnotic in their effect on her.

Sheer physical attraction had caused her to react the way she had on the beach—a release from long pent-up emotions, she decided. It must not happen again, or she would be trapped by her own emotions. What had Brett said about "risk"? He was ready to risk—to be vulnerable. She was not. And she must not give her newly discovered passion any further opportunity for expression.

"Joy, did you hear me?" Brett was saying. "I said that I love you! You are the one I have waited for all these years. I

105

realize we haven't known each other long, but I want to marry you. I want you to be my wife.''

The color drained from Joy's face, nerves tensed as if she had received a sudden blow to her body. Surely she had misunderstood Brett. He couldn't have asked her to marry him. Why would he do that just as she was beginning to get her head together and they were building a comfortable relationship? She felt herself spinning dizzily, pulled against her will into a violent whirlpool of doubts and fears.

''Brett, you know I can't marry you.'' Her reply sounded harsh even to her own ears, though she had not intended it so. ''You knew that I needed some time to adjust, to work some things out for myself. ''Please—don't rush me!''

Brett's dark eyes clouded. He rose abruptly, towering over her. His face was contorted with pain and anger.

''I don't believe you, Joy! You felt the same way I did down on the beach. Don't bother to deny it! I don't want to have a casual affair with you. I want to marry you—yet you treat my proposal like an insult. I can't stand much more of this torture—of being with you and not having you. Tonight I thought you were finally ready to climb out of your dark cave and join the rest of the human race. But I was wrong—very wrong. Well, don't worry! I won't be around to intrude on your privacy. You can be alone to your heart's content. Please excuse me if I don't escort you to your room. Since you are so intent on doing things on your own, you can find your way, I'm sure. Good night!''

Brett's words, like physical blows, forced the breath from her body, leaving her speechless and battered.

He turned on his heel and stalked angrily toward the hotel, not waiting to hear Joy's explanation—that she didn't want to risk hurting him or being hurt until she had sorted out her other problems. And now she faced the most staggering realization of all—that she did, indeed, love Brett McCort! Joy could see nothing but lights swimming in a pool of water as tears flowed in dark rivulets down her face. Her breathing became labored and she sobbed uncontrollably.

Curling up on the bench, she cried until she was exhausted. Her sobs became dry rasping gasps. When all of her tears were spent, she could not will her body to stand. Staring at the fountain, she raised her swollen eyes to the "Lady of Boca." What was her secret? How could she smile when Joy's world was crumbling around her?

Finally Joy rubbed her eyes so that she could look at her watch. She discovered that she had been lying on the hard tile for over two hours. Her body ached all over, but the pain she felt within her made the other seem insignificant. With the corner of her shawl, she wiped her mascara-stained face. Quietly she slipped into the lobby and up to her room, hoping no one would notice her disheveled appearance.

Walking into the bathroom, she stripped off the lovely dress that was now soiled with both sand and make-up, and dropped it in the middle of the floor. Her delicate, lace-trimmed underclothes followed. When she had undressed, she walked across the clothing as if it were not there, and stepped into the shower. Icy spears of water stung her face and body. She had hoped that they would wake her sleeping brain so that she could make some sense of the evening. The water washed away the dark streaks from her face, but she made no attempt to move.

Questions ran through Joy's mind. Why had she been left when everyone she had ever loved had been taken? Why did she have to endure life without them? Was this the reason she had refused to let herself love again, why it was so difficult to say the words *I love you?* Was this a punishment for something she had done? Why did God seem so very far away—now, of all times, when she needed Him most.

The icy water finally took its toll on Joy's body, and she began to shake violently. Turning the water off, she reached for a towel, dripping water on the pile of clothes as she walked across it once more. Toweling herself dry, she grabbed the first gown she could find, slid it over her head, and fell across the bed.

Raising her head for a moment she listened intently, hoping to hear some sound from Brett's room. There was only deathly silence, though the sound of his angry accusations reverberated through her brain. Ironically, "their" song played inharmoniously in the background, spinning around and around like a broken record. The words and melody were haunting. The light had left her life, but the music lingered on.

Suddenly Joy's eyes fell on Ellen's Bible. She had placed it on the bedside table when unpacking on that first day. It had not been opened since. Now she found herself fingering the pages, velvety from much use, scanning once-familiar passages:

The Lord is my shepherd, I shall lack for nothing.
He makes me lie down in green pastures, he leads me beside quiet waters, he restores my soul . . .

Could it have been the Lord who had brought her to this place of green tranquillity and still waters—to be restored, renewed? The Psalmist continued:

I will be glad and rejoice in your love, for you saw my affliction and know the anguish of my soul . . .

Her Creator knew her so well. He had seen her tears, her aching heart, her anguished soul—and He loved her in spite of her fragile faith!

*I sought the Lord, and he answered me, he delivered me
from all my fears.*

Had she really sought the Lord? Or was she, as Brett had
insisted, still intent on working things out for herself? Well,
she had to admit, she had certainly made a royal mess of
things. She read on:

*Delight yourself in the Lord and he will give you the
desires of your heart.*

Was this marvelous promise really hers? The desires of
her heart—a love-filled marriage, children—seemed more
remote than ever. When Brett walked out, her heart had
almost stopped beating. Yet the promise was preceded by a
condition—"Delight yourself in the Lord." That was it!
Her priorities were badly out of order. Here in Boca she had
been seeking rest for her body and mind when what she
really needed was rest for her spirit. She buried her face in
the pages of Ellen's Bible and wept. This time, the tears
were tears of repentance and healing.

Feeling somewhat refreshed, Joy stepped into the bathroom to wash her tear-stained face. Her innately tidy nature
recoiled at the sight of the sodden pile of clothing still lying
on the bathroom floor. She bent down and scooped up the
armload of silky fabric, and then she smelled the fragrance
—sandalwood. The scent clung to the dress she had worn,
assailing her senses, invading her heart and mind.

She must see Brett again—if only to apologize for her
strange behavior. Somehow, whatever the future held for
them, Joy knew she would never be completely alone again.

CHAPTER 10

THE SUN WAS ALREADY shining brightly when Joy opened her swollen eyelids. She was groggy from the after-effects of the traumatic evening, but her heart was lighter. Today she would make things right with Brett. She must dress quickly and talk with him before he left for work. Taking almost no thought of her appearance, she grabbed the pink jump suit and stepped into it hurriedly. Rather than flattering her complexion, the bright color emphasized its pallor. There was nothing that she could do to remove the puffiness from her face, but at least she could try to hide the chalky whiteness, broken by the large indigo circles under her eyes. She slathered on foundation, more blush than usual, and touched a bright pink lipstick to her lips. All of her efforts were insufficient to cover the devastation of the evening before. Only her eyes revealed a new serenity.

Dumping the contents from her evening bag into her shoulder tote, she then picked up the key which she had slung across the desk the night before and rushed toward the elevator. Surely, she thought, she would be able to catch

Brett before he left the dining room. Everything would be all right if she could just speak with him.

As she walked into the lobby, she glanced out the tall, arched windows and saw Brett. He was wearing a business suit rather than the familiar work garb, and was standing by the airport limo. What was he doing? Where was he going? Why hadn't he told her that he was leaving?

The driver of the limousine had finished stowing the luggage and Brett was climbing into the automobile before she could reach the doors of the hotel. Having run all the way across the long lobby, Joy was breathing heavily as she pushed open the front doors without waiting for the doorman's assistance. Just as she stepped outside, the car pulled away. She wanted to call out to the driver to stop, but the words caught in her throat. It was too late. She stood frozen. But thoughts and questions toppled over each other in an effort to bring some semblance of order to the devastating turn of events.

Brett hadn't told her he was leaving, she was sure of that. Was he so angry with her that he would ignore his job here and just take off without a word of explanation? Where was he going? And why? Why? The questions pounded in her mind like an angry surf, eroding the measure of peace that had come to her through Ellen's Bible.

Once more the tears welled up in her eyes. How could there be any tears left? She turned, walked stiffly back into the hotel, and took the elevator to her floor.

When she reached her room, she fell across the bed. Then she smelled it again . . . the sandalwood cologne. His fragrance lingered, but now he was gone—and this time she had lost him forever!

If she had only controlled her long-denied passions . . . If she hadn't responded to his ardent kisses . . . If he hadn't asked her to marry him—then she would have had more time to straighten out her life—a life that would now never include Brett McCort.

The room became a prison. She prowled about like a caged tiger. The sight of the Banyan tree did nothing to ease her pain, nor did the Bible that lay open to the book of Psalms. Overnight everything had changed. All of the bright beauty had turned to ugly shades of gray and black. She flung herself across the bed and wept tears that had been hidden in some recess of her body only to spring forth anew when it appeared that the supply had been exhausted.

It was almost evening before Joy became aware that she had not eaten in almost twenty-four hours. She called room service and ordered a salad and hot tea. She winced when she thought of the happy dinners she had shared with Brett, and his playful teasing. Well, she had no appetite tonight.

Joy didn't taste a bite of the lovely salad. Robot-like, she lifted the fork to her mouth, chewed, and swallowed. After the waiter had removed the table, she was once more alone with her thoughts. They were anything but good company.

Brett, I love you, she thought. *Please listen to me— wherever you are. I love you. Why can't I speak those words when I'm with you? I'm sure God sent you to me to help me work out my problems just by your presence and under- standing. He knew you could teach me to love again. You were a part of the plan all along! Brett, can you hear me? I love you, I love you, I love you . . .*

Golfers dotted the fairways and greens beyond Joy's win- dow, and the groundskeepers were busy with their assigned tasks before she made any attempt to stir. She looked to- ward the window, and the brilliance of the sun's rays sad-

112

dened her. How could the sun shine so brightly when her mood was dark and somber? She pulled the sheet over her head and lay motionless. If she did not move, maybe she could erase the memory of the events that had led to this state of black depression. But the more she tried to forget, the more the memories rushed back to haunt her.

With a determined effort Joy pushed back the covers and raised her body to a sitting position. Her legs moved sluggishly and mechanically. Like a zombie she walked toward the bathroom and splashed water on her face. There seemed to be no reason to dress. She located a robe that she had thrown on the floor and struggled to slip it on. Standing in the center of the room, she looked around as if she could not decide where she was and had no idea what she should do next.

The ringing of the phone broke the silence. Its insistent, piercing noise caused Joy's body to jerk involuntarily. She put her hands to her ears in an attempt to stop the deafening sound. Then, hoping it might be Brett, she lifted the receiver.

"Joy, it's Ellen. How are you dear?"

Usually Ellen's voice was mellow and calm, but today there was a distinct note of hysteria.

"Ellen, are you all right? Is Granny Okay?" What's wrong?" Joy was suddenly concerned.

"I'm fine and Granny is fine. But I really do need to talk with you. I was going to call last night, but decided that morning would be a better time," Ellen continued.

"A better time for what?"

"Well, the news is good, but the timing couldn't be worse. All the customers, who were so understanding while we finished the gowns for the hospital balls, are impatient to know when this dress and that dress will be ready. And the mothers of the debutantes are anxious to pick up their daughters' gowns so they can have their portraits done. To top it all off, we are already getting orders for next year's charity balls. They just won't listen to anything I tell them. They want to talk with you—and nobody else. I hated to call you, but my nerves are just about shredded, Joy. When can you come home?'' Ellen's litany of complaints was like salt in an open wound.

"Oh, Ellen, things are not going well for me, either. I haven't had time to relax and I don't feel at all like working.'' Joy's normally gentle voice was high and shrill.

Her friend, concerned with her own problems and the pressures of work, made no comment. Of all people, Joy had expected Ellen to sympathize, but she had seemingly ignored Joy's unspoken plea.

When the older woman continued, Joy grasped her head and pressed her fingers to her throbbing temple: "Ellen . . . Ellen, stop a minute and listen to me. . . . Yes, I know how troublesome they can be. . . . Yes, I'll come home. I'll be on the first flight I can get. This is the peak of the tourist season, you know. . . . No, don't bother to meet me. Just try to hold yourself together for a few more days. If things get too bad, just close the shoppe until I get home. Now, hang up and go fix yourself a cup of hot tea. I'll see you soon.''

Joy replaced the receiver and put her head down on the pillow. What else could go wrong? How much more could she take?

Then her tumbled thoughts focused on an idea that had evolved slowly—ever since the day of the shopping spree with Marianna. In the children's clothing stores, Joy had fingered the dainty batiste day gowns and admired the exquisite smocking on the toddler dresses, and the idea had taken shape. A children's boutique! She was committed to designing the ball gowns for the upcoming social season, but she had always longed to create fashions in miniature

—those treasured keepsakes of love that could be handed down from one generation to another. *Such designs only grow more precious and beautiful with time,* she thought, *like fine old silver.*

Joy shook her head impatiently. There would be time later to discuss the idea with Ellen. Right now there was a crisis that demanded every erg of her failing energy. She breathed a prayer for strength, and picked up the phone to make her reservation on the next plane to Atlanta. Just as she had expected, all flights were booked for the next four days. She declined stand-by. If there was anything she disliked, it was being tied to a phone waiting for a ticket agent to report a cancellation.

Her thoughts returned to the conversation with Ellen. Strange that her wise and mature friend should need a shoulder to lean on. Joy had thought her a paragon of strength and faith. *How human we all are,* she mused. Even her beloved parents had not had all the answers, but they had pointed her to the unfailing Source. From that Fountain flowed every resource she would ever need. The realization, however, did not quite remove the pain she still felt at the thought of Brett . . .

Joy did not leave the room for the rest of the day, nor did she bother to eat until late evening when she ordered a light meal of soup and hot tea. The food did little to raise her spirits, but it did slightly dull the throbbing in her head.

She picked up several current magazines she had brought to read and thumbed through the pages. The titles were cruelly ironic: "How to Find Someone Who Will Love You as You Are"; "How to Let Go and Love Again"; "Eight Ways to Tell Whether You Are a Loser in Love"; "How Do You Overcome Your Addiction to Him?"; "Do You Have Enough Initiative to Be Your Own Boss?" When she spotted an article entitled "Living Alone and Having a Ball," Joy flung the magazines into the waste paper basket. No help here. She reached, instead, for Ellen's Bible and turned to the Psalms. David, too, suffered under a heavy burden of his own making.

Later, the quiet of the moonlit night was broken by a bird outside her window, improvising a song of exquisite trills and swells. He poured out the melodious notes, liquid and sweet, in a serenade of ecstasy. Joy had awakened when he began his melodious melody to his mate. It was almost too much to bear, but she listened in reverence to this primitive ritual of love. A phrase from an old song came to her: "His eye is on the sparrow, and I know He watches me." Comforted, she slept.

The next morning Joy showered and dressed, determined to spend a more normal day. Her reflection in the full-length mirror told her she still had a long way to go to recover her customary sparkle.

On her way to the dining room, Domenick inquired if she were feeling ill and asked if there were anything he might do to help. She attempted a weak smile but assured him she would be just fine. His eyes reflected her pain as he watched her slow progress through the lobby.

She picked at her breakfast, eating only a few bites, and then wandered back into the lobby. To pass the time, she decided to browse in DeLoy's, an exclusive boutique offering designer originals, available in this specialty shop alone. Seeing the results of others' creativity might stimulate her own.

Joy admired the fabrics, the workmanship, and the unusual detailing. There was a wide selection of clothing for every type of woman and for any event she might wish to attend.

Joy's attention was suddenly drawn to the colors in a skirt of the softest, sheerest georgette she had ever seen. The fabric was designed with vertical stripes of rainbow colors that looked like a watercolor painting. She was impressed by the ingenious way in which the material had been doubled, with the fold at the hemline. By doubling the georgette, the filmy material was not marred by the thickness of a hem. It was so beautiful that Joy replaced it on the rack with a touch of envy. Oh, how she wished to be creative again. She left the lovely little shop and walked out into the lobby.

She considered writing to Brett. Perhaps a letter explaining her attitude would be more effective. She sat down at one of the little desks that were placed at intervals under the tall windows. At any other time, Joy would have reveled in the lovely tropical palms and plants outside the windows, creating a garden paradise. But at the moment Joy was oblivious to everything except the need to communicate with Brett. With the pen poised over the paper, she stared at the blank pink page bearing the golden crest of the hotel. Her mind went blank. She could think of nothing to write! She rose from the desk and trudged back to her room to spend another restless night.

For the first time since Brett's departure, Joy made a valiant attempt to look like her attractive self. She dressed carefully and applied make-up. The mascara made her eyes look wide and haunted. No matter, she thought. There was no longer anyone whom she was trying to please.

She had ignored the aching protest of her stomach when she neglected to eat breakfast. Now it was rumbling noisily. The feasts of previous days now made the famine of the last two days unbearable. Joy walked into the Expresso, hoping that a light lunch would calm the queasiness within.

Ordinarily she would have been entranced by the Victorian dining room with its "gingerbread trim," bentwood chairs, brass railings, and stained-glass panels that glowed colorfully throughout the room. Today, even the most glorious sights could not distract her.

She ordered a bowl of minestrone. Other diners appeared to be enjoying the food, but Joy could not taste a thing. The soup did nothing to warm the cold interior of her body.

When she left the dining room, she strolled aimlessly, finding herself in the courtyard. She had purposely avoided the fountain since her traumatic scene with Brett the night he had walked out of her life. But she needed to see it again. She could not allow this unhappy episode to tarnish the wonderful attachment she had always felt for the Cloister and its surroundings.

Sitting on one of the benches that was shaded by an orange tree, she tried to look at the fountain. Her eyes welled with tears once more and she had to look away. The golden fruit hanging over her head caught her eye. Without thinking, she reached up and plucked one of the oranges. The instant that she did so, she was sorry. She should have left it there for others to enjoy. If every guest picked one piece of fruit, the trees would soon be bare. Well, she thought, since she couldn't put it back, she would eat it.

Her fingernail would not pierce its shiny surface. Turning the orange around in her hand, she studied it intently. So engrossed was she that she did not see the airport limo arrive, nor did she see Brett emerging from the automobile. He, too, had glanced at the statue and the fountain when the car drove past, and had spotted Joy sitting on the bench. He asked the doorman to take care of his luggage and started for the fountain when he noticed an elderly gentleman approaching Joy.

Joy, too, had been so caught up in her own thoughts that

she was unaware of the man's presence until he appeared before her. He was a miniature Santa Claus. His lively, blue eyes twinkled, and his full head of snow-white hair and beard were to be envied by Santa himself.

"Young lady," he asked, "would you like to borrow my pocket knife to peel that orange?"

Startled by the voice, Joy looked up into the beaming, friendly face, "Oh, thank you. I would appreciate it."

As the man reached in his pocket, he said, "There is an old superstition about peeling fruit. If you cut off the entire peel without breaking it, turn the peel around three times over your head, and throw it over your shoulder, the paring will form the initial of your lover's name."

He watched as Joy peeled the fruit in one curling ribbon of orange. The jovial, little man wiped the blade of his knife, replaced it in his pocket, and smiled as he strolled away leaving Joy staring at the peel in her hand.

Feeling a little foolish, she circled the peeling around her head three times. *This is silly,* she thought, *a little like kissing the turned-up hem of your skirt in the hope of getting a new dress.* Nevertheless, she tossed it over her shoulder and turned to see a perfectly formed, golden "B" on the ground. She gasped and rushed blindly from the courtyard toward the Banyan tree.

Brett had stood in the shadow of the trees, listening to the conversation. He walked to where Joy had been sitting and looked down to see the initial glowing against the dark earth. He followed the path that Joy had taken, and when he reached the corner of the building, turned and looked for her. It appeared that she had vanished. Then he saw her sitting on the grass with her hands and face pressed against the trunk of the Banyan tree. As he moved closer, he could hear the desperate sobs coming from the small, forlorn figure.

"Joy, honey, don't cry like that. Please don't cry. I can't stand to see you so unhappy," he pleaded.

Jumping up suddenly, she stared at him incredulously. He had come back! He must still care for her! As quickly as the tears had begun, they disappeared, leaving only dark rivers of mascara trailing down her face. A radiant smile transformed her face for the first time in days.

Brett grasped Joy to him and she flung her arms around his neck. His lips crushed hers, hungry for the sweetness of her kisses after the days of separation. Running her fingers through the thick, dark hair at the back of his neck, she found herself inhaling the familiar sandalwood fragrance. But this time *Brett was here!* His closeness was reassuring and comforting.

They held each other as if their very lives depended on the safe harbor they had found in the other's arms. The entire world around them was forgotten.

"Oh, Brett, I thought you were gone forever—that I would never see you again." Joy was ecstatic. "It was so important that I talk to you, explain to you . . ."

"Hold it! Let me go first," Brett interrupted. "Please forgive me for letting my temper run away with me the other night. I'm afraid that is one of my worst faults. I leap before I look and regret it later. I was the one to blame. I should have waited—given you more time. But when I finally found what I had been looking for all my life, I just couldn't help myself. I was afraid that you might slip away from me."

"But I should not have been so abrupt," Joy insisted. "It was just an involuntary reflex—like jerking your hand away from a hot stove. I had been burned so badly once before. I need you, Brett. But it took the shock of your leaving me to make me realize it."

"Honey, I didn't leave you. I had been trying to tell you

all evening that I had business in Atlanta the next day. But I was dreading the separation. As angry as I was at that moment, I never had any intention of leaving you. You will just have to put up with my hanging around until you are ready for me to ask you again to be my wife," Brett said as he kissed her cheek gently.

"Oh, Brett, I missed you so much. You don't know what these days without you have been like. I have relived every moment we have spent together. You were right the first day we met when you said that maybe you could help. You see, I think God sent you to me. That may sound strange to you . . . but so many things have happened since I have been here that it *couldn't* be coincidence. I need your strength, your happy disposition, your love. I need *you*."

He looked longingly into the blue eyes that were now streaked with red, and puffy from hours of crying.

"Joy, please forgive me for hurting you so. When I left, I thought it would be best not to call you—that you needed time alone. It never occurred to me that you would think I had deserted you. I'll try to be patient until you are ready. What you have told me does not surprise me at all. While we were apart, I did my share of praying, too, and I am convinced that God intended us for each other—to love and to cherish."

He took Joy in his arms once again and kissed her tenderly. As he held her, Joy looked up at the canopy of greenery formed by the branches of the Banyan tree. Then the thought struck her: The characteristics of the Banyan tree—compassion, strength, support, sturdiness, protection, and faith—were all qualities that Brett possessed! He had been the one she had searched for since she was a little girl. With Brett's help she could learn to face the future unafraid.

CHAPTER 11

JOY TOOK GREAT PAINS in selecting the dress she would wear for dinner that evening. After much consideration she decided on an eye-catching, one-shoulder design. She loved to combine unorthodox colors, and the geranium-pink georgette dress with its American Beauty red sash was one of her finest creations. Tonight, above all nights, she wanted to look her very best for Brett.

She had stayed in the sun a little longer than usual after her swim, hoping to turn the pallor of her complexion to a rosy hue. Her smooth skin now glowed.

As Joy deftly applied her make-up, she remembered the one time she had treated herself to a salon evaluation during one of her visits to New York. Her face had been labeled "a fantasy face"—no hard edges—a face of natural beauty, contrived and complicated, but showing strength." The world-famous cosmetician had said, "You love the enchanting . . . the organdies, chiffons, slipper satins, taffeta, draped and flowing in a mist of impressionists' pallets."

Great care had been taken in pressing the dress so that the

folds of the skirt flowed softly from her waist. The luscious pink fabric that draped across her breasts was held by tiny spaghetti ties at one shoulder, and the softness of the lines was enhanced by the startling scarlet sash. The dramatic touch of color added just the right amount of spice to the delicious creation, she thought, as she twirled in front of the mirror. She smiled at the reflection as her skirt rippled in waves about her feet.

Remembering how the fragrance of Brett's cologne had lingered long after he was gone, Joy daubed some perfume behind each ear and at the pulse points of her wrists. Heavy perfumes had never suited her and she had taken great care in selecting this one—a light souffle that was supposed to haunt the wearer and incite curiosity. She hoped that the "Gloria Vanderbilt" perfume would have just that effect on Brett.

She was ready long before she heard Brett's knock. When she opened the door, he stood for a long moment gazing at her in silent admiration.

"Brett!" she breathed his name. He was stunning in a white dinner jacket.

"Hello, Princess." His voice was low and husky as he pulled her toward him. "You are even more beautiful than I remembered."

His slow, sensual kiss sent Joy's pulse racing. She stirred uneasily in his arms, and he moved away, sensing her discomfort.

"Don't be afraid, Joy. You can trust me . . ." Then, in a less serious tone, he said, "I think we had better get you something to eat. You have lost several pounds while I was away. Haven't you been eating?" Brett scolded.

"Well, I guess I lost my appetite . . ."

"In that case, let's go find it. Maybe they will kill the fatted calf for their prodigal guest," he grinned, taking her arm and ushering her ceremoniously from the room.

When they arrived in the Patio Royale, they found it transformed into a coral fantasia by the mellow glow of candlelight. Ornamental fig trees growing in large urns sparkled with tiny, white lights. And Addison Mizner's passion for arches was in evidence throughout the room. Pointed arches framed the soaring windows and tall, white, rounded ones crowned the massive wooden doors. Baskets of ferns were suspended from the center of another row of graceful arches, supported by twin columns that spanned the width of the room.

Joy and Brett were seated on a raised balcony overlooking the main part of the dining room. From the windows they could see a sleek cabin cruiser docking at the hotel's marina on Lake Boca Raton. It was an enchanted evening —a new beginning for them.

Caught up in the spirit of the occasion, Brett said, "Let's celebrate our reunion with a toast." He caught her hand in his and dropped a light kiss in the palm.

"I feel like celebrating! It's so good to have you back. You can't possibly know how lonely it was while you were away," Joy told him.

"You couldn't have been any more unhappy than I. I could just imagine some man sweeping you off your feet before I could get back," he admitted.

"I had to fight them off with a big stick," Joy said as her soft laughter bubbled once again.

She studied the deeply tanned face that had become so precious to her. The cleft in his chin was more prominent by candlelight, and the lines that creased downward beside his mouth deepened with his smile. Then his eyes caught hers. She felt a tingle race up her spine. His eyes affected her in the strangest way. They seemed to caress her face and speak to her in a voice all their own. His eyes had been the first thing she had noticed about him on the drive from the airport. They still intrigued her.

The cooler was placed beside their table and the waiter poured a little of the Perrier in each glass. After the waiter had left the table, Brett raised his glass, "It isn't champagne, but I want to propose a toast to the loveliest lady in the room: Never above you—never below you—always beside you."

As they touched their glasses, Joy looked at him and said, "That was lovely. I don't think I've heard it before."

"It means that I never want to dominate you or be dominated by you, but I'll be there beside you whenever you need me."

"Thank you, Brett," Joy whispered. "Now," she said brightly, "what am I going to have for dinner?"

"Anything you like. Tell me what you want, and I promise I will order for you without comment."

She proceeded to list the items she had selected from the extensive list: Chilled bay shrimp with avocado and grapefruit sections, spinach soup, hearts of lettuce salad with blue cheese dressing, roast Long Island duckling with wild rice and brandied Bing cherries, carrots, and a baked potato.

True to his word, Brett did not utter a word as she named the various foods. But one eyebrow flew up and a sly grin creased his face as he tried to remember her choices. Remarkably he was able to relay the order to the waiter.

Crunching on crispy vegetables from the relish tray before them, they chatted happily. The old happy-go-lucky feeling returned gradually. The tension both of them had felt slowly ebbed away and they lingered over the meal. At times Brett felt himself on the verge of making some comment, but he cautiously refrained. Joy was such a sensitive, beautiful woman and her emotions had been on a seesaw for quite a while. He would have to be very careful not to upset the momentary balance by a careless remark.

Much later, he asked, "Do you want any dessert?"

"If you will have some with me, I'll have some pear sherbet. It's such a delicacy that we can't get it in Atlanta," Joy grinned.

"Only if you'll promise me that afterwards we can go in the El Lago room and hear Van Smith and the band. They're playing there tonight. That guy who plays the trumpet makes me wish I had continued with my trumpet lessons."

"I'd love it!" she agreed.

The elegant room they entered was one that Joy had never seen before, and she swiveled her head to take in all of the decor. The lights in the gleaming chandelier had been dimmed, casting a soft glow over the entire room. She was amazed that such a huge room could feel so cozy. Conversation and laughter mingled with the melodious sound of the orchestra.

The waiter had just pulled out Joy's chair when she felt someone's eyes on her. Turning toward the band, she saw Van Smith at the piano, nodding and smiling. Returning his smile, she settled herself comfortably, and Brett took a seat beside her. Suddenly she was aware that the orchestra was playing a familiar melody.

"Brett, did you request 'You Light Up My Life'?" she asked.

"No, honest, I didn't. You must have made quite an impression on Mr. Smith the night I asked him to play it for you."

The maestro's touch on the piano keys lent a quality to the song that Joy had never heard before. When he moved his right hand to play the melody on the celeste, the bell-like tones added another dimension that enhanced the impromptu score. From their table Brett and Joy watched the pianist's hands moving gracefully from one instrument to another. Not once did he look at the keyboards, but was constantly scanning the faces of the people in the audience.

When the song had ended, Joy and Brett rose from their table and walked over to thank the pianist.

"Mr. Smith," Joy began, "of all the people who have enjoyed your music, how did you ever remember *us?*"

The orchestra leader's eyes twinkled. "People are my hobby," he said. "I enjoy trying to put faces and tunes together. Bringing pleasure to others is a real source of satisfaction for me. Then, of course," he added, maintaining the melody with one hand while including the band members with a sweep of the other, "I have a great group of musicians who do an outstanding job of improvisation."

"Well, it certainly does a lot for the ego to be remembered. Thanks again for giving us such a beautiful memory." Joy flashed a brilliant smile as Brett bowed, giving a smart salute to the other members of the band.

"It was our pleasure. If you have another song you want to hear, just let me know," Smith said as his hands moved across the keyboard, never missing a beat.

At their table, Joy turned to study the now-familiar face in profile as Brett listened to the music. Questions wandered about, unchecked, in her head. What would it be like to be married to Brett? How would it feel to "belong" to someone? She realized that she was one of the few women her age who had never experienced the ultimate expression of love, and at times she bitterly resented those friends who did not believe her. She had clung tenaciously to that principle of her faith, though, in recent days, the temptation to yield to Brett's ardor had been almost overwhelming.

As she pondered, she knew that she had already made up her mind that she wanted to live with Brett for the rest of her life. She should have told him that she would marry him, but a niggling doubt always managed to creep in just when she was on the brink of decision.

Her thoughts were interrupted when she heard Brett say, "Mmmm, you smell good tonight. Is that a new perfume?"

"I'm glad you noticed," she colored beneath her light tan. "Yes, it is, and I hope it will haunt you like your sandalwood has haunted me."

"I didn't know you liked sandalwood," he said with surprise.

"Only when *you* are wearing it, and only when you are here with me," she stated emphatically.

Brett's arm was now resting on the table. He draped the other casually around the back of his chair as he turned to talk with Joy.

He did not touch her. In fact, his chair was a full two feet away. But as he continued his conversation, she looked into his eyes, the color shifting from bronze to amber and back to rich mahogany. It was as if his eyes were a thing apart, beckoning her, inviting her to lose herself in their warm depths.

As they sparkled and scintillated, they began to move across her face slowly in an almost tangible caress—first to one eye; then, to the other, skimming the tip of her delicate nose, then dropping to linger on the sweet curve of her lips. She could almost feel his lips on hers—warm, firm, desirous. Though she didn't hear a word he was saying, she was held captive by those searching, probing eyes.

They shifted to her jawline, stroking the tender curve of her cheek, moving to touch the hollow at the base of her throat. She felt herself feeling strangely breathless. How incredible. The man had not laid a hand on her, yet she felt the physical warmth of his embrace—and a rising excitement yet to be named. It was an electrifying moment—unlike anything Joy had ever experienced.

When the music ended, breaking the spell, she felt both regret and relief. She excused herself from the table and hurried to the powder room to compose herself. She splashed cold water on her burning face and held her wrists under the faucet, allowing the cooling flow to still her racing pulse. She felt as if she had run a marathon race.

When she returned to the table, Brett rose to seat her, concerned that she might have become ill.

"Did I say anything to cause you to leave so suddenly?" he asked. "I've wracked my brain, but I couldn't imagine how a recital of dull facts about my childhood could have upset you!"

"It really wasn't anything you said, Brett," Joy assured him. "Maybe someday I'll tell you—when I understand it better myself."

CHAPTER 12

THE WORLD HAD NEVER been brighter than it appeared to Joy the following morning when she awakened. Glistening droplets of dew clung to the grass. With the eye of an artist, Joy's mind transformed the scene into a dress of white moiré silk that would shimmer and change as light caught the wavy patterns. Never without a note pad nearby, she recorded her impressions to incorporate later into a dress design.

Suddenly her thoughts returned to her conversation with Ellen about the Debutante Ball. She had not been able to create a design for April Munroe. April would look stunning in a white moiré gown. Aha! she thought. That was the answer to one of the gowns that had been baffling her for so long.

Beauty filled her eyes wherever she looked that morning. The Banyan tree's waxy leaves glimmered in the early morning sunlight. Was this the same view she had seen only yesterday morning? How could one's attitude and state of mind alter so drastically the appearance of things?

Standing before the open window, she breathed in great gulps of air and the fragrances that greeted her were as lovely as the sights. The lingering scent of the night-blooming jasmine near her window was now a romantic and lovely aroma. Only yesterday it had brought tears to her eyes. *What a difference a day makes*, she thought—trite, maybe, but so very true.

Exhilarated, she hurried into the bathroom and stepped into the shower. As the refreshing spray hit her face and then pelted her back, she began to hum. The hum progressed to a "tra la la." Before she knew it she was singing . . . happy songs, love songs, fun songs. Her spirits soared.

With thirty minutes remaining before she was to meet Brett for breakfast, she would still be able to dress leisurely. Reflecting on the events of the evening before, she remembered that Brett had told her he had a business meeting tonight and wouldn't be able to have dinner with her. "If I have to leave day after tomorrow, I want to make the most of every minute we have together," she said aloud. "After breakfast, I'll complete some sketches. This is the first time in months that I've been excited about working."

Deciding that she would go to the beach and sketch after breakfast, she selected a bright watermelon pink swimsuit with grass-green laces that secured the deep plunging front of the suit. She had asked one of the seamstresses to make her a simple boat-necked top and a wrap skirt in grass green, trimmed with the same watermelon shade as the suit. Slices of watermelons were appliqued on both the skirt and the top. It was a nice cover to wear to the dining room, and could be easily removed for swimming and sunbathing.

Joy doubted that wrap skirts would ever drift into complete disfavor with the average homemaker or working woman. They were so comfortable and convenient for quick trips to the supermarket or other errands. She made a mental note to be sure to have plenty of unusual wraps in the boutique for the summer.

She stashed all of her art supplies in a big tote bag, added a towel, and was ready for the day. She had wasted so much time while Brett was away. Today she would make up for all of those unhappy and unproductive days, she promised herself.

Brett was already seated at a table when she entered the dining room. He was intently watching something outside the windows and did not see her until the maitre d' had escorted her to his table.

"What is so interesting out there this morning?" she asked.

"I was just admiring the shuttle yacht, *Mizner's Dream,* in the marina. Why haven't we ridden it to the Beach Club yet?"

"I think it only sails during the daytime. I'm going to the beach after breakfast, so I'll try it out," Joy replied.

"Wish I could go with you and we could just soak up sun all day." He looked wistfully in the direction of the ocean.

"Nope, not today. This morning is going to be all work and little play for me. I intend to accomplish a great deal today. I feel inspired!"

"I'm glad to hear that, and Ellen certainly will be, too, from what you told me about her crisis call. But, besides the dresses for the Debutante Ball, what's the rush?" Brett inquired. "I thought the charity balls were almost a year away."

"I wondered that, too, when Mother would start working on the new gowns almost as soon as the completed ones had been delivered. But since each dress is an original, it takes a lot of time to create just the right design for each client. Then the fabric must be located and purchased.

132

"Even the trims can be frustrating beyond belief. Several times I have had to change designs completely because none of the suppliers had an item in stock!" Joy tried to explain in layman's terms all of the intricasies of designing, obtaining the materials, and making the patterns to fit the individual. Only then could the dressmakers begin the actual construction and fitting of the garments.

"Good grief! I had no idea dress-designing was so complicated. When you come down to it, it is very much like architecture, isn't it? We design the building, specify all materials to be used, and see that the structure is built properly. Guess we are in the same line of work when you think about it," Brett observed.

"Hey, you know, you're right!" Joy turned to the waiter who was dispensing croissants, muffins, Danish pastries, and other delicacies from a huge metal warmer which hung around his neck. "I think I'll have another of those bran muffins." The waiter lifted out one of the toasty warm muffins with his tongs and placed it on her bread-and-butter plate.

Brett's eyes crinkled with merriment. "Joy, watching you eat is almost as much fun as eating my own meal. I remember when I was a little boy visiting my grandfather, it seemed that everything he ate appeared to taste better than whatever I was eating. He could make a biscuit with butter and syrup look like the treat of a lifetime."

Joy laughed at the thought of Brett as a small boy and finished her bowl of strawberries, selected from a table containing fruits of all descriptions. The waiter brought her broiled fish with grilled tomatoes and potatoes and refilled her coffee cup.

"You can have your fish for breakfast. Just give me good old country ham and eggs. By the way, can you cook?" he asked as an afterthought.

"I'll have you know that I'm a very good cook. Those frozen dinners are a cinch. Just poke them in the oven, set the timer, and voila—instant dinner!" she smiled impishly.

"You have to be kidding! I had enough of those when Mother and Dad would go out to dinner, and leave us kids with the old TV-dinner routine. Seriously, can you cook—I mean good old 'down-home' Southern cooking?" His face had become very solemn as he waited for her reply.

Joy laughed at his anguished expression. "I'm teasing, of course. I enjoy cooking the good old stand-bys like fried chicken, rice and gravy, and grits. Mother taught me when I was just a little girl. She was excellent in the kitchen as well as a talented artist, businesswoman, and an especially good wife and mother. I always hoped I could be like her someday." Joy's face revealed the pride and love she felt for her mother, as well as a wistful expression of hope for her own future.

"I wanted to be sure that you could cook. If you had to eat in a restaurant all of your life, it would take a millionaire just to pay for your meals!" Brett laughed, knowing that she would be indignant.

"Enough about my appetite! You don't turn down much food yourself, I've noticed," Joy frowned in mock anger.

"Uh, oh! I did say that I wouldn't tease you anymore. By the way, Joy, I'm sorry that I can't have dinner with you tonight. But don't forget to eat," he reminded her. "I don't want you wasting away again."

"Do you really have to go to a business meeting tonight? I have to catch the early flight out day after tomorrow to go back to Atlanta," she asked, secretly hoping that he would cancel his plans.

"I'm afraid so. It's something that can't wait," he stated firmly and her face mirrored her disappointment.

"Well, I'll probably just stop in the Court of Four Lions

and have a bite after I get through with today's sketches. Have a good day . . . I'll miss you." Her voice softened. "I'll miss you, too, Princess. You take care, hear?" Brett said as he left her to finish her coffee.

When she reached the beach, Joy removed her skirt and top and walked into the surf to test the temperature of the water. Finding it a little too cool for an early morning swim, she returned to the lounge chair with its canvas awning which she could use later to block the sun. She stretched out on the lounge and stared at the ocean. Her creative mind went to work at once, conjuring the vision of a dress that would capture some of the beauty of the Atlantic.

Quickly she unpacked her materials and sketched a long dress of ombre chiffon in shades of greens and blues. Diagonal rows of ruffles extended from one shoulder downward to the floor-length hemline, giving the appearance of waves rolling toward the beach. She added a long, sheer shawl of the same fabric. It added an ethereal quality to the dress when draped around the throat in front, and when the wearer walked, the fabric would float softly in her wake.

And I know just the woman to wear it, she thought. No one would look better in it than Doris Key. Her naturally blonde hair would shine like the sun coming up over the ocean. That was it! Doris would look like Botticelli's Venus. Unlike Venus, however, she would be clothed in a gown the color of the sea. Excitement mounted as she gazed around the shoreline for other inspirations.

She walked down the beach and found a long, white feather, probably from one of the seagulls that followed the boats which plied the inlet, she thought. Looking at the feather, she sketched a mental picture of a long, black

135

strapless taffeta dress with no ornamentation except for one extraordinary white feather which would be fashioned from organza. It would be tacked across the bodice diagonally with only the tip of the feather extending above the bodice. Ah, perfect! Simple, but elegant.

Hurrying back to her lounge chair, she captured the image on paper, along with a long flowing gown of creamy, sand-colored georgette, sprinkled with beads the colors of the small shells that lay strewn over the beach.

Her hands moved rapidly now as she concocted a pale gold dress with a handkerchief skirt that emulated the now-endangered sea oats which waved so gracefully in the ocean breeze. Those little points of the skirt, if made of soft chiffon, would ripple with movement—giving the appearance of sea oats swaying gently. As she put the final touches to the dress, she smiled broadly

To clear her head, Joy raced into the ocean and dived into a wave. She rose exuberantly to catch another huge wave, riding it almost to the beach. Childlike, she rushed back and forth as if she might miss one moment of the wondrous experience.

Finally, exhausted from her exertion, she struggled out of the water and shook her golden head. Vibrant energy replaced the depression that had drained her and left her listless.

Joy strolled along the beach, letting her body dry in the warm breeze. She stooped to pick up a shell and stared at it thoughtfully, turning it around and around in her hand. *How very beautiful,* she thought. *I wonder where this shell began its long journey?*

The beauty of the shell inspired yet another idea for a dress. It must be a strapless dress, she decided, and the fabric would stand away slightly from the body at the top. Satin—that would be the only fabric to duplicate the sheen of the shell. But it had to be lined with satin as well. Yes, the dress would be shell pink, and the lining which would peek above the top of the bodice would be a deeper shade of pink, just like the inside of the shell she was holding. A vision of the skirt took shape in her imagination. It would be long in the back and curve gradually upward to knee-length in the front so that the deep pink lining could be seen. Delighted with her final idea, Joy ran back to sketch the dress. Afterward she relaxed contentedly in the sun.

When her hearty appetite surfaced once more, she walked to the Cabana Terrace for a quick bite of lunch—her reward for a successful morning's work. Long ago Joy had decided that, even if she were dieting, she would never skip breakfast. Her body craved some nourishment when she awakened so that she could have enough energy for the day. If she missed any meal, it would have to be lunch. Then she tried to have dinner early enough so that she would have time to work off some of the calories before going to bed. She was able to keep her weight under control with this routine, or by cutting down the size of the portions.

Leisurely she enjoyed the fresh seafood salad and entertained herself with her favorite pastime—people-watching. A little boy about four years old walked toward the nearby pool. She couldn't help but notice his dark brown eyes and his sturdy, little legs. He could have been a miniature of Brett, she decided. Should she and Brett marry and have children, their little boys would all have legs like that—and large, chocolate-brown eyes!

Did she know Brett well enough to marry him? What would she say if he asked her again? Her outburst the night that he had proposed had certainly been enough to discourage any man, especially after the way she had responded to his kisses on the beach. Yes, he had every right to have been angry and confused. And why had she not told him that she would marry him when he returned from Atlanta?

She wanted Brett. She needed him. He had become a part of her life, and the thought of losing him was unbearable. Just how long would he wait for her to make up her mind? Surely even his patience had a limit. Perhaps she should just tell him that she wanted to be his wife.

That wouldn't really be proposing to him, since he had already asked her to marry him. Things were completely different now. Yet she hesitated. Perhaps she was still playing the role of a Southern lady of an earlier era.

She certainly didn't agree with many of the ideas her friends held. Quite a few of them considered her peculiar because she already felt equal to men and saw no need for legislation to guarantee that equality. In some ways she felt that the scale tipped in the direction of women, giving them a favored position. She liked the idea of men opening doors for her, helping her with her coat, pulling out her chair, and paying for dinner or the theatre. No, she didn't want to be subservient, but she did like the respect and protection of men. Brett gave her the impression of cherishing her without dominating her. Was there another man like him in the whole world?

He had made it perfectly clear that he wanted to know when Joy was ready to marry him. *I'll just have to call him tonight when he gets back from his meeting and say, "I'm ready for you to ask me,"* she thought. *No, that doesn't sound right. Oh, well! By tonight, I'll think of something.*

CHAPTER 13

THERE SEEMED LITTLE NEED to dress for dinner, but Joy had promised Brett. At the last minute she decided to dine in the Patio Royale, where she could enjoy the music of the orchestra rather than in the Court of Four Lions, where she would have only her own thoughts to keep her company.

Since she would not be seeing Brett that evening, Joy took no particular pains with her dress. She grabbed a simple long-sleeved shirtwaist, applied transparent powder to tone down her sunburned face, some mascara, and a touch of lipstick. Running a brush through her hair, she noticed that it was at least two shades lighter. She would have to be more careful in the sun tomorrow.

As she walked through the lobby, she spoke to Domenick who was openly appreciative of the lovely girl in the sapphire blue dress. The color made her eyes sparkle like pale blue crystals, and her face glowed with pleasure when she saw her old friend.

Once again she was grateful that the hotel had not abandoned some of the timeless traditions of service. There was something so coldly impersonal about self-service which had replaced such personnel as the bell captain and bellmen in many of the large hotel chains. It was unthinkable, in her mind, that there should not be a Domenick who remembered the names of guests from former days and was now welcoming their children. Joy decided that there was something inherent in her being that resisted such progress as the building of condos and the self-operated elevators. She wondered if she would be considered a "maverick" had she lived out West rather than in the South. And why should she change for the sake of change, even if hers was not a popular stand—or even if it was in opposition to Brett's?

She studied the menu. Brett would have loved hearing her order, she thought. Ah, but she could almost taste the marinated zucchini sticks with Genoa salami and the chilled melon and fruit soup. Her mouth watered in anticipation. She smiled to herself. *Joy, you are becoming an impossible 'foodaholic.'*

The music, as on previous evenings, was varied enough to please all of the diners, and its quality was unmatched. Joy had grown to love dining while listening to live music. Like Mr. Smith, each of the musicians seemed to enjoy bringing pleasure to the guests.

When the entreé was served, Joy had tasted only a few bites when she glanced toward the orchestra once more. As her eyes shifted, she caught sight of a familiar figure being seated at a table just in front of the orchestra. Startled, she jerked her head back in that direction. It was Brett! And he was not alone. Seated with him was a gorgeous strawberry blonde. So this was the business that "couldn't wait."

I've seen that girl somewhere before . . . Joy struggled to remember. *But where? I know—it was the day I had lunch with Marianna!*

Heartsick, Joy slumped in her chair, fearful that Brett would spot her. She had believed every word he had told her. Yet here he was with another woman only hours after his passionate declaration of love! What's more—he had probably been seeing her all along. Anger and indignation seethed within.

Though her first inclination had been to bolt and run, her instinctive curiosity outweighed the decision. She shifted a little lower into her chair so that she could study the couple. There was little chance that Brett would see her, however, because his eyes were riveted on the woman's face. And he was not by himself.

All of the men at surrounding tables were casting appreciative glances at her. Men who were not with female companions stared unashamedly at the gorgeous creature. *Men!* Joy thought. *They're all alike!*

The woman with Brett could have been a high-fashion model if judged by her face alone. Her figure was equally devastating. Reddish-blonde hair fell in shining waves around her shoulders. And the shoulders that it brushed were bare. *Too bare,* Joy thought. Her dress was a simple, black affair with tiny spaghetti straps. Joy gritted her teeth as she watched the woman who was now laughing at something that Brett had said.

He was undeniably charming. *Keep 'em laughing, Brett. That's your motto, isn't it? But you made your big mistake tonight,* Joy thought bitterly. *You thought that I would be having dinner in the Court of Four Lions, so I would never find out about your little tête-á-tête, didn't you? Well, tonight your plan backfired!*

Then the anger that had erupted began to turn to self-pity. Tears welled in Joy's eyes. Brett just used me and then tossed me aside when he saw something more interesting, she grieved. Tears coursed down her face, and she grabbed

141

the coral linen napkin and tried to staunch the flow.

With a terrible sense of timing, the waiter appeared to ask Joy if she were not feeling well or if her scallopini were not to her liking. Through her sobs Joy managed to convey that the food was just fine, but that she felt a little ill. It was true. She was sick with humiliation!

She asked the waiter for the check, suddenly eager to escape the sight of Brett and his lovely dinner companion. He reached into the breast pocket of his jacket and produced the bill. As he did so, he asked solicitously if there were anything that he could do to help. Joy bit her tongue. It was a temptation to tell him what he could do to the couple who were now dancing to the music that she had been enjoying only moments before. She would like to see the entire plate of scallopini dumped over Brett's head! Instead, she nodded negatively and signed the check.

Knowing that she would have to traverse the entire length of the dining room to get to the nearest exit, she looked for the darkest and quickest route. The last thing she wanted was for Brett to see her. She would never give him the satisfaction of knowing how he had upset her. He and the woman were seated at their table again, and the route she had chosen would take her directly into his line of vision. Well, she would just have to leave as inconspicuously as possible.

Mustering all of her courage, she rose and turned her head toward the wall. Maybe Brett wouldn't recognize her from the back. The distance seemed interminable—like miles before she reached the door. Outside, she hurried down the brightly carpeted steps that led into the lobby. *I made it!* she thought with relief.

Unexpectedly a hand touched her shoulder. She jumped. Then Brett had his arms around her. He really had nerve to follow her as if nothing had happened! Joy seethed with anger. She tried to push his arms away, but she could not speak. Struggling to break his hold on her, she glanced at his eyes and wondered why she could have been struck both deaf and dumb when she looked into them.

"Joy, honey, what's wrong?" Brett asked. "Where have you been? I've tried to reach you all day. I even tried your room just before coming here. Have you eaten? Come on back and sit with me while I finish my meal, will you?"

She stared at him in disbelief. Did he suppose that she hadn't seen him and *that woman?* Did he really expect her to follow him meekly and be a fifth wheel to their cozy little twosome? Words continued to fail her.

"Joy, what in the world is wrong with you? Are you sick or something? I just wanted you to come in and sit with Sam and me while we have dinner." His face showed no evidence of repentance.

Then all of the words that had remained trapped spewed forth with unexpected venom. "You expect me to go and sit with you and your date while the two of you have dinner! You were the one who had such an important *business meeting* tonight! Business, hah! And I believed you when you told me that you loved me and wanted to marry me. Then the minute my back is turned, you are dancing with a strawberry-blonde bombshell! Well, Brett, you have done one good thing for me—no, two. First, I have finally gotten my spunk back after a very long time. And, second, I won't ever trust another man as long as I live!"

"Hold it! Hold it!" Brett interrupted her tirade. "I said that I wanted you to meet *Sam*. That 'strawberry-blonde bombshell,' as you call her, is *Samantha*—'Sam' for short. She's one of the engineers on the condo job. When I told her that I hated not being with you tonight, she insisted that the three of us have dinner together. We could talk business, and I could still be with you. Now, does that smooth your

143

ruffled feathers a little? Sam really is a very nice lady. And by the way, she is very much married.''

His long dissertation had given Joy time to weigh the situation. His explanation sounded plausible. Then she asked weakly, ''But why didn't you ever tell me that Sam was a *woman?*''

''Honestly, honey, the thought never occurred to me. She is just an engineer as far as I'm concerned. After I met you, do you think I could be interested in another woman, even if she *were* available?'' He smiled down at her and kissed the tip of her sunburned nose. Joy's anger melted, to be replaced with utter contrition.

''You are really rotten to the core!'' she stormed at him in mock indignation. ''Do you realize that I wasn't able to eat my veal scallopini after I saw you with her? I wasted all of that good food, plus my baked eggplant!''

Brett threw back his head and laughed heartily. Then he countered, ''Now I know the way to your heart. Come on back with me. Never let it be said that you left the table without finishing a meal on my account.''

He put his arm around her waist possessively and guided her back to the table where Sam sat alone. When she saw them, Sam's face lighted with pleasure.

''At last I get to meet the 'Joy' of Brett's life,'' she said with sincerity. ''He has talked about you so much that it would have been a shame not to have met you.''

Joy could not help but warm to the woman's friendly smile and pleasant personality. Brett proceeded to tell Sam about Joy's misconceptions about her and soon they were all laughing.

''This certainly isn't the first time that my name has gotten me in trouble,'' Sam commented. ''Many a wife has stared holes through me before they realize that I am strictly an engineer when I'm at work. Breaking up other relationships just isn't my style. My mother and father were divorced because of 'the other woman' and I go out of my way to keep associations with other men on a professional level. It is hard enough, at times, to be a woman engineer without having my name cause problems, too.''

Joy smiled at her and said, ''Well, I'm certainly glad that you're happily married. I'd hate to have you as my competition. You outshine everyone around.''

''Not in Brett's eyes. I don't think he even realized that I was a woman until Frank broke the news that I would be taking a leave of absence soon to have a baby.'' Sam's reassuring smile calmed any lingering fears.

The conversation was mostly happy talk regarding the arrival of the new baby and Joy's work. Then the two women teased Brett unmercifully about his near-fatal error in neglecting to tell Joy that Sam was a woman. Being outnumbered, he changed the subject to the construction of the condo.

While Brett and Sam discussed business, Joy reflected on what Sam had said. So Brett had meant it when he told Joy that she was the only woman in the world for him. Well, after tonight, she would have to make sure that he asked her again to marry him. There was no longer any question what her answer would be.

CHAPTER 14

AFTER THEY HAD DRIVEN Sam home and Joy had promised to keep in touch, Brett swung the car around and headed up A1A. Joy struggled not to comment as they passed the high-rise buildings that hugged the shoreline. She wanted to avoid another controversy about the buildings. Instead, she asked Brett what made him decide to study architecture and why he had chosen Auburn instead of Georgia Tech, which was so close to home.

"Well, to tell the truth, I needed to get away from home. Cut the apron strings, you know. Auburn has a good school of architecture. Several of my friends were there, and, besides, I really did want the chance to play football with "Shug" Jordan as my coach. As it turned out, I didn't get to play too much because I happened to be on campus when Pat Sullivan and Terry Beasley had their 'dynamic duo' going. Since I played the same position that Terry played, I sat on the bench most of the season. But I'm not complaining. They worked well together."

"They were something else, weren't they?" Joy inter-

146

jected. "I was so happy when Pat got the Heisman Trophy. But when Auburn beat Alabama by a score of 17-16 with two blocked punts, you must have been going crazy down there!"

"Hey, Love, you've been holding out on me. How does such a feminine little thing know so much about football?" Brett asked in disbelief.

"I've loved football since I was a little girl," she explained. "My father took me to my brother's Little League football practices every afternoon. Even in high school I was an oddity because I really enjoyed the games. My girl friends were never able to understand it. But tell me more! What was it like when Auburn beat Alabama?" Joy's interested questioning was all Brett needed.

"Pandemonium broke out all over the state. Records of the last few minutes of the ballgame were broadcast from a loudspeaker at the front of the bookstore. Toomers' Corner, the main intersection in front of the campus, was a madhouse. It was Mardi Gras, the Fourth of July, and New Year's Eve, all rolled up into one! When we got back to the campus, the party was still going strong. For days, as I worked in the architecture building, I could look out and see streamers hanging from all of the old oaks, magnolias, and telephone lines. Samford Hall, the main building, looked like a Christmas tree covered with tinsel.

"The guys who lived in Alabama were more excited than anyone else because of the big cross-state rivalry. But every year I just hope that Auburn beats Tech and those Georgia Bulldogs. Then I don't have to take the teasing from all of the folks in Atlanta. . . . Hey!" he exclaimed, looking over at her. "I order two season tickets every year for the games at Auburn. Would you like to go this fall? It would be fun showing you the campus and being able to talk football with my date rather than having to explain everything that is happening on the field." Brett was intrigued with Joy's interest in the game he loved—and delighted to discover that they had something else in common.

"I'd love to! I haven't seen too many games since Bill was killed. Now that my father is gone, I usually watch the games on TV or go by myself. I haven't found a woman who shares my love for football and, unfortunately, the man I was engaged to went to the games only if he were trying to impress someone." She thought about John and realized that there was no trace of bitterness. Changing the subject, she said, "Why don't you try your hand at coaching Little League football? You would be great with kids, I bet."

"I've thought about it, but my schedule is so crazy that I can't be there early enough for practice. And when I have to go out of town, I would have to miss practice completely. It really wouldn't be fair to the kids. But I owe a lot to my Little League coach." Brett stopped and turned to Joy, a look of incredulity on his face as realization dawned.

"Bill Lawrence must have been your brother! Joy, I had not made the connection until just now! I played football with him in Little League and, later, in high school. And you were the kid sister who always came to watch him practice. Now I remember you! You had chubby, little legs and big, blue eyes, and the same happy smile you have now. Everyone called you 'Kitten,' probably because you were so cute and cuddly. How could I have forgotten?"

Joy's face was illumined with instant recognition. "Then that's why *your* name was so familiar to me! I kept wondering why the name 'McCort' kept coming back to me. But you weren't called 'Brett' then. Didn't they call you 'Buddy'?"

Brett threw back his head and laughed. "You're right! And if I hadn't put my foot down and demanded that the family start calling me 'Brett,' I would have one day been known as 'Grandpa Buddy.' Can you picture that?"

Joy felt a slight blush burn her face as she said, "But you still don't know the whole story. I had the worst crush on you then, and you didn't even know that I was alive. I pestered Bill constantly to invite you over to the house. But when you came, you ignored me like the plague."

"Well, Honey, I must have been blind. Of course, the age difference did mean a lot back when I was all of fourteen or fifteen and you must have been only eight or nine. Now, I know why I waited all these years to find the right girl. I had been waiting for that little 'Kitten' to grow up." Brett smiled at her, and she felt a warm, pleasurable sensation sweep through her body.

She had found a link with the past that had been stored in her attic of memories for so many years. He and Bill had been good friends, and their families had enjoyed sharing their sons' athletic accomplishments. It was natural that, with the passing of years, they had grown apart until they had lost all track of each other. How incredible that she had known Brett all these years, only to find her 'first love' again in Boca.

The rest of the drive was spent in comfortable silence as they reviewed the past. Soon Brett was turning into El Camino Real and they were back at the Cloister. After he had left the car with the parking attendant, he took Joy's arm and steered her toward the fountain.

"Now, we are going to sit and enjoy the fountain tonight and forget that other unhappy scene," he said firmly.

This is the time, Joy thought happily. Surely he would ask her now. They sat on the same bench where Joy had shed so many tears on that other dreadful night. But this was a new and beautiful beginning. She would not spoil it.

Brett put his arms around her and kissed her tenderly.

Then she heard her own voice murmuring, "Brett, I love

you so much." Had she really said the words? Had he heard her? The answer to her questions was instantaneous.

Brett grasped her shoulders and looked into her eyes. "Do you really mean that, Joy? Look at me and tell me again."

When she stared into his dark brown hypnotic eyes, her heart began its accelerated thumping. The pounding moved upward into her throat. She knew she was on the verge of making what might be a binding commitment, and fear swept her once again. But this time she squelched the apprehension.

"I do love you, Brett," she said firmly as his stunned expression changed to one of overwhelming relief and love.

Without a word he grasped her to him as if he would never let her go. She could feel his heart bearing like a tom-tom, matching the wild rhythm of her own. The strong arms that enveloped her were like balm to her aching heart. His strength flowed into her own veins. He was the shelter she had found in the 'winter of her life,' like the promise of the cherry blossom. He was her Banyan tree, her friend, her link to the past and to the future. He was her first love—and her last—the one God had chosen for her.

Having breakfast with Brett the following morning, Joy feasted on his eyes, his face, his smile. Her appetite had not lessened. Instead, the beautiful new feeling that existed between them enhanced the flavor of her food and renewed her zest for living.

Happily she told him her plans for her last day in Boca. As she enumerated the things that she hoped to accomplish, his eyebrows rose in astonishment.

"Whoa! How in the world are you going to do all of that in only one day? Are you sure that you can't stay a little longer?" he pleaded.

"Brett, there is nothing I would like more than to stay here at the Cloister with you. But Ellen needs me, and I can't let her down. Will you be coming to Atlanta soon?"

"I certainly hope so. Pete Jennings seems to be feeling better. When his leg heals, he can take over the project here. By the way, will you have dinner with me tonight? It may be our last for quite a while," he said with a touch of unhappiness.

"What a perfect ending to my visit. I'll be ready whenever you say," Joy replied.

It was she who left the dining room first that morning. So many things remained to be done that she knew she must not waste a minute. Now that Brett was back, she felt a strong resurgence of life and creative energy. Her step was buoyant and her heart light as she walked away.

Joy hurried into the Mizner Garden with its two huge fountains embellished with the colorfully decorated tiles. Each in its own way was a work of art, but her favorite would always be the Lady of Boca's fountain, she decided.

The flowers that surrounded her gave her the same inspiration for dress designs as had the ocean and the beach. Quickly she sketched a dress that gave the impression of a poinsettia. Ruffles made from a series of triangles formed layers of pointed petals which stood away from the floor-length straight scarlet skirt.

The Jacaranda tree with its lavender blossoms called to mind a pale orchid taffeta with a bell-shaped skirt and a whisper of a pale green sash just as soft as the fern-like leaves of the tree.

The yellow hibiscus with its rich green foliage inspired a green chiffon formal with a high neck in front and low in the back, with soft folds of fabric falling from the shoulders to the waist where a large, silk yellow hibiscus flower would be attached.

But then she looked at the bougainvillea and her imagination drew from the blooming vine the most elegant dress of all. With this dress she would capture the charm of the Old World as Addison Mizner had when he built the Cloister. The gown would be a traditional Spanish dress as worn by the original flamenco dancers, the Andelusian gypsies, hugging the body to the knees. There, a bouffant ruffle would fall to the floor giving room for the dancer to move her feet freely. The fabric would be fuschia taffeta overlaid with sheer white lace, revealing the bright color beneath. To complete the look, she would use a tall Spanish comb for the hair. From this comb would fall a mantilla of white lace which would be attached by tiny, fuschia silk blossoms that would emulate the bougainvillea blooms. *Maybe this will be my very own dress,* she thought, *to remind me of the beginning of a new life.*

She put her sketch pad away and rushed back into the lobby, remembering the skirt she had seen in DeLoy's. Perhaps it was still there. Though it was a rare occurrence when she bought clothes from other shops, she wanted the lovely creation to wear to dinner with Brett.

She rushed into the boutique and tried on the skirt. It was a perfect fit! But she needed a blouse to complete the ensemble. Instantly her eye was drawn to a pale turquoise design, with a single soft layer of ruffles at the neck and down the front of the blouse.

Brett would love it! But would he sweep her into his arms and ask her to marry him tonight? Suddenly she was impatient to see him. She had never been more sure of any decision in her life.

Her shopping adventure could not have been more successful. When Brett saw her in the rainbow skirt and turquoise blouse, he let out a long, low whistle of approval. He put his arm around her waist, holding her close to him, as they followed the maitre d' to their table that evening.

For the first time since she had known Brett, she ordered her meal without thought for the tempting selections on the menu. Butterflies fluttered in her stomach in anticipation of the question which would decide her future.

To her dismay, as the meal progressed, Brett chatted about mundane things—his work, the boutique, the weather. Nothing at all was said about their relationship. In fact she might have been having a conversation with a perfect stranger. With each course, her brilliant smile faded until, by the time the entrée was served, her spirits had drooped.

The Smith orchestra was playing in the dining room that evening. Again, the strains of the lovely melody that had come to have such a special meaning for them rippled through the room. Brett moved toward her and kissed her lightly on the cheek. Joy held her breath. If he were going to ask her, now was the opportune time. But once more she was disappointed. They listened in silence.

When the band completed the medley they were playing, the audience applauded appreciatively. Joy tried to keep her smile firmly in place, but the effort was becoming almost too much. The waiter asked if he could remove her plate which still contained half of her main course. She nodded miserably.

When he picked up the plate, she saw it! Tucked under one corner of the plate lay a pale blue velvet box! She looked at Brett questioningly. A faint smile played on his lips. But he said nothing.

She picked up the box and opened it. There, nestled in a bed of white satin, was the most beautiful pear-shaped diamond ring she had ever seen. She gasped.

"Honey," Brett said, "I was afraid to ask you to marry me again, so I decided to let the ring do it for me. Before you run away or tell me to wait, I'm going to try once more. Joy, will you marry me as soon as I can get back to Atlanta? I love you and need you with me for the rest of my life."

"Oh, Brett, I was so afraid you wouldn't ask me again! Yes, yes, yes! I'll marry you! Whenever you say!" The sparkling tears in Joy's eyes rivaled the brilliance of the diamond that Brett had slipped on her finger.

Joy's voice quivered with emotion as she looked at her hand which was now adorned with the beautiful ring. "Brett, there is a quotation that keeps running through my mind when I'm with you. I hope I can remember it because it must have been intended for just this moment. 'I love you, not only for what you are, but for what I am when I am with you.'"

Brett held her hands in his as he responded, "And I love you for lighting my life and giving it new meaning . . . Now, there are two things you need to do when you get home. Reserve the church, and call the seamstress and tell her you have a rush job. Your very first design *has* to be your wedding dress. We will do this up in fine style because it is going to be the *only wedding* either of us will ever have. Understood?"

"Understood!" she replied.

The following morning Joy said her goodbyes to some of the hotel employees who had been especially kind to her. When she spoke to Domenick, she promised him that she wouldn't stay away so long. Perhaps, Joy mused, Brett would even surprise her with a honeymoon trip to Boca— where they could begin their own family tradition.

She stood for a moment, savoring again the elegant surroundings, grateful that the beauty of the grand old hotel was not merely a facade, but a spirit, offering refuge and loving concern to the weary travelers who entered its doors. Some of them were looking for physical rest and a change of pace. Others, like herself, were looking for something far more significant. She had been so right to come here to recover the love and security of her childhood. In doing so she had found once more the security of God's perfect love. It was as though He were saying, *My child, now you know the meaning of real joy—and Brett is only one sign of my love for you. I will be with you always* . . .

Brett stood patiently waiting for her to board the airport limousine. His reluctance to let her go showed clearly in his countenance. When he kissed her, she clung to him, fearful that leaving him would break the spell. But as he released her, his warm smile and the love in his eyes told her eloquently that their reunion would be forever.

"Don't forget! You'd look beautiful in a burlap bag, but your wedding dress is a priority." he reminded, as he closed the door of the car.

Looking back through a veil of happy tears at this man who would belong to her until death parted them, Joy spotted the fountain beyond. "The Lady," clothed in sunlight, seemed to glow with an ethereal splendor. The source of her smile would forever remain a mystery, but Joy suspected that she was pleased with the events that had transpired under her watchful eye.

As the sun grew visibly brighter, it touched the cascade of sparkling water flowing from the fountain. Instantly it was transformed in Joy's mind into a shimmering bridal veil, sprinkled with pearls and opalescent crystal beads. The Lady smiled on . . .

MEET THE AUTHORS

VELMA SEAWELL DANIELS has always been passionately in love with books. She is a native of Florida, where she has earned the title of "The Book Lady." She is an NBC television hostess, librarian, book reviewer, newspaper and magazine columnist, and popular seminar and conference speaker. Velma is married to her "first-grade" sweetheart, Dexter, a championship golfer and business executive. Velma writes for *Guideposts* and is the author of three inspirational best-sellers—*Patches of Joy, Kat* (the true story of her calico cat), and *Celebrate Joy.*

PEGGY ESKEW KING grew up in Anderson, South Carolina, where she studied art and fashion design at Winthrop College. She delights in creating and sewing original designs for her personal wardrobe as well as for family and friends. Peggy has won numerous awards, including the title of Mrs. Columbus and runner-up to Mrs. Georgia. She travels extensively and is a voracious reader —logging as many as 400 books per year. Peggy now resides in Winter Haven, Florida, where she welcomes her minister sons and their families for frequent visits.